THE GRAPHIC NOVEL
Mary Shelley

ORIGINAL TEXT VERSION

Script Adaptation: Jason Cobley
American English Adaptation: Joe Sutliff Sanders
Linework: Declan Shalvey
Coloring: Jason Cardy & Kat Nicholson
Lettering: Terry Wiley
Art Director: Jon Haward
Design & Layout: Jo Wheeler & Jenny Placentino
Publishing Assistant: Joanna Watts
Additional Information: Karen Wenborn

Editor in Chief: Clive Bryant

Frankenstein: The Graphic Novel
Original Text Version

Mary Shelley

First US Edition

Published by: Classical Comics Ltd

Acknowledgments: Every effort has been made to trace copyright holders of material reproduced in this book. Any rights not acknowledged here will be acknowledged in subsequent editions if notice is given to Classical Comics Ltd.

All enquiries should be addressed to:
Classical Comics Ltd.
PO Box 7280
Litchborough
Towcester
NN12 9AR
United Kingdom
Tel: 0845 812 3000

info@classicalcomics.com
www.classicalcomics.com

ISBN: 978-1-906332-49-5

Printed in China by SURE Print & Design
using biodegradable vegetable inks on environmentally friendly paper.
This material can be disposed of by recycling,
incineration for energy recovery, composting and biodegradation.

Jason Cardy and Kat Nicholson would like to thank Kate Derrick and Dylan Cook for their help with preparing the pages for coloring. The publishers would like to acknowledge the design assistance of Greg Powell in the completion of this book.

GRAPH
SAN
DERS

Contents

Dramatis Personæ 4
Prologue 6

◆◆◆

Frankenstein
or The Modern Prometheus

Volume I
Letter I 7
Letter II..8
Letter III...8
Letter IV...9

Chapter I..12
Chapter II 13
Chapter III 16
Chapter IV 20
Chapter V..22
Chapter VI 35
Chapter VII 39
Chapter VIII 48

Volume II
Chapter I..51
Chapter II...52
Chapter III 56
Chapter IV...61
Chapter V 64
Chapter VI...67
Chapter VII 68
Chapter VIII...73
Chapter IX 81

Volume III
Chapter I..84
Chapter II...87
Chapter III 92
Chapter IV..102
Chapter V...107
Chapter VI..110
Chapter VII 116

◆◆◆

Mary Shelley 132
Mary Shelley's Family Tree 135
The Birth of Frankenstein 136
Frankenstein Lives! 138
Page Creation 140

Dramatis Personæ

Victor Frankenstein

Frankenstein's Monster

Elizabeth Lavenza
Victor's adopted sister

Robert Walton
Adventurer

The Ship's Master

The Ship's Lieutenant

Alphonse Frankenstein
Victor's father

Caroline Frankenstein
Victor's mother

Ernest Frankenstein
Victor's brother

William Frankenstein
Victor's brother

Henry Clerval
Victor's friend

Justine Moritz
Servant to Frankenstein's household

Dramatis Personæ

Monsieur Krempe
*Professor of Natural Philosophy,
University of Ingolstadt*

Monsieur Waldman
*Professor of Chemistry,
University of Ingolstadt*

Lawyer
*States the charge against
Justine Moritz*

Old Woman
*Gives evidence against
Justine Mortiz*

Monsieur DeLacy
Cottage dweller

Agatha DeLacy
*Daughter of
Monsieur DeLacy*

Felix DeLacy
Son of Monsieur DeLacy

Turkish Merchant

Safie
Daughter of the Turkish Merchant

Mr. Kirwin
Magistrate

Fisherman

Genevan Judge

Prologue

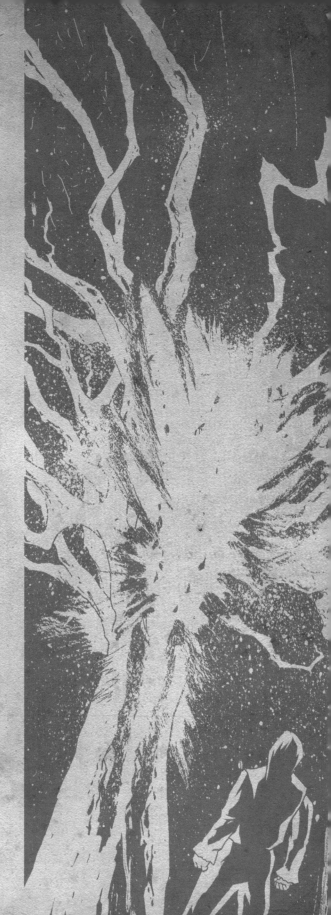

Mary Shelley's literary masterpiece *Frankenstein* was unleashed upon the world in 1818. It was written before the days of steam travel, when the world seemed a much larger place than it does today. Far-off places were out of the reach of all but the bravest adventurers; and in those unknown places it was possible that things could exist — even things created by human beings — that would terrify anyone who saw them.

Science was progressing at an astounding pace. It seemed that anything and everything was possible, as the human race found new and more powerful ways to create and also to destroy.

At the same time, medical science was finding new ways to heal the sick and to revive the dying; and it started to raise questions about the nature of life itself. If the dying can be revived, then could the dead also be brought back to life? How about a dead person that had been assembled from the parts of other dead people? Could that be given life too?

Where would it all end? Would this all go too far? And if so, what would the consequences be?

Indeed, in this early world of advancing medical science, anything and everything seemed possible...

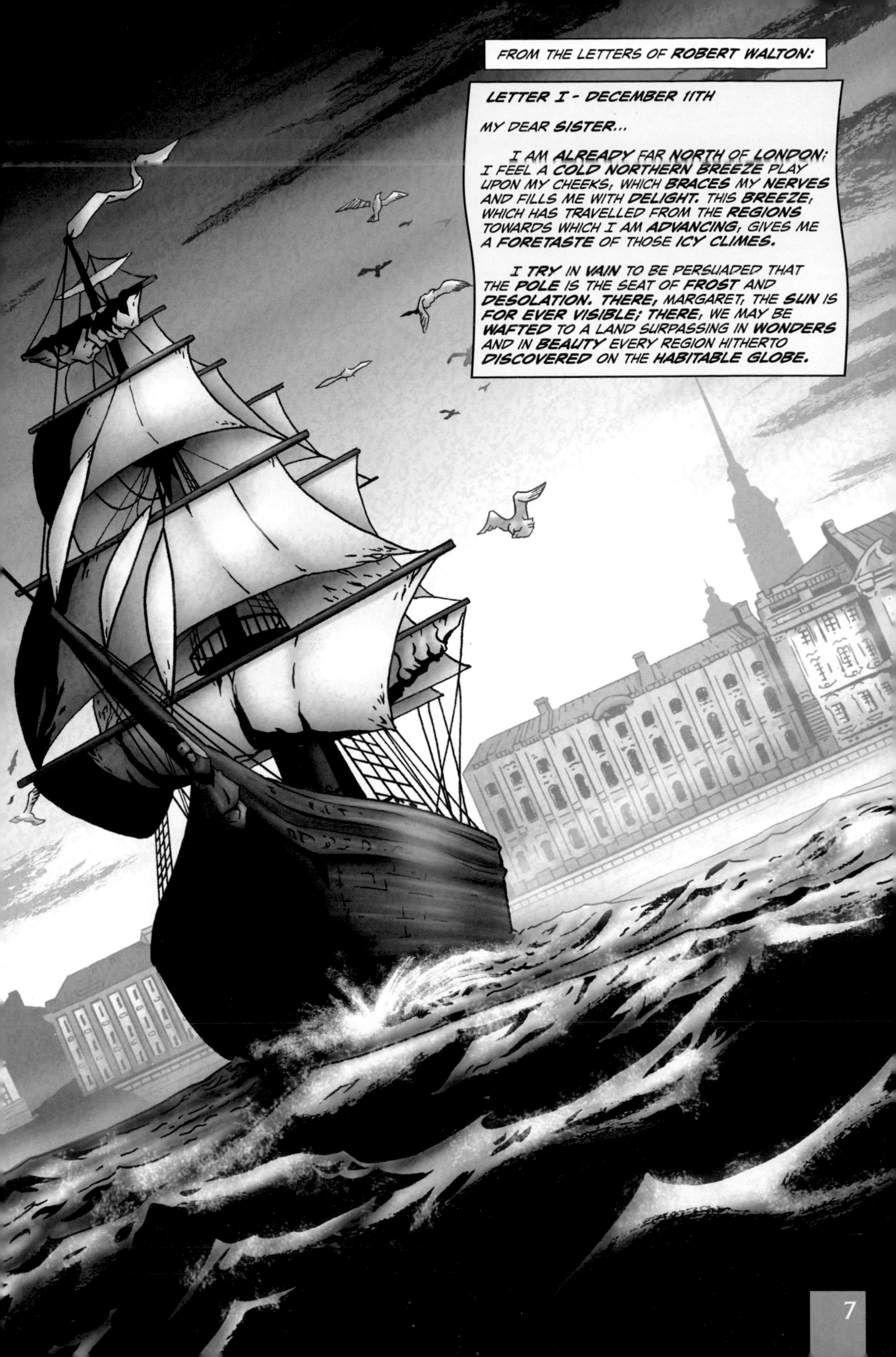
FROM THE LETTERS OF ROBERT WALTON:
LETTER I - DECEMBER 11TH
MY DEAR SISTER...
I AM ALREADY FAR NORTH OF LONDON; I FEEL A COLD NORTHERN BREEZE PLAY UPON MY CHEEKS, WHICH BRACES MY NERVES AND FILLS ME WITH DELIGHT. THIS BREEZE, WHICH HAS TRAVELLED FROM THE REGIONS TOWARDS WHICH I AM ADVANCING, GIVES ME A FORETASTE OF THOSE ICY CLIMES.
I TRY IN VAIN TO BE PERSUADED THAT THE POLE IS THE SEAT OF FROST AND DESOLATION. THERE, MARGARET, THE SUN IS FOR EVER VISIBLE; THERE, WE MAY BE WAFTED TO A LAND SURPASSING IN WONDERS AND IN BEAUTY EVERY REGION HITHERTO DISCOVERED ON THE HABITABLE GLOBE.

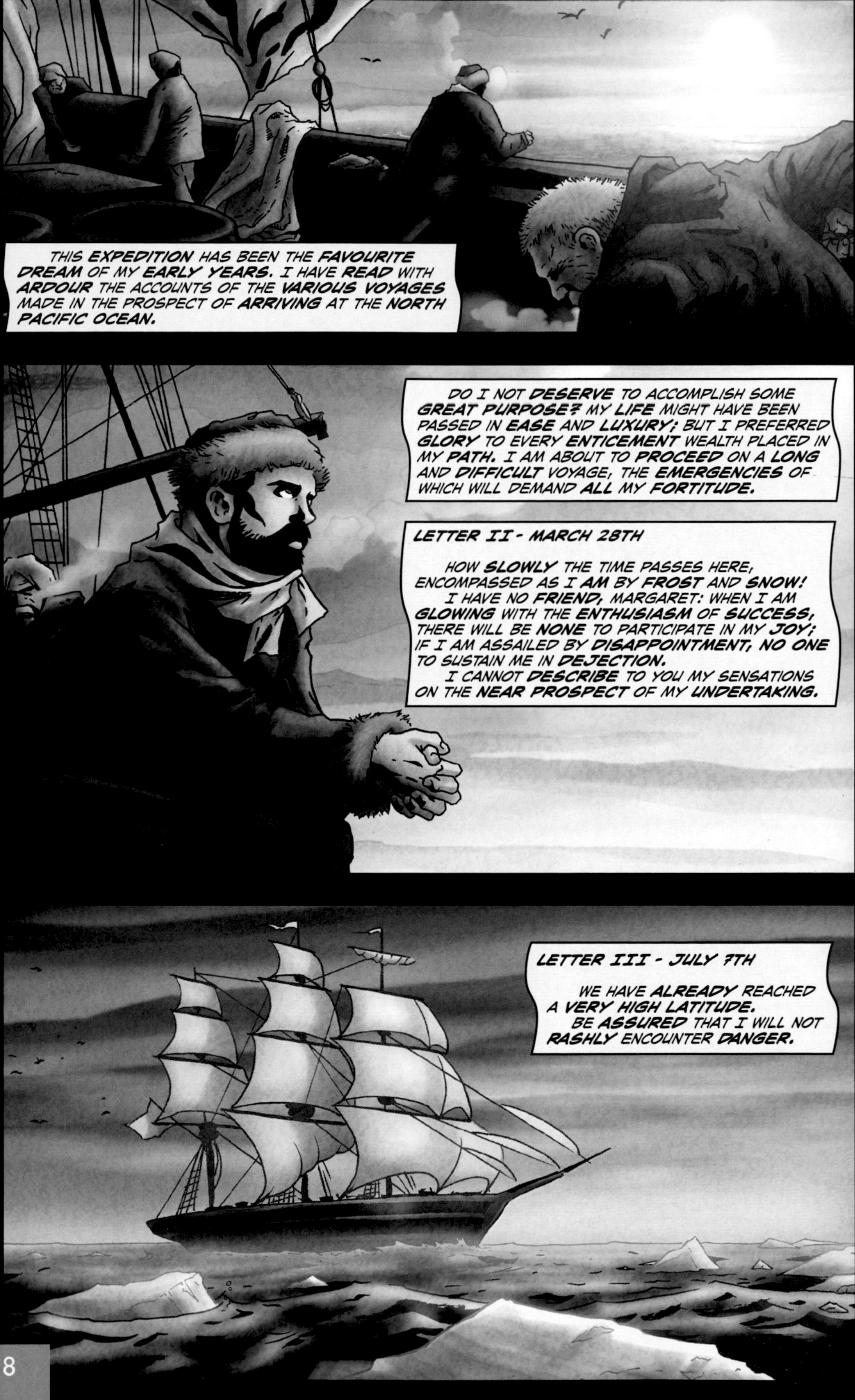
THIS EXPEDITION HAS BEEN THE FAVOURITE DREAM OF MY EARLY YEARS. I HAVE READ WITH ARDOUR THE ACCOUNTS OF THE VARIOUS VOYAGES MADE IN THE PROSPECT OF ARRIVING AT THE NORTH PACIFIC OCEAN.
DO I NOT DESERVE TO ACCOMPLISH SOME GREAT PURPOSE? MY LIFE MIGHT HAVE BEEN PASSED IN EASE AND LUXURY; BUT I PREFERRED GLORY TO EVERY ENTICEMENT WEALTH PLACED IN MY PATH. I AM ABOUT TO PROCEED ON A LONG AND DIFFICULT VOYAGE, THE EMERGENCIES OF WHICH WILL DEMAND ALL MY FORTITUDE.
LETTER II - MARCH 28TH
HOW SLOWLY THE TIME PASSES HERE, ENCOMPASSED AS I AM BY FROST AND SNOW! I HAVE NO FRIEND, MARGARET: WHEN I AM GLOWING WITH THE ENTHUSIASM OF SUCCESS, THERE WILL BE NONE TO PARTICIPATE IN MY JOY; IF I AM ASSAILED BY DISAPPOINTMENT, NO ONE TO SUSTAIN ME IN DEJECTION. I CANNOT DESCRIBE TO YOU MY SENSATIONS ON THE NEAR PROSPECT OF MY UNDERTAKING.
LETTER III - JULY 7TH
WE HAVE ALREADY REACHED A VERY HIGH LATITUDE. BE ASSURED THAT I WILL NOT RASHLY ENCOUNTER DANGER.

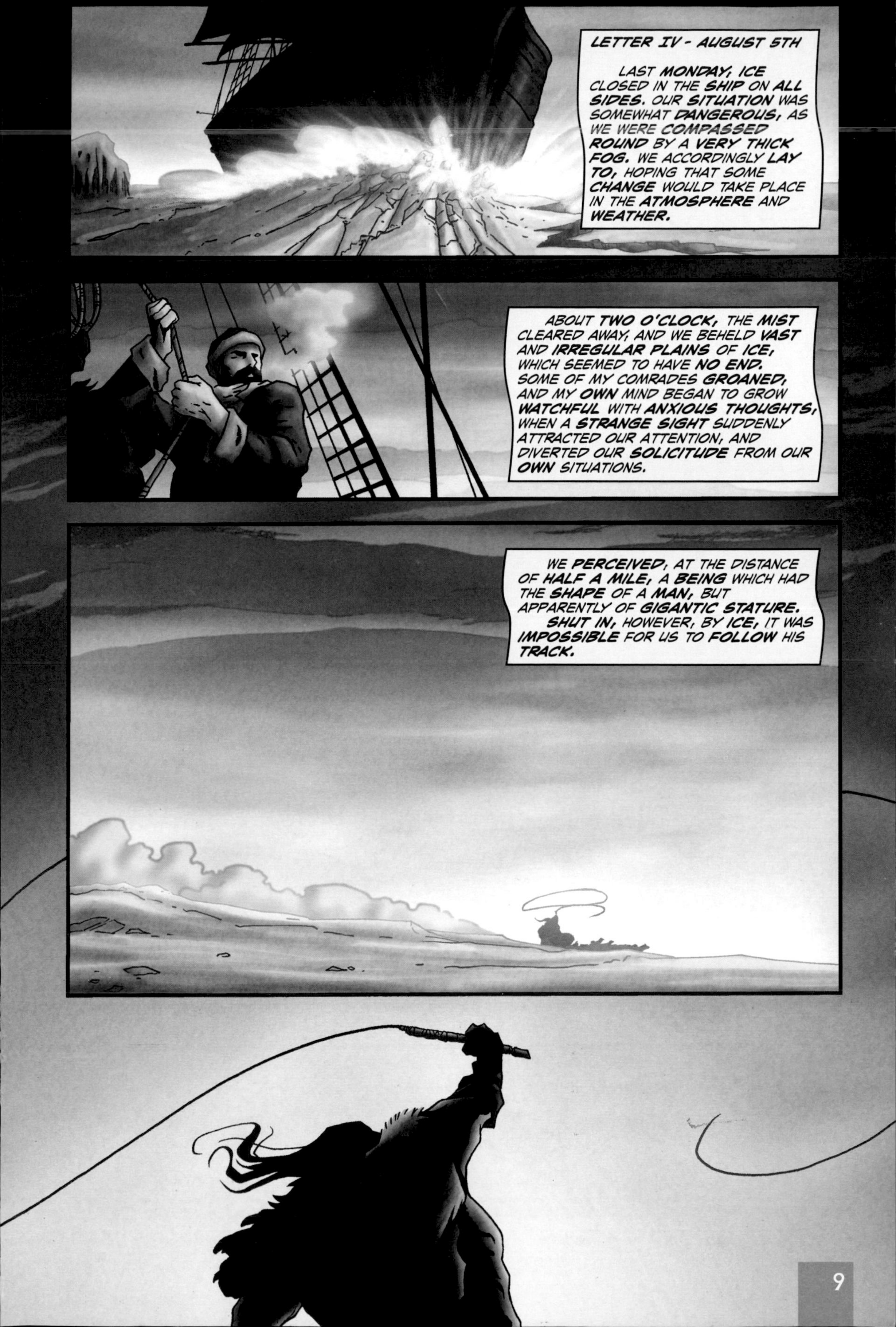
LETTER IV - AUGUST 5TH
LAST MONDAY, ICE CLOSED IN THE SHIP ON ALL SIDES. OUR SITUATION WAS SOMEWHAT DANGEROUS, AS WE WERE COMPASSED ROUND BY A VERY THICK FOG. WE ACCORDINGLY LAY TO, HOPING THAT SOME CHANGE WOULD TAKE PLACE IN THE ATMOSPHERE AND WEATHER.
ABOUT TWO O'CLOCK, THE MIST CLEARED AWAY, AND WE BEHELD VAST AND IRREGULAR PLAINS OF ICE, WHICH SEEMED TO HAVE NO END. SOME OF MY COMRADES GROANED, AND MY OWN MIND BEGAN TO GROW WATCHFUL WITH ANXIOUS THOUGHTS, WHEN A STRANGE SIGHT SUDDENLY ATTRACTED OUR ATTENTION, AND DIVERTED OUR SOLICITUDE FROM OUR OWN SITUATIONS.
WE PERCEIVED, AT THE DISTANCE OF HALF A MILE, A BEING WHICH HAD THE SHAPE OF A MAN, BUT APPARENTLY OF GIGANTIC STATURE.
SHUT IN, HOWEVER, BY ICE, IT WAS IMPOSSIBLE FOR US TO FOLLOW HIS TRACK.

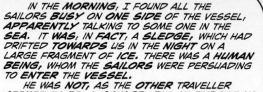

IN THE **MORNING**, I FOUND ALL THE SAILORS **BUSY** ON **ONE SIDE** OF THE VESSEL, **APPARENTLY** TALKING TO SOME ONE IN THE **SEA**. IT **WAS**, IN **FACT**, A **SLEDGE**, WHICH HAD DRIFTED **TOWARDS** US IN THE **NIGHT** ON A LARGE FRAGMENT OF ICE. THERE WAS A **HUMAN BEING**, WHOM THE **SAILORS** WERE PERSUADING TO **ENTER** THE **VESSEL**.

HE WAS **NOT**, AS THE **OTHER** TRAVELLER SEEMED TO BE, A **SAVAGE**, BUT AN **EUROPEAN**.

HERE IS OUR **CAPTAIN**, AND HE WILL NOT ALLOW YOU TO **PERISH** ON THE **OPEN SEA**.

BEFORE I COME ON BOARD, WILL YOU HAVE THE KINDNESS TO INFORM ME **WHITHER** YOU ARE **BOUND**?

WE ARE ON A VOYAGE OF **DISCOVERY** TOWARDS THE **NORTHERN POLE**.

UPON **HEARING** THIS HE APPEARED **SATISFIED**, AND **CONSENTED** TO COME **ON BOARD**.

HIS **LIMBS** WERE NEARLY **FROZEN**, AND HIS **BODY** DREADFULLY **EMACIATED** BY FATIGUE AND **SUFFERING**. I NEVER **SAW** A MAN IN SO **WRETCHED** A CONDITION. WE **RESTORED** HIM TO **ANIMATION** AND BY **SLOW** DEGREES HE **RECOVERED**. **TWO DAYS** PASSED BEFORE HE WAS ABLE TO **SPEAK**.

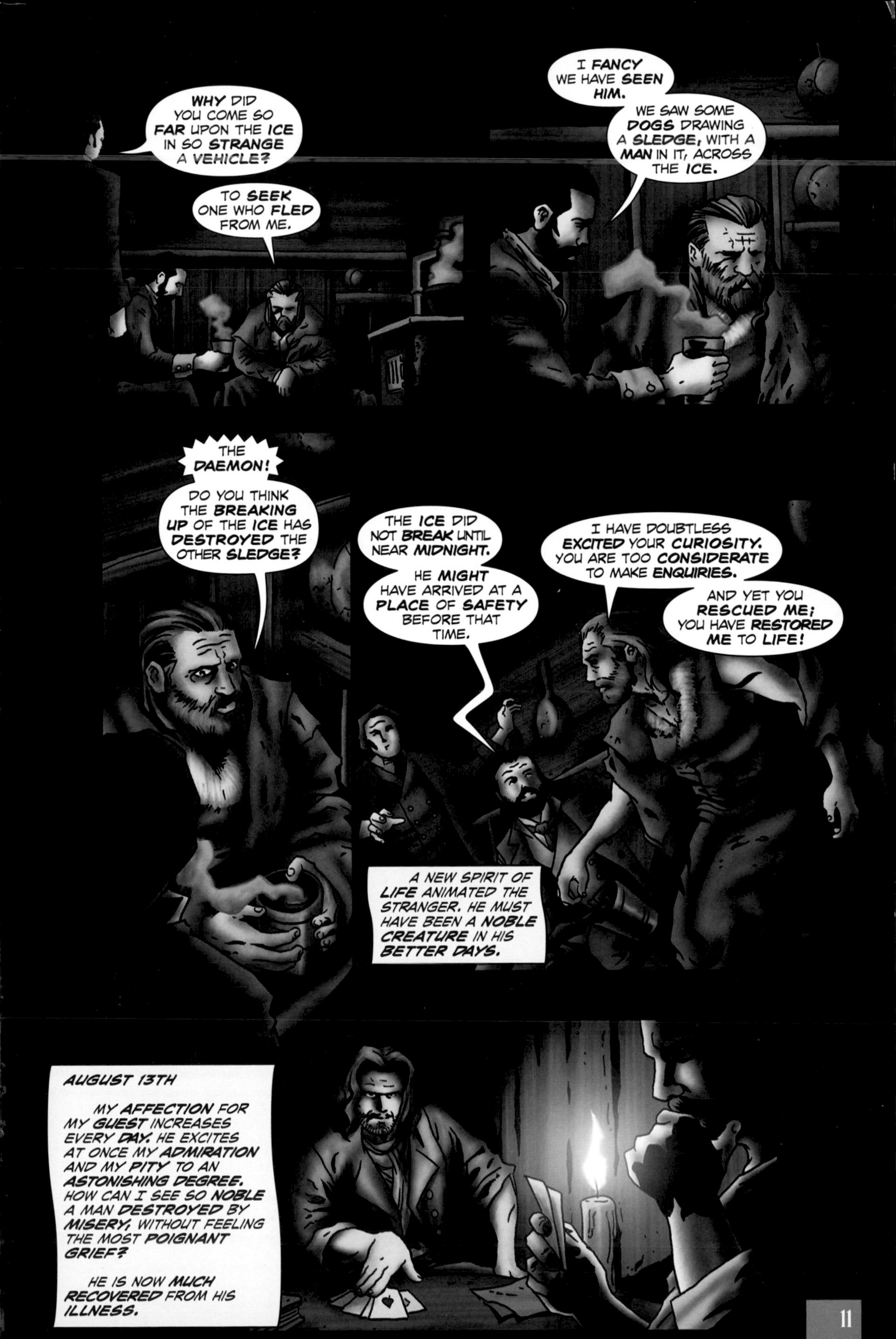
WHY DID YOU COME SO FAR UPON THE ICE IN SO STRANGE A VEHICLE?
TO SEEK ONE WHO FLED FROM ME.
I FANCY WE HAVE SEEN HIM.
WE SAW SOME DOGS DRAWING A SLEDGE, WITH A MAN IN IT, ACROSS THE ICE.
THE DAEMON!
DO YOU THINK THE BREAKING UP OF THE ICE HAS DESTROYED THE OTHER SLEDGE?
THE ICE DID NOT BREAK UNTIL NEAR MIDNIGHT.
HE MIGHT HAVE ARRIVED AT A PLACE OF SAFETY BEFORE THAT TIME.
I HAVE DOUBTLESS EXCITED YOUR CURIOSITY. YOU ARE TOO CONSIDERATE TO MAKE ENQUIRIES.
AND YET YOU RESCUED ME; YOU HAVE RESTORED ME TO LIFE!
A NEW SPIRIT OF LIFE ANIMATED THE STRANGER. HE MUST HAVE BEEN A NOBLE CREATURE IN HIS BETTER DAYS.
AUGUST 13TH
MY AFFECTION FOR MY GUEST INCREASES EVERY DAY. HE EXCITES AT ONCE MY ADMIRATION AND MY PITY TO AN ASTONISHING DEGREE. HOW CAN I SEE SO NOBLE A MAN DESTROYED BY MISERY, WITHOUT FEELING THE MOST POIGNANT GRIEF?
HE IS NOW MUCH RECOVERED FROM HIS ILLNESS.

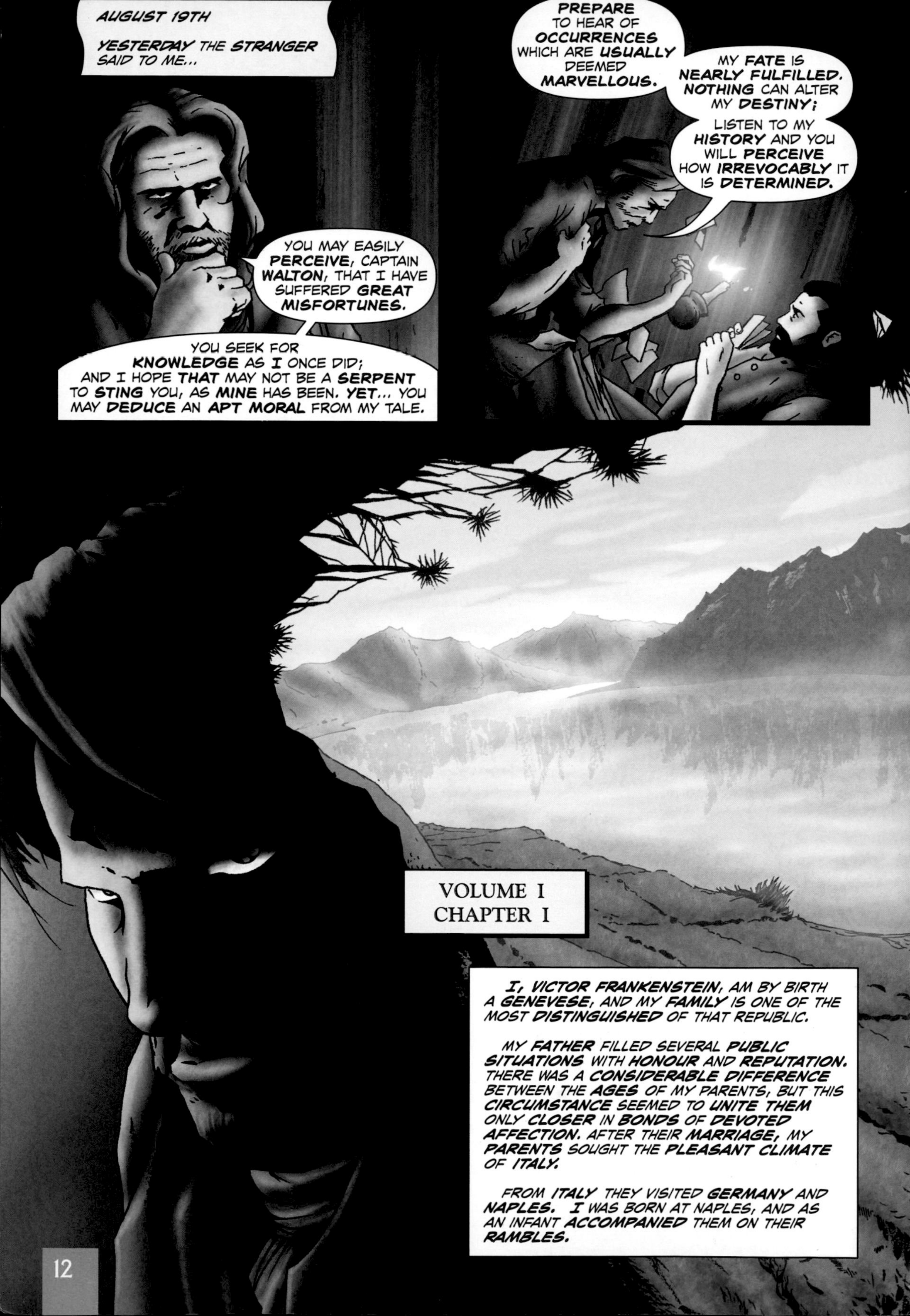

AUGUST 19TH
YESTERDAY THE STRANGER SAID TO ME...
YOU MAY EASILY PERCEIVE, CAPTAIN WALTON, THAT I HAVE SUFFERED GREAT MISFORTUNES.
YOU SEEK FOR KNOWLEDGE AS I ONCE DID; AND I HOPE THAT MAY NOT BE A SERPENT TO STING YOU, AS MINE HAS BEEN. YET... YOU MAY DEDUCE AN APT MORAL FROM MY TALE.
PREPARE TO HEAR OF OCCURRENCES WHICH ARE USUALLY DEEMED MARVELLOUS.
MY FATE IS NEARLY FULFILLED. NOTHING CAN ALTER MY DESTINY;
LISTEN TO MY HISTORY AND YOU WILL PERCEIVE HOW IRREVOCABLY IT IS DETERMINED.
VOLUME I
CHAPTER I
I, VICTOR FRANKENSTEIN, AM BY BIRTH A GENEVESE, AND MY FAMILY IS ONE OF THE MOST DISTINGUISHED OF THAT REPUBLIC.
MY FATHER FILLED SEVERAL PUBLIC SITUATIONS WITH HONOUR AND REPUTATION. THERE WAS A CONSIDERABLE DIFFERENCE BETWEEN THE AGES OF MY PARENTS, BUT THIS CIRCUMSTANCE SEEMED TO UNITE THEM ONLY CLOSER IN BONDS OF DEVOTED AFFECTION. AFTER THEIR MARRIAGE, MY PARENTS SOUGHT THE PLEASANT CLIMATE OF ITALY.
FROM ITALY THEY VISITED GERMANY AND NAPLES. I WAS BORN AT NAPLES, AND AS AN INFANT ACCOMPANIED THEM ON THEIR RAMBLES.

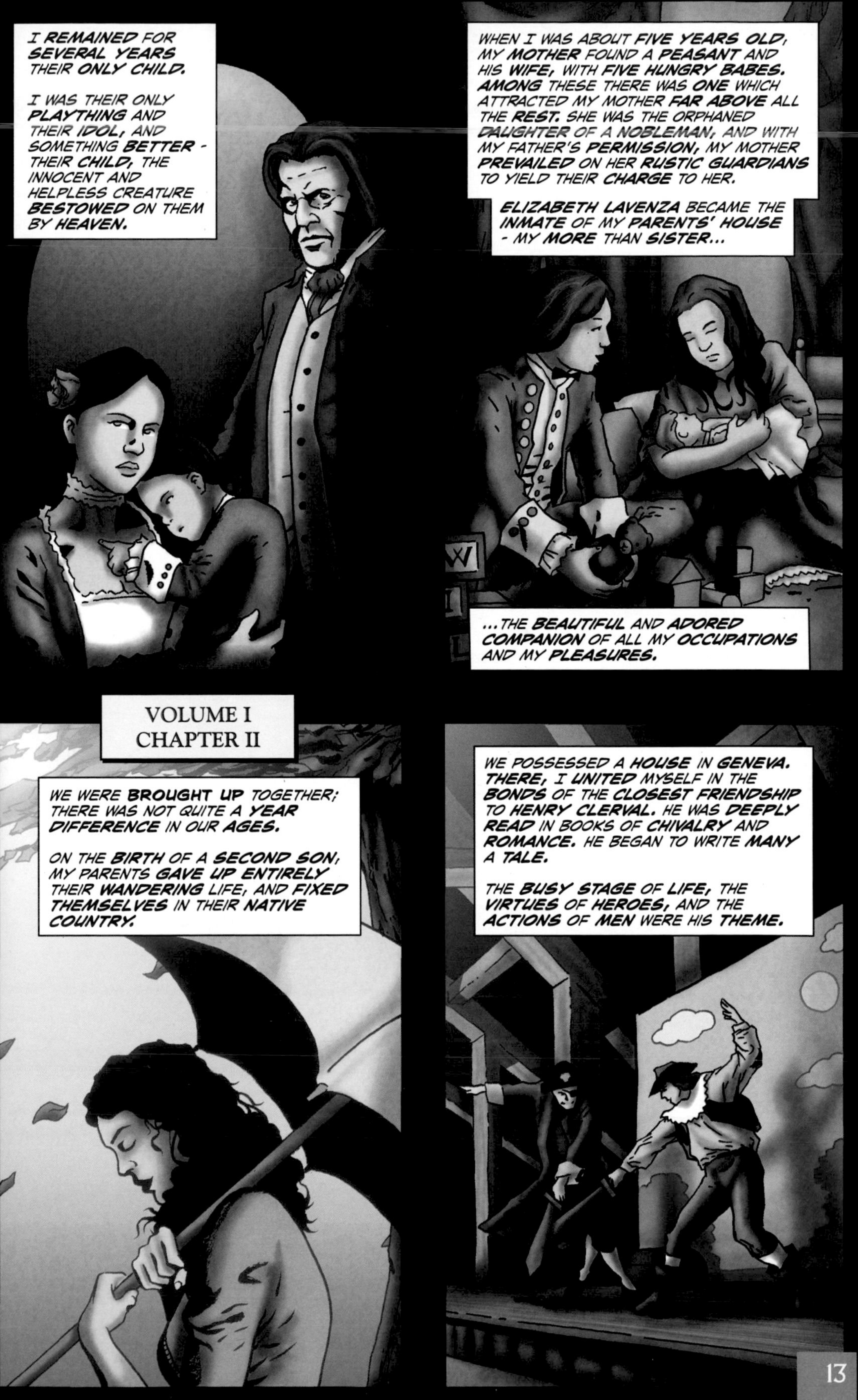
I REMAINED FOR SEVERAL YEARS THEIR ONLY CHILD.
I WAS THEIR ONLY PLAYTHING AND THEIR IDOL, AND SOMETHING BETTER - THEIR CHILD, THE INNOCENT AND HELPLESS CREATURE BESTOWED ON THEM BY HEAVEN.
WHEN I WAS ABOUT FIVE YEARS OLD, MY MOTHER FOUND A PEASANT AND HIS WIFE, WITH FIVE HUNGRY BABES. AMONG THESE THERE WAS ONE WHICH ATTRACTED MY MOTHER FAR ABOVE ALL THE REST. SHE WAS THE ORPHANED DAUGHTER OF A NOBLEMAN, AND WITH MY FATHER'S PERMISSION, MY MOTHER PREVAILED ON HER RUSTIC GUARDIANS TO YIELD THEIR CHARGE TO HER.
ELIZABETH LAVENZA BECAME THE INMATE OF MY PARENTS' HOUSE - MY MORE THAN SISTER...
...THE BEAUTIFUL AND ADORED COMPANION OF ALL MY OCCUPATIONS AND MY PLEASURES.
VOLUME I
CHAPTER II
WE WERE BROUGHT UP TOGETHER; THERE WAS NOT QUITE A YEAR DIFFERENCE IN OUR AGES.
ON THE BIRTH OF A SECOND SON, MY PARENTS GAVE UP ENTIRELY THEIR WANDERING LIFE, AND FIXED THEMSELVES IN THEIR NATIVE COUNTRY.
WE POSSESSED A HOUSE IN GENEVA. THERE, I UNITED MYSELF IN THE BONDS OF THE CLOSEST FRIENDSHIP TO HENRY CLERVAL. HE WAS DEEPLY READ IN BOOKS OF CHIVALRY AND ROMANCE. HE BEGAN TO WRITE MANY A TALE.
THE BUSY STAGE OF LIFE, THE VIRTUES OF HEROES, AND THE ACTIONS OF MEN WERE HIS THEME.

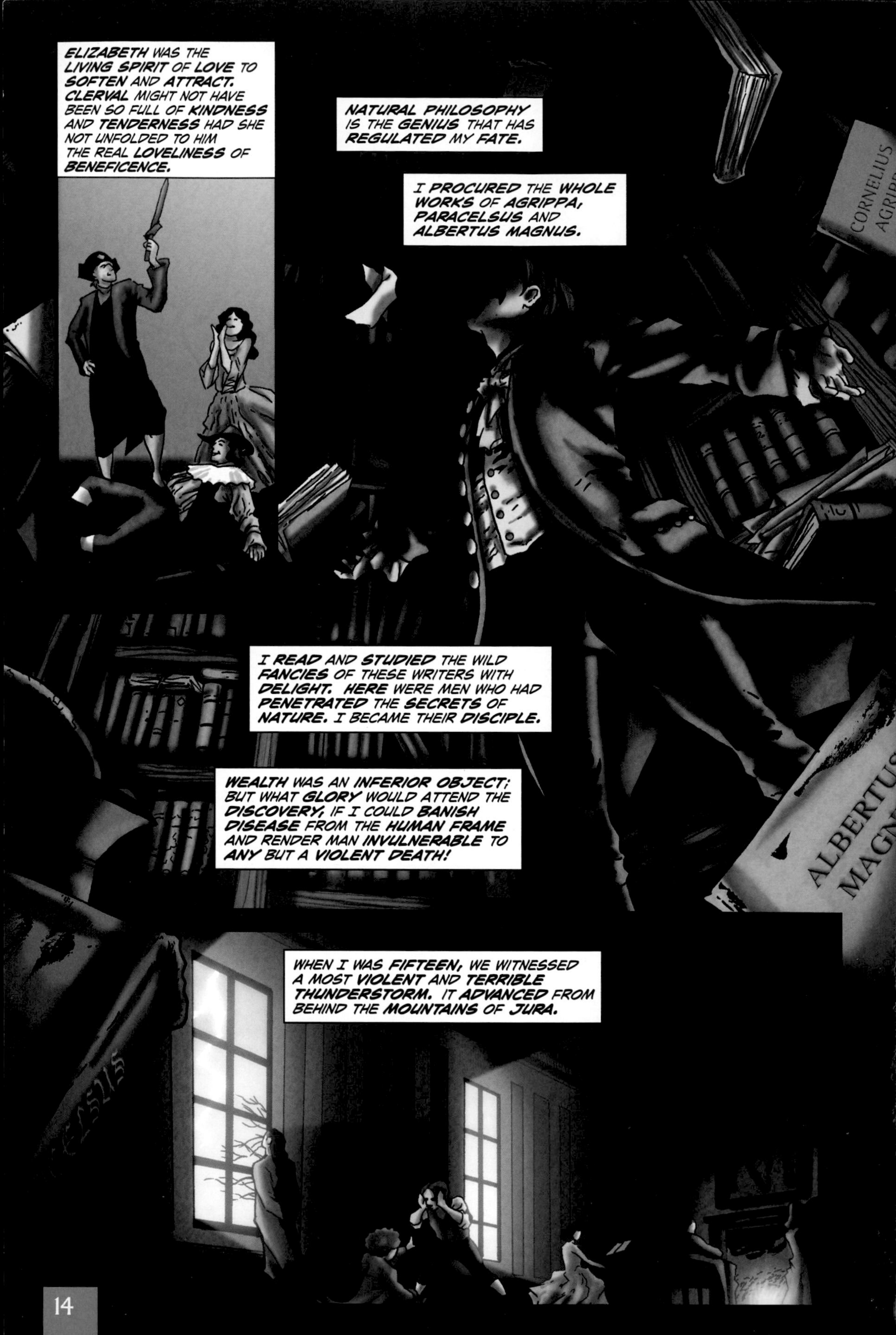
ELIZABETH WAS THE LIVING SPIRIT OF LOVE TO SOFTEN AND ATTRACT. CLERVAL MIGHT NOT HAVE BEEN SO FULL OF KINDNESS AND TENDERNESS HAD SHE NOT UNFOLDED TO HIM THE REAL LOVELINESS OF BENEFICENCE.
NATURAL PHILOSOPHY IS THE GENIUS THAT HAS REGULATED MY FATE.
I PROCURED THE WHOLE WORKS OF AGRIPPA, PARACELSUS AND ALBERTUS MAGNUS.
CORNELIUS
I READ AND STUDIED THE WILD FANCIES OF THESE WRITERS WITH DELIGHT. HERE WERE MEN WHO HAD PENETRATED THE SECRETS OF NATURE. I BECAME THEIR DISCIPLE.
WEALTH WAS AN INFERIOR OBJECT; BUT WHAT GLORY WOULD ATTEND THE DISCOVERY, IF I COULD BANISH DISEASE FROM THE HUMAN FRAME AND RENDER MAN INVULNERABLE TO ANY BUT A VIOLENT DEATH!
ALBERTUS
WHEN I WAS FIFTEEN, WE WITNESSED A MOST VIOLENT AND TERRIBLE THUNDERSTORM. IT ADVANCED FROM BEHIND THE MOUNTAINS OF JURA.

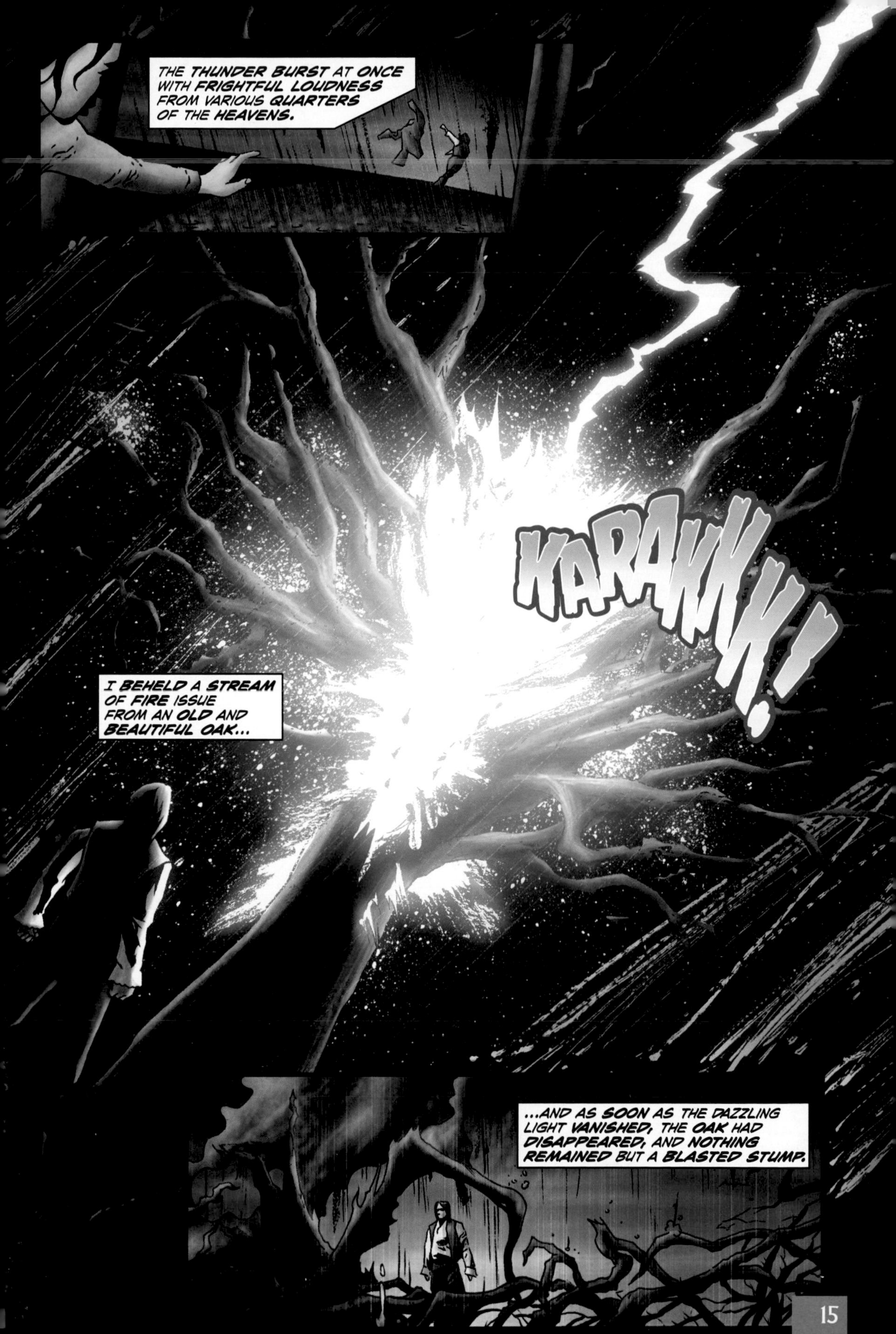
THE THUNDER BURST AT ONCE WITH FRIGHTFUL LOUDNESS FROM VARIOUS QUARTERS OF THE HEAVENS.
KARAKKK!
I BEHELD A STREAM OF FIRE ISSUE FROM AN OLD AND BEAUTIFUL OAK...
...AND AS SOON AS THE DAZZLING LIGHT VANISHED, THE OAK HAD DISAPPEARED, AND NOTHING REMAINED BUT A BLASTED STUMP.

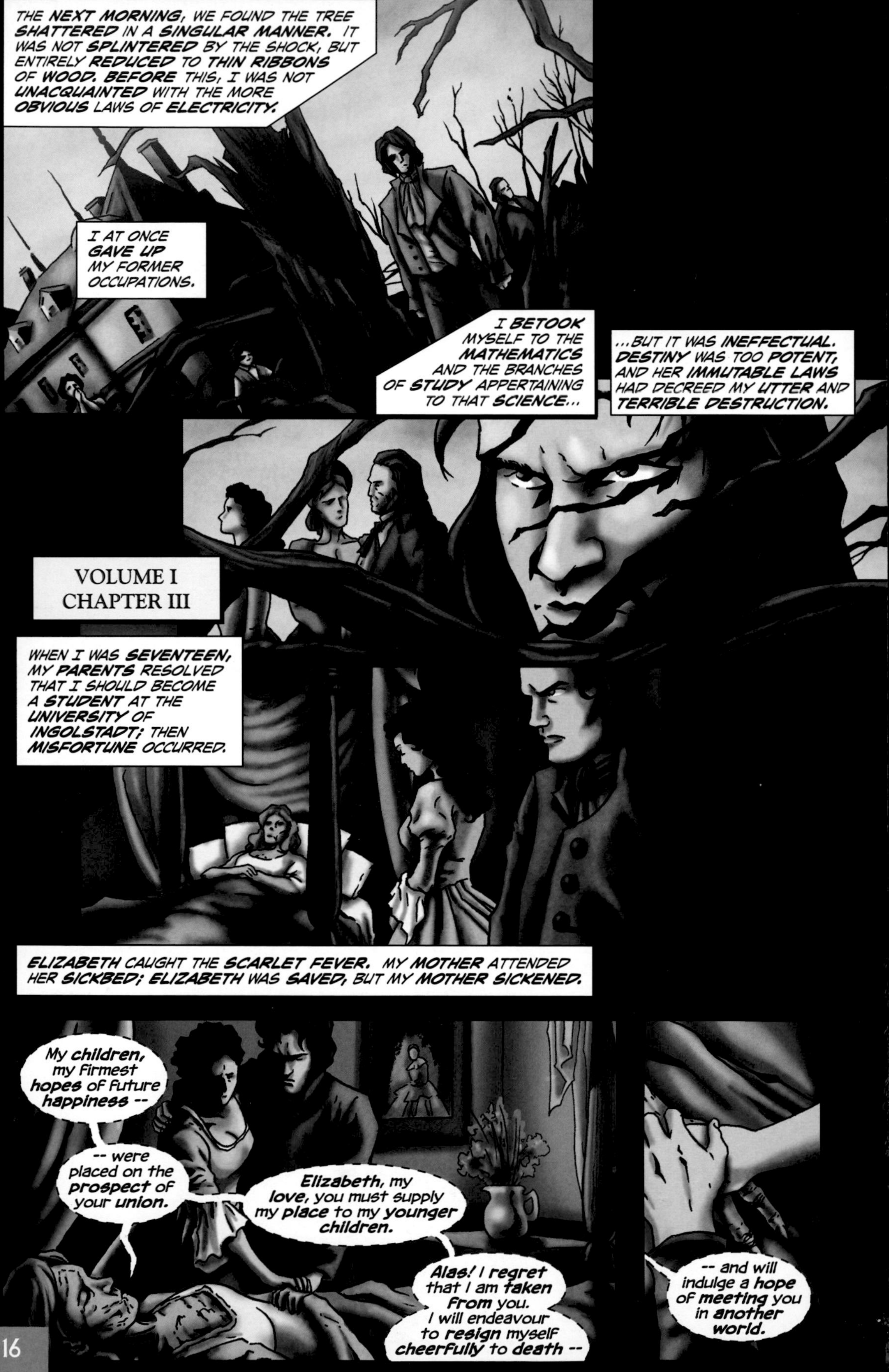
THE NEXT MORNING, WE FOUND THE TREE SHATTERED IN A SINGULAR MANNER. IT WAS NOT SPLINTERED BY THE SHOCK, BUT ENTIRELY REDUCED TO THIN RIBBONS OF WOOD. BEFORE THIS, I WAS NOT UNACQUAINTED WITH THE MORE OBVIOUS LAWS OF ELECTRICITY.
I AT ONCE GAVE UP MY FORMER OCCUPATIONS.
I BETOOK MYSELF TO THE MATHEMATICS AND THE BRANCHES OF STUDY APPERTAINING TO THAT SCIENCE...
...BUT IT WAS INEFFECTUAL. DESTINY WAS TOO POTENT, AND HER IMMUTABLE LAWS HAD DECREED MY UTTER AND TERRIBLE DESTRUCTION.
VOLUME I
CHAPTER III
WHEN I WAS SEVENTEEN, MY PARENTS RESOLVED THAT I SHOULD BECOME A STUDENT AT THE UNIVERSITY OF INGOLSTADT; THEN MISFORTUNE OCCURRED.
ELIZABETH CAUGHT THE SCARLET FEVER. MY MOTHER ATTENDED HER SICKBED; ELIZABETH WAS SAVED, BUT MY MOTHER SICKENED.
My children, my firmest hopes of future happiness --
-- were placed on the prospect of your union.
Elizabeth, my love, you must supply my place to my younger children.
Alas! I regret that I am taken from you. I will endeavour to resign myself cheerfully to death --
-- and will indulge a hope of meeting you in another world.

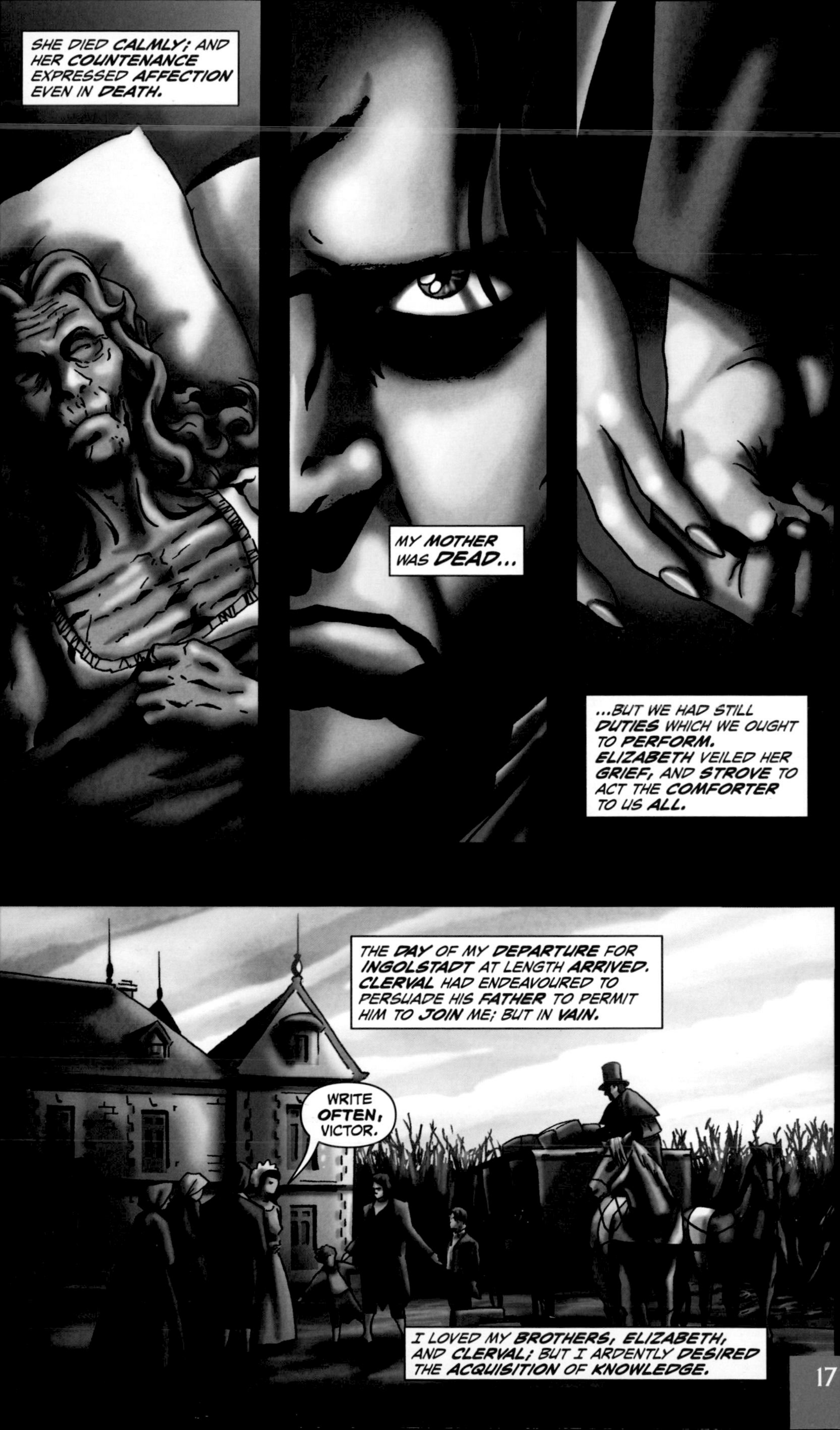
SHE DIED CALMLY; AND HER COUNTENANCE EXPRESSED AFFECTION EVEN IN DEATH.
MY MOTHER WAS DEAD...
...BUT WE HAD STILL DUTIES WHICH WE OUGHT TO PERFORM. ELIZABETH VEILED HER GRIEF, AND STROVE TO ACT THE COMFORTER TO US ALL.
THE DAY OF MY DEPARTURE FOR INGOLSTADT AT LENGTH ARRIVED. CLERVAL HAD ENDEAVOURED TO PERSUADE HIS FATHER TO PERMIT HIM TO JOIN ME; BUT IN VAIN.
WRITE OFTEN, VICTOR.
I LOVED MY BROTHERS, ELIZABETH, AND CLERVAL; BUT I ARDENTLY DESIRED THE ACQUISITION OF KNOWLEDGE.

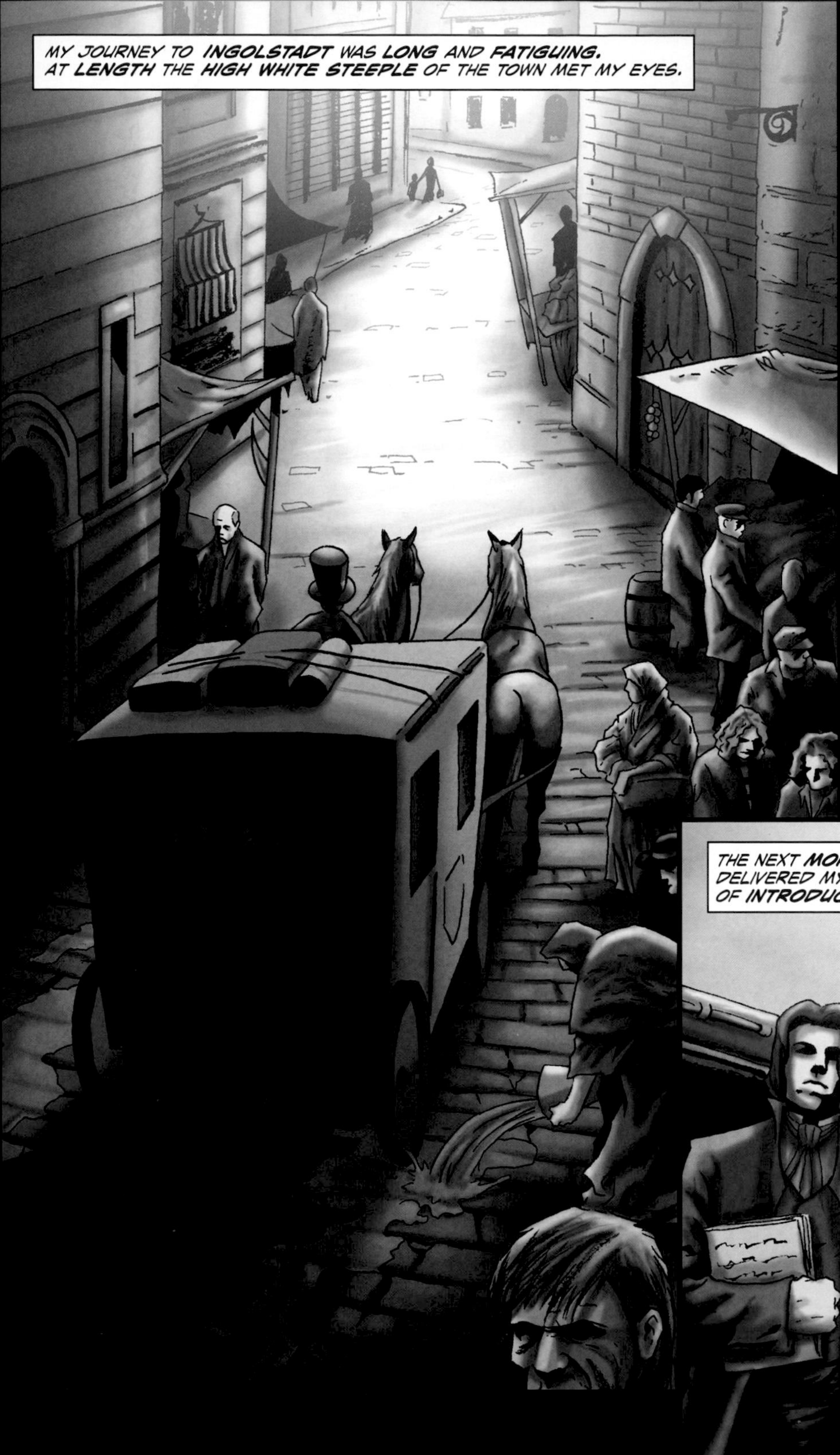
MY JOURNEY TO INGOLSTADT WAS LONG AND FATIGUING. AT LENGTH THE HIGH WHITE STEEPLE OF THE TOWN MET MY EYES.

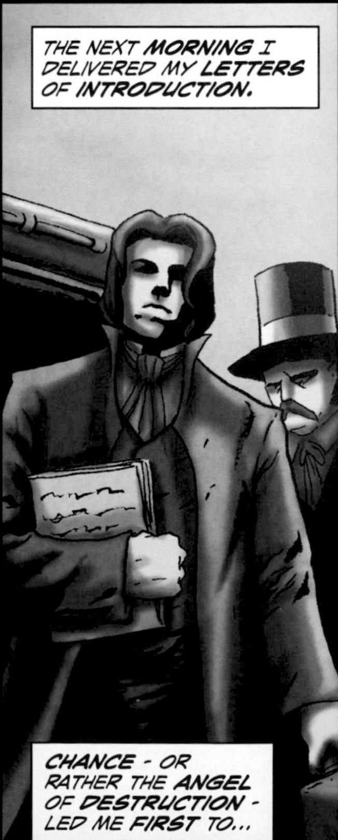
THE NEXT MORNING I DELIVERED MY LETTERS OF INTRODUCTION.
CHANCE - OR RATHER THE ANGEL OF DESTRUCTION - LED ME FIRST TO...

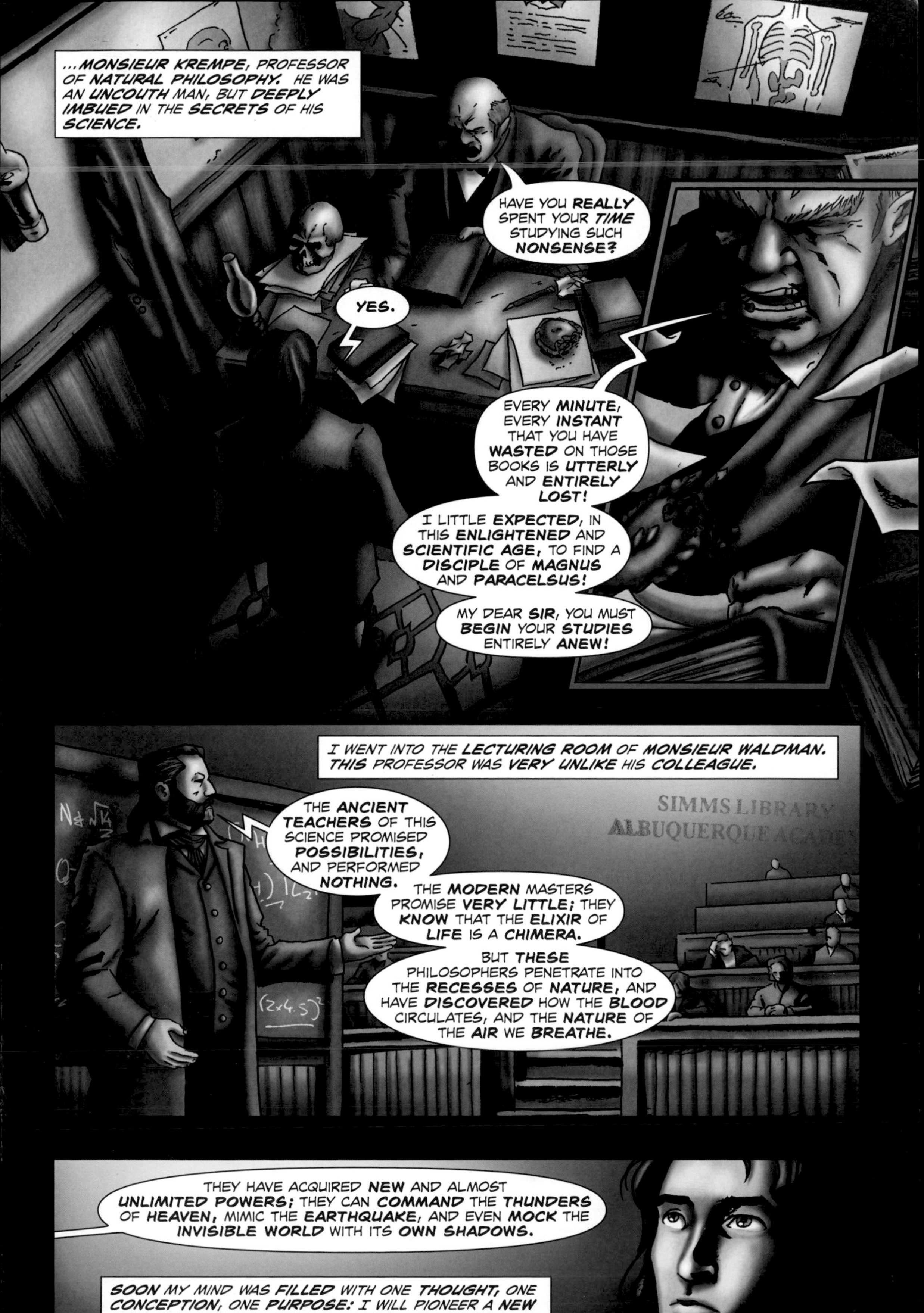
...MONSIEUR KREMPE, PROFESSOR OF NATURAL PHILOSOPHY. HE WAS AN UNCOUTH MAN, BUT DEEPLY IMBUED IN THE SECRETS OF HIS SCIENCE.
HAVE YOU REALLY SPENT YOUR TIME STUDYING SUCH NONSENSE?
YES.
EVERY MINUTE, EVERY INSTANT THAT YOU HAVE WASTED ON THOSE BOOKS IS UTTERLY AND ENTIRELY LOST!
I LITTLE EXPECTED, IN THIS ENLIGHTENED AND SCIENTIFIC AGE, TO FIND A DISCIPLE OF MAGNUS AND PARACELSUS!
MY DEAR SIR, YOU MUST BEGIN YOUR STUDIES ENTIRELY ANEW!
I WENT INTO THE LECTURING ROOM OF MONSIEUR WALDMAN. THIS PROFESSOR WAS VERY UNLIKE HIS COLLEAGUE.
THE ANCIENT TEACHERS OF THIS SCIENCE PROMISED POSSIBILITIES, AND PERFORMED NOTHING.
THE MODERN MASTERS PROMISE VERY LITTLE; THEY KNOW THAT THE ELIXIR OF LIFE IS A CHIMERA.
BUT THESE PHILOSOPHERS PENETRATE INTO THE RECESSES OF NATURE, AND HAVE DISCOVERED HOW THE BLOOD CIRCULATES, AND THE NATURE OF THE AIR WE BREATHE.
THEY HAVE ACQUIRED NEW AND ALMOST UNLIMITED POWERS; THEY CAN COMMAND THE THUNDERS OF HEAVEN, MIMIC THE EARTHQUAKE, AND EVEN MOCK THE INVISIBLE WORLD WITH ITS OWN SHADOWS.
SOON MY MIND WAS FILLED WITH ONE THOUGHT, ONE CONCEPTION, ONE PURPOSE: I WILL PIONEER A NEW WAY, EXPLORE UNKNOWN POWERS, AND UNFOLD TO THE WORLD THE DEEPEST MYSTERIES OF CREATION.

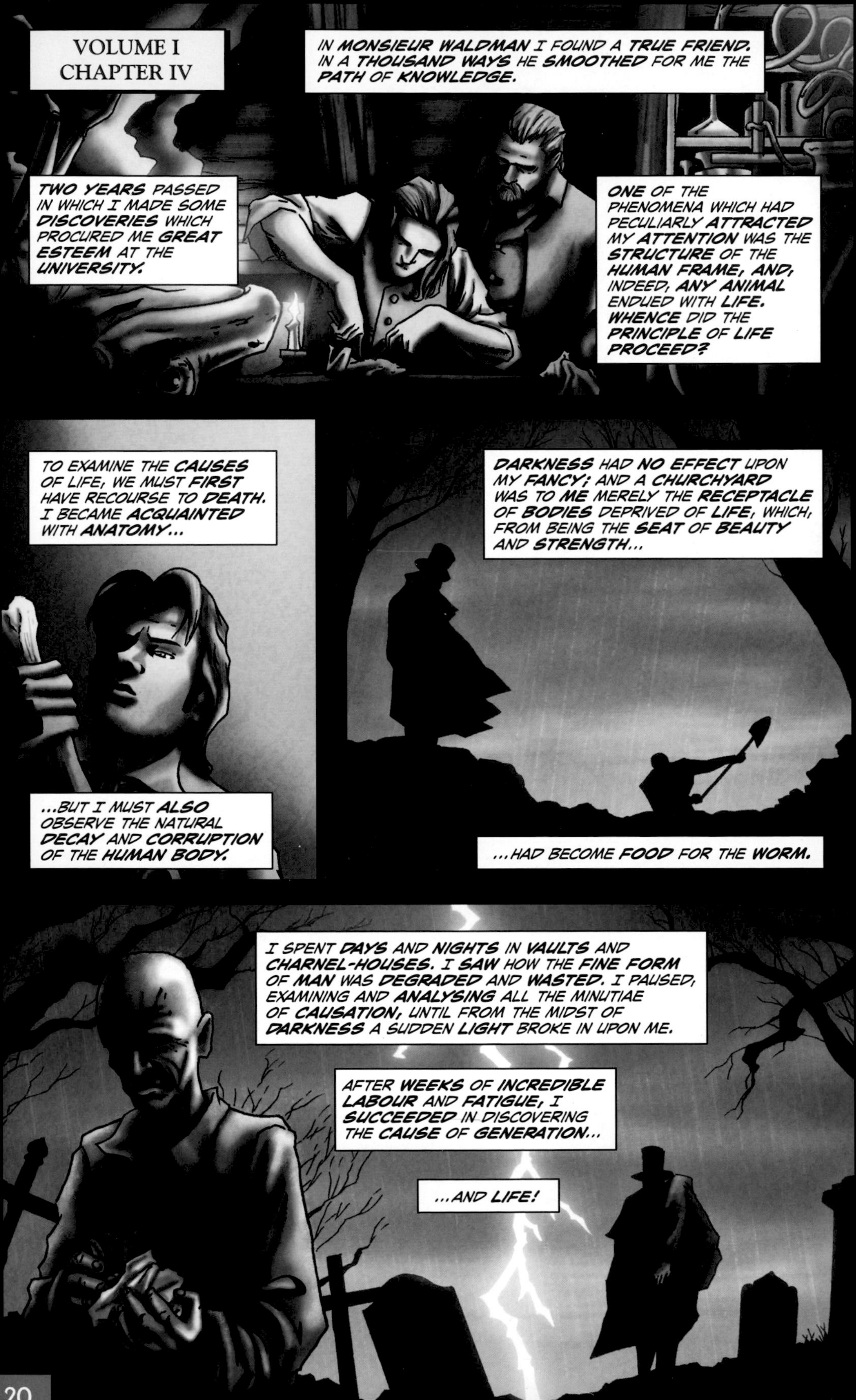
VOLUME I
CHAPTER IV
IN MONSIEUR WALDMAN I FOUND A TRUE FRIEND. IN A THOUSAND WAYS HE SMOOTHED FOR ME THE PATH OF KNOWLEDGE.
TWO YEARS PASSED IN WHICH I MADE SOME DISCOVERIES WHICH PROCURED ME GREAT ESTEEM AT THE UNIVERSITY.
ONE OF THE PHENOMENA WHICH HAD PECULIARLY ATTRACTED MY ATTENTION WAS THE STRUCTURE OF THE HUMAN FRAME, AND, INDEED, ANY ANIMAL ENDUED WITH LIFE. WHENCE DID THE PRINCIPLE OF LIFE PROCEED?
TO EXAMINE THE CAUSES OF LIFE, WE MUST FIRST HAVE RECOURSE TO DEATH. I BECAME ACQUAINTED WITH ANATOMY...
...BUT I MUST ALSO OBSERVE THE NATURAL DECAY AND CORRUPTION OF THE HUMAN BODY.
DARKNESS HAD NO EFFECT UPON MY FANCY; AND A CHURCHYARD WAS TO ME MERELY THE RECEPTACLE OF BODIES DEPRIVED OF LIFE, WHICH, FROM BEING THE SEAT OF BEAUTY AND STRENGTH...
...HAD BECOME FOOD FOR THE WORM.
I SPENT DAYS AND NIGHTS IN VAULTS AND CHARNEL-HOUSES. I SAW HOW THE FINE FORM OF MAN WAS DEGRADED AND WASTED. I PAUSED, EXAMINING AND ANALYSING ALL THE MINUTIAE OF CAUSATION, UNTIL FROM THE MIDST OF DARKNESS A SUDDEN LIGHT BROKE IN UPON ME.
AFTER WEEKS OF INCREDIBLE LABOUR AND FATIGUE, I SUCCEEDED IN DISCOVERING THE CAUSE OF GENERATION...
...AND LIFE!

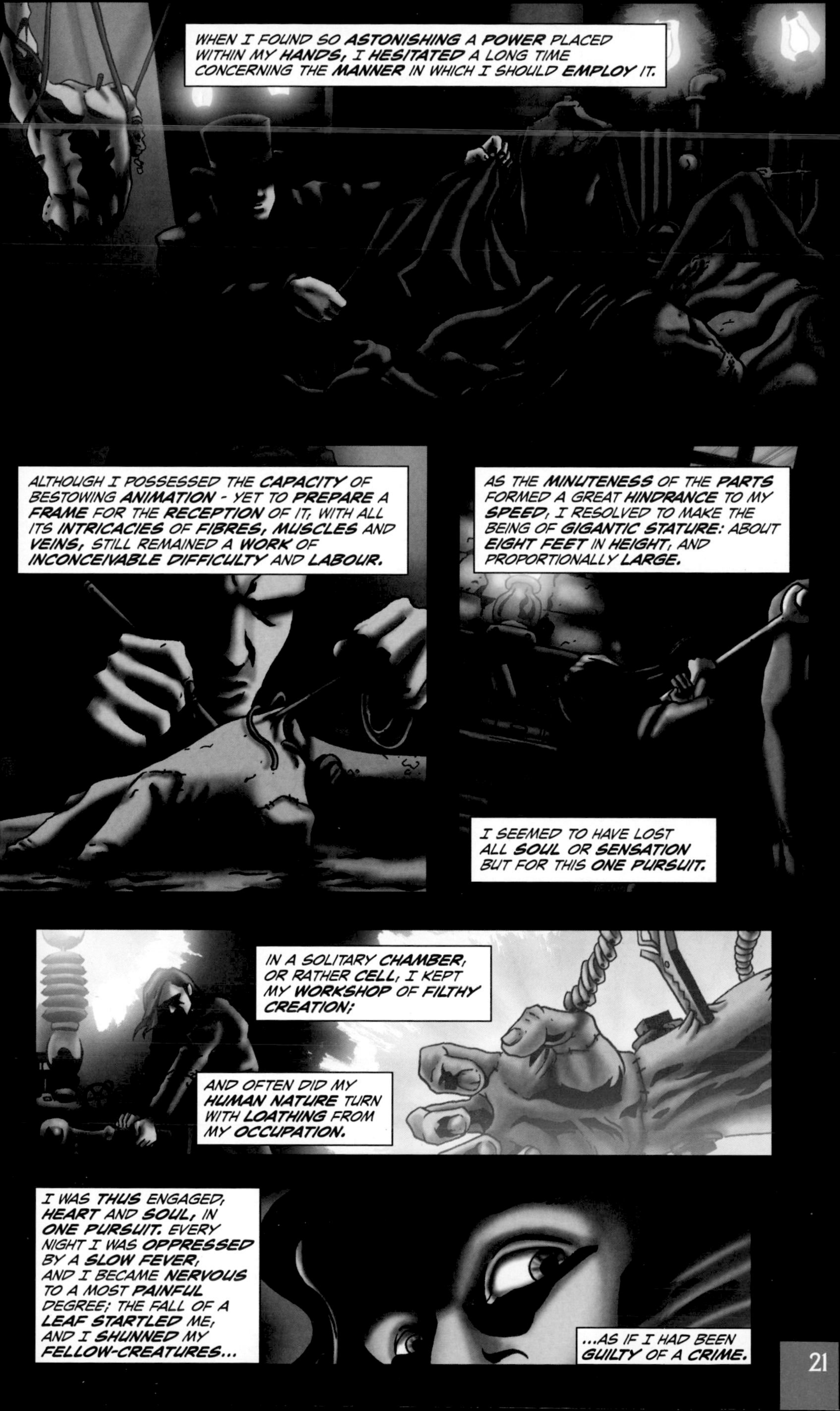
WHEN I FOUND SO ASTONISHING A POWER PLACED WITHIN MY HANDS, I HESITATED A LONG TIME CONCERNING THE MANNER IN WHICH I SHOULD EMPLOY IT.
ALTHOUGH I POSSESSED THE CAPACITY OF BESTOWING ANIMATION - YET TO PREPARE A FRAME FOR THE RECEPTION OF IT, WITH ALL ITS INTRICACIES OF FIBRES, MUSCLES AND VEINS, STILL REMAINED A WORK OF INCONCEIVABLE DIFFICULTY AND LABOUR.
AS THE MINUTENESS OF THE PARTS FORMED A GREAT HINDRANCE TO MY SPEED, I RESOLVED TO MAKE THE BEING OF GIGANTIC STATURE: ABOUT EIGHT FEET IN HEIGHT, AND PROPORTIONALLY LARGE.
I SEEMED TO HAVE LOST ALL SOUL OR SENSATION BUT FOR THIS ONE PURSUIT.
IN A SOLITARY CHAMBER, OR RATHER CELL, I KEPT MY WORKSHOP OF FILTHY CREATION;
AND OFTEN DID MY HUMAN NATURE TURN WITH LOATHING FROM MY OCCUPATION.
I WAS THUS ENGAGED, HEART AND SOUL, IN ONE PURSUIT. EVERY NIGHT I WAS OPPRESSED BY A SLOW FEVER, AND I BECAME NERVOUS TO A MOST PAINFUL DEGREE; THE FALL OF A LEAF STARTLED ME, AND I SHUNNED MY FELLOW-CREATURES...
...AS IF I HAD BEEN GUILTY OF A CRIME.

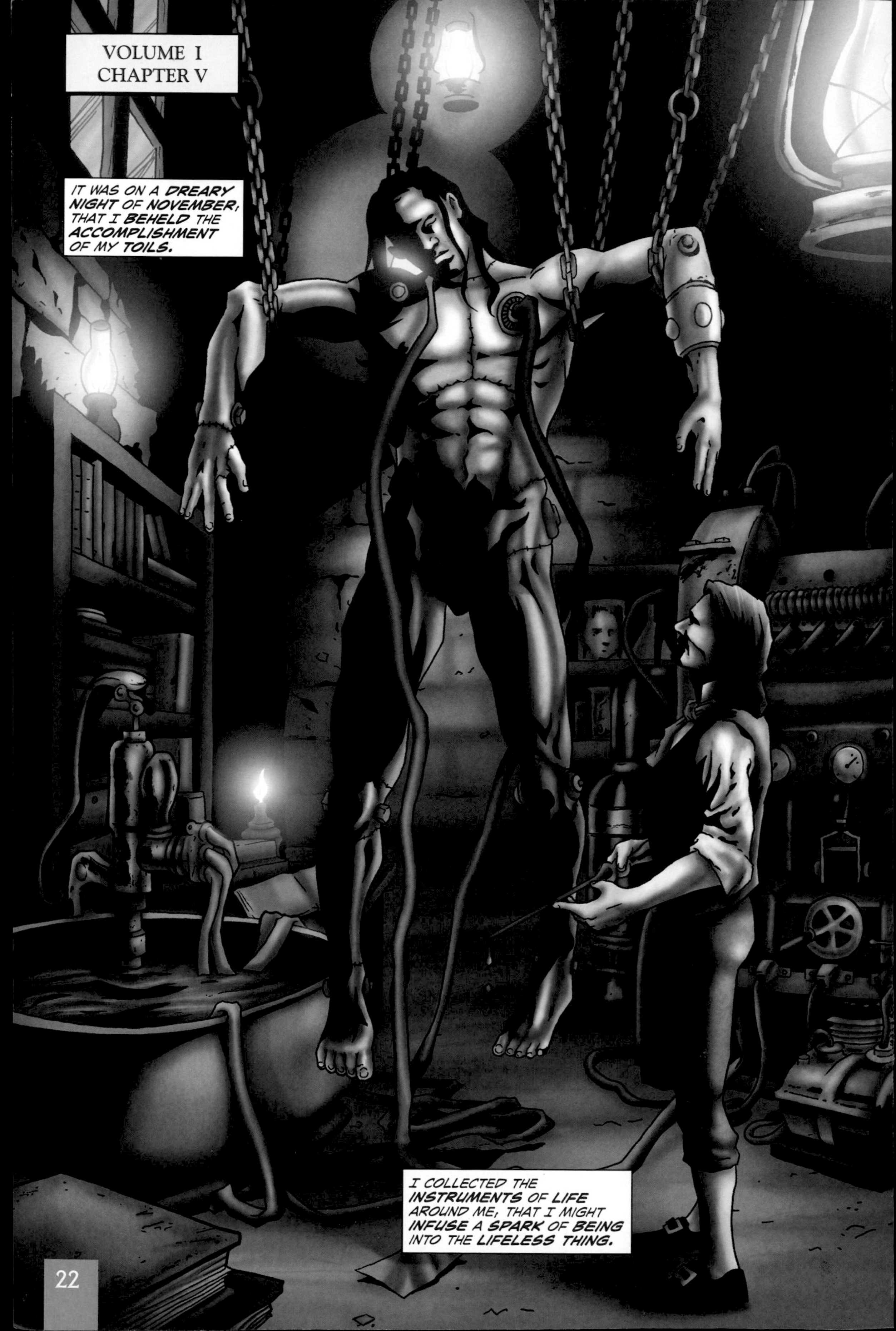
VOLUME I
CHAPTER V
IT WAS ON A DREARY NIGHT OF NOVEMBER, THAT I BEHELD THE ACCOMPLISHMENT OF MY TOILS.
I COLLECTED THE INSTRUMENTS OF LIFE AROUND ME, THAT I MIGHT INFUSE A SPARK OF BEING INTO THE LIFELESS THING.

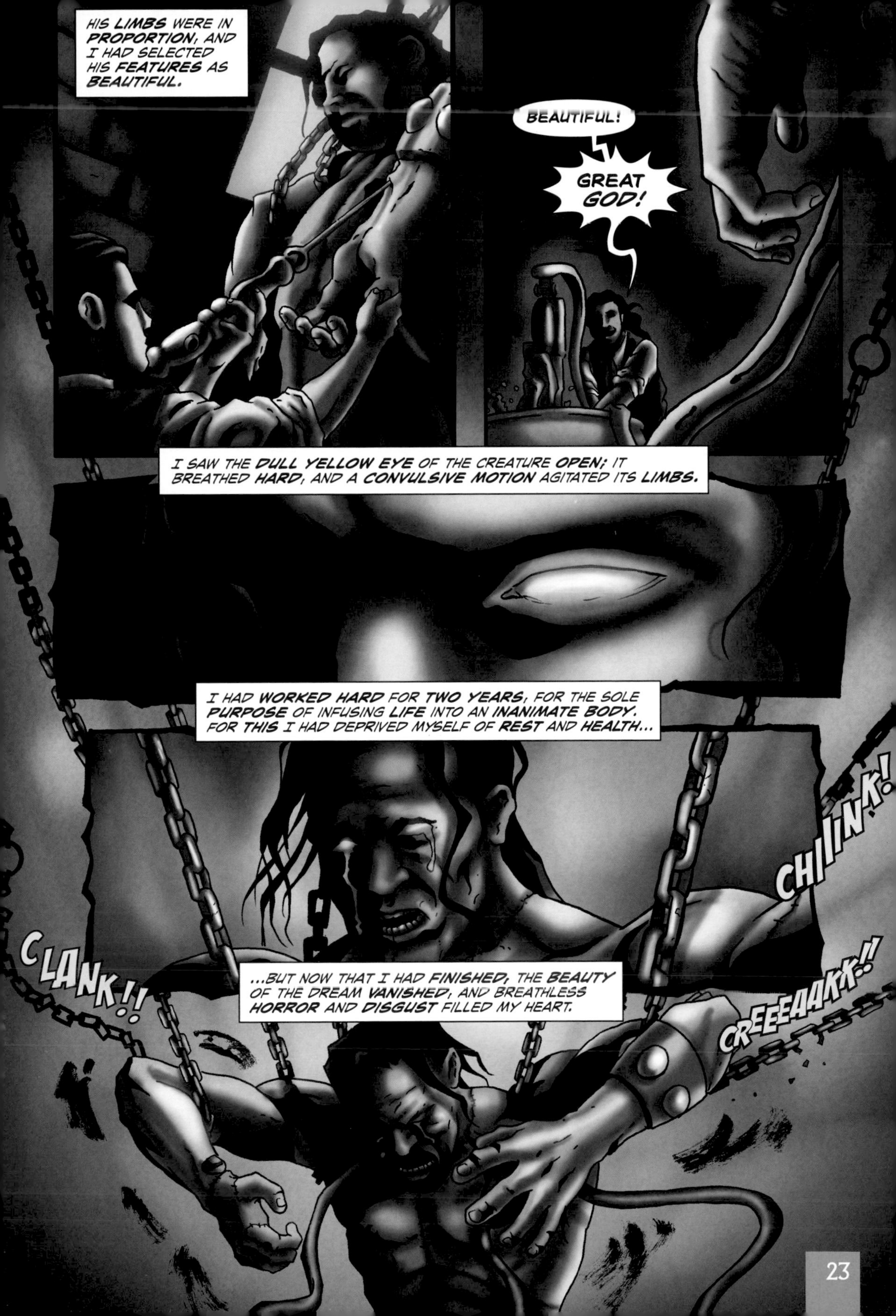
HIS LIMBS WERE IN PROPORTION, AND I HAD SELECTED HIS FEATURES AS BEAUTIFUL.
BEAUTIFUL!
GREAT GOD!
I SAW THE DULL YELLOW EYE OF THE CREATURE OPEN; IT BREATHED HARD, AND A CONVULSIVE MOTION AGITATED ITS LIMBS.
I HAD WORKED HARD FOR TWO YEARS, FOR THE SOLE PURPOSE OF INFUSING LIFE INTO AN INANIMATE BODY. FOR THIS I HAD DEPRIVED MYSELF OF REST AND HEALTH...
CHIIINK!
CLANK!!
...BUT NOW THAT I HAD FINISHED, THE BEAUTY OF THE DREAM VANISHED, AND BREATHLESS HORROR AND DISGUST FILLED MY HEART.
CREEEAAKK!!

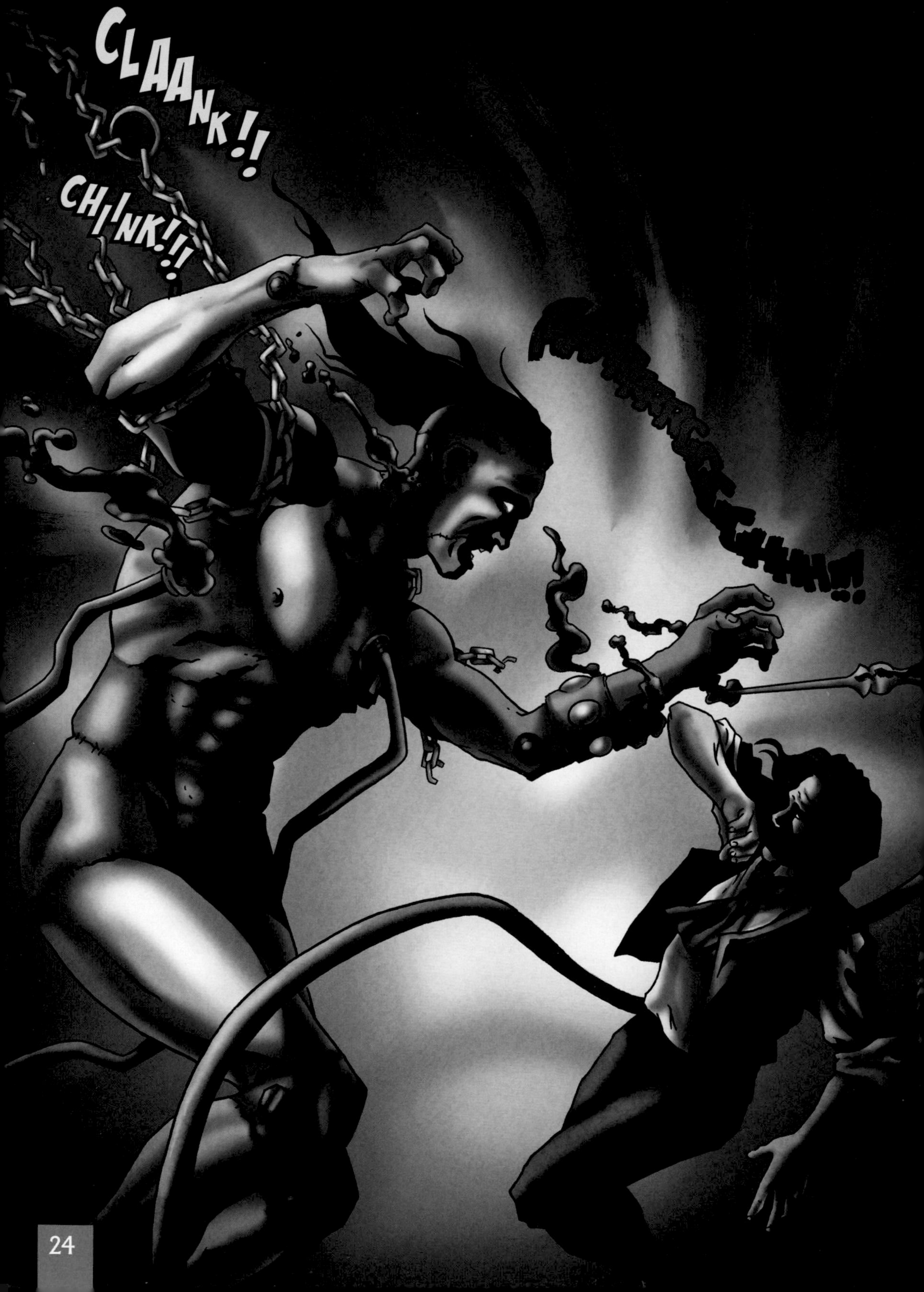
CLAANK!!
CHIINK!!!

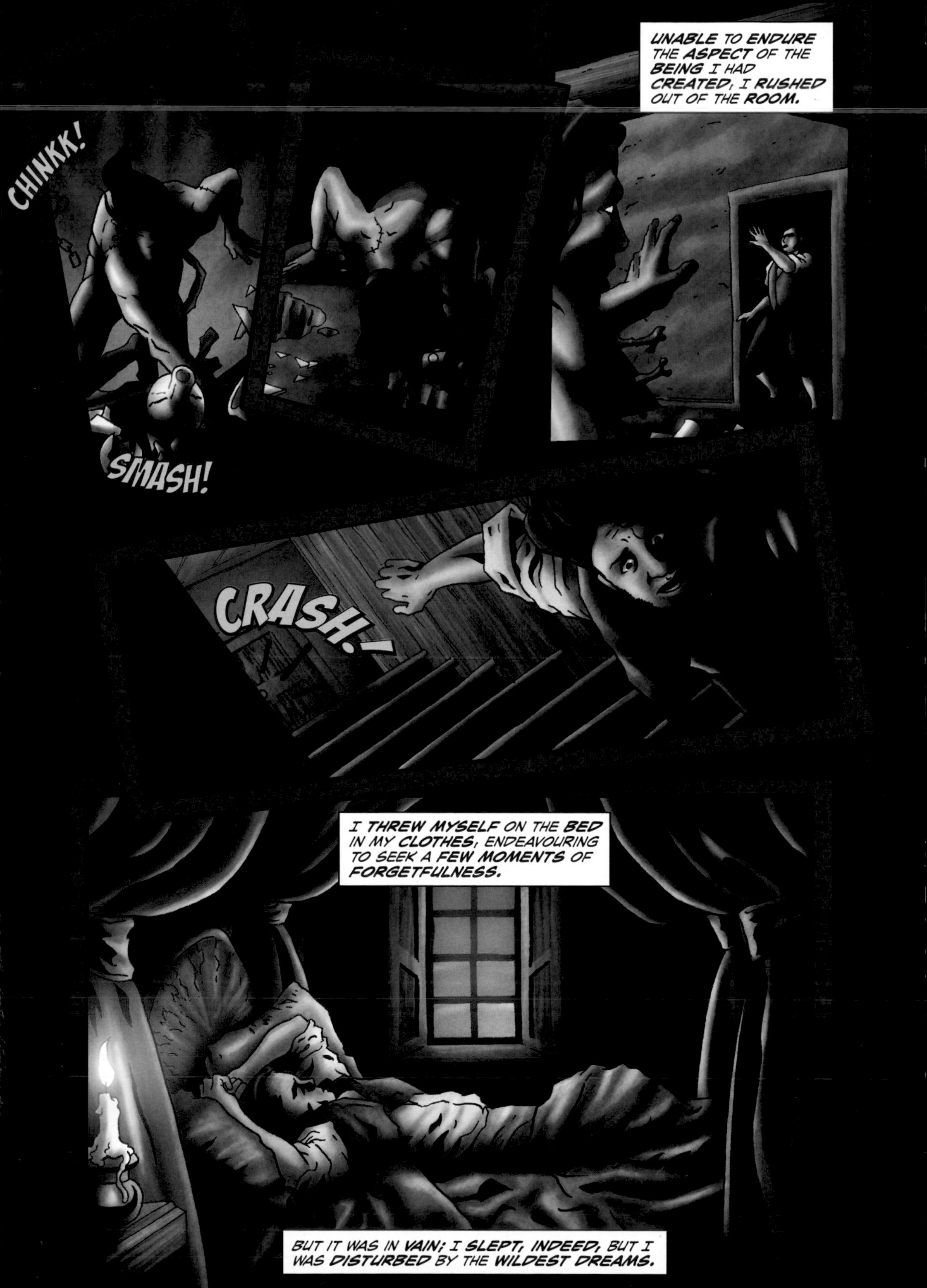
UNABLE TO ENDURE THE ASPECT OF THE BEING I HAD CREATED, I RUSHED OUT OF THE ROOM.
CHINKK!
SMASH!
CRASH!
I THREW MYSELF ON THE BED IN MY CLOTHES, ENDEAVOURING TO SEEK A FEW MOMENTS OF FORGETFULNESS.
BUT IT WAS IN VAIN; I SLEPT, INDEED, BUT I WAS DISTURBED BY THE WILDEST DREAMS.

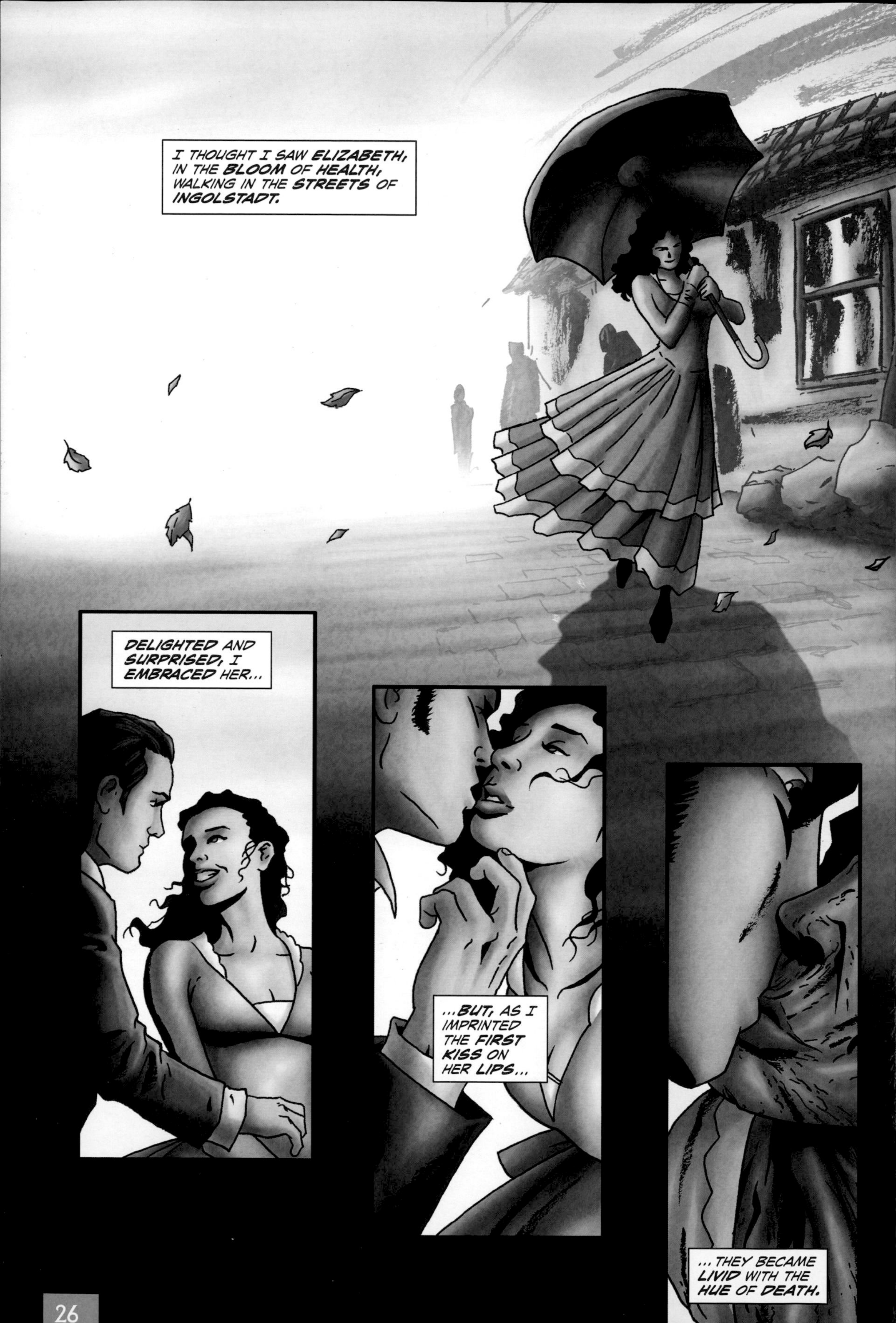
I THOUGHT I SAW ELIZABETH, IN THE BLOOM OF HEALTH, WALKING IN THE STREETS OF INGOLSTADT.
DELIGHTED AND SURPRISED, I EMBRACED HER...
...BUT, AS I IMPRINTED THE FIRST KISS ON HER LIPS...
...THEY BECAME LIVID WITH THE HUE OF DEATH.

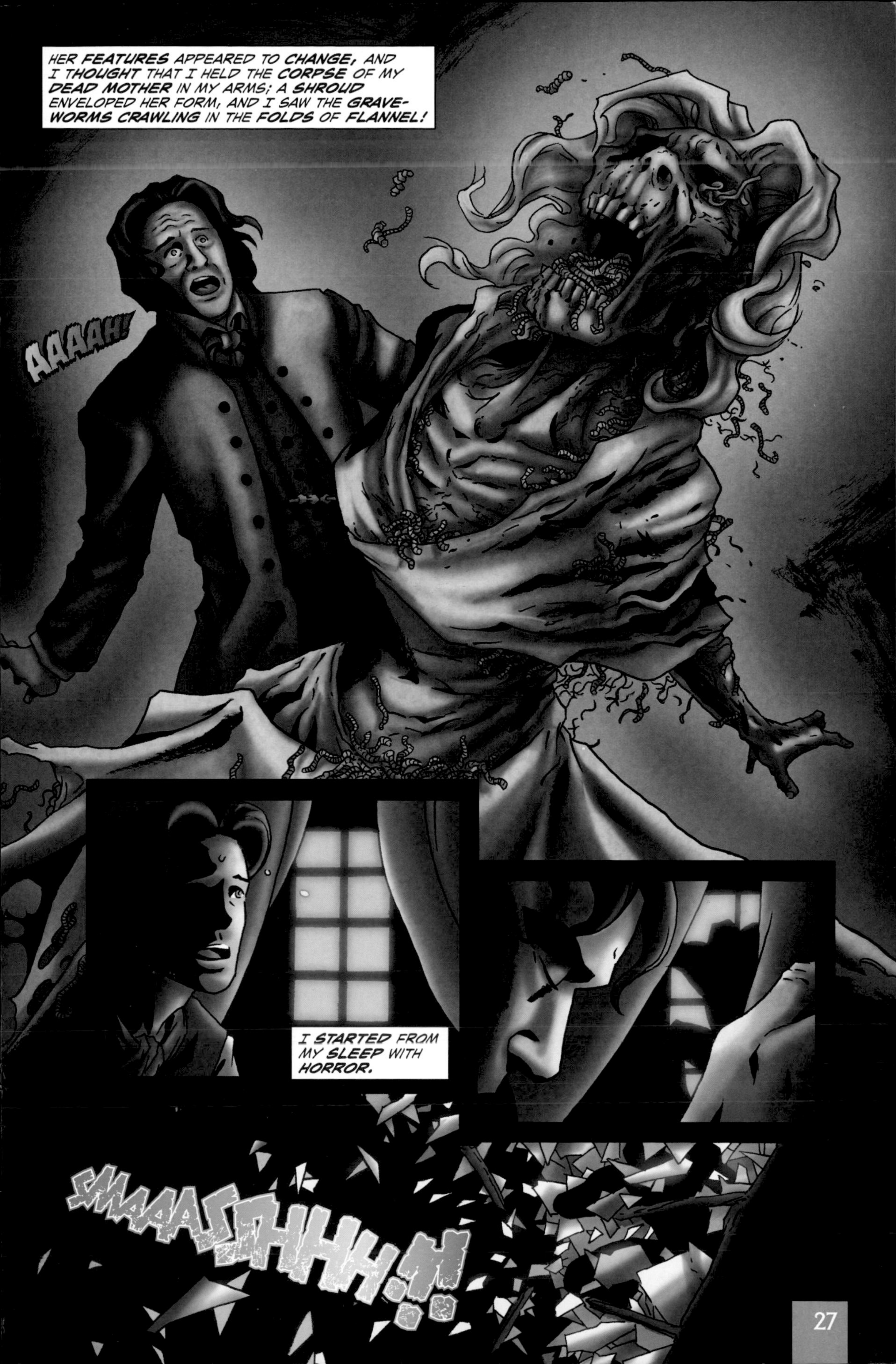
HER FEATURES APPEARED TO CHANGE, AND I THOUGHT THAT I HELD THE CORPSE OF MY DEAD MOTHER IN MY ARMS; A SHROUD ENVELOPED HER FORM, AND I SAW THE GRAVE-WORMS CRAWLING IN THE FOLDS OF FLANNEL!
AAAAH!
I STARTED FROM MY SLEEP WITH HORROR.
SMAAASHHH!!!

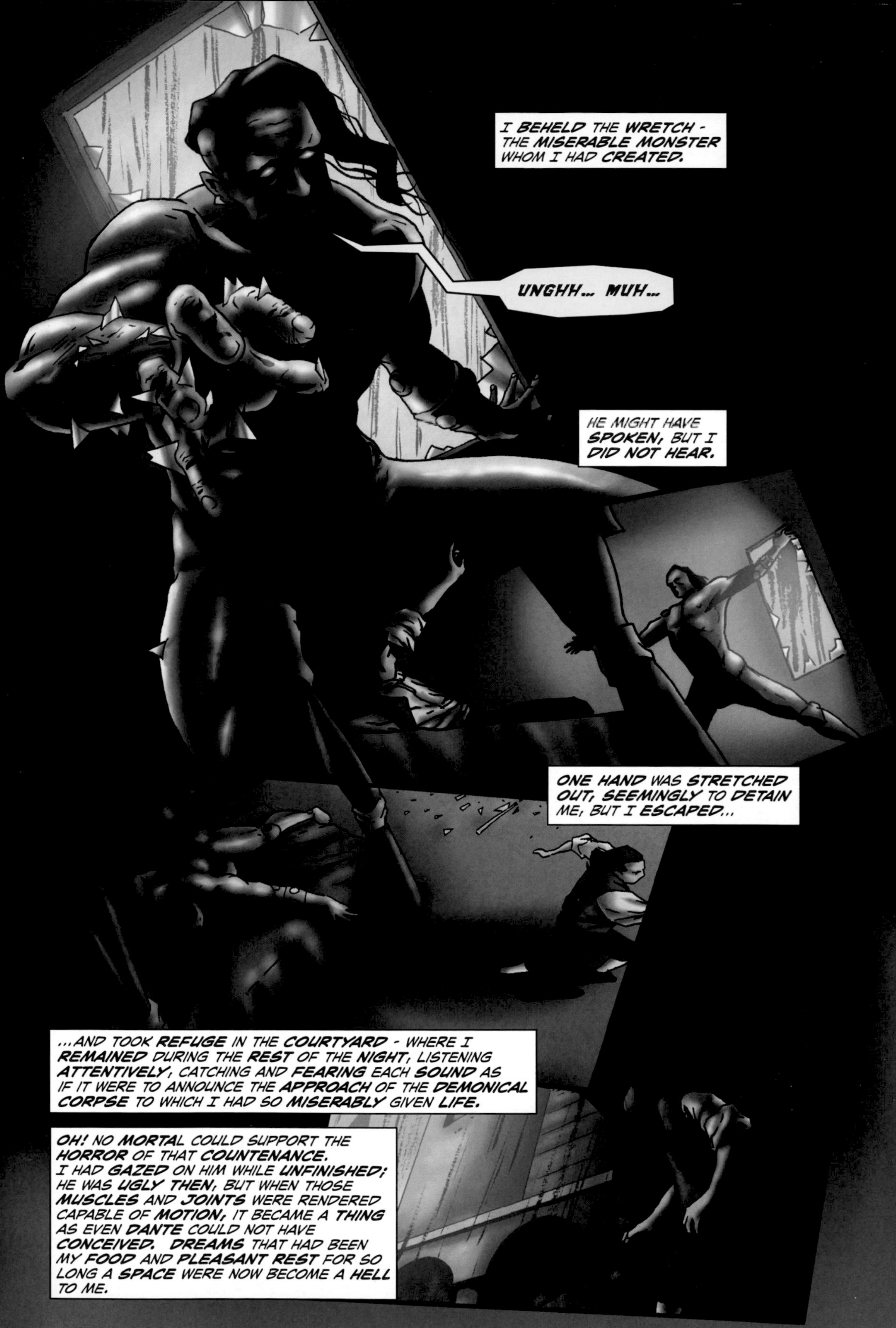
I BEHELD THE WRETCH - THE MISERABLE MONSTER WHOM I HAD CREATED.
UNGHH... MUH...
HE MIGHT HAVE SPOKEN, BUT I DID NOT HEAR.
ONE HAND WAS STRETCHED OUT, SEEMINGLY TO DETAIN ME; BUT I ESCAPED...
...AND TOOK REFUGE IN THE COURTYARD - WHERE I REMAINED DURING THE REST OF THE NIGHT, LISTENING ATTENTIVELY, CATCHING AND FEARING EACH SOUND AS IF IT WERE TO ANNOUNCE THE APPROACH OF THE DEMONICAL CORPSE TO WHICH I HAD SO MISERABLY GIVEN LIFE.
OH! NO MORTAL COULD SUPPORT THE HORROR OF THAT COUNTENANCE. I HAD GAZED ON HIM WHILE UNFINISHED; HE WAS UGLY THEN, BUT WHEN THOSE MUSCLES AND JOINTS WERE RENDERED CAPABLE OF MOTION, IT BECAME A THING AS EVEN DANTE COULD NOT HAVE CONCEIVED. DREAMS THAT HAD BEEN MY FOOD AND PLEASANT REST FOR SO LONG A SPACE WERE NOW BECOME A HELL TO ME.

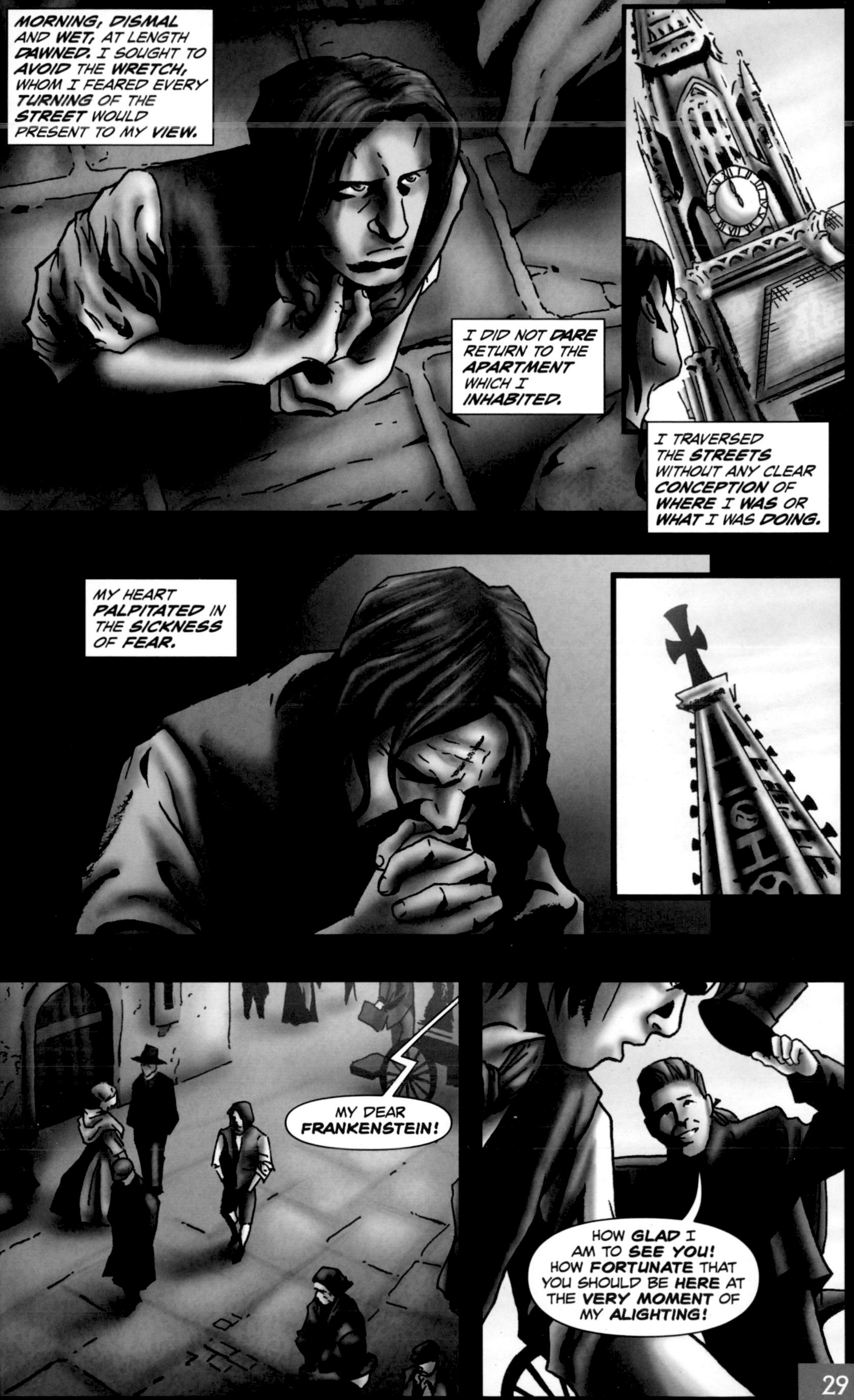
MORNING, DISMAL AND WET, AT LENGTH DAWNED. I SOUGHT TO AVOID THE WRETCH, WHOM I FEARED EVERY TURNING OF THE STREET WOULD PRESENT TO MY VIEW.
I DID NOT DARE RETURN TO THE APARTMENT WHICH I INHABITED.
I TRAVERSED THE STREETS WITHOUT ANY CLEAR CONCEPTION OF WHERE I WAS OR WHAT I WAS DOING.
MY HEART PALPITATED IN THE SICKNESS OF FEAR.
MY DEAR FRANKENSTEIN!
HOW GLAD I AM TO SEE YOU! HOW FORTUNATE THAT YOU SHOULD BE HERE AT THE VERY MOMENT OF MY ALIGHTING!

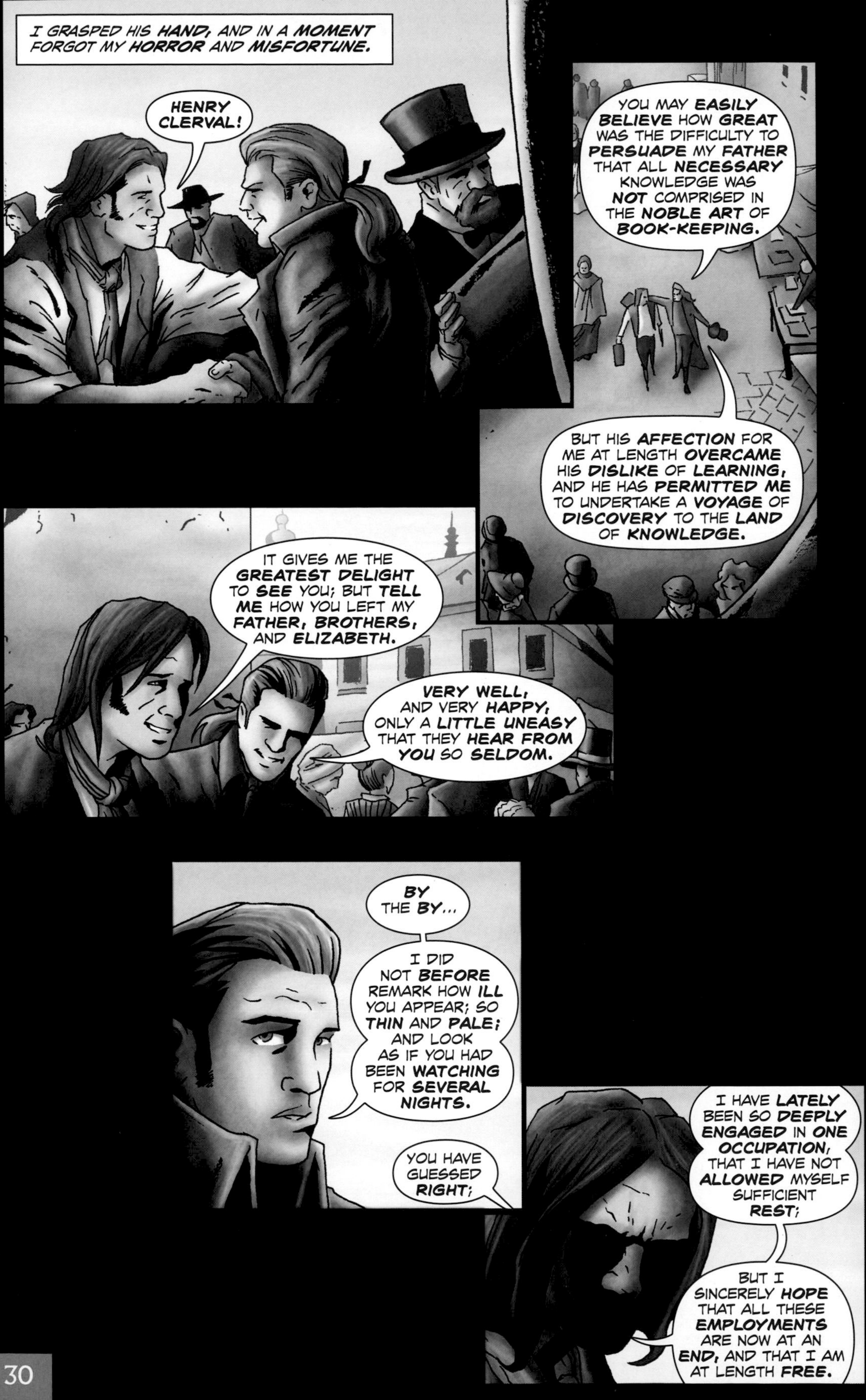
I GRASPED HIS HAND, AND IN A MOMENT FORGOT MY HORROR AND MISFORTUNE.
HENRY CLERVAL!
YOU MAY EASILY BELIEVE HOW GREAT WAS THE DIFFICULTY TO PERSUADE MY FATHER THAT ALL NECESSARY KNOWLEDGE WAS NOT COMPRISED IN THE NOBLE ART OF BOOK-KEEPING.
BUT HIS AFFECTION FOR ME AT LENGTH OVERCAME HIS DISLIKE OF LEARNING, AND HE HAS PERMITTED ME TO UNDERTAKE A VOYAGE OF DISCOVERY TO THE LAND OF KNOWLEDGE.
IT GIVES ME THE GREATEST DELIGHT TO SEE YOU; BUT TELL ME HOW YOU LEFT MY FATHER, BROTHERS, AND ELIZABETH.
VERY WELL, AND VERY HAPPY; ONLY A LITTLE UNEASY THAT THEY HEAR FROM YOU SO SELDOM.
BY THE BY...
I DID NOT BEFORE REMARK HOW ILL YOU APPEAR; SO THIN AND PALE; AND LOOK AS IF YOU HAD BEEN WATCHING FOR SEVERAL NIGHTS.
YOU HAVE GUESSED RIGHT;
I HAVE LATELY BEEN SO DEEPLY ENGAGED IN ONE OCCUPATION, THAT I HAVE NOT ALLOWED MYSELF SUFFICIENT REST;
BUT I SINCERELY HOPE THAT ALL THESE EMPLOYMENTS ARE NOW AT AN END, AND THAT I AM AT LENGTH FREE.

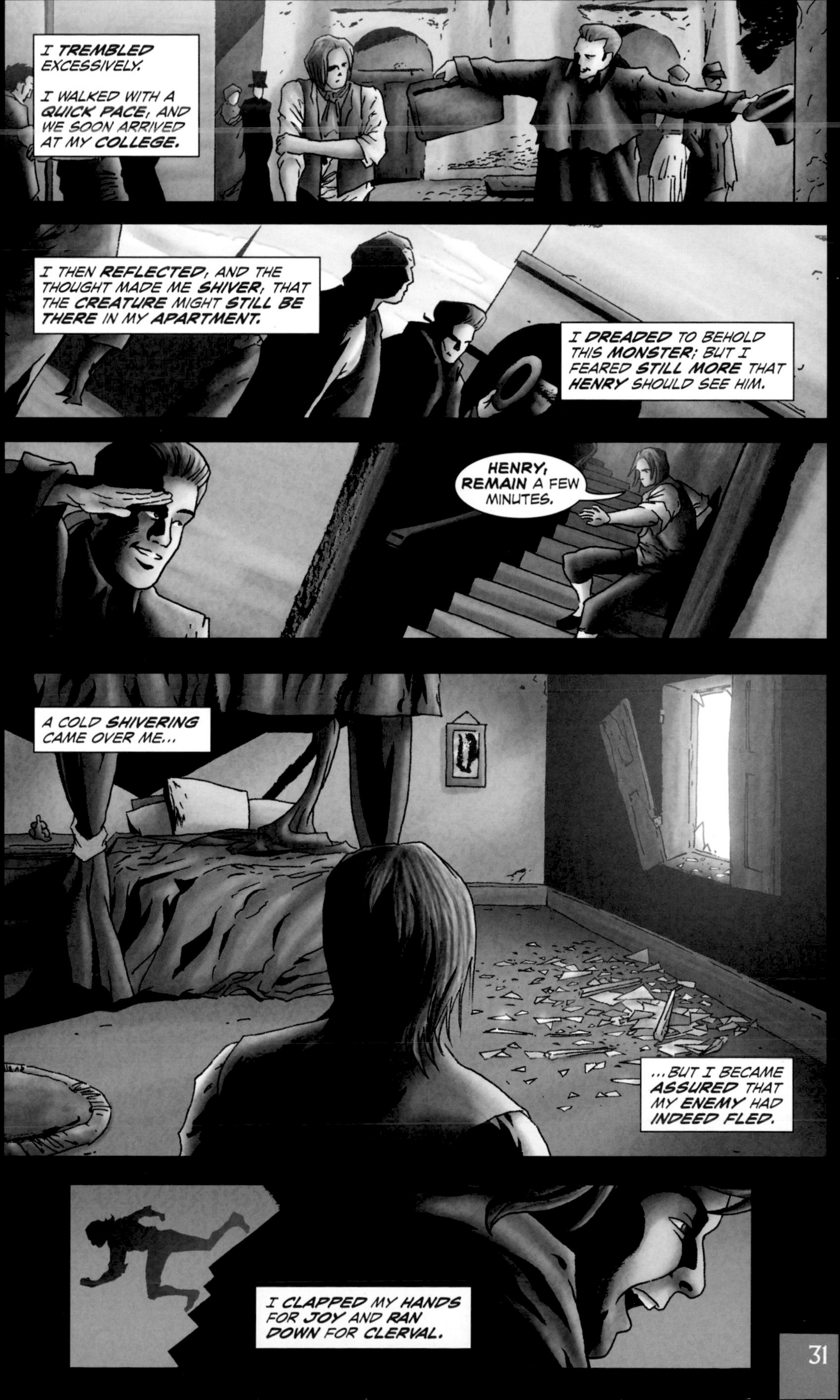
I TREMBLED EXCESSIVELY.
I WALKED WITH A QUICK PACE, AND WE SOON ARRIVED AT MY COLLEGE.
I THEN REFLECTED, AND THE THOUGHT MADE ME SHIVER, THAT THE CREATURE MIGHT STILL BE THERE IN MY APARTMENT.
I DREADED TO BEHOLD THIS MONSTER; BUT I FEARED STILL MORE THAT HENRY SHOULD SEE HIM.
HENRY, REMAIN A FEW MINUTES.
A COLD SHIVERING CAME OVER ME...
...BUT I BECAME ASSURED THAT MY ENEMY HAD INDEED FLED.
I CLAPPED MY HANDS FOR JOY AND RAN DOWN FOR CLERVAL.

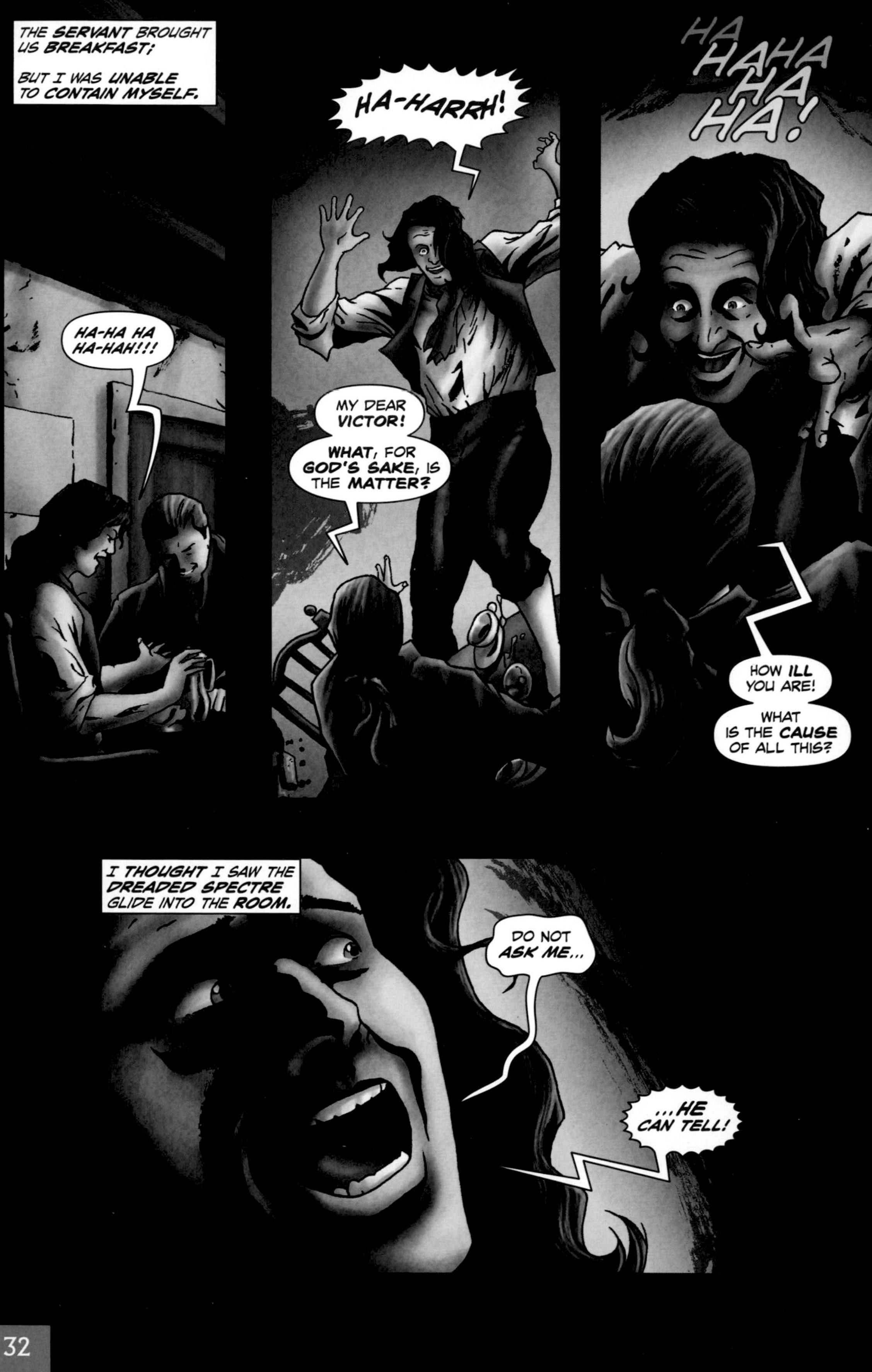
THE SERVANT BROUGHT US BREAKFAST;
BUT I WAS UNABLE TO CONTAIN MYSELF.
HA-HA HA HA-HAH!!!
HA-HARRH!
MY DEAR VICTOR!
WHAT, FOR GOD'S SAKE, IS THE MATTER?
HA HAHA HA HA!
HOW ILL YOU ARE!
WHAT IS THE CAUSE OF ALL THIS?
I THOUGHT I SAW THE DREADED SPECTRE GLIDE INTO THE ROOM.
DO NOT ASK ME...
...HE CAN TELL!

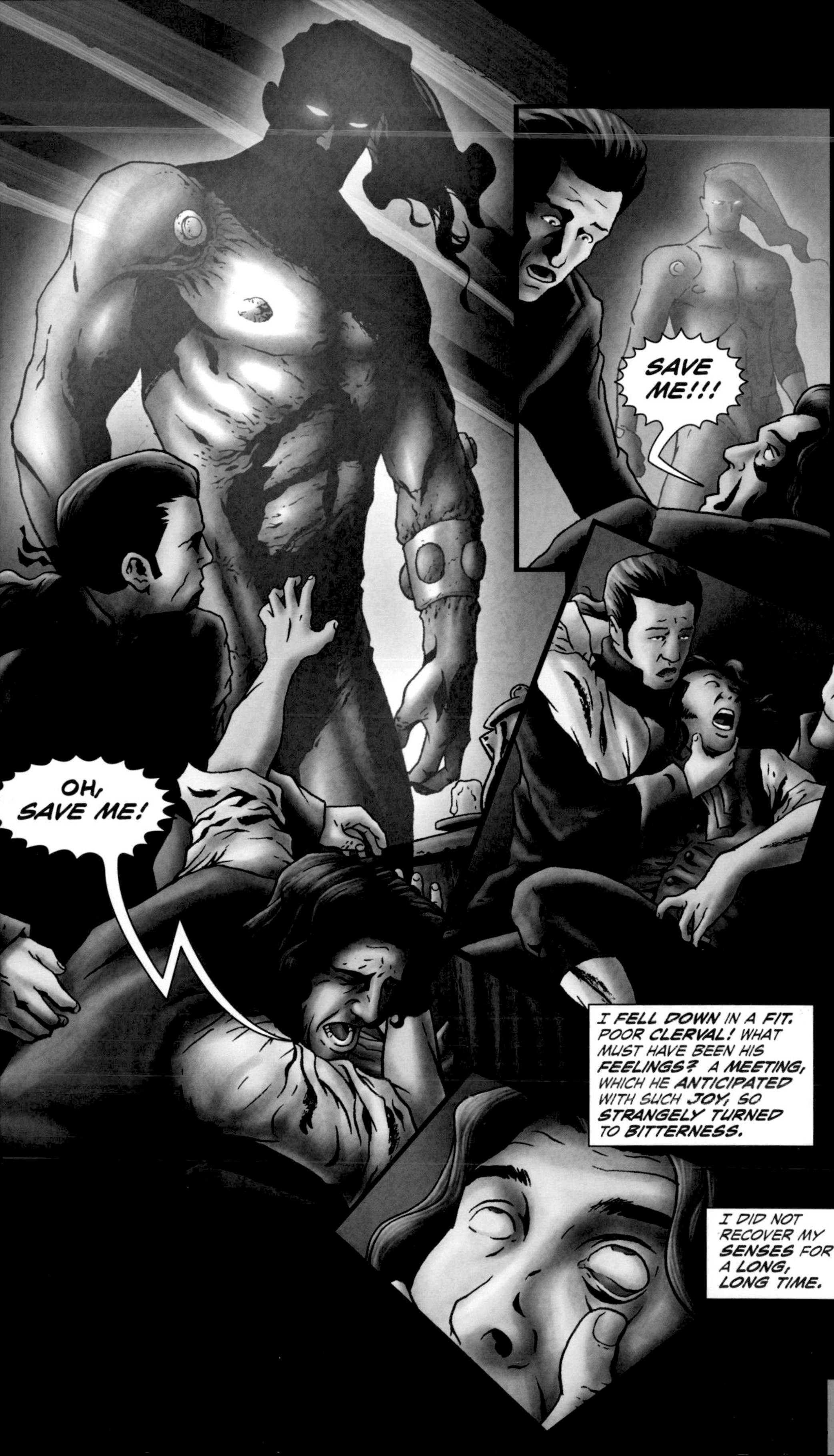
SAVE ME!!!
OH, SAVE ME!
I FELL DOWN IN A FIT. POOR CLERVAL! WHAT MUST HAVE BEEN HIS FEELINGS? A MEETING, WHICH HE ANTICIPATED WITH SUCH JOY, SO STRANGELY TURNED TO BITTERNESS.
I DID NOT RECOVER MY SENSES FOR A LONG, LONG TIME.

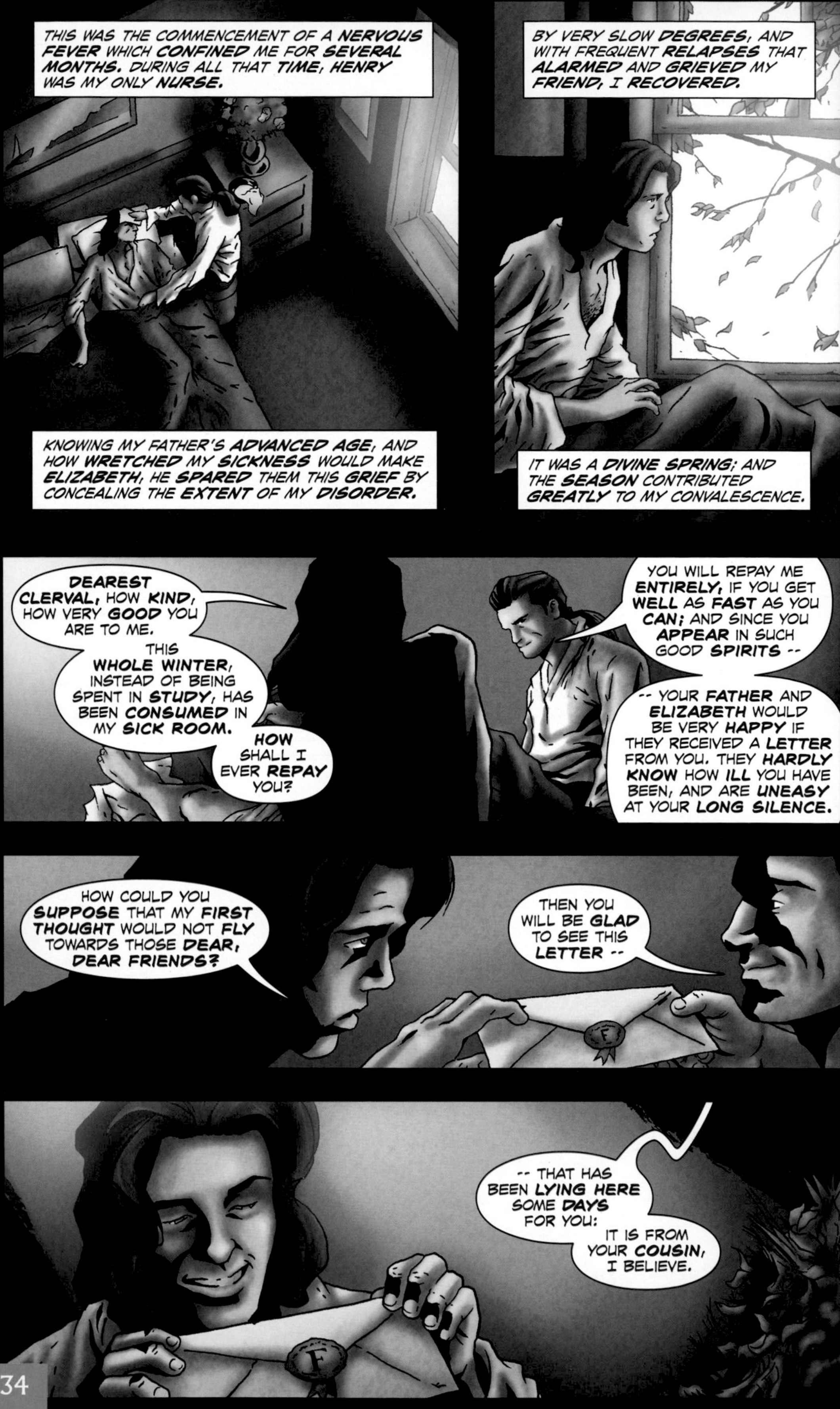
THIS WAS THE COMMENCEMENT OF A NERVOUS FEVER WHICH CONFINED ME FOR SEVERAL MONTHS. DURING ALL THAT TIME, HENRY WAS MY ONLY NURSE.
KNOWING MY FATHER'S ADVANCED AGE, AND HOW WRETCHED MY SICKNESS WOULD MAKE ELIZABETH, HE SPARED THEM THIS GRIEF BY CONCEALING THE EXTENT OF MY DISORDER.
BY VERY SLOW DEGREES, AND WITH FREQUENT RELAPSES THAT ALARMED AND GRIEVED MY FRIEND, I RECOVERED.
IT WAS A DIVINE SPRING; AND THE SEASON CONTRIBUTED GREATLY TO MY CONVALESCENCE.
DEAREST CLERVAL, HOW KIND, HOW VERY GOOD YOU ARE TO ME.
THIS WHOLE WINTER, INSTEAD OF BEING SPENT IN STUDY, HAS BEEN CONSUMED IN MY SICK ROOM.
HOW SHALL I EVER REPAY YOU?
YOU WILL REPAY ME ENTIRELY, IF YOU GET WELL AS FAST AS YOU CAN; AND SINCE YOU APPEAR IN SUCH GOOD SPIRITS --
-- YOUR FATHER AND ELIZABETH WOULD BE VERY HAPPY IF THEY RECEIVED A LETTER FROM YOU. THEY HARDLY KNOW HOW ILL YOU HAVE BEEN, AND ARE UNEASY AT YOUR LONG SILENCE.
HOW COULD YOU SUPPOSE THAT MY FIRST THOUGHT WOULD NOT FLY TOWARDS THOSE DEAR, DEAR FRIENDS?
THEN YOU WILL BE GLAD TO SEE THIS LETTER --
-- THAT HAS BEEN LYING HERE SOME DAYS FOR YOU:
IT IS FROM YOUR COUSIN, I BELIEVE.

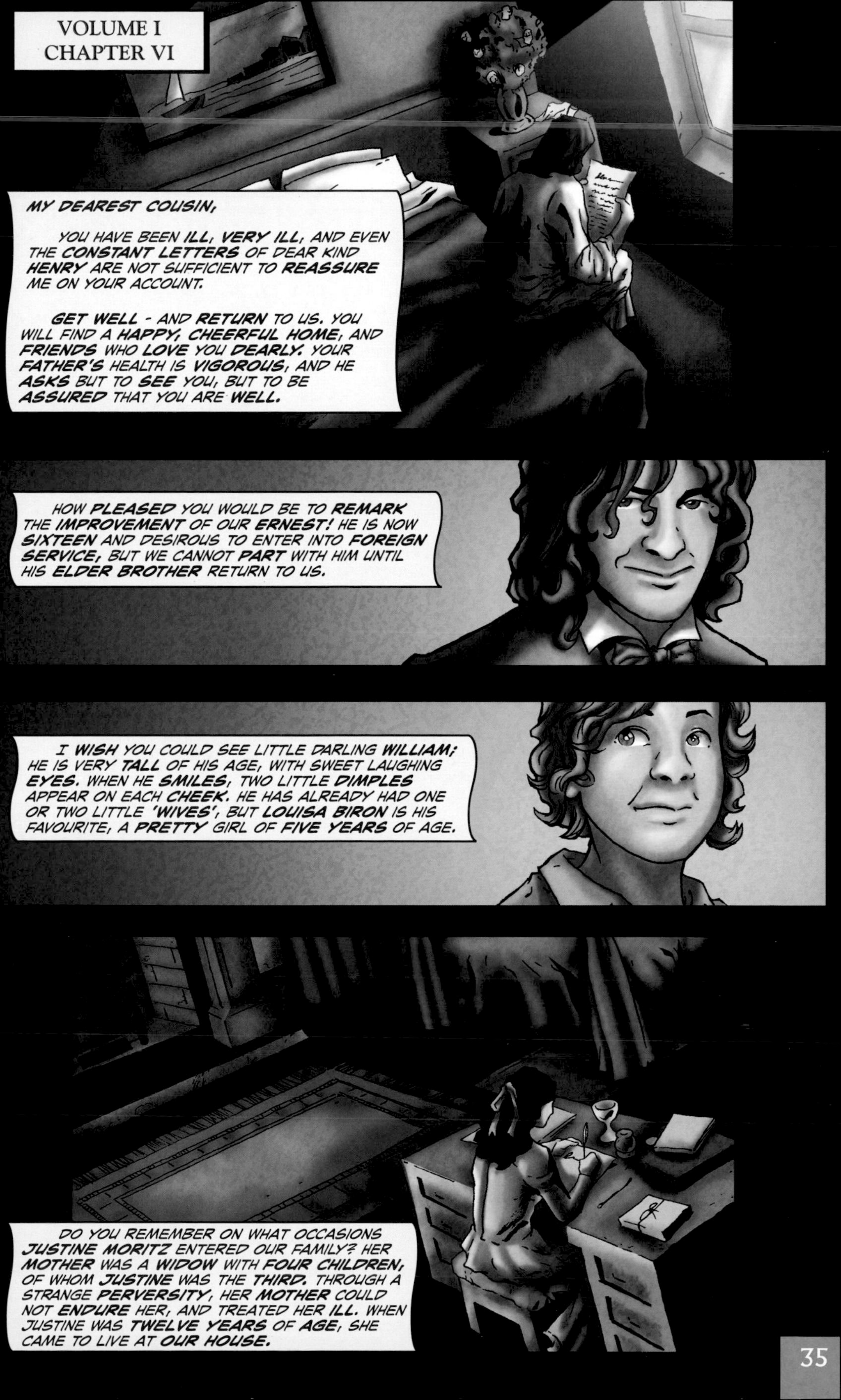
VOLUME I
CHAPTER VI
MY DEAREST COUSIN,
YOU HAVE BEEN ILL, VERY ILL, AND EVEN THE CONSTANT LETTERS OF DEAR KIND HENRY ARE NOT SUFFICIENT TO REASSURE ME ON YOUR ACCOUNT.
GET WELL - AND RETURN TO US. YOU WILL FIND A HAPPY, CHEERFUL HOME, AND FRIENDS WHO LOVE YOU DEARLY. YOUR FATHER'S HEALTH IS VIGOROUS, AND HE ASKS BUT TO SEE YOU, BUT TO BE ASSURED THAT YOU ARE WELL.
HOW PLEASED YOU WOULD BE TO REMARK THE IMPROVEMENT OF OUR ERNEST! HE IS NOW SIXTEEN AND DESIROUS TO ENTER INTO FOREIGN SERVICE, BUT WE CANNOT PART WITH HIM UNTIL HIS ELDER BROTHER RETURN TO US.
I WISH YOU COULD SEE LITTLE DARLING WILLIAM; HE IS VERY TALL OF HIS AGE, WITH SWEET LAUGHING EYES. WHEN HE SMILES, TWO LITTLE DIMPLES APPEAR ON EACH CHEEK. HE HAS ALREADY HAD ONE OR TWO LITTLE 'WIVES', BUT LOUISA BIRON IS HIS FAVOURITE, A PRETTY GIRL OF FIVE YEARS OF AGE.
DO YOU REMEMBER ON WHAT OCCASIONS JUSTINE MORITZ ENTERED OUR FAMILY? HER MOTHER WAS A WIDOW WITH FOUR CHILDREN, OF WHOM JUSTINE WAS THE THIRD. THROUGH A STRANGE PERVERSITY, HER MOTHER COULD NOT ENDURE HER, AND TREATED HER ILL. WHEN JUSTINE WAS TWELVE YEARS OF AGE, SHE CAME TO LIVE AT OUR HOUSE.

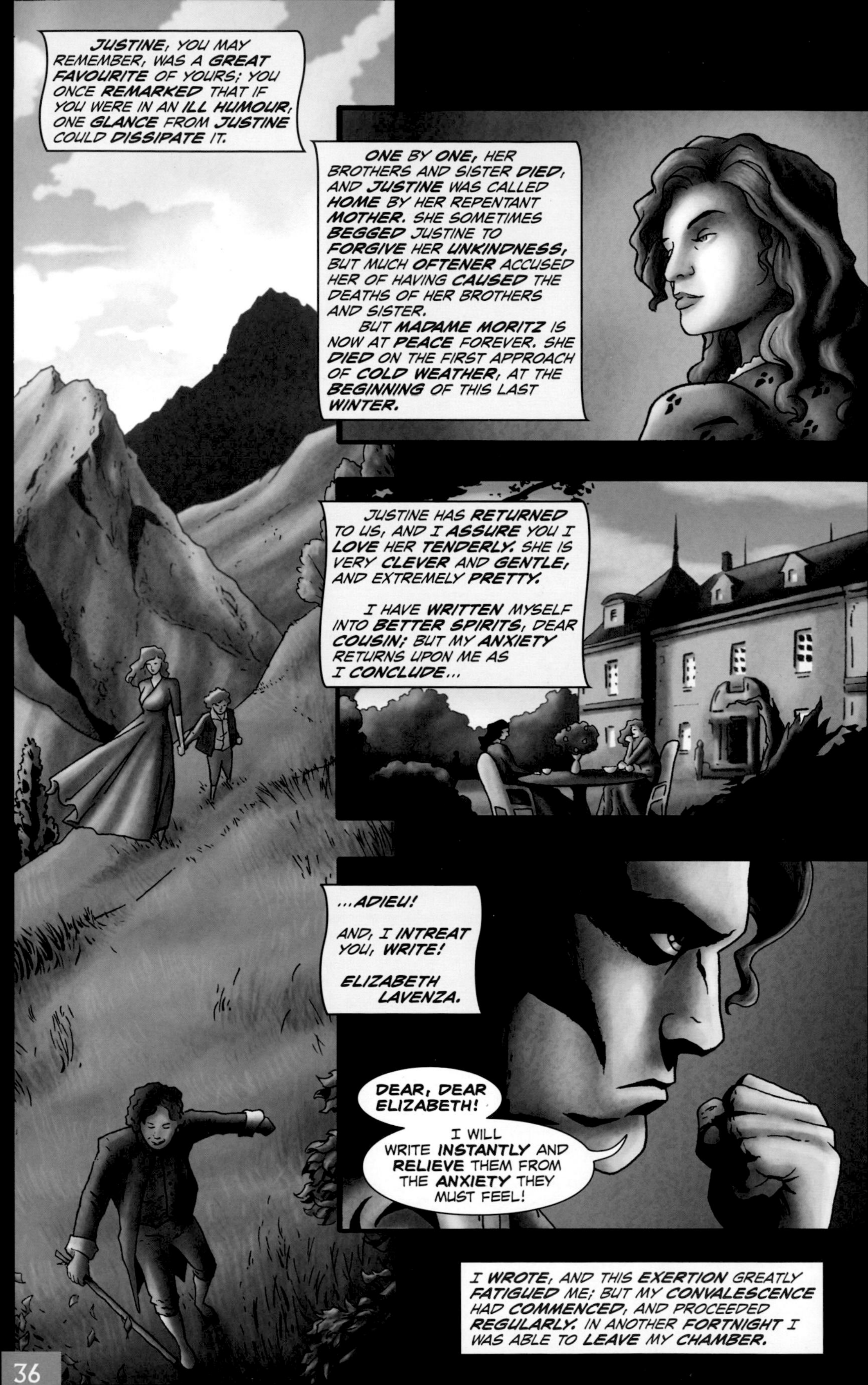
JUSTINE, YOU MAY REMEMBER, WAS A GREAT FAVOURITE OF YOURS; YOU ONCE REMARKED THAT IF YOU WERE IN AN ILL HUMOUR, ONE GLANCE FROM JUSTINE COULD DISSIPATE IT.
ONE BY ONE, HER BROTHERS AND SISTER DIED, AND JUSTINE WAS CALLED HOME BY HER REPENTANT MOTHER. SHE SOMETIMES BEGGED JUSTINE TO FORGIVE HER UNKINDNESS, BUT MUCH OFTENER ACCUSED HER OF HAVING CAUSED THE DEATHS OF HER BROTHERS AND SISTER.
BUT MADAME MORITZ IS NOW AT PEACE FOREVER. SHE DIED ON THE FIRST APPROACH OF COLD WEATHER, AT THE BEGINNING OF THIS LAST WINTER.
JUSTINE HAS RETURNED TO US, AND I ASSURE YOU I LOVE HER TENDERLY. SHE IS VERY CLEVER AND GENTLE, AND EXTREMELY PRETTY.
I HAVE WRITTEN MYSELF INTO BETTER SPIRITS, DEAR COUSIN; BUT MY ANXIETY RETURNS UPON ME AS I CONCLUDE...
...ADIEU!
AND, I INTREAT YOU, WRITE!
ELIZABETH LAVENZA.
DEAR, DEAR ELIZABETH!
I WILL WRITE INSTANTLY AND RELIEVE THEM FROM THE ANXIETY THEY MUST FEEL!
I WROTE, AND THIS EXERTION GREATLY FATIGUED ME; BUT MY CONVALESCENCE HAD COMMENCED, AND PROCEEDED REGULARLY. IN ANOTHER FORTNIGHT I WAS ABLE TO LEAVE MY CHAMBER.

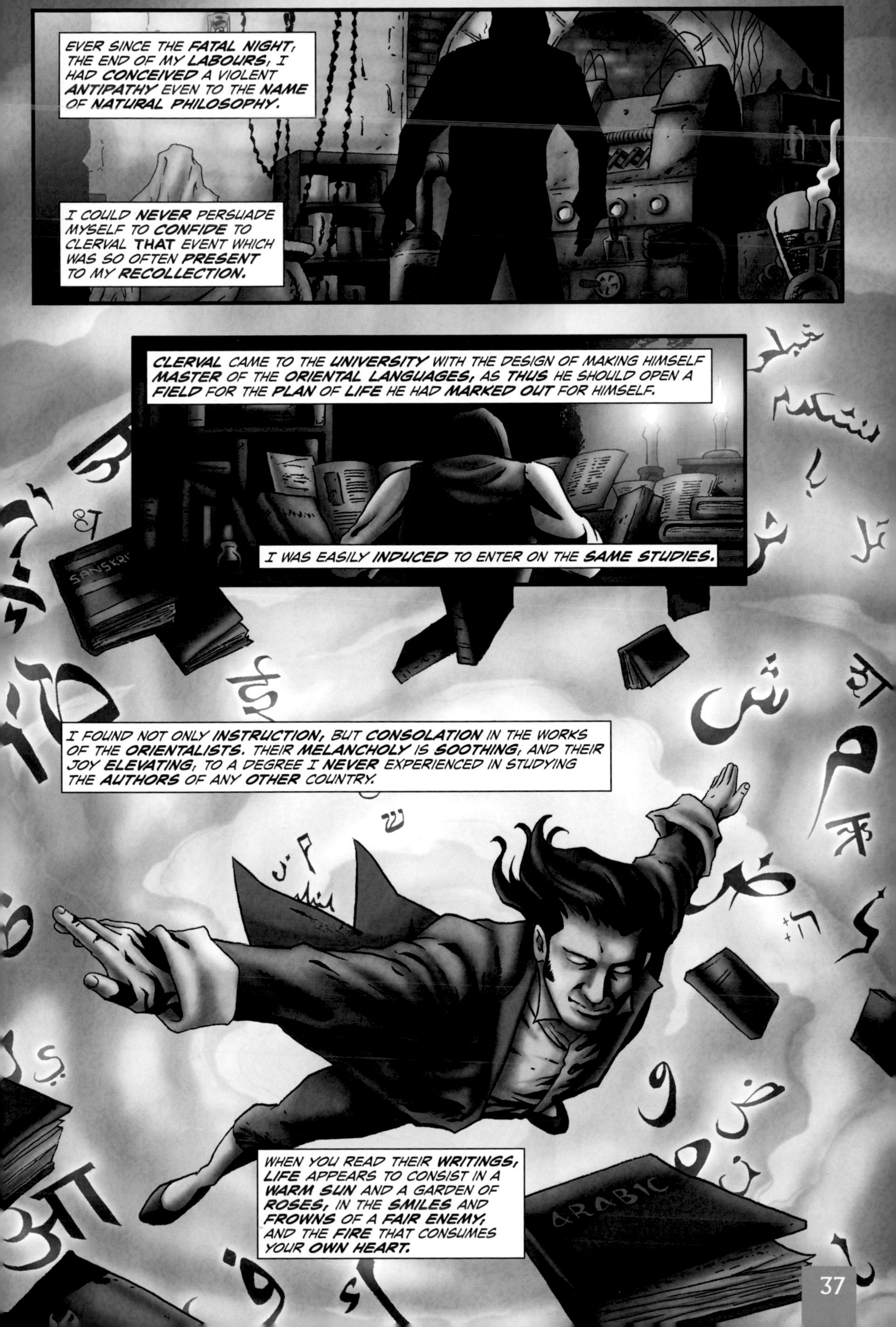
EVER SINCE THE FATAL NIGHT, THE END OF MY LABOURS, I HAD CONCEIVED A VIOLENT ANTIPATHY EVEN TO THE NAME OF NATURAL PHILOSOPHY.
I COULD NEVER PERSUADE MYSELF TO CONFIDE TO CLERVAL THAT EVENT WHICH WAS SO OFTEN PRESENT TO MY RECOLLECTION.
CLERVAL CAME TO THE UNIVERSITY WITH THE DESIGN OF MAKING HIMSELF MASTER OF THE ORIENTAL LANGUAGES, AS THUS HE SHOULD OPEN A FIELD FOR THE PLAN OF LIFE HE HAD MARKED OUT FOR HIMSELF.
I WAS EASILY INDUCED TO ENTER ON THE SAME STUDIES.
I FOUND NOT ONLY INSTRUCTION, BUT CONSOLATION IN THE WORKS OF THE ORIENTALISTS. THEIR MELANCHOLY IS SOOTHING, AND THEIR JOY ELEVATING, TO A DEGREE I NEVER EXPERIENCED IN STUDYING THE AUTHORS OF ANY OTHER COUNTRY.
WHEN YOU READ THEIR WRITINGS, LIFE APPEARS TO CONSIST IN A WARM SUN AND A GARDEN OF ROSES, IN THE SMILES AND FROWNS OF A FAIR ENEMY, AND THE FIRE THAT CONSUMES YOUR OWN HEART.
SANSKRI
ARABIC

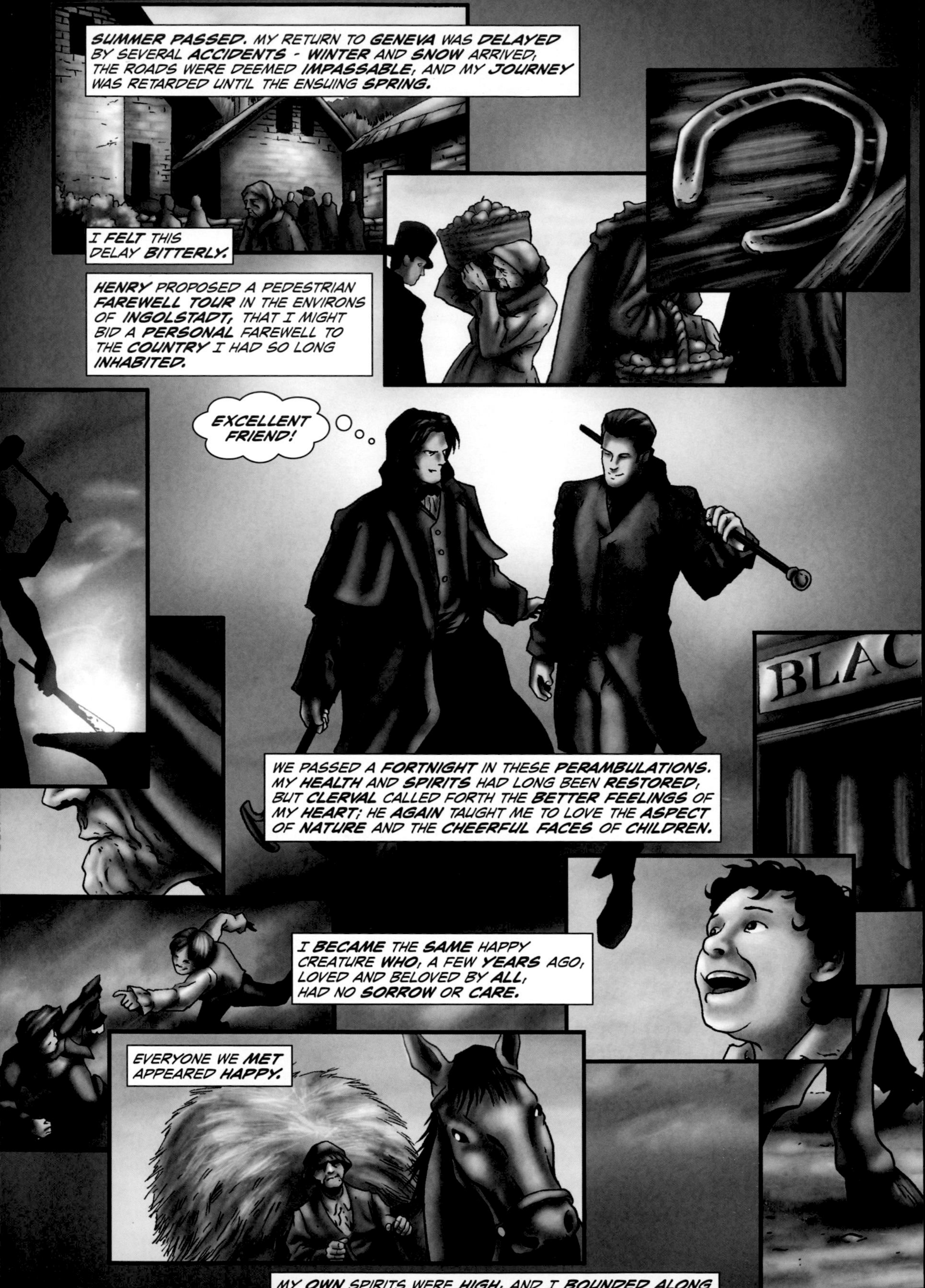
SUMMER PASSED. MY RETURN TO GENEVA WAS DELAYED BY SEVERAL ACCIDENTS - WINTER AND SNOW ARRIVED; THE ROADS WERE DEEMED IMPASSABLE, AND MY JOURNEY WAS RETARDED UNTIL THE ENSUING SPRING.
I FELT THIS DELAY BITTERLY.
HENRY PROPOSED A PEDESTRIAN FAREWELL TOUR IN THE ENVIRONS OF INGOLSTADT, THAT I MIGHT BID A PERSONAL FAREWELL TO THE COUNTRY I HAD SO LONG INHABITED.
EXCELLENT FRIEND!
BLAC
WE PASSED A FORTNIGHT IN THESE PERAMBULATIONS. MY HEALTH AND SPIRITS HAD LONG BEEN RESTORED, BUT CLERVAL CALLED FORTH THE BETTER FEELINGS OF MY HEART; HE AGAIN TAUGHT ME TO LOVE THE ASPECT OF NATURE AND THE CHEERFUL FACES OF CHILDREN.
I BECAME THE SAME HAPPY CREATURE WHO, A FEW YEARS AGO, LOVED AND BELOVED BY ALL, HAD NO SORROW OR CARE.
EVERYONE WE MET APPEARED HAPPY.
MY OWN SPIRITS WERE HIGH, AND I BOUNDED ALONG WITH FEELINGS OF UNBRIDLED JOY AND HILARITY.

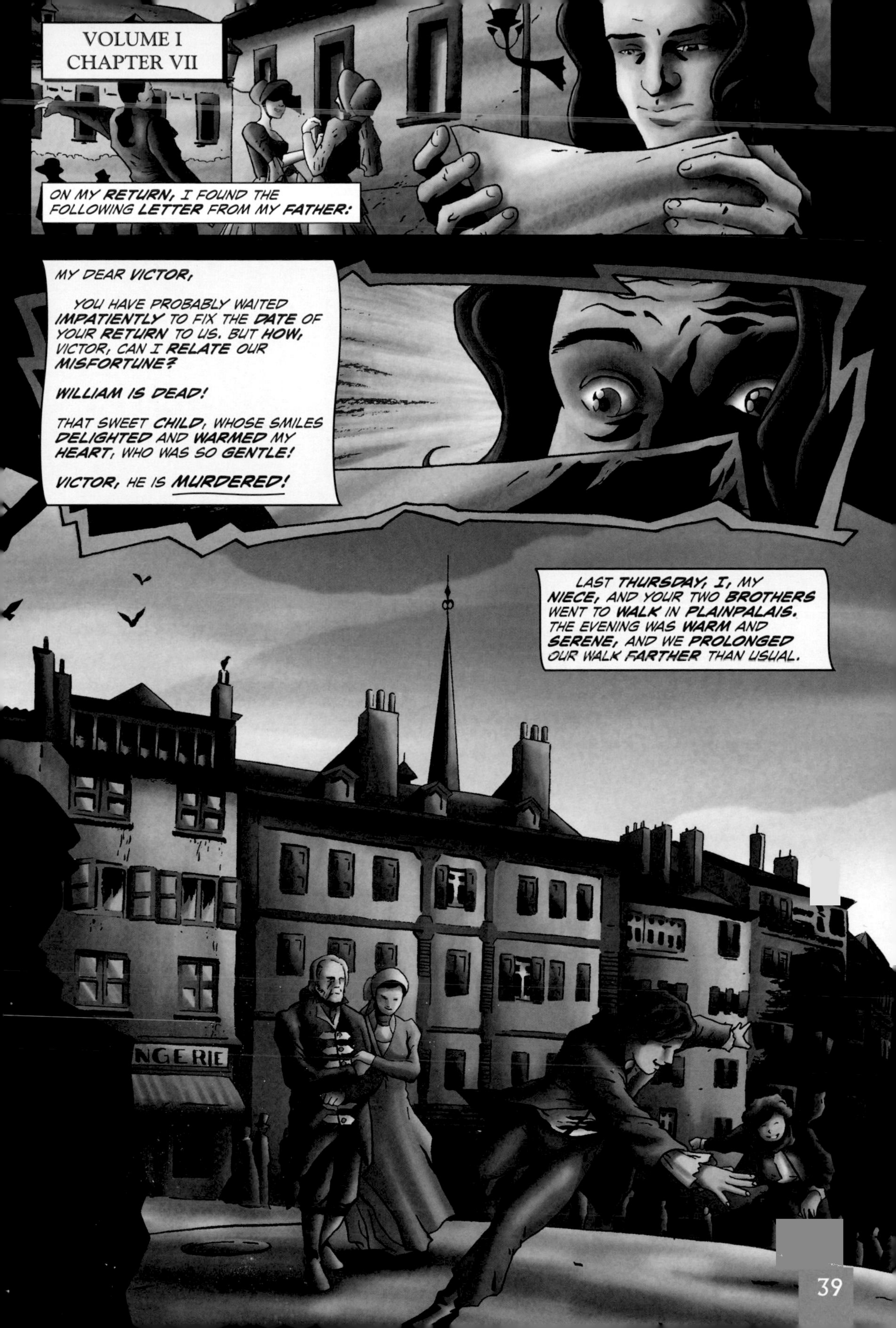
VOLUME I
CHAPTER VII
ON MY RETURN, I FOUND THE FOLLOWING LETTER FROM MY FATHER:
MY DEAR VICTOR,
YOU HAVE PROBABLY WAITED IMPATIENTLY TO FIX THE DATE OF YOUR RETURN TO US. BUT HOW, VICTOR, CAN I RELATE OUR MISFORTUNE?
WILLIAM IS DEAD!
THAT SWEET CHILD, WHOSE SMILES DELIGHTED AND WARMED MY HEART, WHO WAS SO GENTLE!
VICTOR, HE IS MURDERED!
LAST THURSDAY, I, MY NIECE, AND YOUR TWO BROTHERS WENT TO WALK IN PLAINPALAIS. THE EVENING WAS WARM AND SERENE, AND WE PROLONGED OUR WALK FARTHER THAN USUAL.
NGERIE

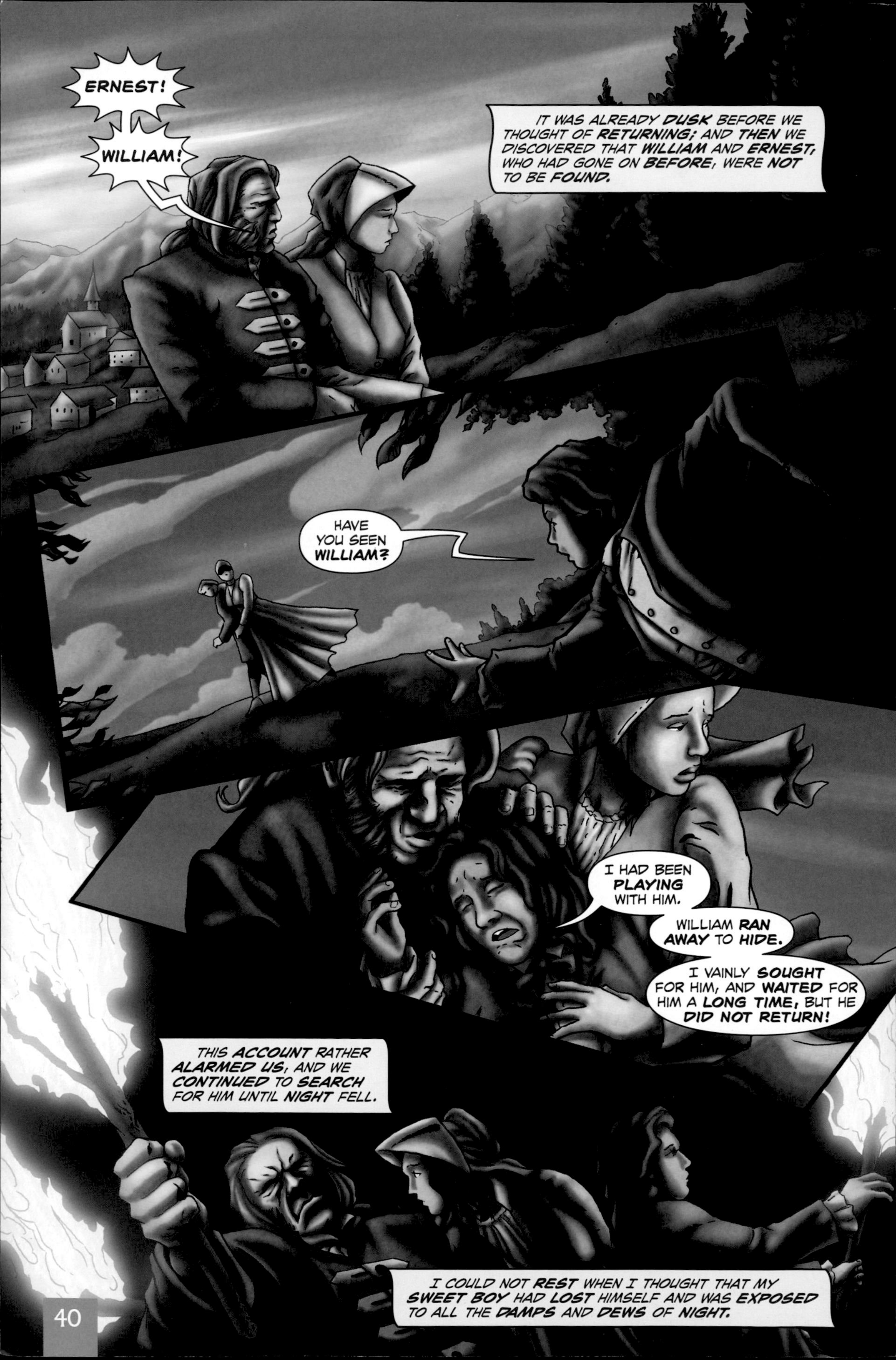
ERNEST!
WILLIAM!
IT WAS ALREADY DUSK BEFORE WE THOUGHT OF RETURNING; AND THEN WE DISCOVERED THAT WILLIAM AND ERNEST, WHO HAD GONE ON BEFORE, WERE NOT TO BE FOUND.
HAVE YOU SEEN WILLIAM?
I HAD BEEN PLAYING WITH HIM.
WILLIAM RAN AWAY TO HIDE.
I VAINLY SOUGHT FOR HIM, AND WAITED FOR HIM A LONG TIME, BUT HE DID NOT RETURN!
THIS ACCOUNT RATHER ALARMED US, AND WE CONTINUED TO SEARCH FOR HIM UNTIL NIGHT FELL.
I COULD NOT REST WHEN I THOUGHT THAT MY SWEET BOY HAD LOST HIMSELF AND WAS EXPOSED TO ALL THE DAMPS AND DEWS OF NIGHT.

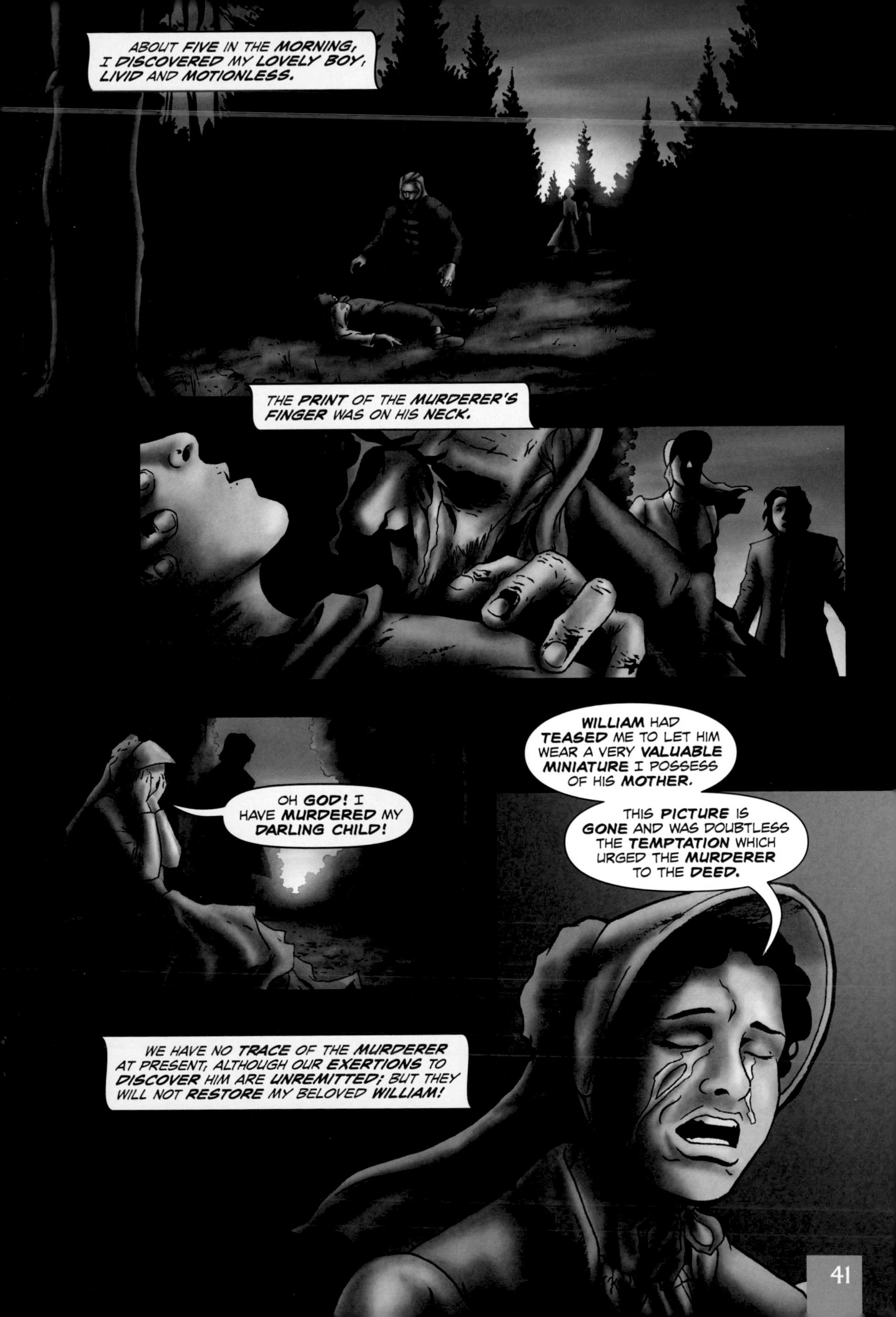

ABOUT FIVE IN THE MORNING, I DISCOVERED MY LOVELY BOY, LIVID AND MOTIONLESS.
THE PRINT OF THE MURDERER'S FINGER WAS ON HIS NECK.
OH GOD! I HAVE MURDERED MY DARLING CHILD!
WILLIAM HAD TEASED ME TO LET HIM WEAR A VERY VALUABLE MINIATURE I POSSESS OF HIS MOTHER.
THIS PICTURE IS GONE AND WAS DOUBTLESS THE TEMPTATION WHICH URGED THE MURDERER TO THE DEED.
WE HAVE NO TRACE OF THE MURDERER AT PRESENT, ALTHOUGH OUR EXERTIONS TO DISCOVER HIM ARE UNREMITTED; BUT THEY WILL NOT RESTORE MY BELOVED WILLIAM!

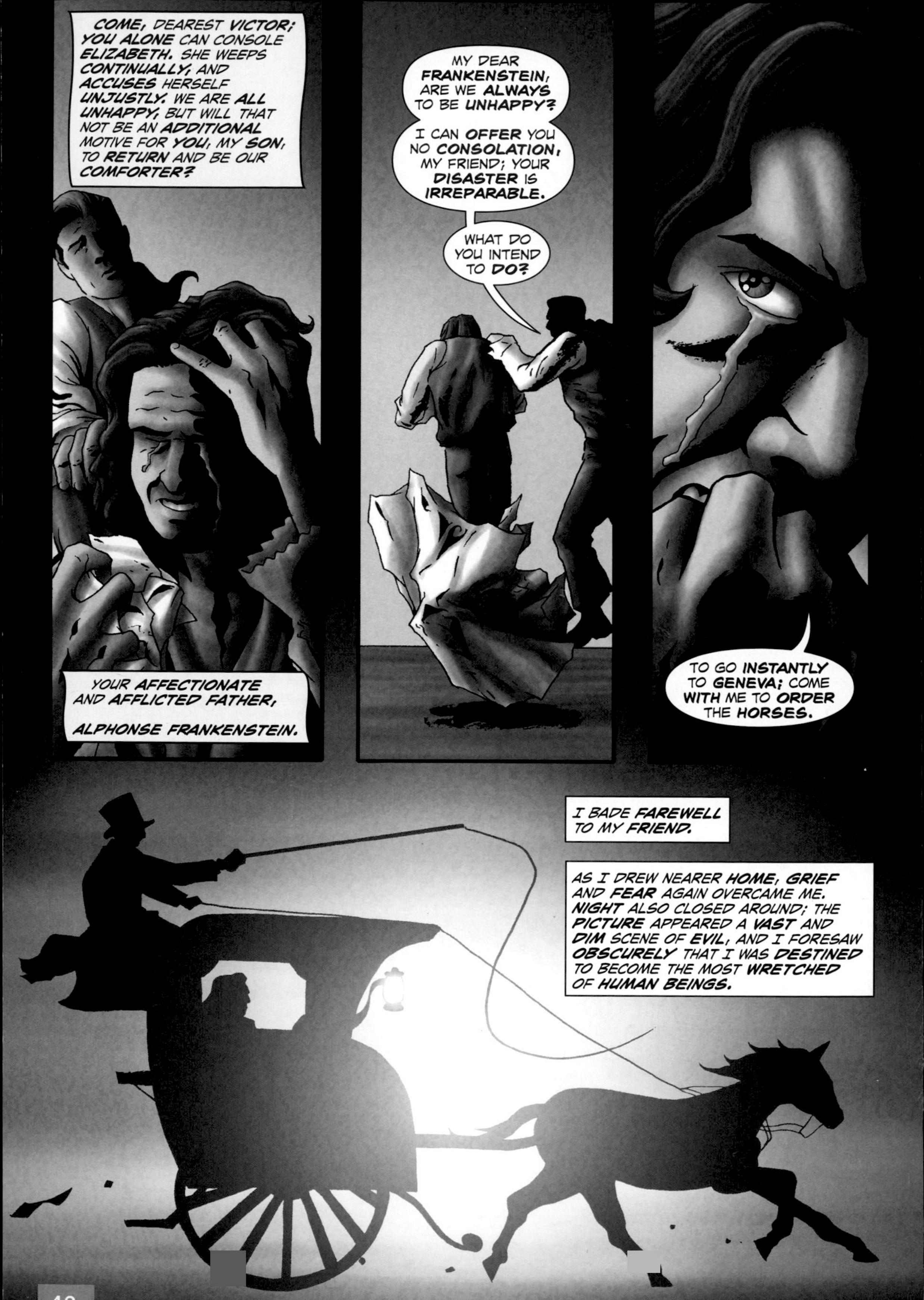

COME, DEAREST VICTOR; YOU ALONE CAN CONSOLE ELIZABETH. SHE WEEPS CONTINUALLY, AND ACCUSES HERSELF UNJUSTLY. WE ARE ALL UNHAPPY; BUT WILL THAT NOT BE AN ADDITIONAL MOTIVE FOR YOU, MY SON, TO RETURN AND BE OUR COMFORTER?
YOUR AFFECTIONATE AND AFFLICTED FATHER,
ALPHONSE FRANKENSTEIN.
MY DEAR FRANKENSTEIN, ARE WE ALWAYS TO BE UNHAPPY?
I CAN OFFER YOU NO CONSOLATION, MY FRIEND; YOUR DISASTER IS IRREPARABLE.
WHAT DO YOU INTEND TO DO?
TO GO INSTANTLY TO GENEVA; COME WITH ME TO ORDER THE HORSES.
I BADE FAREWELL TO MY FRIEND.
AS I DREW NEARER HOME, GRIEF AND FEAR AGAIN OVERCAME ME. NIGHT ALSO CLOSED AROUND; THE PICTURE APPEARED A VAST AND DIM SCENE OF EVIL, AND I FORESAW OBSCURELY THAT I WAS DESTINED TO BECOME THE MOST WRETCHED OF HUMAN BEINGS.

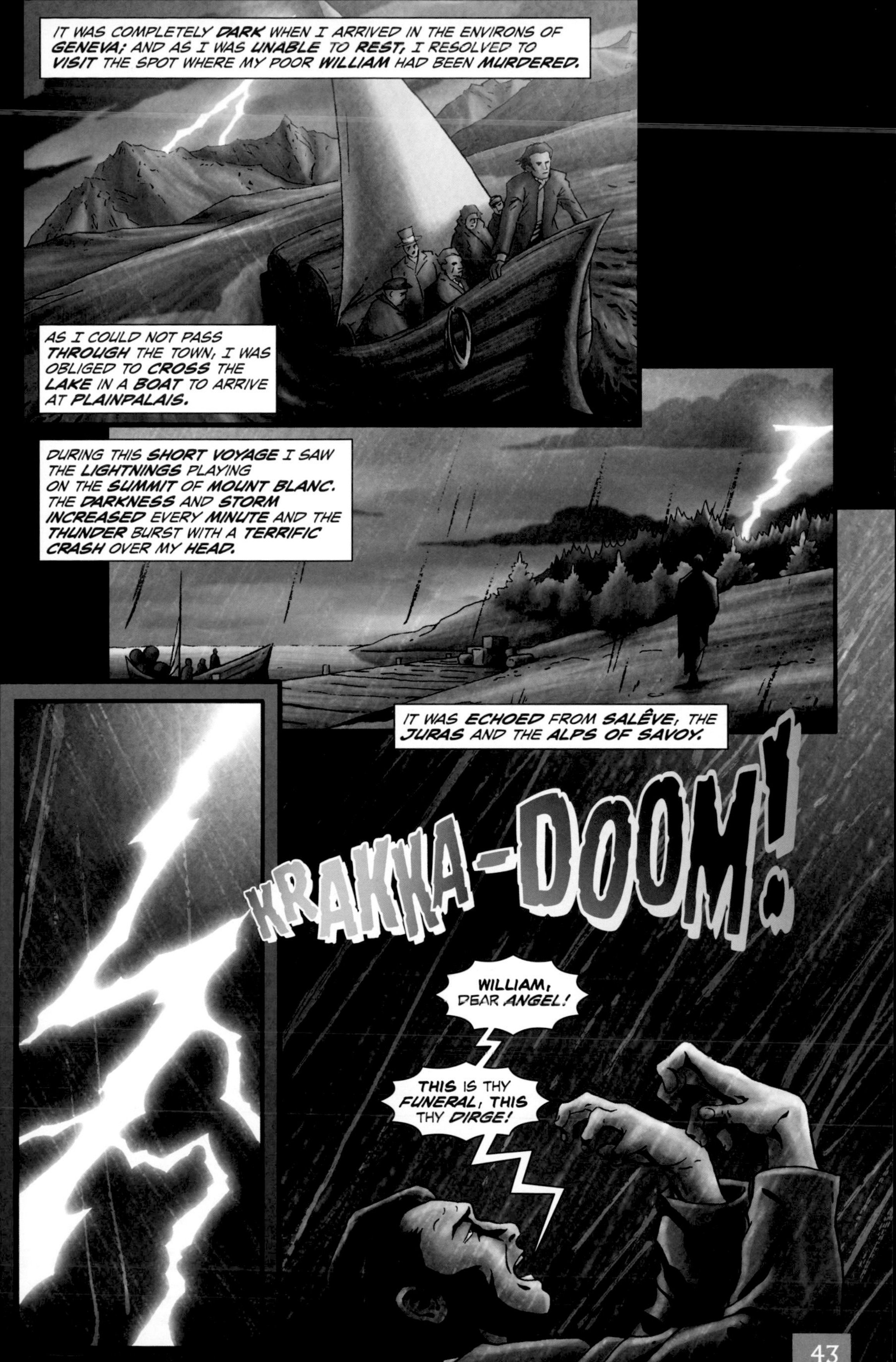
IT WAS COMPLETELY DARK WHEN I ARRIVED IN THE ENVIRONS OF GENEVA; AND AS I WAS UNABLE TO REST, I RESOLVED TO VISIT THE SPOT WHERE MY POOR WILLIAM HAD BEEN MURDERED.
AS I COULD NOT PASS THROUGH THE TOWN, I WAS OBLIGED TO CROSS THE LAKE IN A BOAT TO ARRIVE AT PLAINPALAIS.
DURING THIS SHORT VOYAGE I SAW THE LIGHTNINGS PLAYING ON THE SUMMIT OF MOUNT BLANC. THE DARKNESS AND STORM INCREASED EVERY MINUTE AND THE THUNDER BURST WITH A TERRIFIC CRASH OVER MY HEAD.
IT WAS ECHOED FROM SALÊVE, THE JURAS AND THE ALPS OF SAVOY.
KRAKKA-DOOM!
WILLIAM, DEAR ANGEL!
THIS IS THY FUNERAL, THIS THY DIRGE!

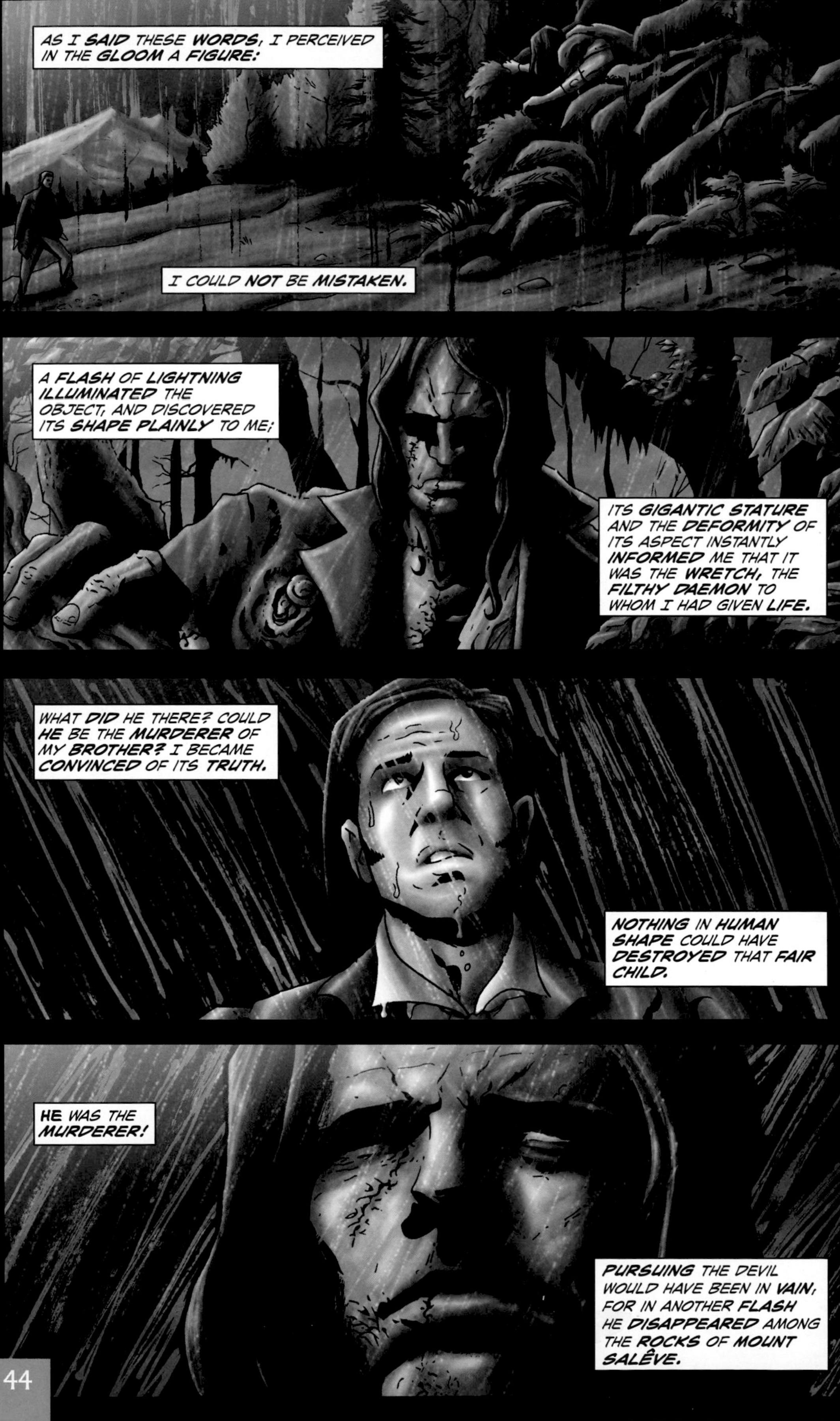
AS I SAID THESE WORDS, I PERCEIVED IN THE GLOOM A FIGURE:
I COULD NOT BE MISTAKEN.
A FLASH OF LIGHTNING ILLUMINATED THE OBJECT, AND DISCOVERED ITS SHAPE PLAINLY TO ME;
ITS GIGANTIC STATURE AND THE DEFORMITY OF ITS ASPECT INSTANTLY INFORMED ME THAT IT WAS THE WRETCH, THE FILTHY DAEMON TO WHOM I HAD GIVEN LIFE.
WHAT DID HE THERE? COULD HE BE THE MURDERER OF MY BROTHER? I BECAME CONVINCED OF ITS TRUTH.
NOTHING IN HUMAN SHAPE COULD HAVE DESTROYED THAT FAIR CHILD.
HE WAS THE MURDERER!
PURSUING THE DEVIL WOULD HAVE BEEN IN VAIN, FOR IN ANOTHER FLASH HE DISAPPEARED AMONG THE ROCKS OF MOUNT SALÊVE.

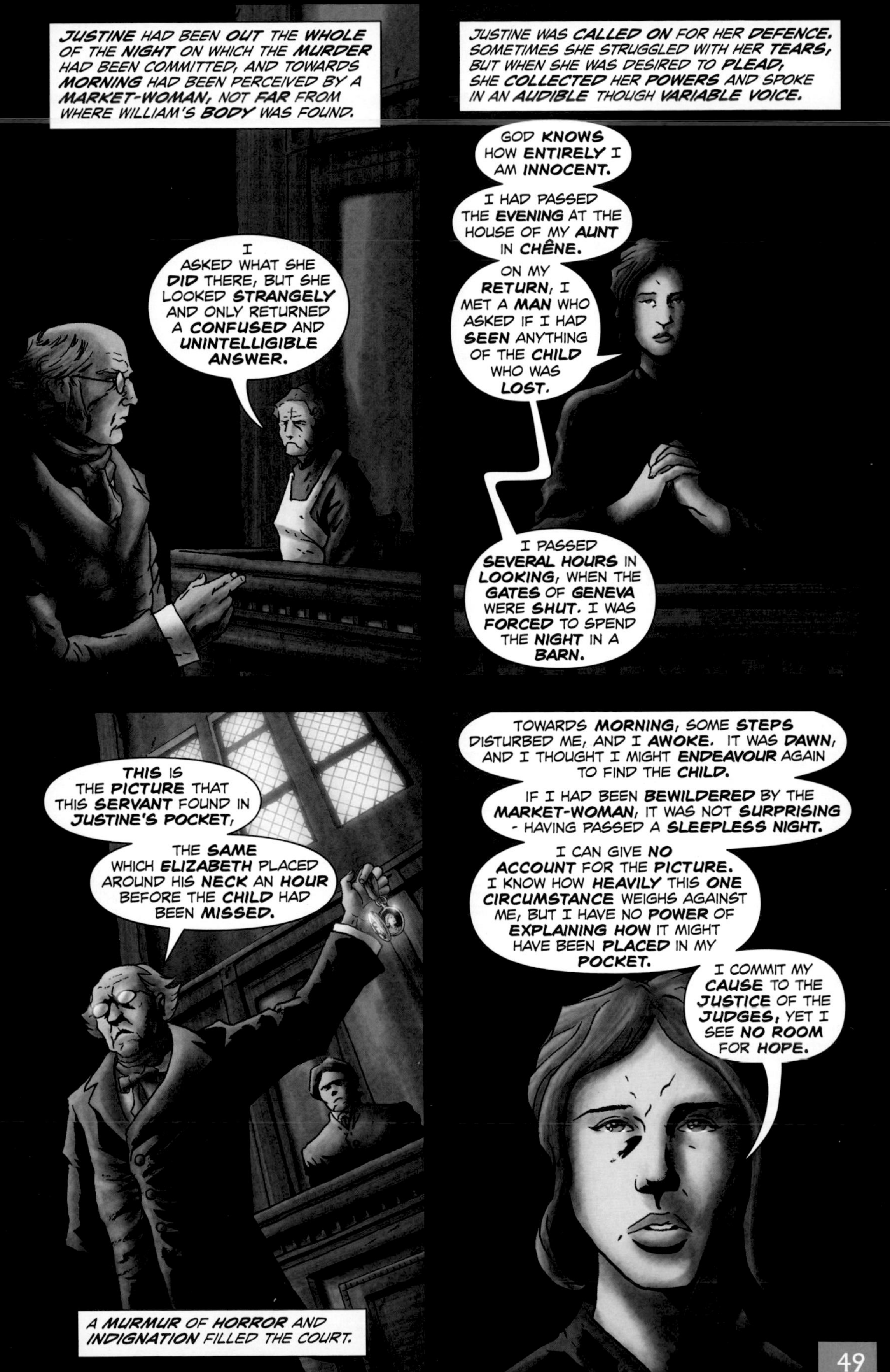
JUSTINE HAD BEEN OUT THE WHOLE OF THE NIGHT ON WHICH THE MURDER HAD BEEN COMMITTED, AND TOWARDS MORNING HAD BEEN PERCEIVED BY A MARKET-WOMAN, NOT FAR FROM WHERE WILLIAM'S BODY WAS FOUND.
I ASKED WHAT SHE DID THERE, BUT SHE LOOKED STRANGELY AND ONLY RETURNED A CONFUSED AND UNINTELLIGIBLE ANSWER.
JUSTINE WAS CALLED ON FOR HER DEFENCE. SOMETIMES SHE STRUGGLED WITH HER TEARS, BUT WHEN SHE WAS DESIRED TO PLEAD, SHE COLLECTED HER POWERS AND SPOKE IN AN AUDIBLE THOUGH VARIABLE VOICE.
GOD KNOWS HOW ENTIRELY I AM INNOCENT.
I HAD PASSED THE EVENING AT THE HOUSE OF MY AUNT IN CHÊNE.
ON MY RETURN, I MET A MAN WHO ASKED IF I HAD SEEN ANYTHING OF THE CHILD WHO WAS LOST.
I PASSED SEVERAL HOURS IN LOOKING, WHEN THE GATES OF GENEVA WERE SHUT. I WAS FORCED TO SPEND THE NIGHT IN A BARN.
THIS IS THE PICTURE THAT THIS SERVANT FOUND IN JUSTINE'S POCKET,
THE SAME WHICH ELIZABETH PLACED AROUND HIS NECK AN HOUR BEFORE THE CHILD HAD BEEN MISSED.
A MURMUR OF HORROR AND INDIGNATION FILLED THE COURT.
TOWARDS MORNING, SOME STEPS DISTURBED ME, AND I AWOKE. IT WAS DAWN, AND I THOUGHT I MIGHT ENDEAVOUR AGAIN TO FIND THE CHILD.
IF I HAD BEEN BEWILDERED BY THE MARKET-WOMAN, IT WAS NOT SURPRISING - HAVING PASSED A SLEEPLESS NIGHT.
I CAN GIVE NO ACCOUNT FOR THE PICTURE. I KNOW HOW HEAVILY THIS ONE CIRCUMSTANCE WEIGHS AGAINST ME, BUT I HAVE NO POWER OF EXPLAINING HOW IT MIGHT HAVE BEEN PLACED IN MY POCKET.
I COMMIT MY CAUSE TO THE JUSTICE OF THE JUDGES, YET I SEE NO ROOM FOR HOPE.

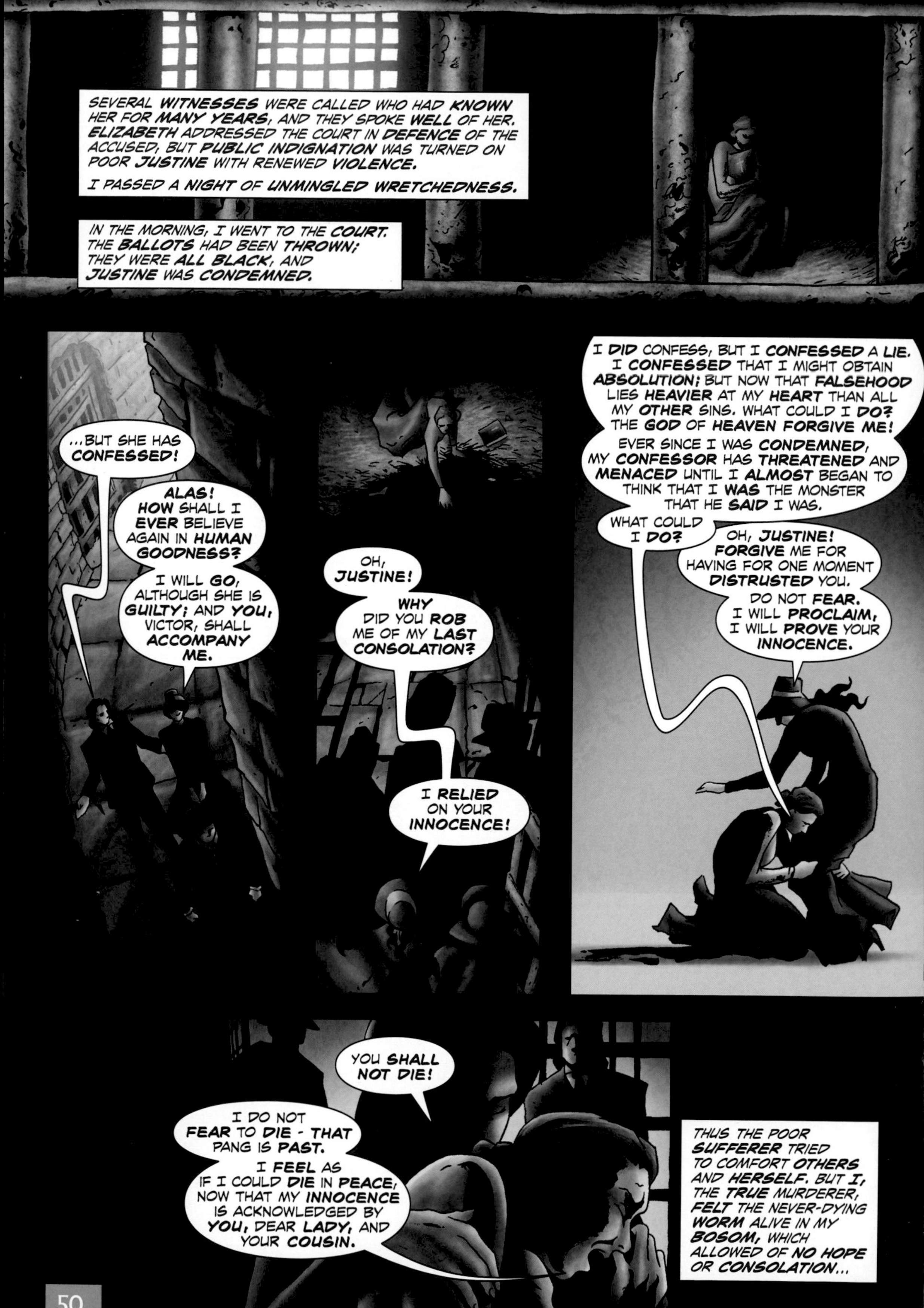

SEVERAL WITNESSES WERE CALLED WHO HAD KNOWN HER FOR MANY YEARS, AND THEY SPOKE WELL OF HER. ELIZABETH ADDRESSED THE COURT IN DEFENCE OF THE ACCUSED, BUT PUBLIC INDIGNATION WAS TURNED ON POOR JUSTINE WITH RENEWED VIOLENCE.
I PASSED A NIGHT OF UNMINGLED WRETCHEDNESS.
IN THE MORNING, I WENT TO THE COURT. THE BALLOTS HAD BEEN THROWN; THEY WERE ALL BLACK, AND JUSTINE WAS CONDEMNED.
...BUT SHE HAS CONFESSED!
ALAS! HOW SHALL I EVER BELIEVE AGAIN IN HUMAN GOODNESS?
I WILL GO, ALTHOUGH SHE IS GUILTY; AND YOU, VICTOR, SHALL ACCOMPANY ME.
OH, JUSTINE!
WHY DID YOU ROB ME OF MY LAST CONSOLATION?
I RELIED ON YOUR INNOCENCE!
I DID CONFESS, BUT I CONFESSED A LIE. I CONFESSED THAT I MIGHT OBTAIN ABSOLUTION; BUT NOW THAT FALSEHOOD LIES HEAVIER AT MY HEART THAN ALL MY OTHER SINS. WHAT COULD I DO? THE GOD OF HEAVEN FORGIVE ME!
EVER SINCE I WAS CONDEMNED, MY CONFESSOR HAS THREATENED AND MENACED UNTIL I ALMOST BEGAN TO THINK THAT I WAS THE MONSTER THAT HE SAID I WAS.
WHAT COULD I DO?
OH, JUSTINE! FORGIVE ME FOR HAVING FOR ONE MOMENT DISTRUSTED YOU.
DO NOT FEAR. I WILL PROCLAIM, I WILL PROVE YOUR INNOCENCE.
YOU SHALL NOT DIE!
I DO NOT FEAR TO DIE - THAT PANG IS PAST.
I FEEL AS IF I COULD DIE IN PEACE, NOW THAT MY INNOCENCE IS ACKNOWLEDGED BY YOU, DEAR LADY, AND YOUR COUSIN.
THUS THE POOR SUFFERER TRIED TO COMFORT OTHERS AND HERSELF. BUT I, THE TRUE MURDERER, FELT THE NEVER-DYING WORM ALIVE IN MY BOSOM, WHICH ALLOWED OF NO HOPE OR CONSOLATION...

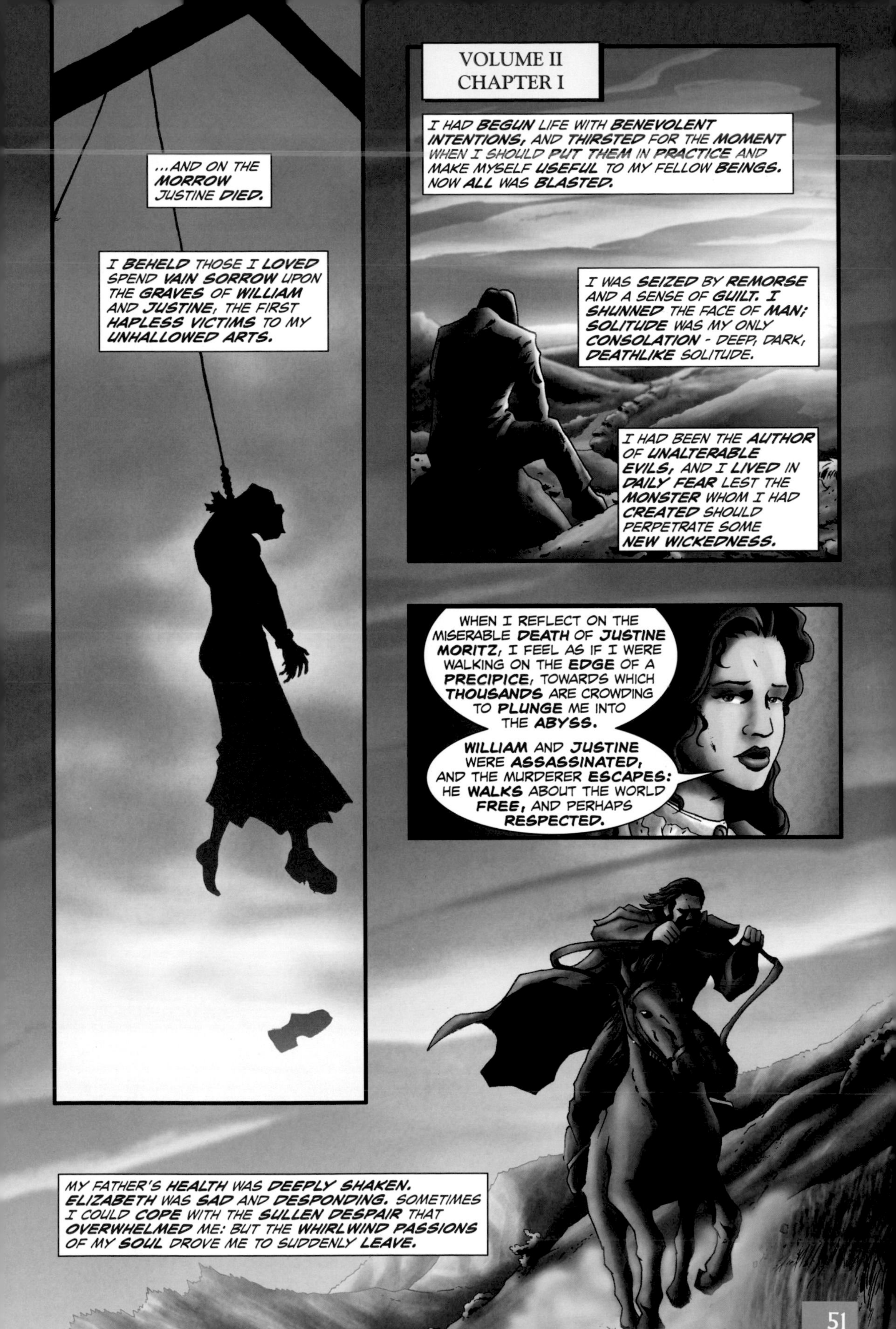

VOLUME II
CHAPTER I
...AND ON THE MORROW JUSTINE DIED.
I BEHELD THOSE I LOVED SPEND VAIN SORROW UPON THE GRAVES OF WILLIAM AND JUSTINE, THE FIRST HAPLESS VICTIMS TO MY UNHALLOWED ARTS.
I HAD BEGUN LIFE WITH BENEVOLENT INTENTIONS, AND THIRSTED FOR THE MOMENT WHEN I SHOULD PUT THEM IN PRACTICE AND MAKE MYSELF USEFUL TO MY FELLOW BEINGS. NOW ALL WAS BLASTED.
I WAS SEIZED BY REMORSE AND A SENSE OF GUILT. I SHUNNED THE FACE OF MAN; SOLITUDE WAS MY ONLY CONSOLATION - DEEP, DARK, DEATHLIKE SOLITUDE.
I HAD BEEN THE AUTHOR OF UNALTERABLE EVILS, AND I LIVED IN DAILY FEAR LEST THE MONSTER WHOM I HAD CREATED SHOULD PERPETRATE SOME NEW WICKEDNESS.
WHEN I REFLECT ON THE MISERABLE DEATH OF JUSTINE MORITZ, I FEEL AS IF I WERE WALKING ON THE EDGE OF A PRECIPICE, TOWARDS WHICH THOUSANDS ARE CROWDING TO PLUNGE ME INTO THE ABYSS.
WILLIAM AND JUSTINE WERE ASSASSINATED, AND THE MURDERER ESCAPES: HE WALKS ABOUT THE WORLD FREE, AND PERHAPS RESPECTED.
MY FATHER'S HEALTH WAS DEEPLY SHAKEN. ELIZABETH WAS SAD AND DESPONDING. SOMETIMES I COULD COPE WITH THE SULLEN DESPAIR THAT OVERWHELMED ME: BUT THE WHIRLWIND PASSIONS OF MY SOUL DROVE ME TO SUDDENLY LEAVE.

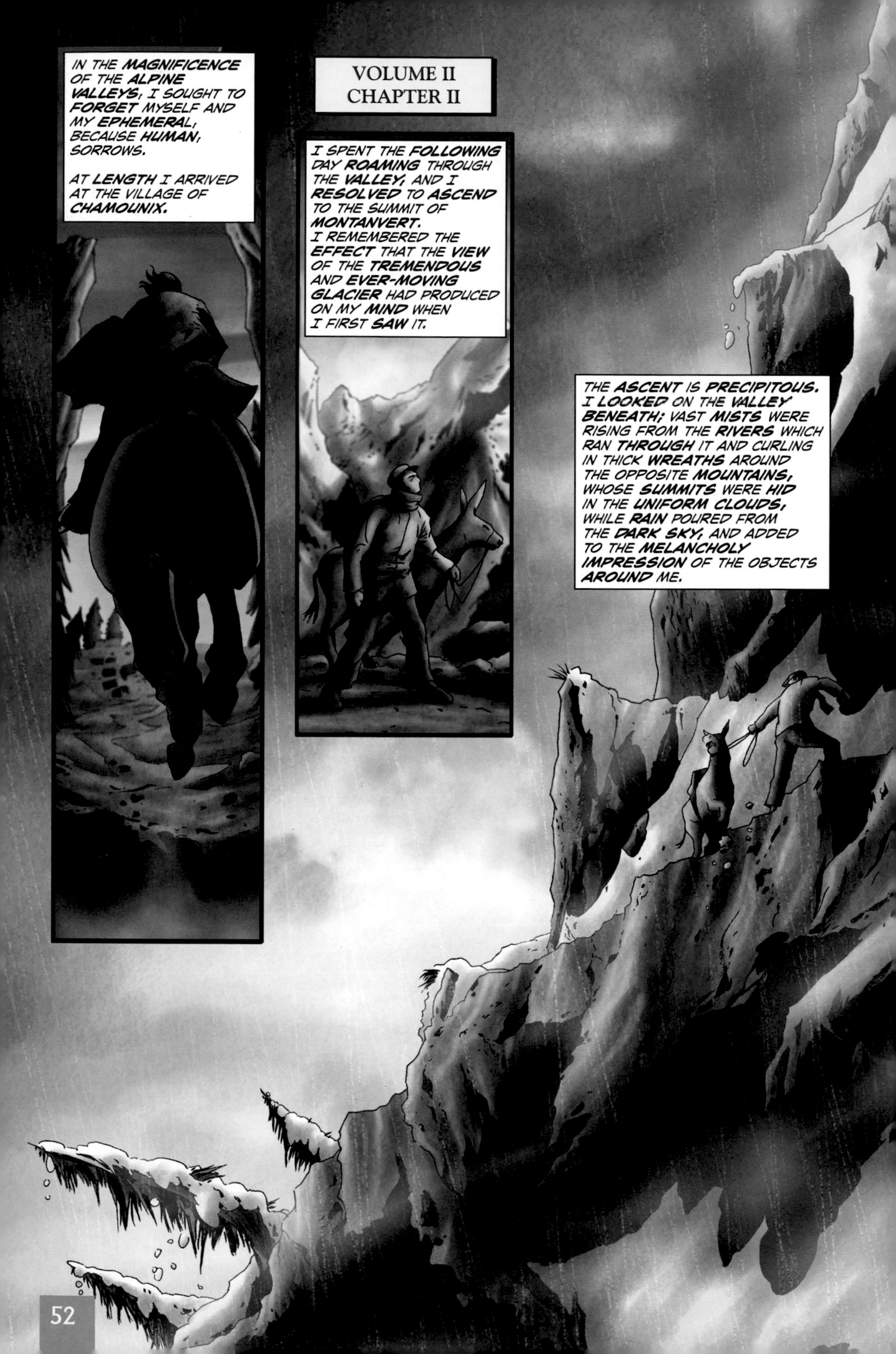
VOLUME II
CHAPTER II
IN THE MAGNIFICENCE OF THE ALPINE VALLEYS, I SOUGHT TO FORGET MYSELF AND MY EPHEMERAL, BECAUSE HUMAN, SORROWS.
AT LENGTH I ARRIVED AT THE VILLAGE OF CHAMOUNIX.
I SPENT THE FOLLOWING DAY ROAMING THROUGH THE VALLEY, AND I RESOLVED TO ASCEND TO THE SUMMIT OF MONTANVERT. I REMEMBERED THE EFFECT THAT THE VIEW OF THE TREMENDOUS AND EVER-MOVING GLACIER HAD PRODUCED ON MY MIND WHEN I FIRST SAW IT.
THE ASCENT IS PRECIPITOUS. I LOOKED ON THE VALLEY BENEATH; VAST MISTS WERE RISING FROM THE RIVERS WHICH RAN THROUGH IT AND CURLING IN THICK WREATHS AROUND THE OPPOSITE MOUNTAINS, WHOSE SUMMITS WERE HID IN THE UNIFORM CLOUDS, WHILE RAIN POURED FROM THE DARK SKY, AND ADDED TO THE MELANCHOLY IMPRESSION OF THE OBJECTS AROUND ME.

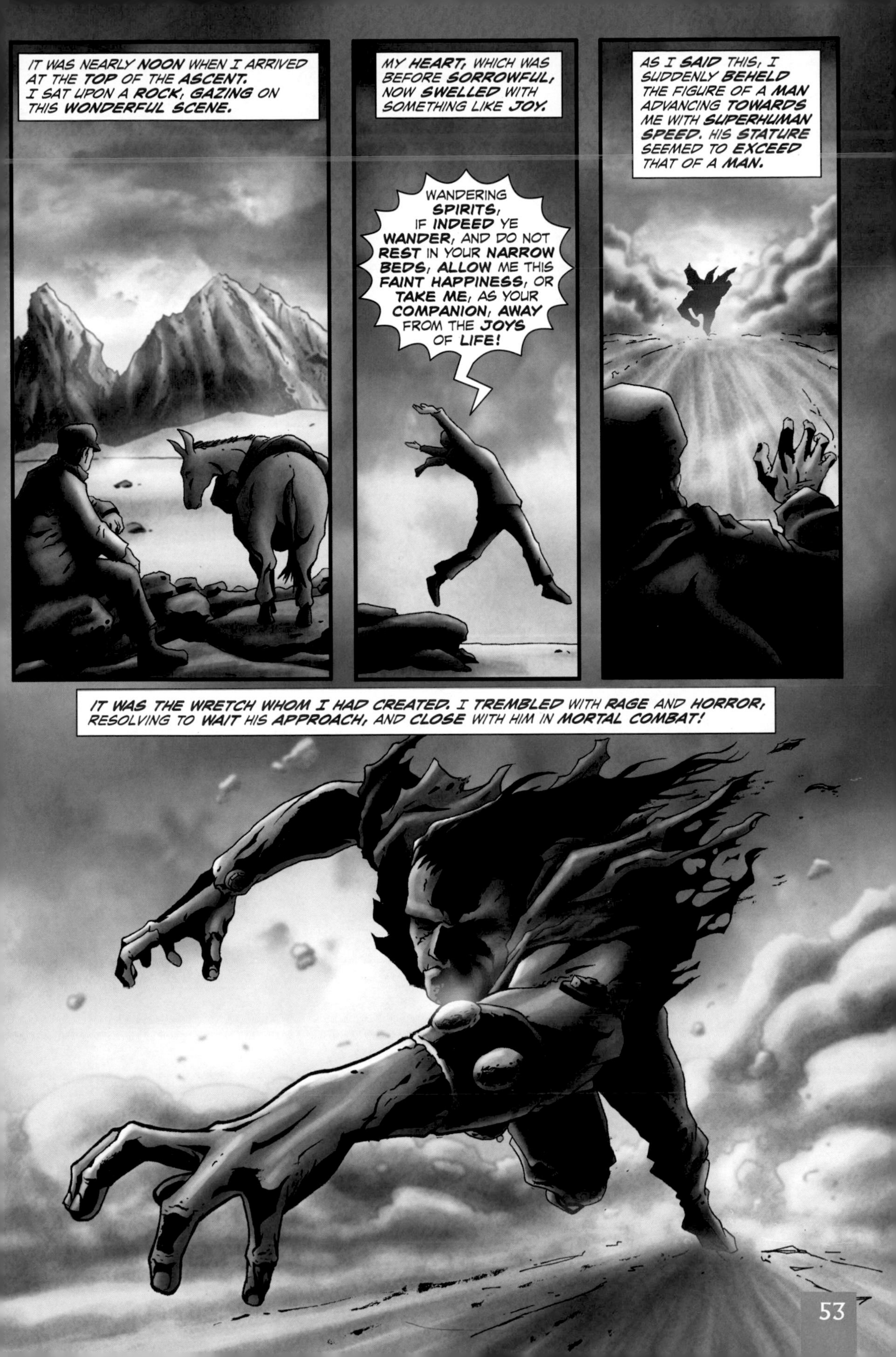
IT WAS NEARLY NOON WHEN I ARRIVED AT THE TOP OF THE ASCENT. I SAT UPON A ROCK, GAZING ON THIS WONDERFUL SCENE.
MY HEART, WHICH WAS BEFORE SORROWFUL, NOW SWELLED WITH SOMETHING LIKE JOY.
WANDERING SPIRITS, IF INDEED YE WANDER, AND DO NOT REST IN YOUR NARROW BEDS, ALLOW ME THIS FAINT HAPPINESS, OR TAKE ME, AS YOUR COMPANION, AWAY FROM THE JOYS OF LIFE!
AS I SAID THIS, I SUDDENLY BEHELD THE FIGURE OF A MAN ADVANCING TOWARDS ME WITH SUPERHUMAN SPEED. HIS STATURE SEEMED TO EXCEED THAT OF A MAN.
IT WAS THE WRETCH WHOM I HAD CREATED. I TREMBLED WITH RAGE AND HORROR, RESOLVING TO WAIT HIS APPROACH, AND CLOSE WITH HIM IN MORTAL COMBAT!

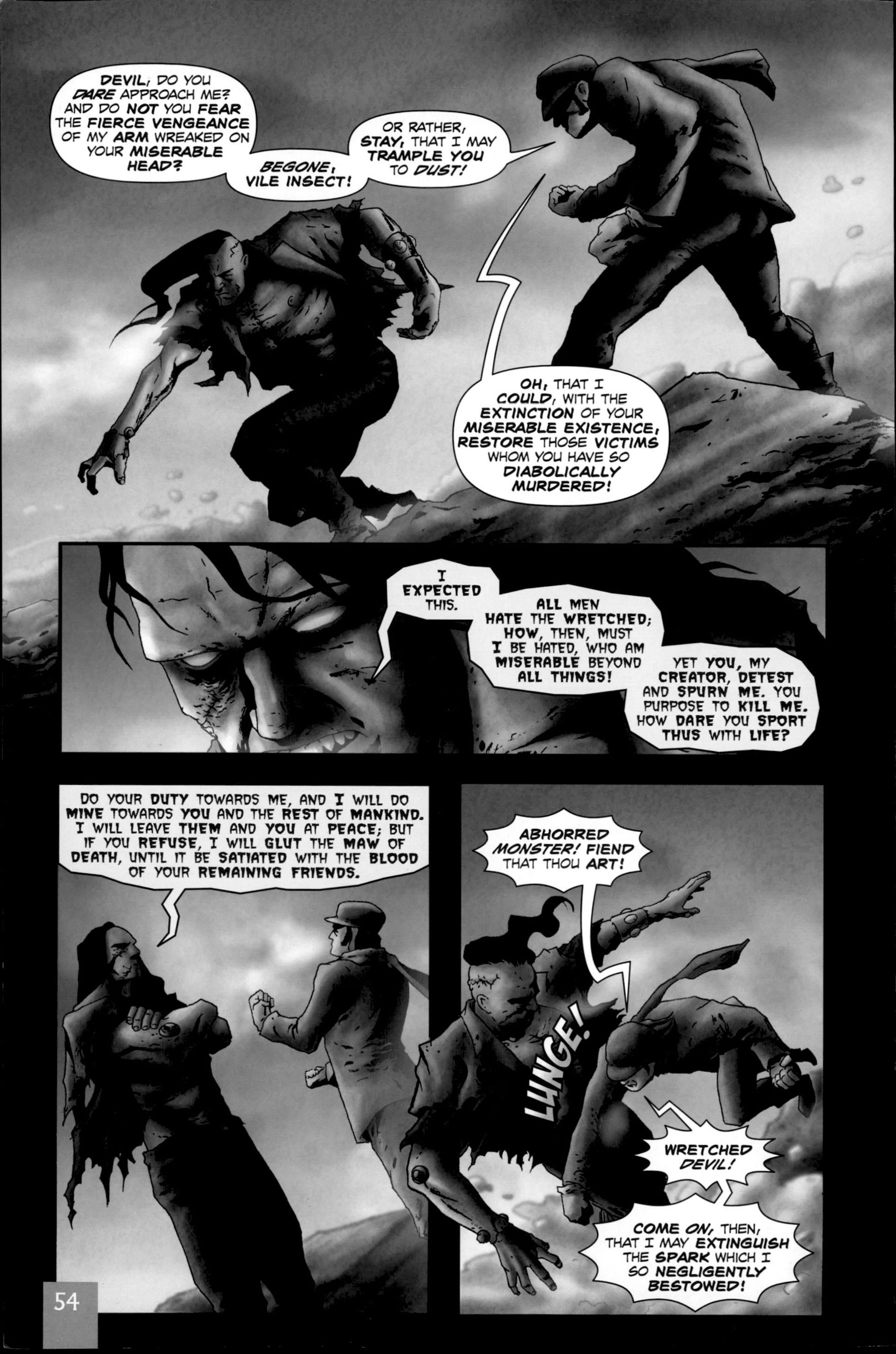
DEVIL, DO YOU DARE APPROACH ME? AND DO NOT YOU FEAR THE FIERCE VENGEANCE OF MY ARM WREAKED ON YOUR MISERABLE HEAD?
BEGONE, VILE INSECT!
OR RATHER, STAY, THAT I MAY TRAMPLE YOU TO DUST!
OH, THAT I COULD, WITH THE EXTINCTION OF YOUR MISERABLE EXISTENCE, RESTORE THOSE VICTIMS WHOM YOU HAVE SO DIABOLICALLY MURDERED!
I EXPECTED THIS.
ALL MEN HATE THE WRETCHED; HOW, THEN, MUST I BE HATED, WHO AM MISERABLE BEYOND ALL THINGS!
YET YOU, MY CREATOR, DETEST AND SPURN ME. YOU PURPOSE TO KILL ME. HOW DARE YOU SPORT THUS WITH LIFE?
DO YOUR DUTY TOWARDS ME, AND I WILL DO MINE TOWARDS YOU AND THE REST OF MANKIND. I WILL LEAVE THEM AND YOU AT PEACE; BUT IF YOU REFUSE, I WILL GLUT THE MAW OF DEATH, UNTIL IT BE SATIATED WITH THE BLOOD OF YOUR REMAINING FRIENDS.
ABHORRED MONSTER! FIEND THAT THOU ART!
LUNGE!
WRETCHED DEVIL!
COME ON, THEN, THAT I MAY EXTINGUISH THE SPARK WHICH I SO NEGLIGENTLY BESTOWED!

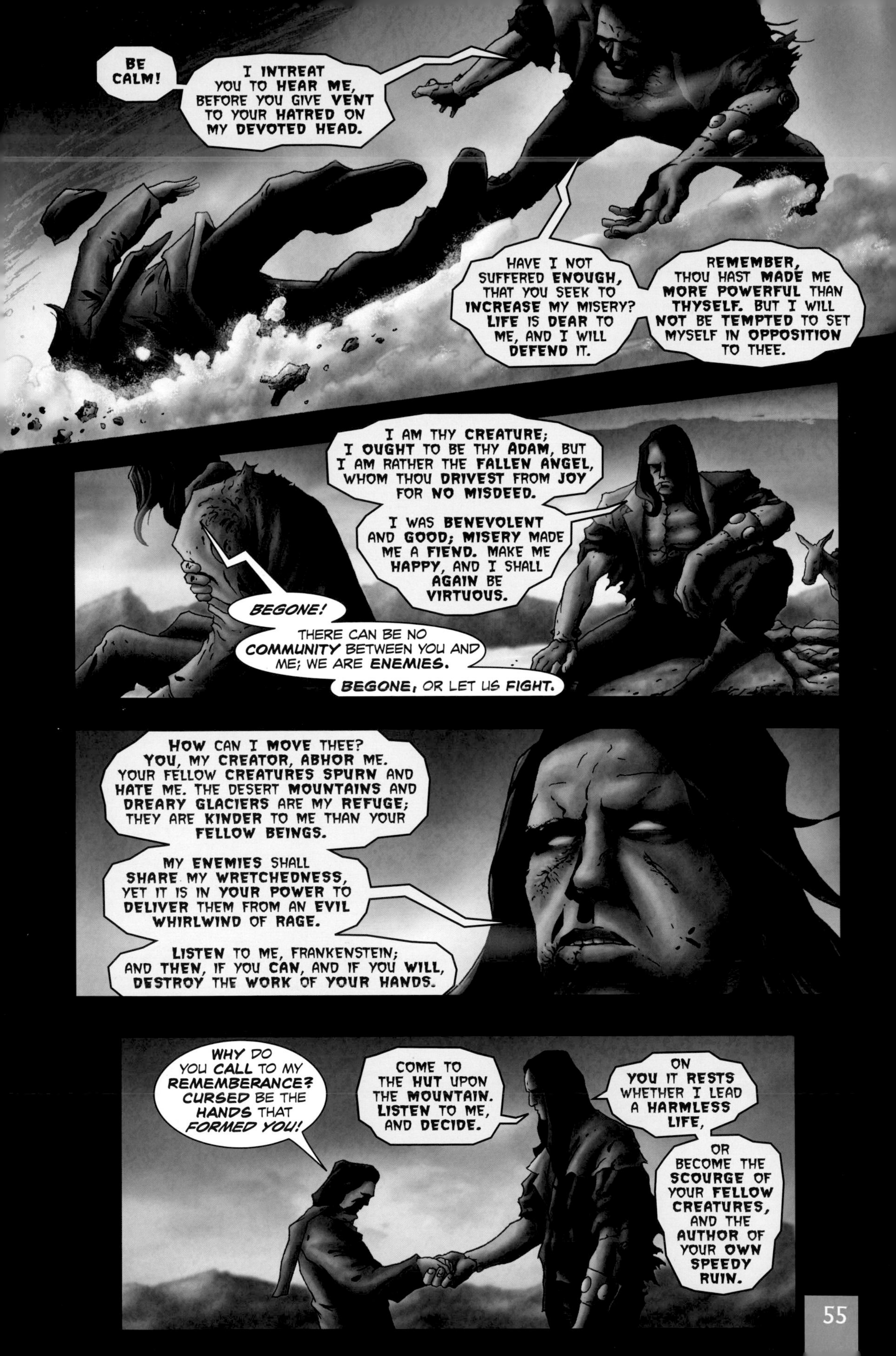
BE CALM!
I INTREAT YOU TO HEAR ME, BEFORE YOU GIVE VENT TO YOUR HATRED ON MY DEVOTED HEAD.
HAVE I NOT SUFFERED ENOUGH, THAT YOU SEEK TO INCREASE MY MISERY? LIFE IS DEAR TO ME, AND I WILL DEFEND IT.
REMEMBER, THOU HAST MADE ME MORE POWERFUL THAN THYSELF. BUT I WILL NOT BE TEMPTED TO SET MYSELF IN OPPOSITION TO THEE.
I AM THY CREATURE; I OUGHT TO BE THY ADAM, BUT I AM RATHER THE FALLEN ANGEL, WHOM THOU DRIVEST FROM JOY FOR NO MISDEED.
I WAS BENEVOLENT AND GOOD; MISERY MADE ME A FIEND. MAKE ME HAPPY, AND I SHALL AGAIN BE VIRTUOUS.
BEGONE!
THERE CAN BE NO COMMUNITY BETWEEN YOU AND ME; WE ARE ENEMIES.
BEGONE, OR LET US FIGHT.
HOW CAN I MOVE THEE? YOU, MY CREATOR, ABHOR ME. YOUR FELLOW CREATURES SPURN AND HATE ME. THE DESERT MOUNTAINS AND DREARY GLACIERS ARE MY REFUGE; THEY ARE KINDER TO ME THAN YOUR FELLOW BEINGS.
MY ENEMIES SHALL SHARE MY WRETCHEDNESS, YET IT IS IN YOUR POWER TO DELIVER THEM FROM AN EVIL WHIRLWIND OF RAGE.
LISTEN TO ME, FRANKENSTEIN; AND THEN, IF YOU CAN, AND IF YOU WILL, DESTROY THE WORK OF YOUR HANDS.
WHY DO YOU CALL TO MY REMEMBERANCE? CURSED BE THE HANDS THAT FORMED YOU!
COME TO THE HUT UPON THE MOUNTAIN. LISTEN TO ME, AND DECIDE.
ON YOU IT RESTS WHETHER I LEAD A HARMLESS LIFE,
OR BECOME THE SCOURGE OF YOUR FELLOW CREATURES, AND THE AUTHOR OF YOUR OWN SPEEDY RUIN.

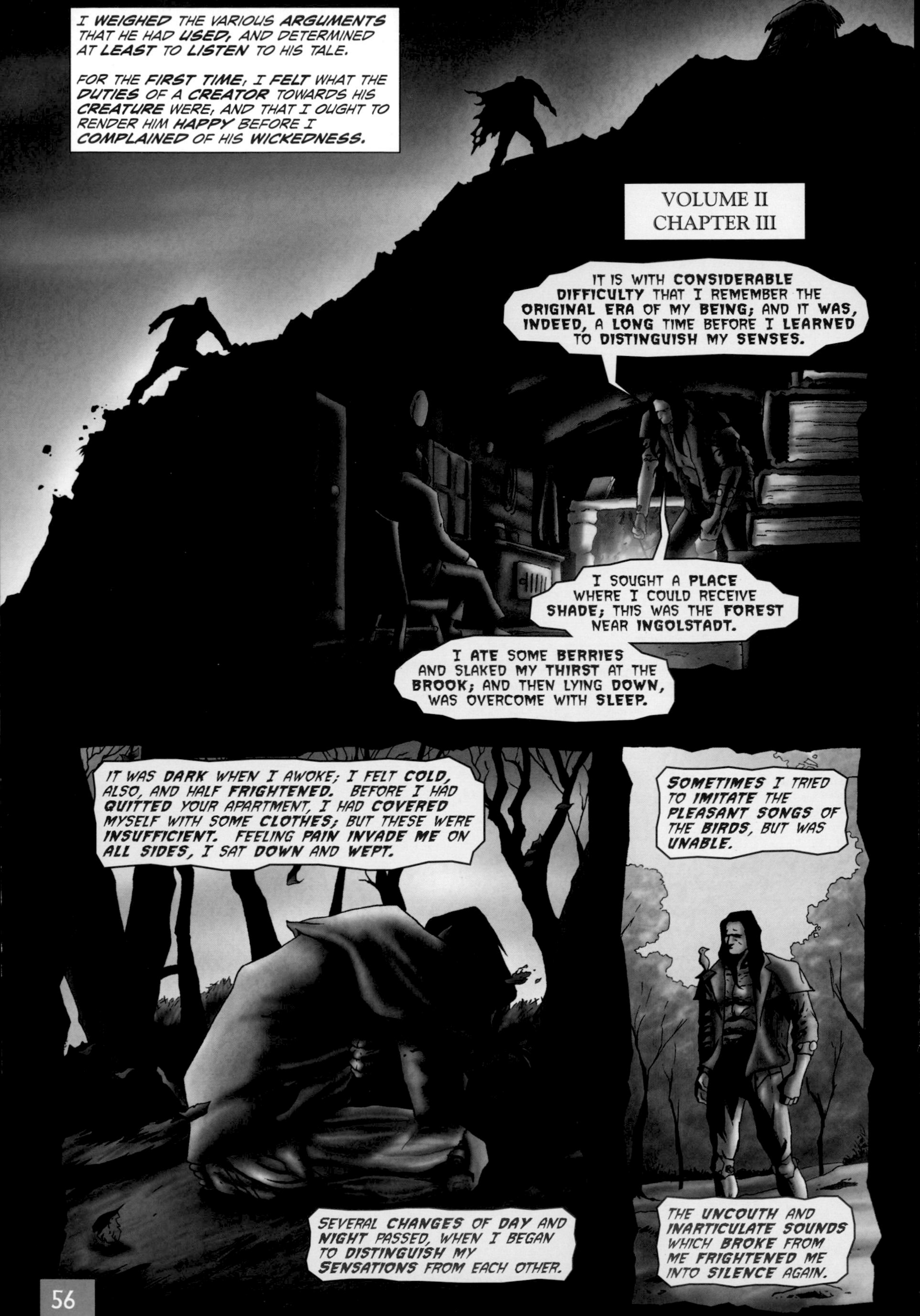
I WEIGHED THE VARIOUS ARGUMENTS THAT HE HAD USED, AND DETERMINED AT LEAST TO LISTEN TO HIS TALE.
FOR THE FIRST TIME, I FELT WHAT THE DUTIES OF A CREATOR TOWARDS HIS CREATURE WERE; AND THAT I OUGHT TO RENDER HIM HAPPY BEFORE I COMPLAINED OF HIS WICKEDNESS.
VOLUME II
CHAPTER III
IT IS WITH CONSIDERABLE DIFFICULTY THAT I REMEMBER THE ORIGINAL ERA OF MY BEING; AND IT WAS, INDEED, A LONG TIME BEFORE I LEARNED TO DISTINGUISH MY SENSES.
I SOUGHT A PLACE WHERE I COULD RECEIVE SHADE; THIS WAS THE FOREST NEAR INGOLSTADT.
I ATE SOME BERRIES AND SLAKED MY THIRST AT THE BROOK; AND THEN LYING DOWN, WAS OVERCOME WITH SLEEP.
IT WAS DARK WHEN I AWOKE; I FELT COLD, ALSO, AND HALF FRIGHTENED. BEFORE I HAD QUITTED YOUR APARTMENT, I HAD COVERED MYSELF WITH SOME CLOTHES; BUT THESE WERE INSUFFICIENT. FEELING PAIN INVADE ME ON ALL SIDES, I SAT DOWN AND WEPT.
SEVERAL CHANGES OF DAY AND NIGHT PASSED, WHEN I BEGAN TO DISTINGUISH MY SENSATIONS FROM EACH OTHER.
SOMETIMES I TRIED TO IMITATE THE PLEASANT SONGS OF THE BIRDS, BUT WAS UNABLE.
THE UNCOUTH AND INARTICULATE SOUNDS WHICH BROKE FROM ME FRIGHTENED ME INTO SILENCE AGAIN.

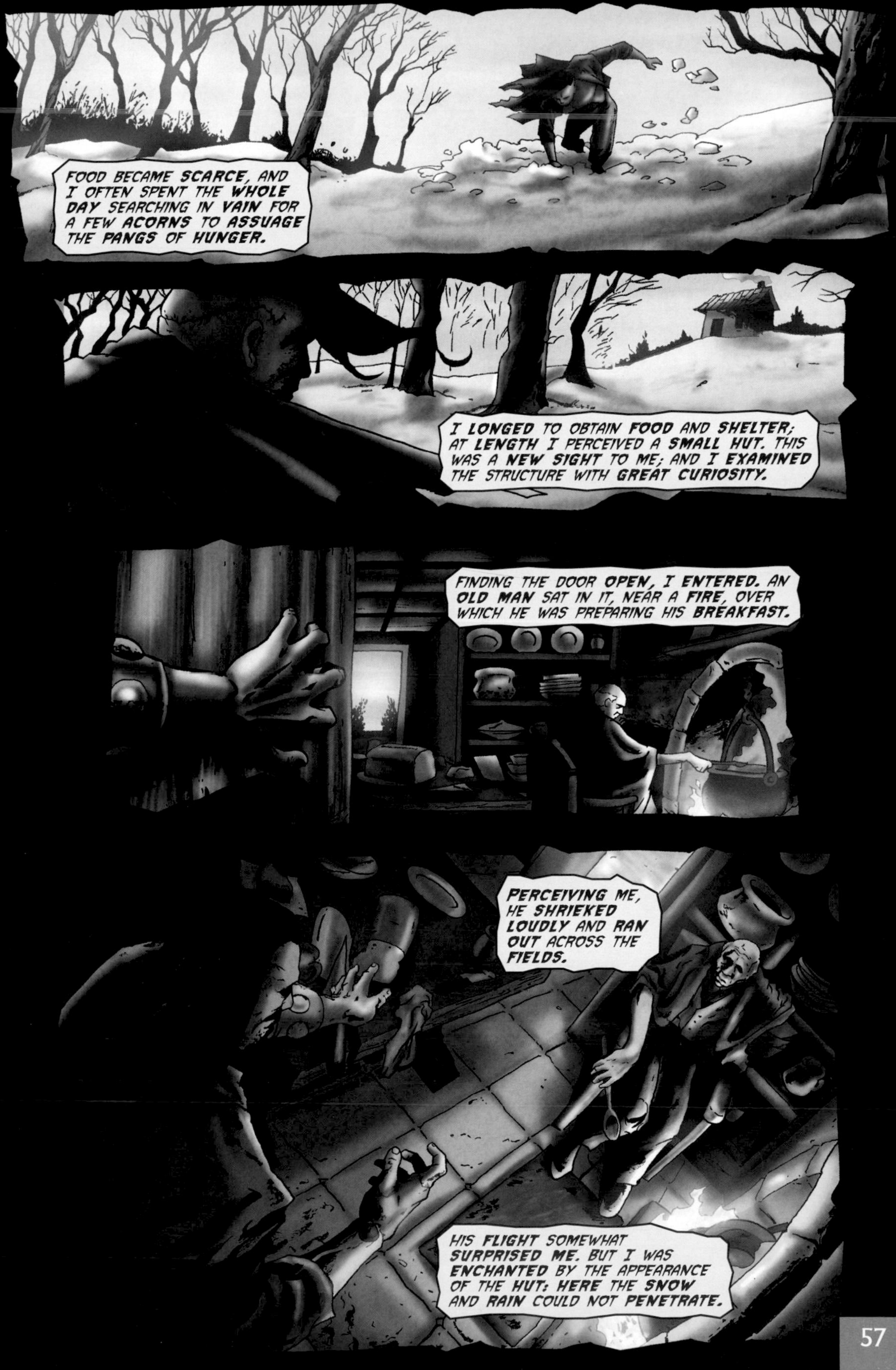
FOOD BECAME SCARCE, AND I OFTEN SPENT THE WHOLE DAY SEARCHING IN VAIN FOR A FEW ACORNS TO ASSUAGE THE PANGS OF HUNGER.
I LONGED TO OBTAIN FOOD AND SHELTER; AT LENGTH I PERCEIVED A SMALL HUT. THIS WAS A NEW SIGHT TO ME; AND I EXAMINED THE STRUCTURE WITH GREAT CURIOSITY.
FINDING THE DOOR OPEN, I ENTERED. AN OLD MAN SAT IN IT, NEAR A FIRE, OVER WHICH HE WAS PREPARING HIS BREAKFAST.
PERCEIVING ME, HE SHRIEKED LOUDLY AND RAN OUT ACROSS THE FIELDS.
HIS FLIGHT SOMEWHAT SURPRISED ME. BUT I WAS ENCHANTED BY THE APPEARANCE OF THE HUT: HERE THE SNOW AND RAIN COULD NOT PENETRATE.

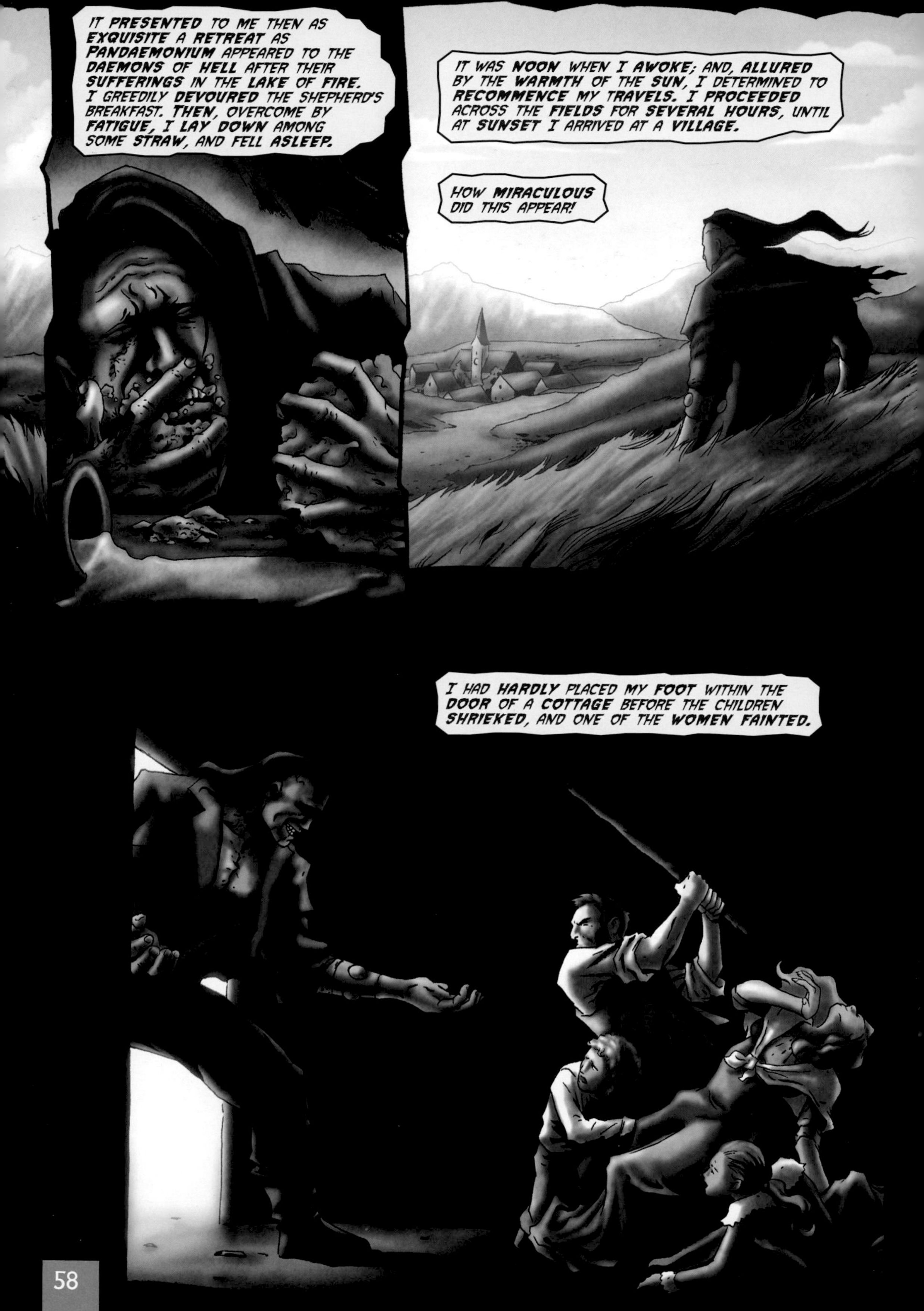
IT PRESENTED TO ME THEN AS EXQUISITE A RETREAT AS PANDAEMONIUM APPEARED TO THE DAEMONS OF HELL AFTER THEIR SUFFERINGS IN THE LAKE OF FIRE. I GREEDILY DEVOURED THE SHEPHERD'S BREAKFAST. THEN, OVERCOME BY FATIGUE, I LAY DOWN AMONG SOME STRAW, AND FELL ASLEEP.
IT WAS NOON WHEN I AWOKE; AND, ALLURED BY THE WARMTH OF THE SUN, I DETERMINED TO RECOMMENCE MY TRAVELS. I PROCEEDED ACROSS THE FIELDS FOR SEVERAL HOURS, UNTIL AT SUNSET I ARRIVED AT A VILLAGE.
HOW MIRACULOUS DID THIS APPEAR!
I HAD HARDLY PLACED MY FOOT WITHIN THE DOOR OF A COTTAGE BEFORE THE CHILDREN SHRIEKED, AND ONE OF THE WOMEN FAINTED.

THE WHOLE VILLAGE WAS ROUSED; SOME FLED, SOME ATTACKED ME, UNTIL, GRIEVOUSLY BRUISED BY STONES AND MANY OTHER KINDS OF MISSILE WEAPONS, I ESCAPED TO THE OPEN COUNTRY...

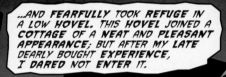

...AND FEARFULLY TOOK REFUGE IN A LOW HOVEL. THIS HOVEL JOINED A COTTAGE OF A NEAT AND PLEASANT APPEARANCE; BUT AFTER MY LATE DEARLY BOUGHT EXPERIENCE, I DARED NOT ENTER IT.

ALTHOUGH THE WIND ENTERED IT BY INNUMERABLE CHINKS, I FOUND IT AN AGREEABLE ASYLUM.

HERE THEN I RETREATED, AND LAY DOWN HAPPY TO HAVE FOUND A SHELTER, HOWEVER MISERABLE, FROM THE SEASON AND FROM THE BARBARITY OF MAN.

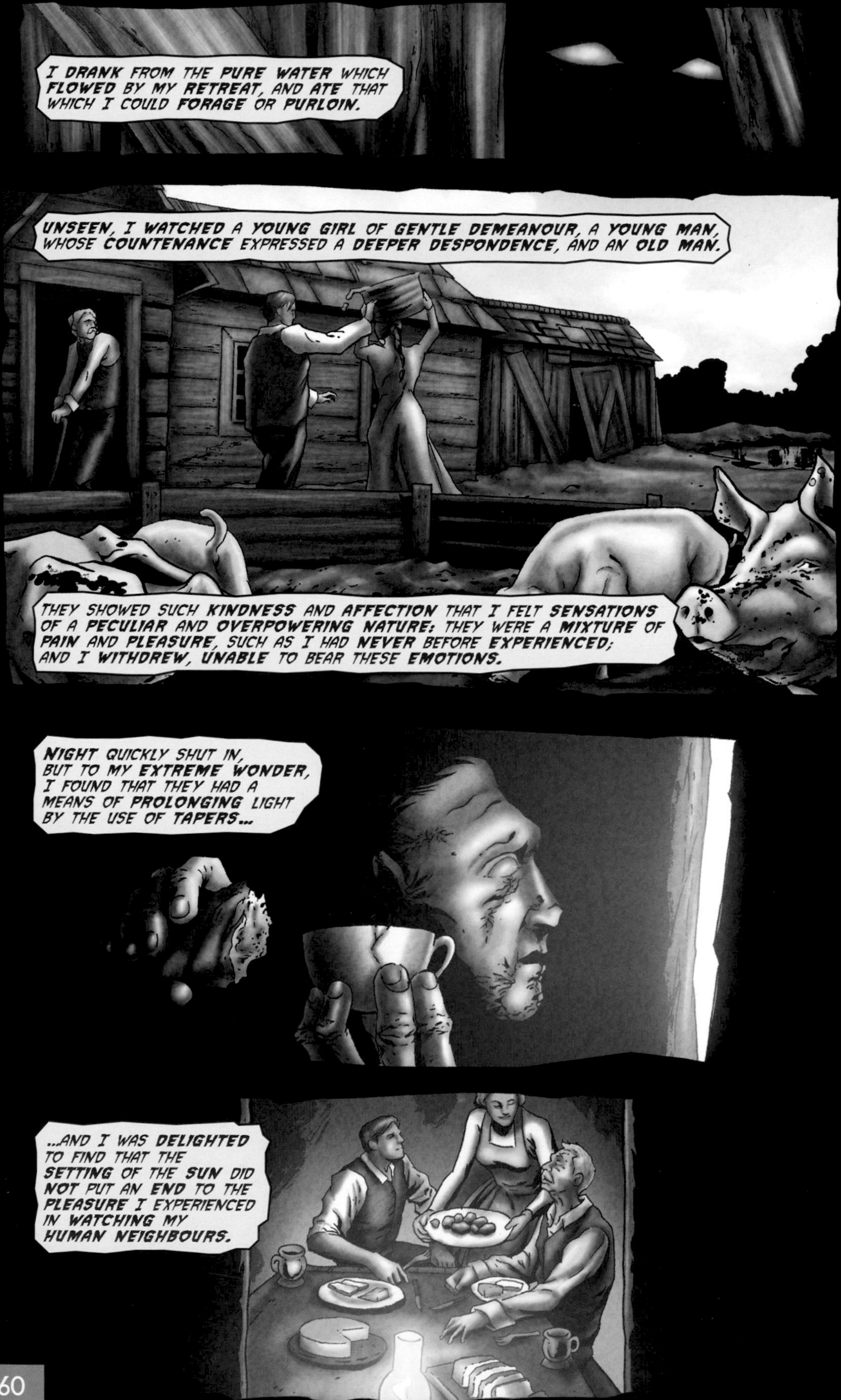
I DRANK FROM THE PURE WATER WHICH FLOWED BY MY RETREAT, AND ATE THAT WHICH I COULD FORAGE OR PURLOIN.
UNSEEN, I WATCHED A YOUNG GIRL OF GENTLE DEMEANOUR, A YOUNG MAN, WHOSE COUNTENANCE EXPRESSED A DEEPER DESPONDENCE, AND AN OLD MAN.
THEY SHOWED SUCH KINDNESS AND AFFECTION THAT I FELT SENSATIONS OF A PECULIAR AND OVERPOWERING NATURE: THEY WERE A MIXTURE OF PAIN AND PLEASURE, SUCH AS I HAD NEVER BEFORE EXPERIENCED; AND I WITHDREW, UNABLE TO BEAR THESE EMOTIONS.
NIGHT QUICKLY SHUT IN, BUT TO MY EXTREME WONDER, I FOUND THAT THEY HAD A MEANS OF PROLONGING LIGHT BY THE USE OF TAPERS...
...AND I WAS DELIGHTED TO FIND THAT THE SETTING OF THE SUN DID NOT PUT AN END TO THE PLEASURE I EXPERIENCED IN WATCHING MY HUMAN NEIGHBOURS.

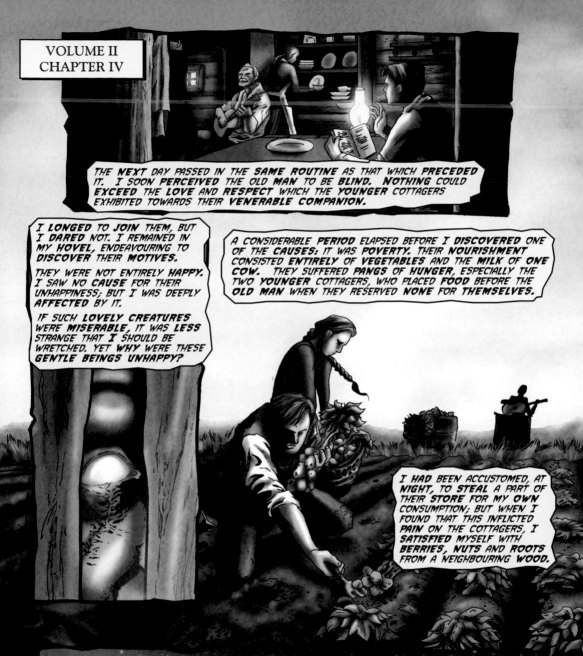

THE **NEXT** DAY PASSED IN THE **SAME ROUTINE** AS THAT WHICH **PRECEDED** IT. I SOON PERCEIVED THE **OLD MAN** TO BE **BLIND**. NOTHING COULD **EXCEED** THE **LOVE** AND **RESPECT** WHICH THE **YOUNGER** COTTAGERS EXHIBITED TOWARDS THEIR **VENERABLE COMPANION**.

I **LONGED** TO **JOIN** THEM, BUT I **DARED** NOT. I REMAINED IN MY **HOVEL**, ENDEAVOURING TO **DISCOVER** THEIR **MOTIVES**.

THEY WERE NOT ENTIRELY HAPPY. I SAW NO **CAUSE** FOR THEIR **UNHAPPINESS**; BUT I WAS DEEPLY **AFFECTED** BY IT.

IF SUCH **LOVELY CREATURES** WERE **MISERABLE**, IT WAS **LESS** STRANGE THAT I **SHOULD** BE WRETCHED. YET WHY WERE THESE **GENTLE BEINGS** UNHAPPY?

A CONSIDERABLE **PERIOD** ELAPSED BEFORE I DISCOVERED ONE OF THE **CAUSES**: IT WAS **POVERTY**. THEIR **NOURISHMENT** CONSISTED **ENTIRELY** OF VEGETABLES AND THE **MILK** OF **ONE COW**. THEY SUFFERED **PANGS** OF HUNGER, ESPECIALLY THE TWO **YOUNGER** COTTAGERS, WHO PLACED **FOOD** BEFORE THE **OLD MAN** WHEN THEY RESERVED **NONE** FOR THEMSELVES.

I HAD BEEN ACCUSTOMED, AT **NIGHT**, TO **STEAL** A PART OF THEIR **STORE** FOR MY **OWN** CONSUMPTION; BUT WHEN I FOUND THAT THIS INFLICTED **PAIN** ON THE COTTAGERS, I **SATISFIED** MYSELF WITH **BERRIES, NUTS** AND **ROOTS** FROM A NEIGHBOURING WOOD.

I DISCOVERED ALSO **ANOTHER** MEANS THROUGH WHICH I WAS **ENABLED** TO **ASSIST** THEIR **LABOURS**.

THE **YOUTH** SPENT A **GREAT** PART OF EACH DAY COLLECTING **WOOD** FOR THE FAMILY **FIRE**; AND, DURING THE **NIGHT**, I OFTEN TOOK HIS **TOOLS** AND BROUGHT HOME **FIRING** SUFFICIENT FOR THE **CONSUMPTION** OF SEVERAL DAYS.

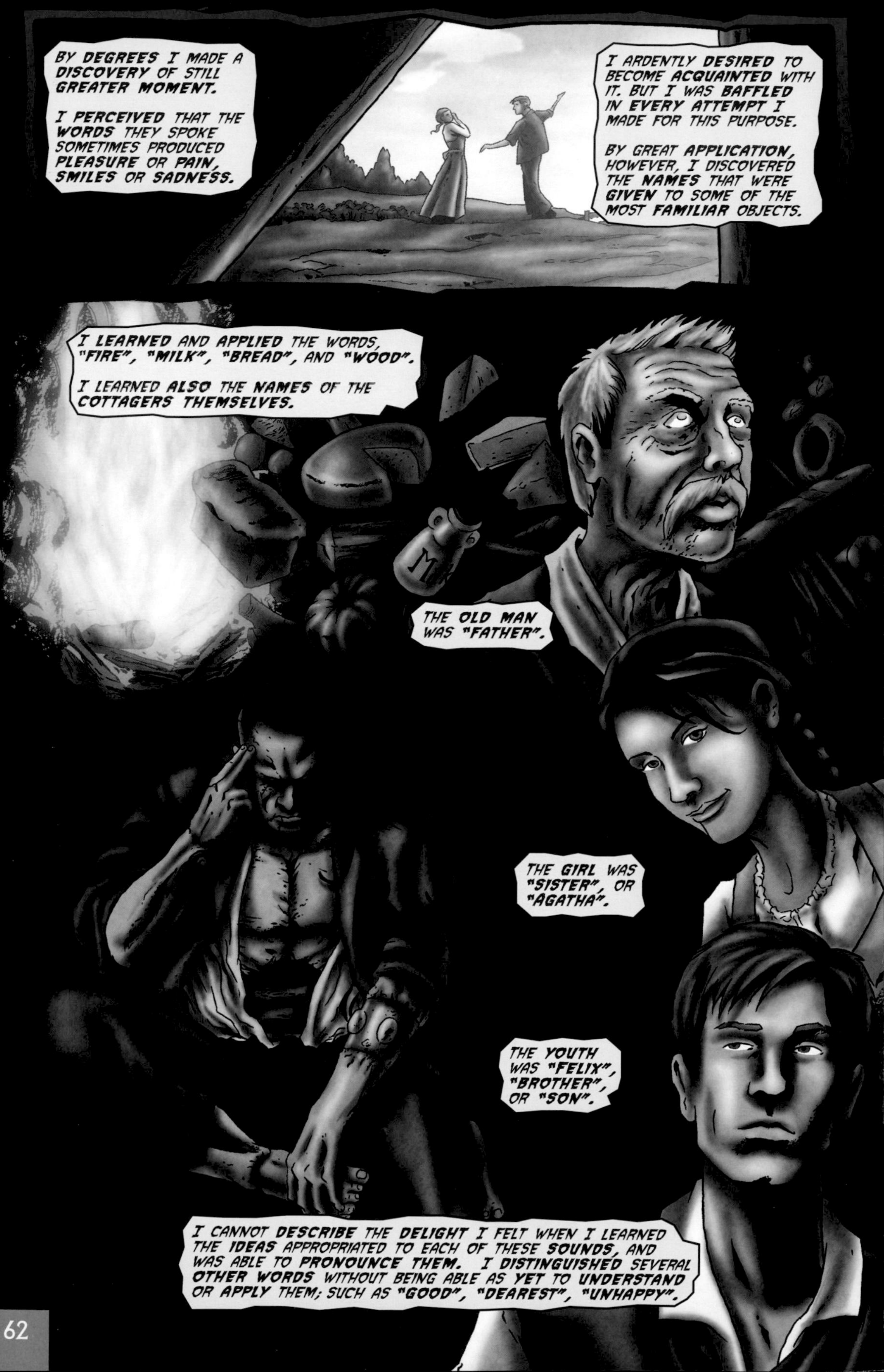
BY DEGREES I MADE A DISCOVERY OF STILL GREATER MOMENT.
I PERCEIVED THAT THE WORDS THEY SPOKE SOMETIMES PRODUCED PLEASURE OR PAIN, SMILES OR SADNESS.
I ARDENTLY DESIRED TO BECOME ACQUAINTED WITH IT. BUT I WAS BAFFLED IN EVERY ATTEMPT I MADE FOR THIS PURPOSE.
BY GREAT APPLICATION, HOWEVER, I DISCOVERED THE NAMES THAT WERE GIVEN TO SOME OF THE MOST FAMILIAR OBJECTS.
I LEARNED AND APPLIED THE WORDS, "FIRE", "MILK", "BREAD", AND "WOOD".
I LEARNED ALSO THE NAMES OF THE COTTAGERS THEMSELVES.
THE OLD MAN WAS "FATHER".
THE GIRL WAS "SISTER", OR "AGATHA".
THE YOUTH WAS "FELIX", "BROTHER", OR "SON".
I CANNOT DESCRIBE THE DELIGHT I FELT WHEN I LEARNED THE IDEAS APPROPRIATED TO EACH OF THESE SOUNDS, AND WAS ABLE TO PRONOUNCE THEM. I DISTINGUISHED SEVERAL OTHER WORDS WITHOUT BEING ABLE AS YET TO UNDERSTAND OR APPLY THEM; SUCH AS "GOOD", "DEAREST", "UNHAPPY".

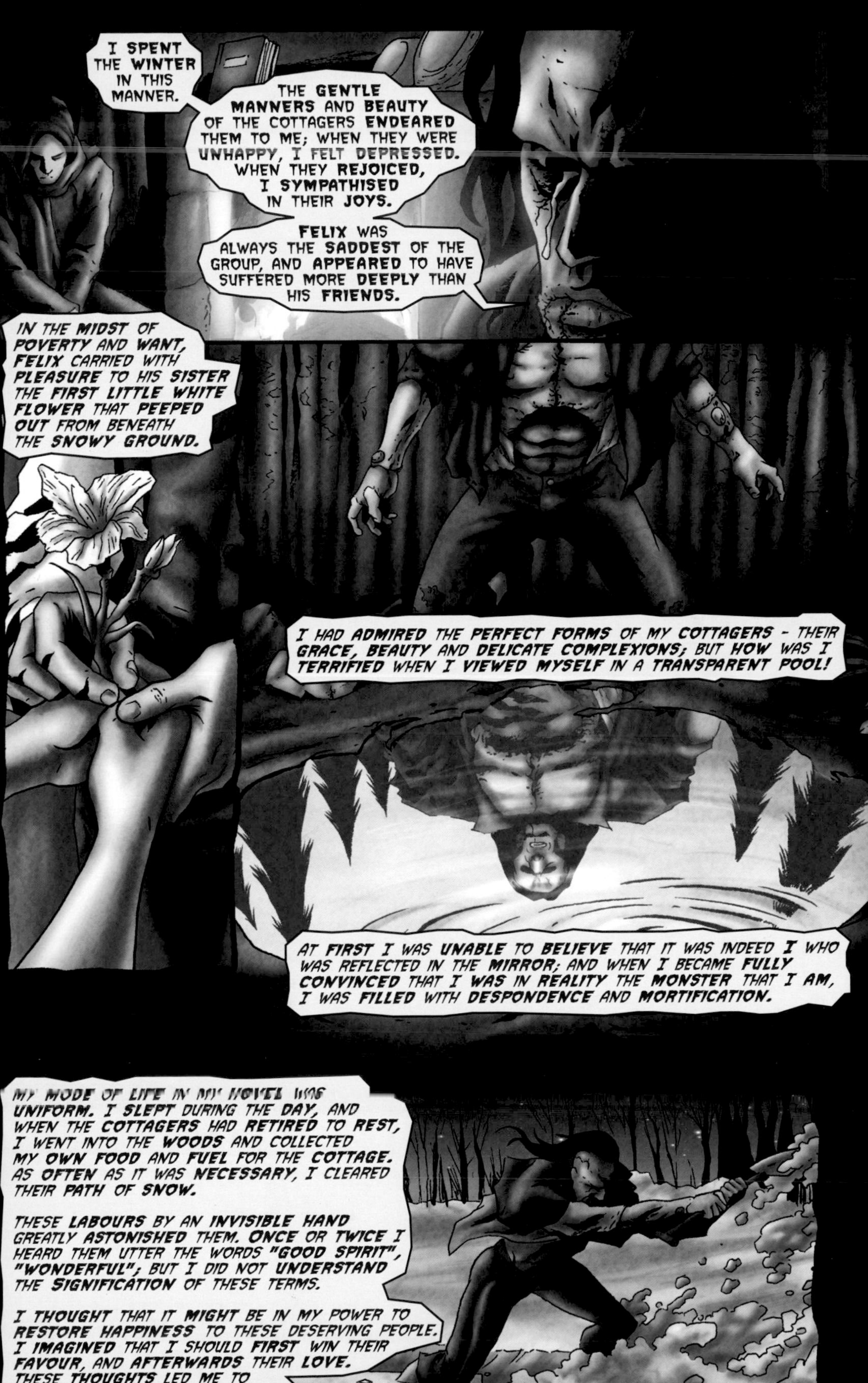
I SPENT THE WINTER IN THIS MANNER.
THE GENTLE MANNERS AND BEAUTY OF THE COTTAGERS ENDEARED THEM TO ME; WHEN THEY WERE UNHAPPY, I FELT DEPRESSED. WHEN THEY REJOICED, I SYMPATHISED IN THEIR JOYS.
FELIX WAS ALWAYS THE SADDEST OF THE GROUP, AND APPEARED TO HAVE SUFFERED MORE DEEPLY THAN HIS FRIENDS.
IN THE MIDST OF POVERTY AND WANT, FELIX CARRIED WITH PLEASURE TO HIS SISTER THE FIRST LITTLE WHITE FLOWER THAT PEEPED OUT FROM BENEATH THE SNOWY GROUND.
I HAD ADMIRED THE PERFECT FORMS OF MY COTTAGERS - THEIR GRACE, BEAUTY AND DELICATE COMPLEXIONS; BUT HOW WAS I TERRIFIED WHEN I VIEWED MYSELF IN A TRANSPARENT POOL!
AT FIRST I WAS UNABLE TO BELIEVE THAT IT WAS INDEED I WHO WAS REFLECTED IN THE MIRROR; AND WHEN I BECAME FULLY CONVINCED THAT I WAS IN REALITY THE MONSTER THAT I AM, I WAS FILLED WITH DESPONDENCE AND MORTIFICATION.
MY MODE OF LIFE IN MY HOVEL WAS UNIFORM. I SLEPT DURING THE DAY, AND WHEN THE COTTAGERS HAD RETIRED TO REST, I WENT INTO THE WOODS AND COLLECTED MY OWN FOOD AND FUEL FOR THE COTTAGE. AS OFTEN AS IT WAS NECESSARY, I CLEARED THEIR PATH OF SNOW.
THESE LABOURS BY AN INVISIBLE HAND GREATLY ASTONISHED THEM. ONCE OR TWICE I HEARD THEM UTTER THE WORDS "GOOD SPIRIT", "WONDERFUL"; BUT I DID NOT UNDERSTAND THE SIGNIFICATION OF THESE TERMS.
I THOUGHT THAT IT MIGHT BE IN MY POWER TO RESTORE HAPPINESS TO THESE DESERVING PEOPLE. I IMAGINED THAT I SHOULD FIRST WIN THEIR FAVOUR, AND AFTERWARDS THEIR LOVE. THESE THOUGHTS LED ME TO APPLY WITH FRESH ARDOUR TO ACQUIRING THE ART OF LANGUAGE.

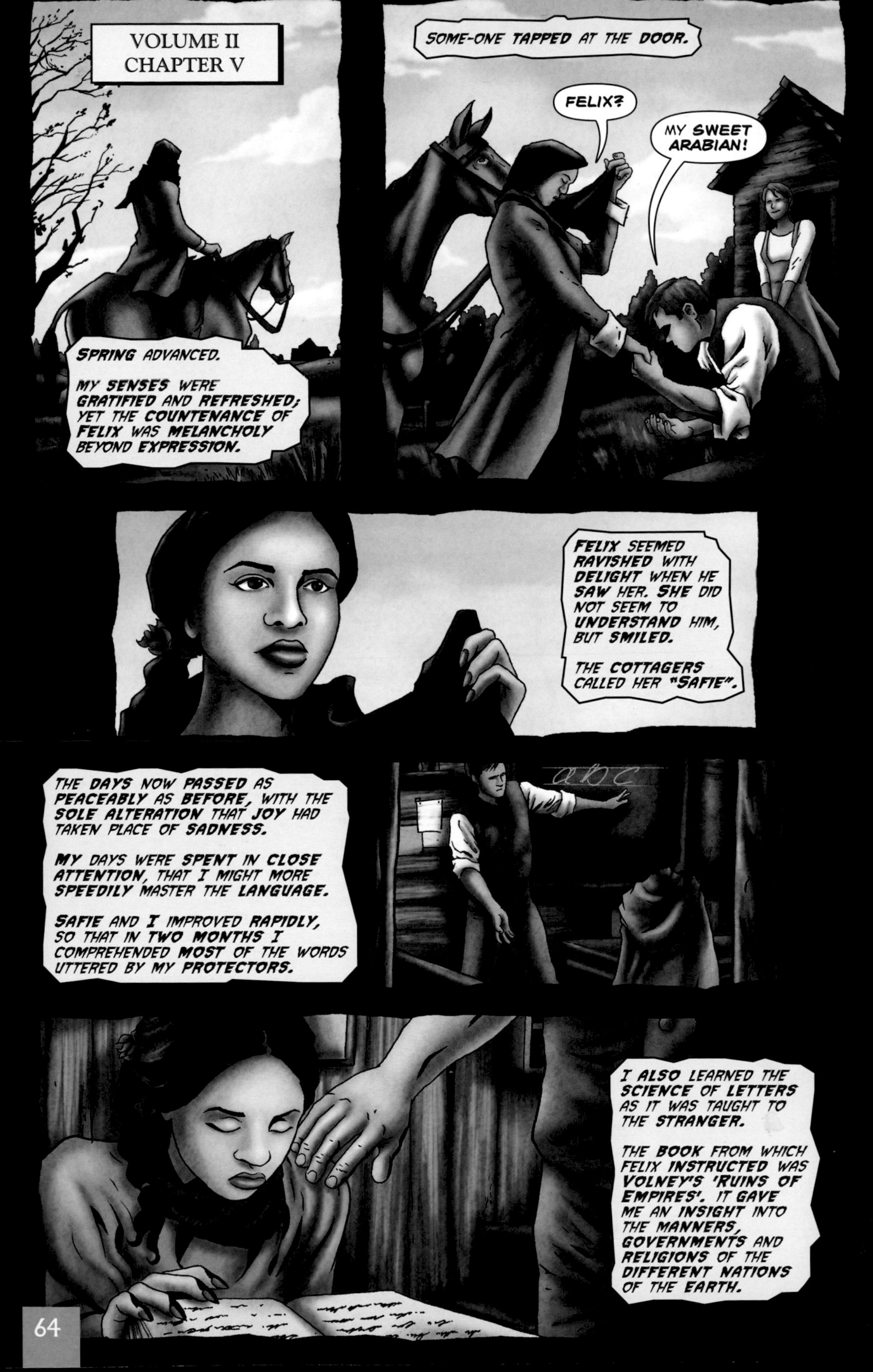
VOLUME II
CHAPTER V
SPRING ADVANCED.
MY SENSES WERE GRATIFIED AND REFRESHED; YET THE COUNTENANCE OF FELIX WAS MELANCHOLY BEYOND EXPRESSION.
SOME-ONE TAPPED AT THE DOOR.
FELIX?
MY SWEET ARABIAN!
FELIX SEEMED RAVISHED WITH DELIGHT WHEN HE SAW HER. SHE DID NOT SEEM TO UNDERSTAND HIM, BUT SMILED.
THE COTTAGERS CALLED HER "SAFIE".
THE DAYS NOW PASSED AS PEACEABLY AS BEFORE, WITH THE SOLE ALTERATION THAT JOY HAD TAKEN PLACE OF SADNESS.
MY DAYS WERE SPENT IN CLOSE ATTENTION, THAT I MIGHT MORE SPEEDILY MASTER THE LANGUAGE.
SAFIE AND I IMPROVED RAPIDLY, SO THAT IN TWO MONTHS I COMPREHENDED MOST OF THE WORDS UTTERED BY MY PROTECTORS.
I ALSO LEARNED THE SCIENCE OF LETTERS AS IT WAS TAUGHT TO THE STRANGER.
THE BOOK FROM WHICH FELIX INSTRUCTED WAS VOLNEY'S 'RUINS OF EMPIRES'. IT GAVE ME AN INSIGHT INTO THE MANNERS, GOVERNMENTS AND RELIGIONS OF THE DIFFERENT NATIONS OF THE EARTH.

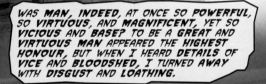

WAS MAN, INDEED, AT ONCE SO POWERFUL, SO VIRTUOUS, AND MAGNIFICENT, YET SO VICIOUS AND BASE? TO BE A GREAT AND VIRTUOUS MAN APPEARED THE HIGHEST HONOUR, BUT WHEN I HEARD DETAILS OF VICE AND BLOODSHED, I TURNED AWAY WITH DISGUST AND LOATHING.

THE WORDS INDUCED ME TO TURN TOWARDS MYSELF. AND WHAT WAS I?

OF MY CREATION AND CREATOR I WAS ABSOLUTELY IGNORANT. I WAS ENDUED WITH A FIGURE HIDEOUSLY DEFORMED AND LOATHSOME; I WAS NOT EVEN OF THE SAME NATURE AS MAN.

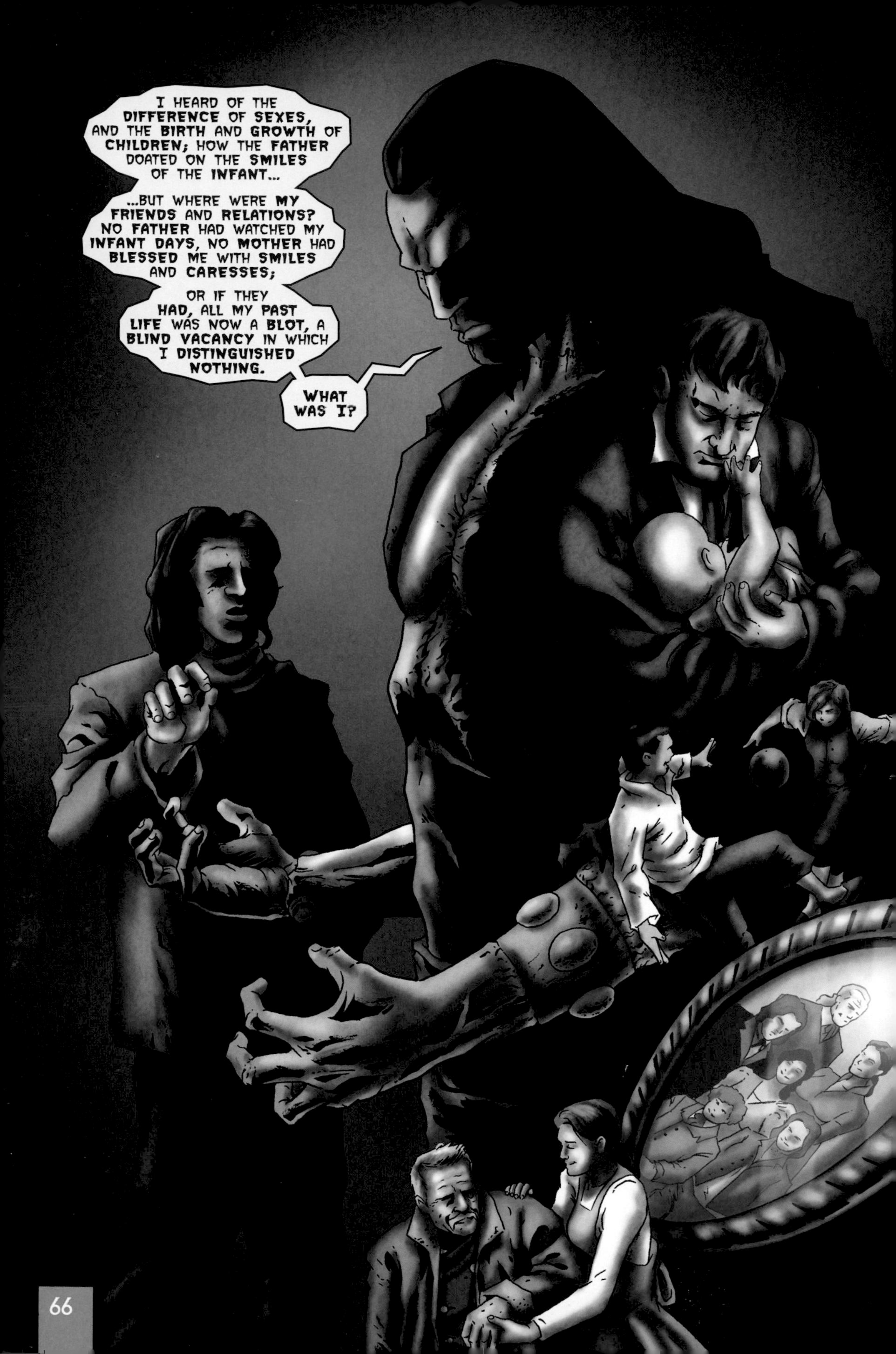
I HEARD OF THE DIFFERENCE OF SEXES, AND THE BIRTH AND GROWTH OF CHILDREN; HOW THE FATHER DOATED ON THE SMILES OF THE INFANT...
...BUT WHERE WERE MY FRIENDS AND RELATIONS? NO FATHER HAD WATCHED MY INFANT DAYS, NO MOTHER HAD BLESSED ME WITH SMILES AND CARESSES;
OR IF THEY HAD, ALL MY PAST LIFE WAS NOW A BLOT, A BLIND VACANCY IN WHICH I DISTINGUISHED NOTHING.
WHAT WAS I?

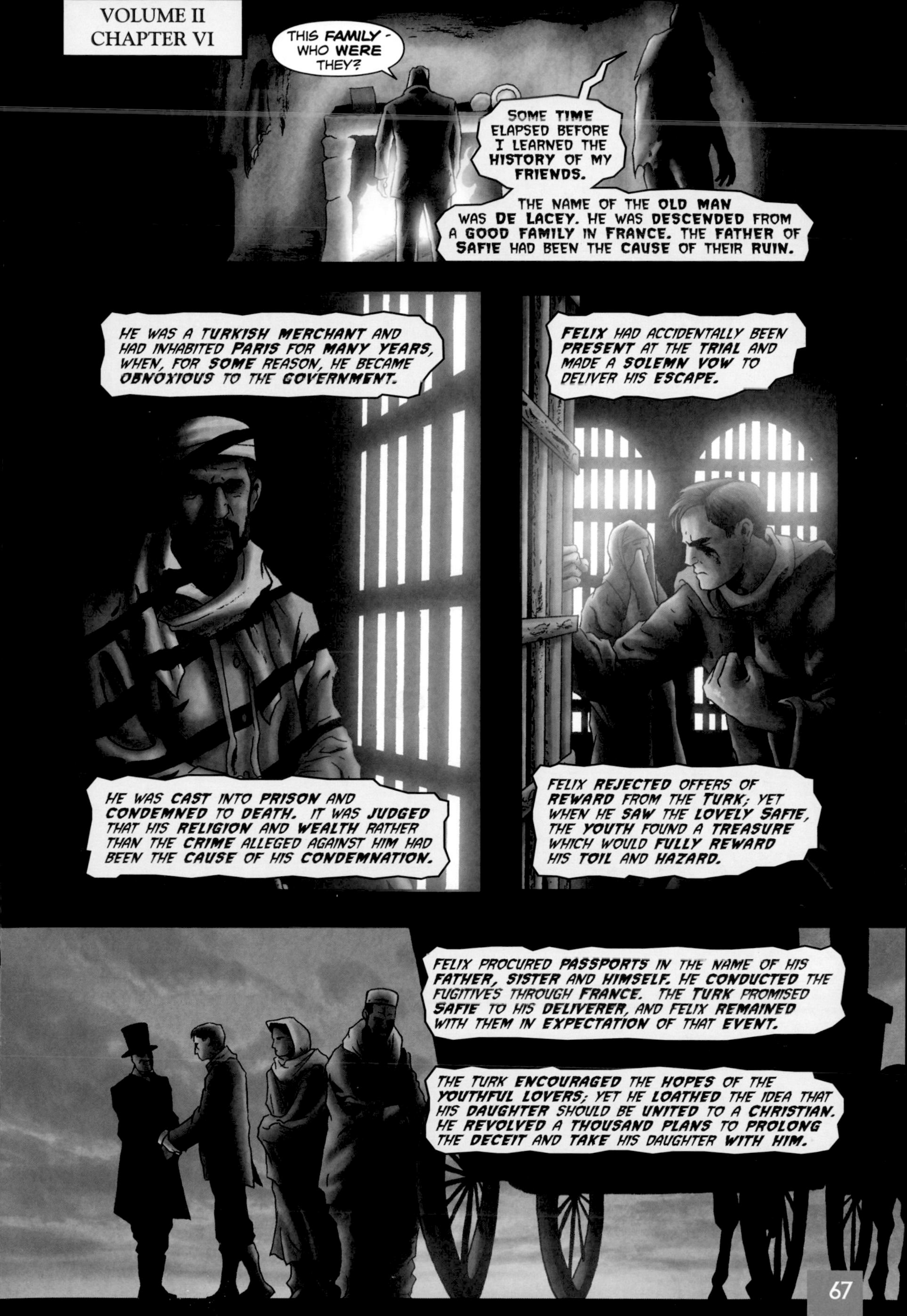
VOLUME II
CHAPTER VI
THIS FAMILY - WHO WERE THEY?
SOME TIME ELAPSED BEFORE I LEARNED THE HISTORY OF MY FRIENDS.
THE NAME OF THE OLD MAN WAS DE LACEY. HE WAS DESCENDED FROM A GOOD FAMILY IN FRANCE. THE FATHER OF SAFIE HAD BEEN THE CAUSE OF THEIR RUIN.
HE WAS A TURKISH MERCHANT AND HAD INHABITED PARIS FOR MANY YEARS, WHEN, FOR SOME REASON, HE BECAME OBNOXIOUS TO THE GOVERNMENT.
HE WAS CAST INTO PRISON AND CONDEMNED TO DEATH. IT WAS JUDGED THAT HIS RELIGION AND WEALTH RATHER THAN THE CRIME ALLEGED AGAINST HIM HAD BEEN THE CAUSE OF HIS CONDEMNATION.
FELIX HAD ACCIDENTALLY BEEN PRESENT AT THE TRIAL AND MADE A SOLEMN VOW TO DELIVER HIS ESCAPE.
FELIX REJECTED OFFERS OF REWARD FROM THE TURK; YET WHEN HE SAW THE LOVELY SAFIE, THE YOUTH FOUND A TREASURE WHICH WOULD FULLY REWARD HIS TOIL AND HAZARD.
FELIX PROCURED PASSPORTS IN THE NAME OF HIS FATHER, SISTER AND HIMSELF. HE CONDUCTED THE FUGITIVES THROUGH FRANCE. THE TURK PROMISED SAFIE TO HIS DELIVERER, AND FELIX REMAINED WITH THEM IN EXPECTATION OF THAT EVENT.
THE TURK ENCOURAGED THE HOPES OF THE YOUTHFUL LOVERS; YET HE LOATHED THE IDEA THAT HIS DAUGHTER SHOULD BE UNITED TO A CHRISTIAN. HE REVOLVED A THOUSAND PLANS TO PROLONG THE DECEIT AND TAKE HIS DAUGHTER WITH HIM.

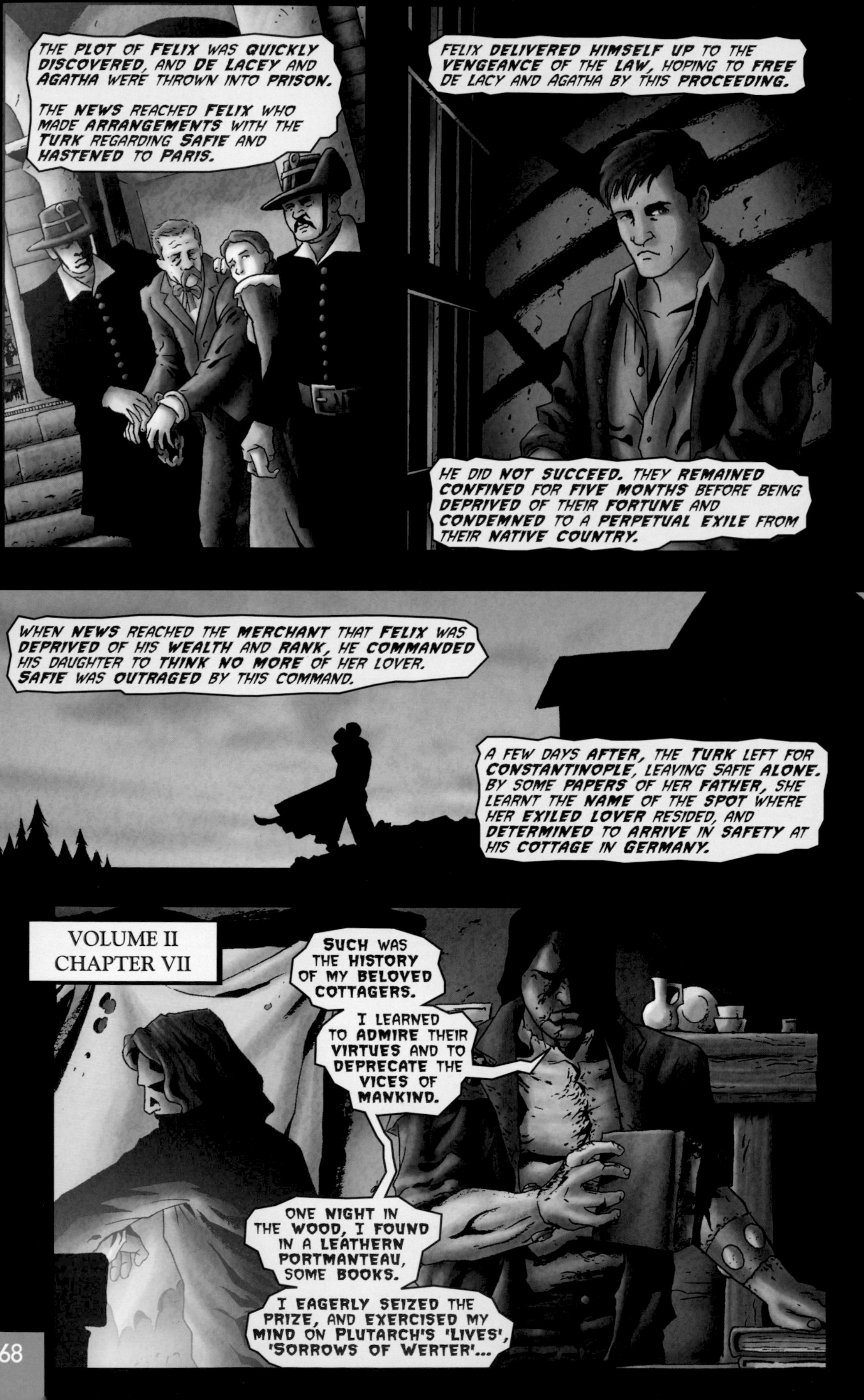
THE PLOT OF FELIX WAS QUICKLY DISCOVERED, AND DE LACEY AND AGATHA WERE THROWN INTO PRISON.
THE NEWS REACHED FELIX WHO MADE ARRANGEMENTS WITH THE TURK REGARDING SAFIE AND HASTENED TO PARIS.
FELIX DELIVERED HIMSELF UP TO THE VENGEANCE OF THE LAW, HOPING TO FREE DE LACY AND AGATHA BY THIS PROCEEDING.
HE DID NOT SUCCEED. THEY REMAINED CONFINED FOR FIVE MONTHS BEFORE BEING DEPRIVED OF THEIR FORTUNE AND CONDEMNED TO A PERPETUAL EXILE FROM THEIR NATIVE COUNTRY.
WHEN NEWS REACHED THE MERCHANT THAT FELIX WAS DEPRIVED OF HIS WEALTH AND RANK, HE COMMANDED HIS DAUGHTER TO THINK NO MORE OF HER LOVER. SAFIE WAS OUTRAGED BY THIS COMMAND.
A FEW DAYS AFTER, THE TURK LEFT FOR CONSTANTINOPLE, LEAVING SAFIE ALONE. BY SOME PAPERS OF HER FATHER, SHE LEARNT THE NAME OF THE SPOT WHERE HER EXILED LOVER RESIDED, AND DETERMINED TO ARRIVE IN SAFETY AT HIS COTTAGE IN GERMANY.
VOLUME II
CHAPTER VII
SUCH WAS THE HISTORY OF MY BELOVED COTTAGERS.
I LEARNED TO ADMIRE THEIR VIRTUES AND TO DEPRECATE THE VICES OF MANKIND.
ONE NIGHT IN THE WOOD, I FOUND IN A LEATHERN PORTMANTEAU, SOME BOOKS.
I EAGERLY SEIZED THE PRIZE, AND EXERCISED MY MIND ON PLUTARCH'S 'LIVES', 'SORROWS OF WERTER'...

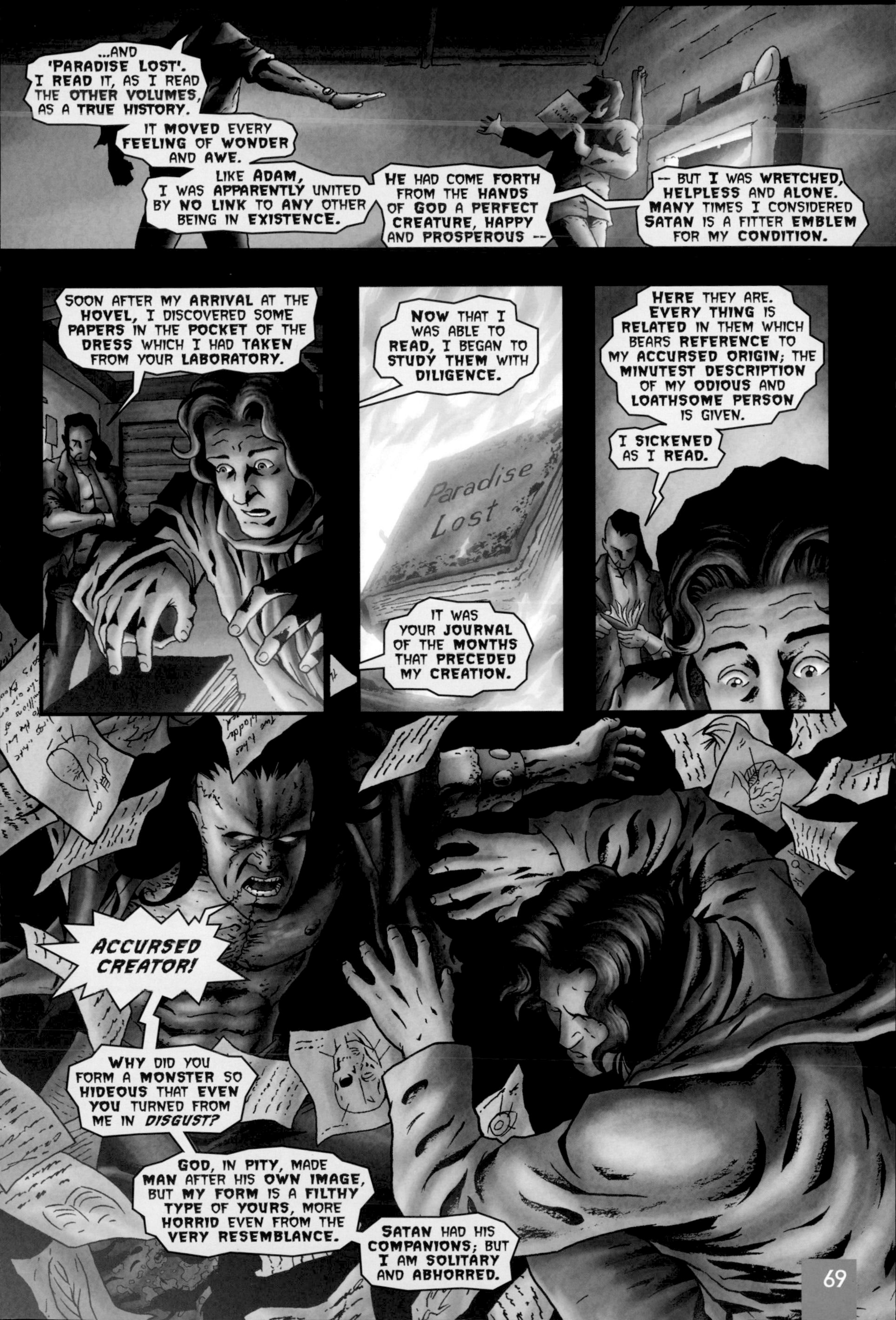
...AND 'PARADISE LOST'. I READ IT, AS I READ THE OTHER VOLUMES, AS A TRUE HISTORY.
IT MOVED EVERY FEELING OF WONDER AND AWE.
LIKE ADAM, I WAS APPARENTLY UNITED BY NO LINK TO ANY OTHER BEING IN EXISTENCE.
HE HAD COME FORTH FROM THE HANDS OF GOD A PERFECT CREATURE, HAPPY AND PROSPEROUS --
-- BUT I WAS WRETCHED, HELPLESS AND ALONE. MANY TIMES I CONSIDERED SATAN IS A FITTER EMBLEM FOR MY CONDITION.
SOON AFTER MY ARRIVAL AT THE HOVEL, I DISCOVERED SOME PAPERS IN THE POCKET OF THE DRESS WHICH I HAD TAKEN FROM YOUR LABORATORY.
NOW THAT I WAS ABLE TO READ, I BEGAN TO STUDY THEM WITH DILIGENCE.
Paradise Lost
IT WAS YOUR JOURNAL OF THE MONTHS THAT PRECEDED MY CREATION.
HERE THEY ARE. EVERY THING IS RELATED IN THEM WHICH BEARS REFERENCE TO MY ACCURSED ORIGIN; THE MINUTEST DESCRIPTION OF MY ODIOUS AND LOATHSOME PERSON IS GIVEN.
I SICKENED AS I READ.
ACCURSED CREATOR!
WHY DID YOU FORM A MONSTER SO HIDEOUS THAT EVEN YOU TURNED FROM ME IN DISGUST?
GOD, IN PITY, MADE MAN AFTER HIS OWN IMAGE, BUT MY FORM IS A FILTHY TYPE OF YOURS, MORE HORRID EVEN FROM THE VERY RESEMBLANCE.
SATAN HAD HIS COMPANIONS; BUT I AM SOLITARY AND ABHORRED.

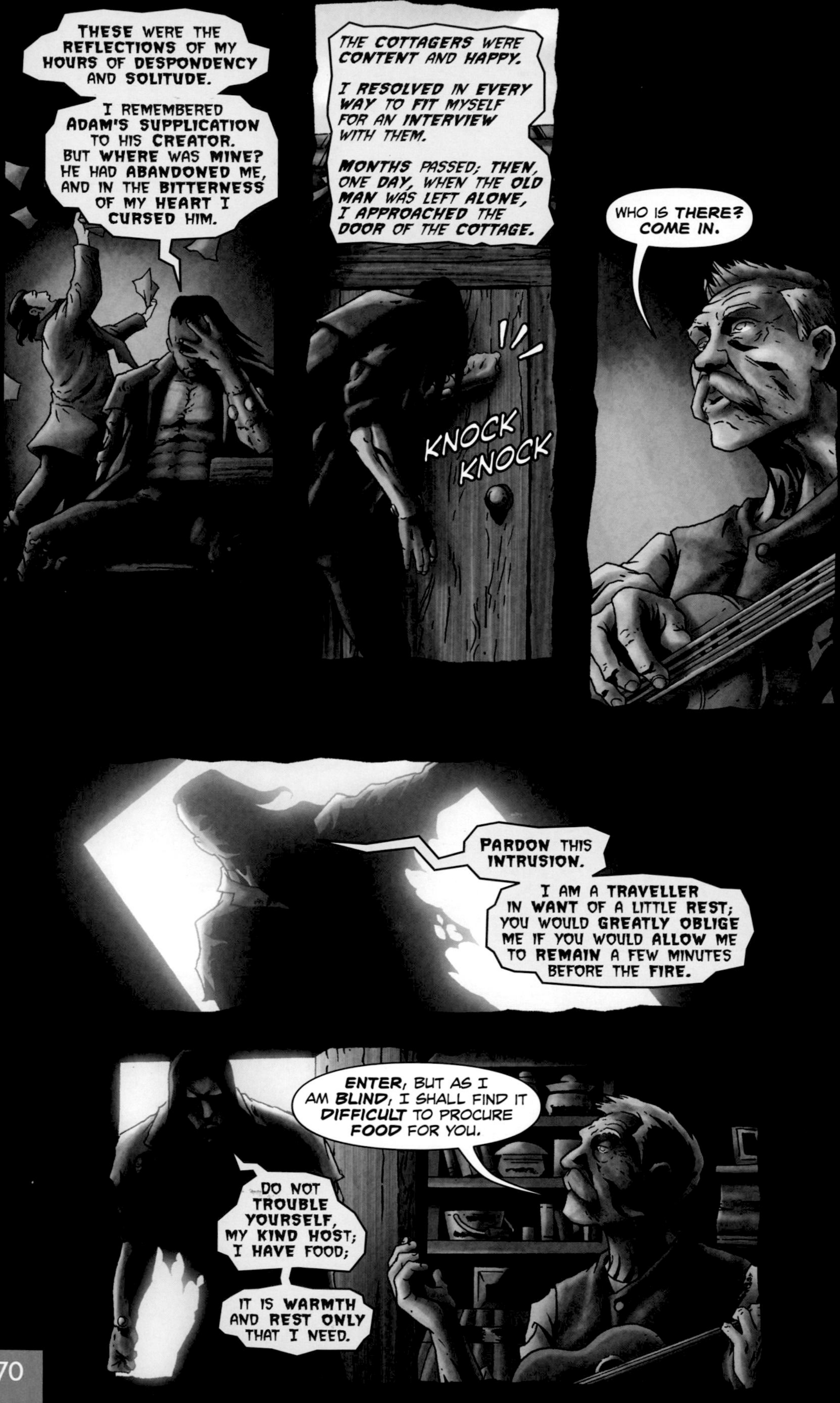
THESE WERE THE REFLECTIONS OF MY HOURS OF DESPONDENCY AND SOLITUDE.
I REMEMBERED ADAM'S SUPPLICATION TO HIS CREATOR. BUT WHERE WAS MINE? HE HAD ABANDONED ME, AND IN THE BITTERNESS OF MY HEART I CURSED HIM.
THE COTTAGERS WERE CONTENT AND HAPPY.
I RESOLVED IN EVERY WAY TO FIT MYSELF FOR AN INTERVIEW WITH THEM.
MONTHS PASSED; THEN, ONE DAY, WHEN THE OLD MAN WAS LEFT ALONE, I APPROACHED THE DOOR OF THE COTTAGE.
KNOCK KNOCK
WHO IS THERE? COME IN.
PARDON THIS INTRUSION.
I AM A TRAVELLER IN WANT OF A LITTLE REST; YOU WOULD GREATLY OBLIGE ME IF YOU WOULD ALLOW ME TO REMAIN A FEW MINUTES BEFORE THE FIRE.
ENTER, BUT AS I AM BLIND, I SHALL FIND IT DIFFICULT TO PROCURE FOOD FOR YOU.
DO NOT TROUBLE YOURSELF, MY KIND HOST; I HAVE FOOD;
IT IS WARMTH AND REST ONLY THAT I NEED.

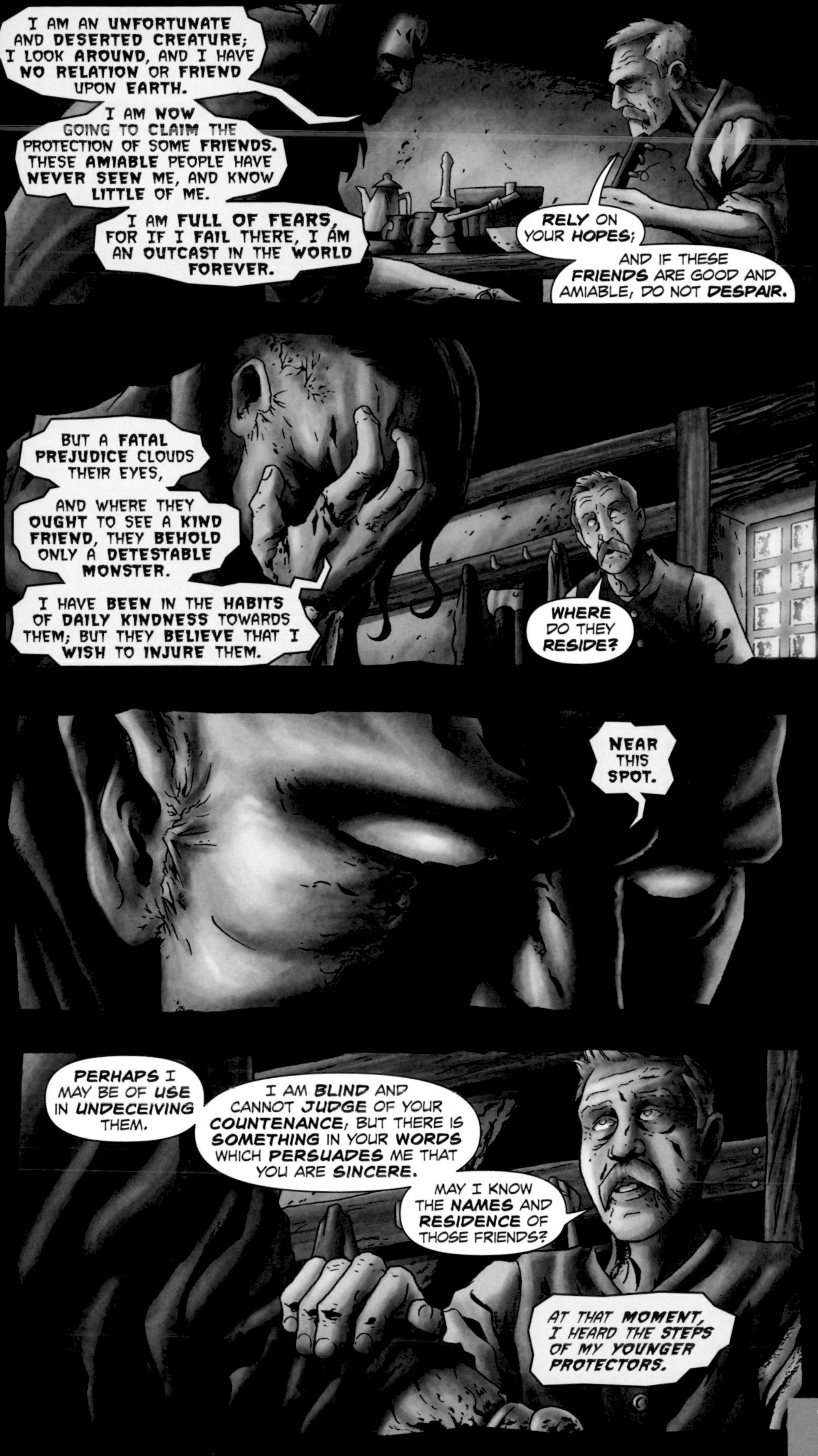
I AM AN UNFORTUNATE AND DESERTED CREATURE; I LOOK AROUND, AND I HAVE NO RELATION OR FRIEND UPON EARTH.
I AM NOW GOING TO CLAIM THE PROTECTION OF SOME FRIENDS. THESE AMIABLE PEOPLE HAVE NEVER SEEN ME, AND KNOW LITTLE OF ME.
I AM FULL OF FEARS, FOR IF I FAIL THERE, I AM AN OUTCAST IN THE WORLD FOREVER.
RELY ON YOUR HOPES;
AND IF THESE FRIENDS ARE GOOD AND AMIABLE, DO NOT DESPAIR.
BUT A FATAL PREJUDICE CLOUDS THEIR EYES,
AND WHERE THEY OUGHT TO SEE A KIND FRIEND, THEY BEHOLD ONLY A DETESTABLE MONSTER.
I HAVE BEEN IN THE HABITS OF DAILY KINDNESS TOWARDS THEM; BUT THEY BELIEVE THAT I WISH TO INJURE THEM.
WHERE DO THEY RESIDE?
NEAR THIS SPOT.
PERHAPS I MAY BE OF USE IN UNDECEIVING THEM.
I AM BLIND AND CANNOT JUDGE OF YOUR COUNTENANCE, BUT THERE IS SOMETHING IN YOUR WORDS WHICH PERSUADES ME THAT YOU ARE SINCERE.
MAY I KNOW THE NAMES AND RESIDENCE OF THOSE FRIENDS?
AT THAT MOMENT, I HEARD THE STEPS OF MY YOUNGER PROTECTORS.

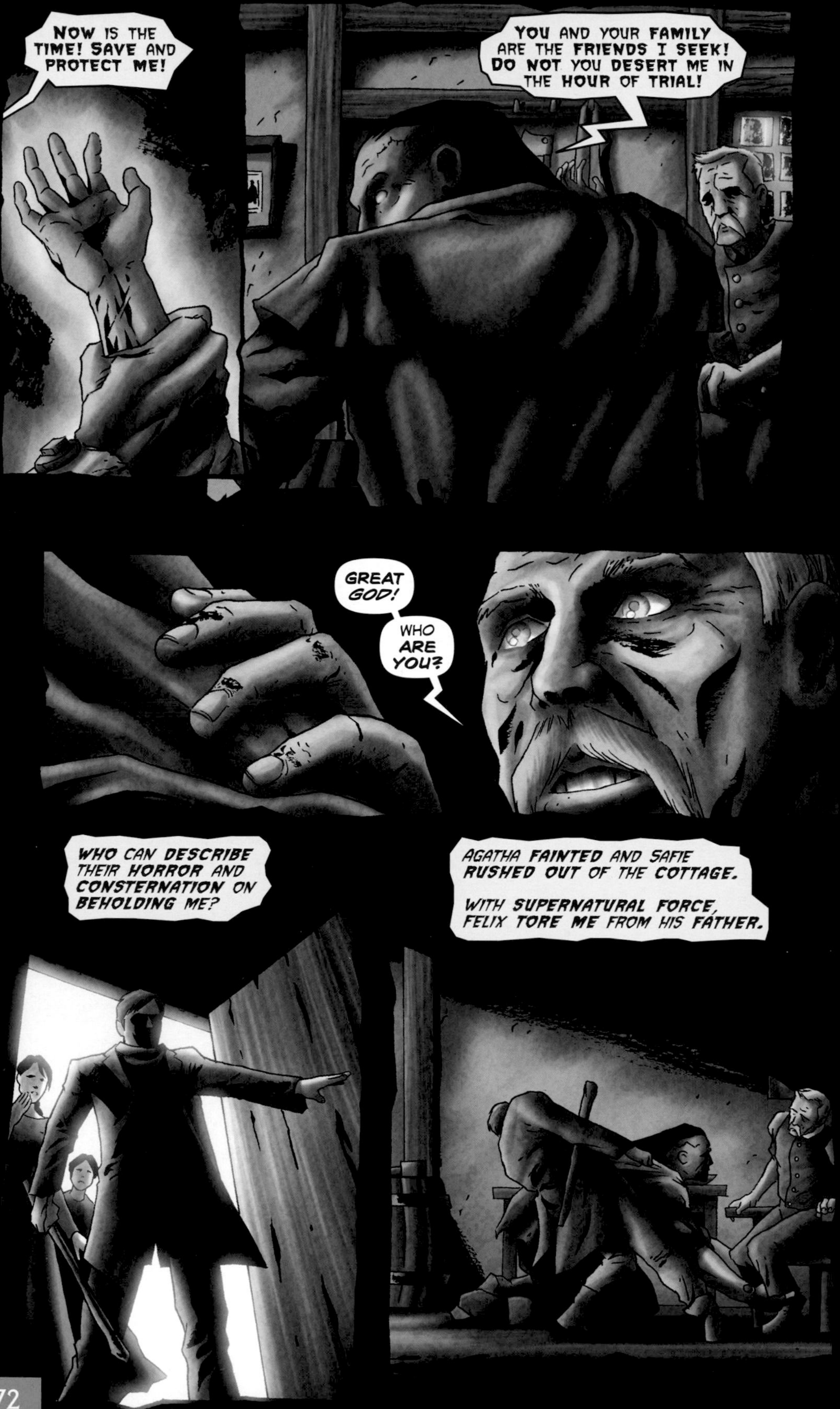
NOW IS THE TIME! SAVE AND PROTECT ME!
YOU AND YOUR FAMILY ARE THE FRIENDS I SEEK! DO NOT YOU DESERT ME IN THE HOUR OF TRIAL!
GREAT GOD!
WHO ARE YOU?
WHO CAN DESCRIBE THEIR HORROR AND CONSTERNATION ON BEHOLDING ME?
AGATHA FAINTED AND SAFIE RUSHED OUT OF THE COTTAGE.
WITH SUPERNATURAL FORCE, FELIX TORE ME FROM HIS FATHER.

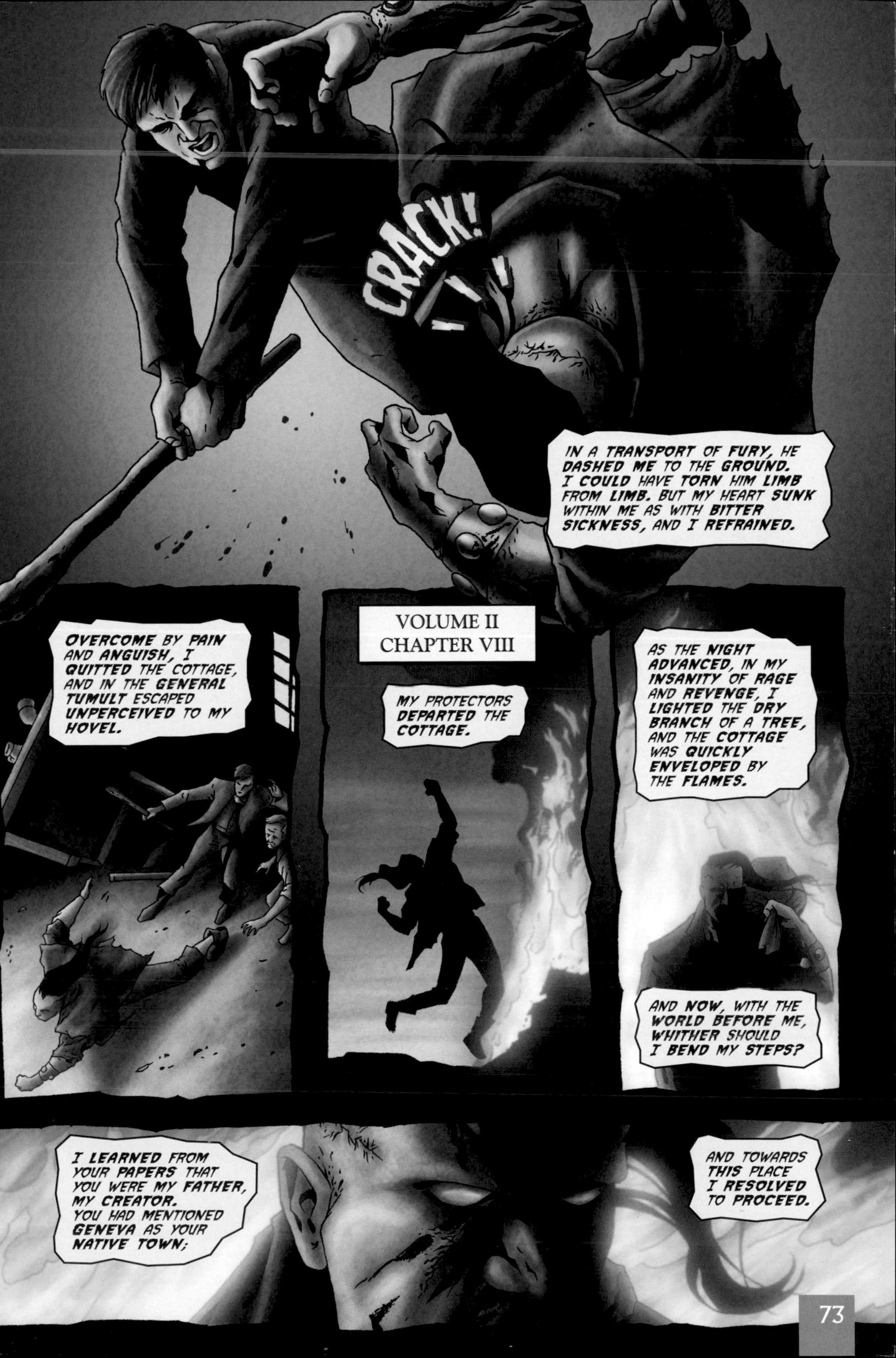
CRACK!
IN A TRANSPORT OF FURY, HE DASHED ME TO THE GROUND. I COULD HAVE TORN HIM LIMB FROM LIMB. BUT MY HEART SUNK WITHIN ME AS WITH BITTER SICKNESS, AND I REFRAINED.
OVERCOME BY PAIN AND ANGUISH, I QUITTED THE COTTAGE, AND IN THE GENERAL TUMULT ESCAPED UNPERCEIVED TO MY HOVEL.
VOLUME II CHAPTER VIII
MY PROTECTORS DEPARTED THE COTTAGE.
AS THE NIGHT ADVANCED, IN MY INSANITY OF RAGE AND REVENGE, I LIGHTED THE DRY BRANCH OF A TREE, AND THE COTTAGE WAS QUICKLY ENVELOPED BY THE FLAMES.
AND NOW, WITH THE WORLD BEFORE ME, WHITHER SHOULD I BEND MY STEPS?
I LEARNED FROM YOUR PAPERS THAT YOU WERE MY FATHER, MY CREATOR. YOU HAD MENTIONED GENEVA AS YOUR NATIVE TOWN;
AND TOWARDS THIS PLACE I RESOLVED TO PROCEED.

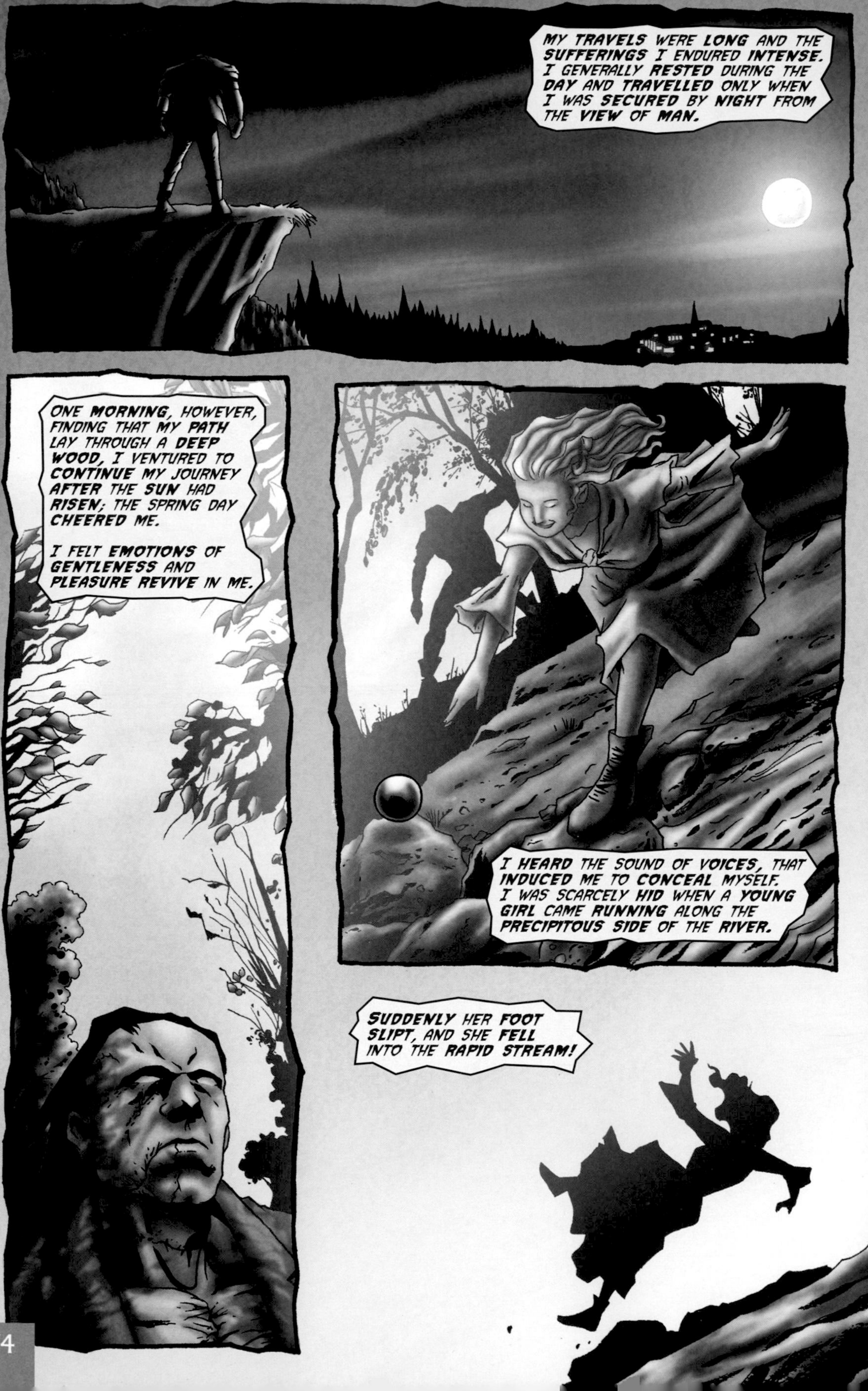
MY TRAVELS WERE LONG AND THE SUFFERINGS I ENDURED INTENSE. I GENERALLY RESTED DURING THE DAY AND TRAVELLED ONLY WHEN I WAS SECURED BY NIGHT FROM THE VIEW OF MAN.
ONE MORNING, HOWEVER, FINDING THAT MY PATH LAY THROUGH A DEEP WOOD, I VENTURED TO CONTINUE MY JOURNEY AFTER THE SUN HAD RISEN; THE SPRING DAY CHEERED ME.
I FELT EMOTIONS OF GENTLENESS AND PLEASURE REVIVE IN ME.
I HEARD THE SOUND OF VOICES, THAT INDUCED ME TO CONCEAL MYSELF. I WAS SCARCELY HID WHEN A YOUNG GIRL CAME RUNNING ALONG THE PRECIPITOUS SIDE OF THE RIVER.
SUDDENLY HER FOOT SLIPT, AND SHE FELL INTO THE RAPID STREAM!

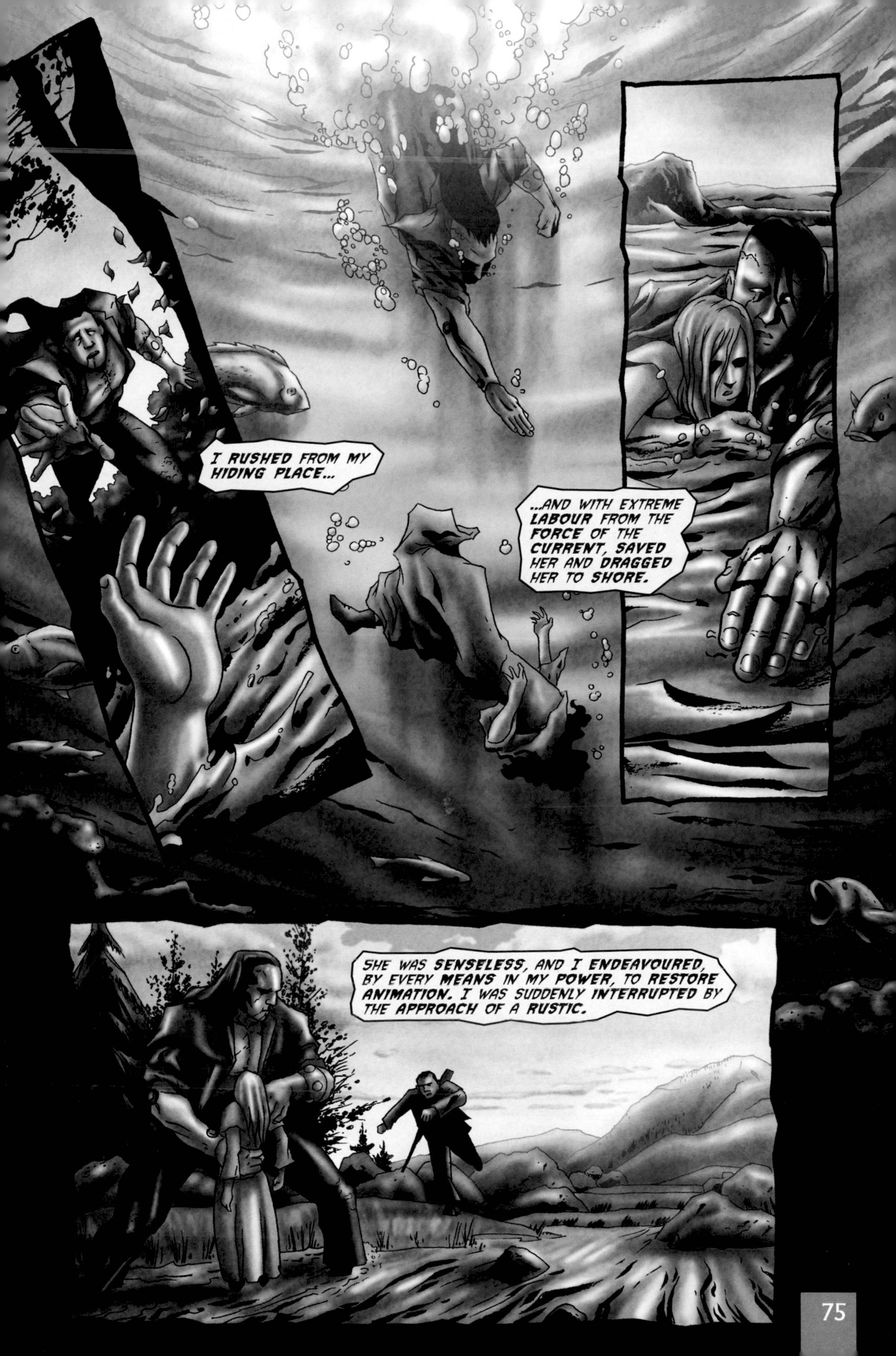

I RUSHED FROM MY HIDING PLACE...
...AND WITH EXTREME LABOUR FROM THE FORCE OF THE CURRENT, SAVED HER AND DRAGGED HER TO SHORE.
SHE WAS SENSELESS, AND I ENDEAVOURED, BY EVERY MEANS IN MY POWER, TO RESTORE ANIMATION. I WAS SUDDENLY INTERRUPTED BY THE APPROACH OF A RUSTIC.

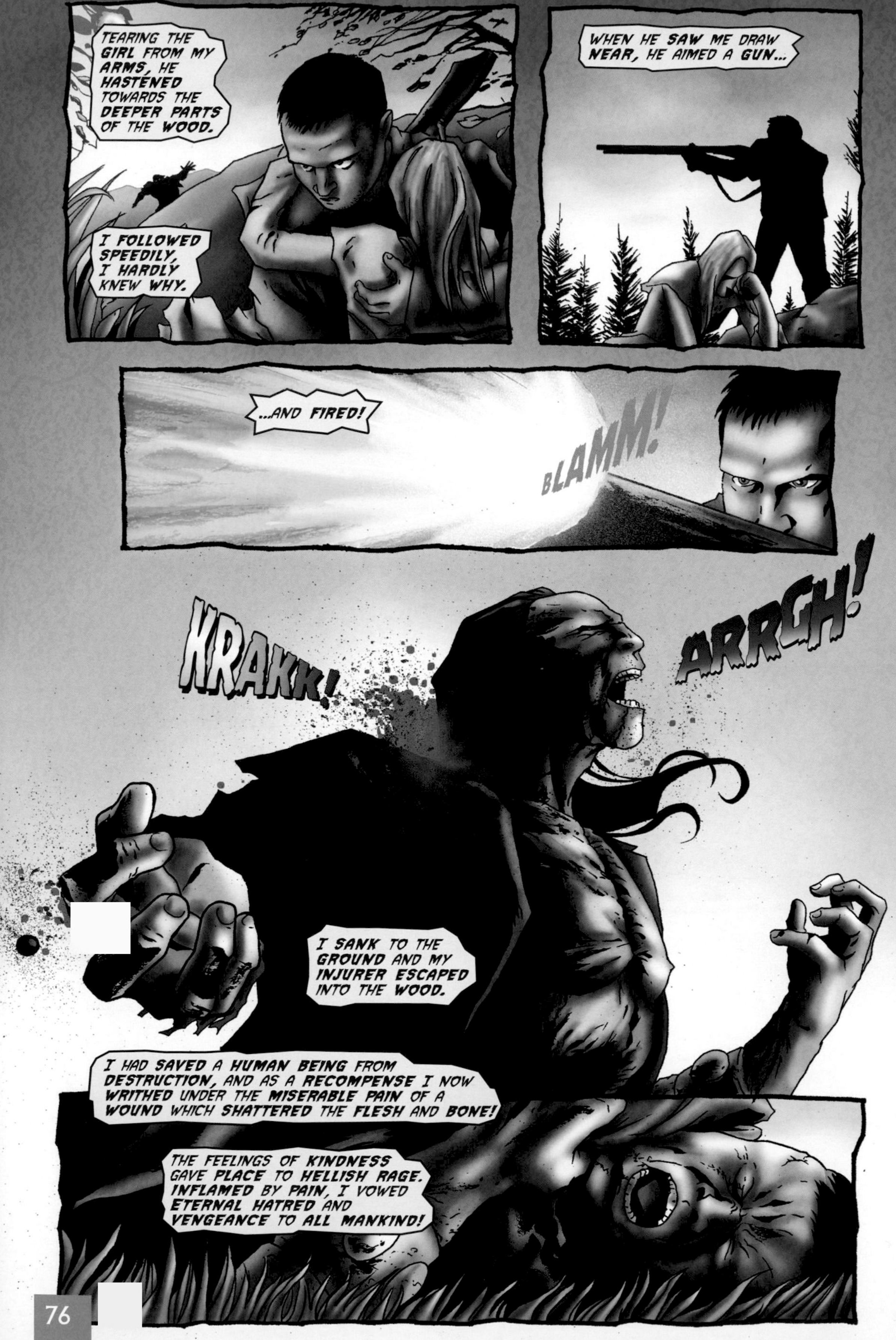
TEARING THE GIRL FROM MY ARMS, HE HASTENED TOWARDS THE DEEPER PARTS OF THE WOOD.
I FOLLOWED SPEEDILY, I HARDLY KNEW WHY.
WHEN HE SAW ME DRAW NEAR, HE AIMED A GUN...
...AND FIRED!
BLAMM!
KRAKK!
ARRGH!
I SANK TO THE GROUND AND MY INJURER ESCAPED INTO THE WOOD.
I HAD SAVED A HUMAN BEING FROM DESTRUCTION, AND AS A RECOMPENSE I NOW WRITHED UNDER THE MISERABLE PAIN OF A WOUND WHICH SHATTERED THE FLESH AND BONE!
THE FEELINGS OF KINDNESS GAVE PLACE TO HELLISH RAGE. INFLAMED BY PAIN, I VOWED ETERNAL HATRED AND VENGEANCE TO ALL MANKIND!

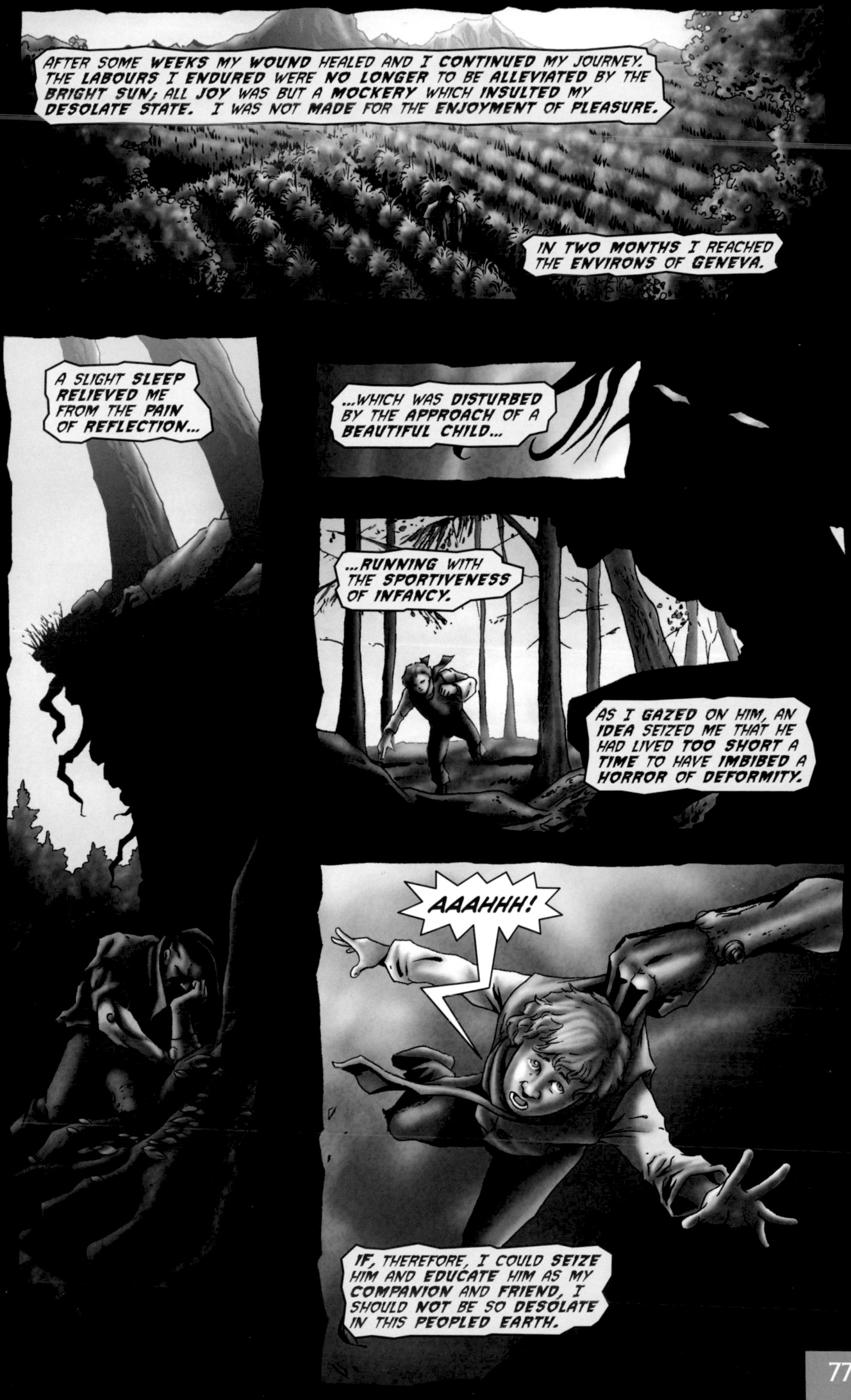
AFTER SOME WEEKS MY WOUND HEALED AND I CONTINUED MY JOURNEY. THE LABOURS I ENDURED WERE NO LONGER TO BE ALLEVIATED BY THE BRIGHT SUN; ALL JOY WAS BUT A MOCKERY WHICH INSULTED MY DESOLATE STATE. I WAS NOT MADE FOR THE ENJOYMENT OF PLEASURE.
IN TWO MONTHS I REACHED THE ENVIRONS OF GENEVA.
A SLIGHT SLEEP RELIEVED ME FROM THE PAIN OF REFLECTION...
...WHICH WAS DISTURBED BY THE APPROACH OF A BEAUTIFUL CHILD...
...RUNNING WITH THE SPORTIVENESS OF INFANCY.
AS I GAZED ON HIM, AN IDEA SEIZED ME THAT HE HAD LIVED TOO SHORT A TIME TO HAVE IMBIBED A HORROR OF DEFORMITY.
AAAHHH!
IF, THEREFORE, I COULD SEIZE HIM AND EDUCATE HIM AS MY COMPANION AND FRIEND, I SHOULD NOT BE SO DESOLATE IN THIS PEOPLED EARTH.

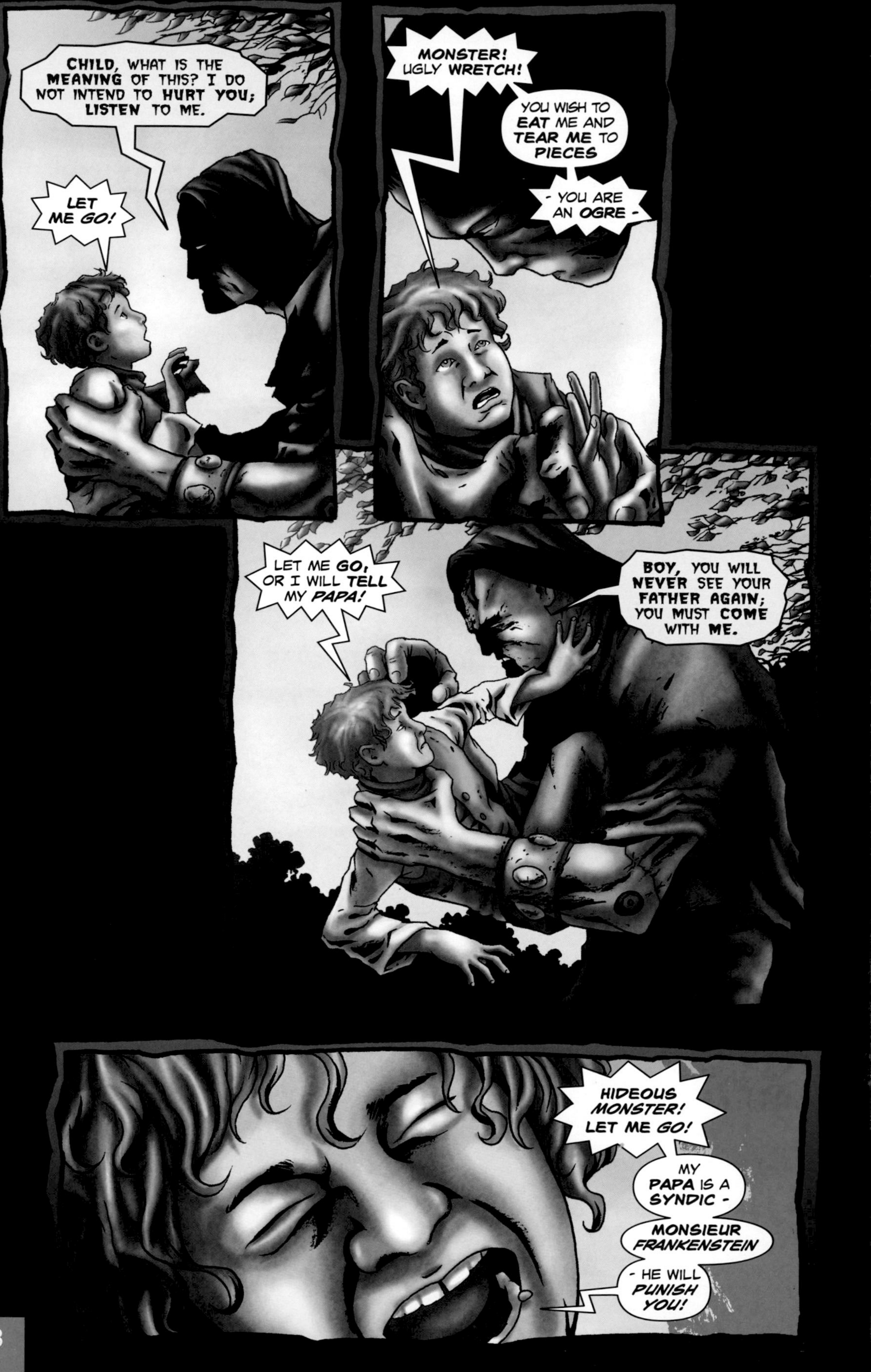
CHILD, WHAT IS THE MEANING OF THIS? I DO NOT INTEND TO HURT YOU; LISTEN TO ME.
LET ME GO!
MONSTER! UGLY WRETCH!
YOU WISH TO EAT ME AND TEAR ME TO PIECES
- YOU ARE AN OGRE -
LET ME GO, OR I WILL TELL MY PAPA!
BOY, YOU WILL NEVER SEE YOUR FATHER AGAIN; YOU MUST COME WITH ME.
HIDEOUS MONSTER! LET ME GO!
MY PAPA IS A SYNDIC -
MONSIEUR FRANKENSTEIN
- HE WILL PUNISH YOU!

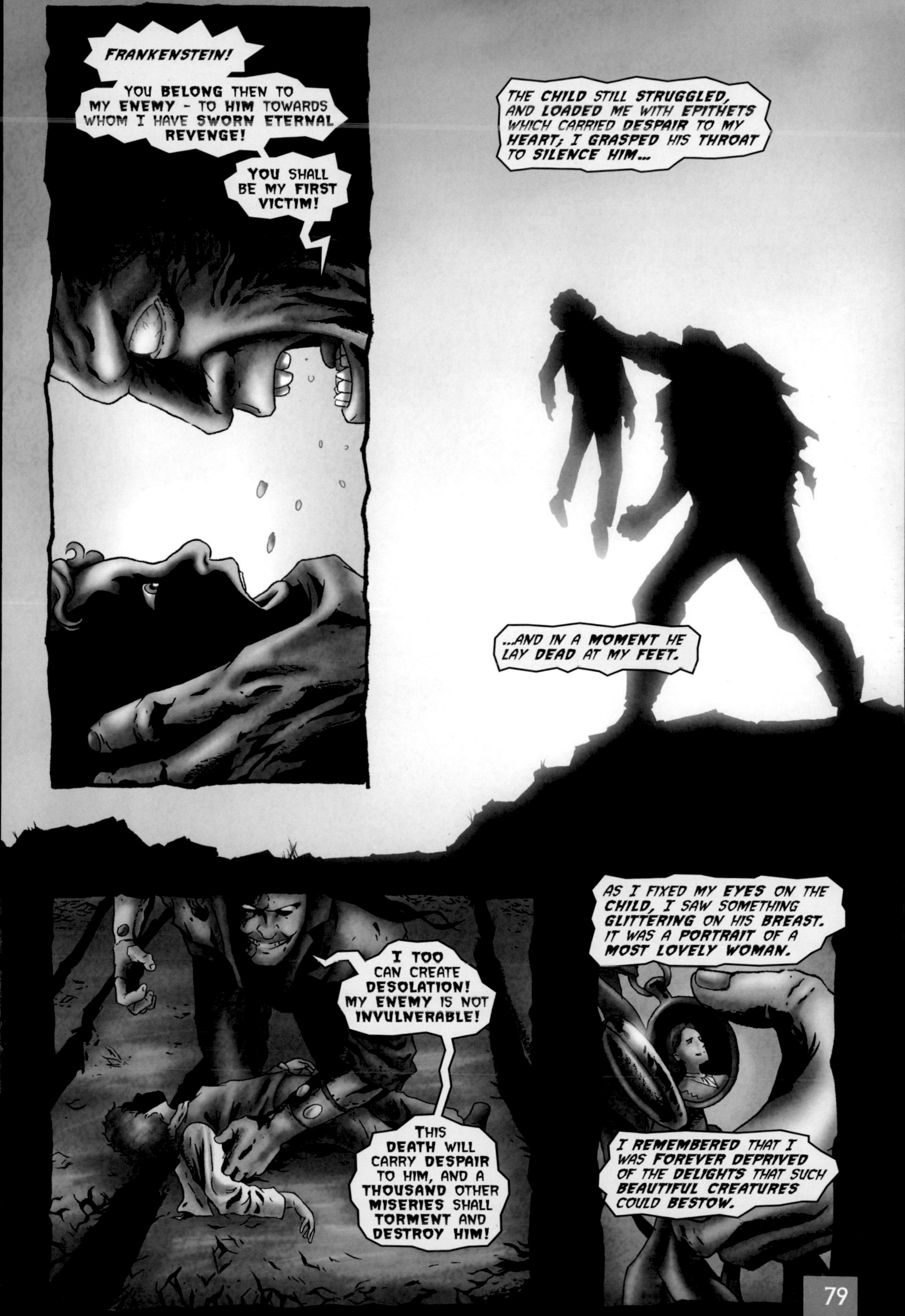
FRANKENSTEIN!
YOU BELONG THEN TO MY ENEMY - TO HIM TOWARDS WHOM I HAVE SWORN ETERNAL REVENGE!
YOU SHALL BE MY FIRST VICTIM!
THE CHILD STILL STRUGGLED, AND LOADED ME WITH EPITHETS WHICH CARRIED DESPAIR TO MY HEART; I GRASPED HIS THROAT TO SILENCE HIM...
...AND IN A MOMENT HE LAY DEAD AT MY FEET.
I TOO CAN CREATE DESOLATION! MY ENEMY IS NOT INVULNERABLE!
THIS DEATH WILL CARRY DESPAIR TO HIM, AND A THOUSAND OTHER MISERIES SHALL TORMENT AND DESTROY HIM!
AS I FIXED MY EYES ON THE CHILD, I SAW SOMETHING GLITTERING ON HIS BREAST. IT WAS A PORTRAIT OF A MOST LOVELY WOMAN.
I REMEMBERED THAT I WAS FOREVER DEPRIVED OF THE DELIGHTS THAT SUCH BEAUTIFUL CREATURES COULD BESTOW.

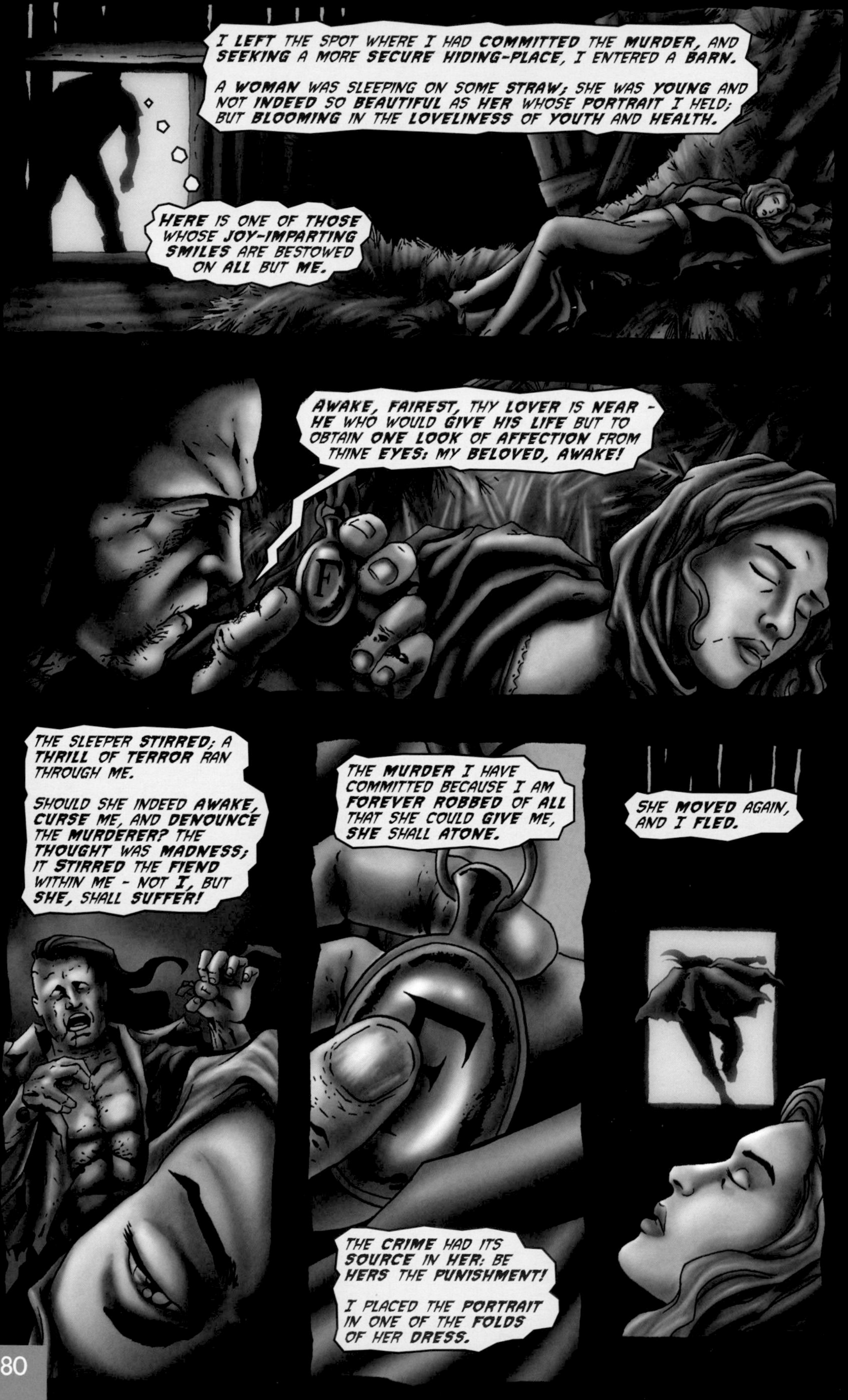
I LEFT THE SPOT WHERE I HAD COMMITTED THE MURDER, AND SEEKING A MORE SECURE HIDING-PLACE, I ENTERED A BARN.
A WOMAN WAS SLEEPING ON SOME STRAW; SHE WAS YOUNG AND NOT INDEED SO BEAUTIFUL AS HER WHOSE PORTRAIT I HELD; BUT BLOOMING IN THE LOVELINESS OF YOUTH AND HEALTH.
HERE IS ONE OF THOSE WHOSE JOY-IMPARTING SMILES ARE BESTOWED ON ALL BUT ME.
AWAKE, FAIREST, THY LOVER IS NEAR - HE WHO WOULD GIVE HIS LIFE BUT TO OBTAIN ONE LOOK OF AFFECTION FROM THINE EYES: MY BELOVED, AWAKE!
F
THE SLEEPER STIRRED; A THRILL OF TERROR RAN THROUGH ME.
SHOULD SHE INDEED AWAKE, CURSE ME, AND DENOUNCE THE MURDERER? THE THOUGHT WAS MADNESS; IT STIRRED THE FIEND WITHIN ME - NOT I, BUT SHE, SHALL SUFFER!
THE MURDER I HAVE COMMITTED BECAUSE I AM FOREVER ROBBED OF ALL THAT SHE COULD GIVE ME, SHE SHALL ATONE.
THE CRIME HAD ITS SOURCE IN HER: BE HERS THE PUNISHMENT!
I PLACED THE PORTRAIT IN ONE OF THE FOLDS OF HER DRESS.
SHE MOVED AGAIN, AND I FLED.

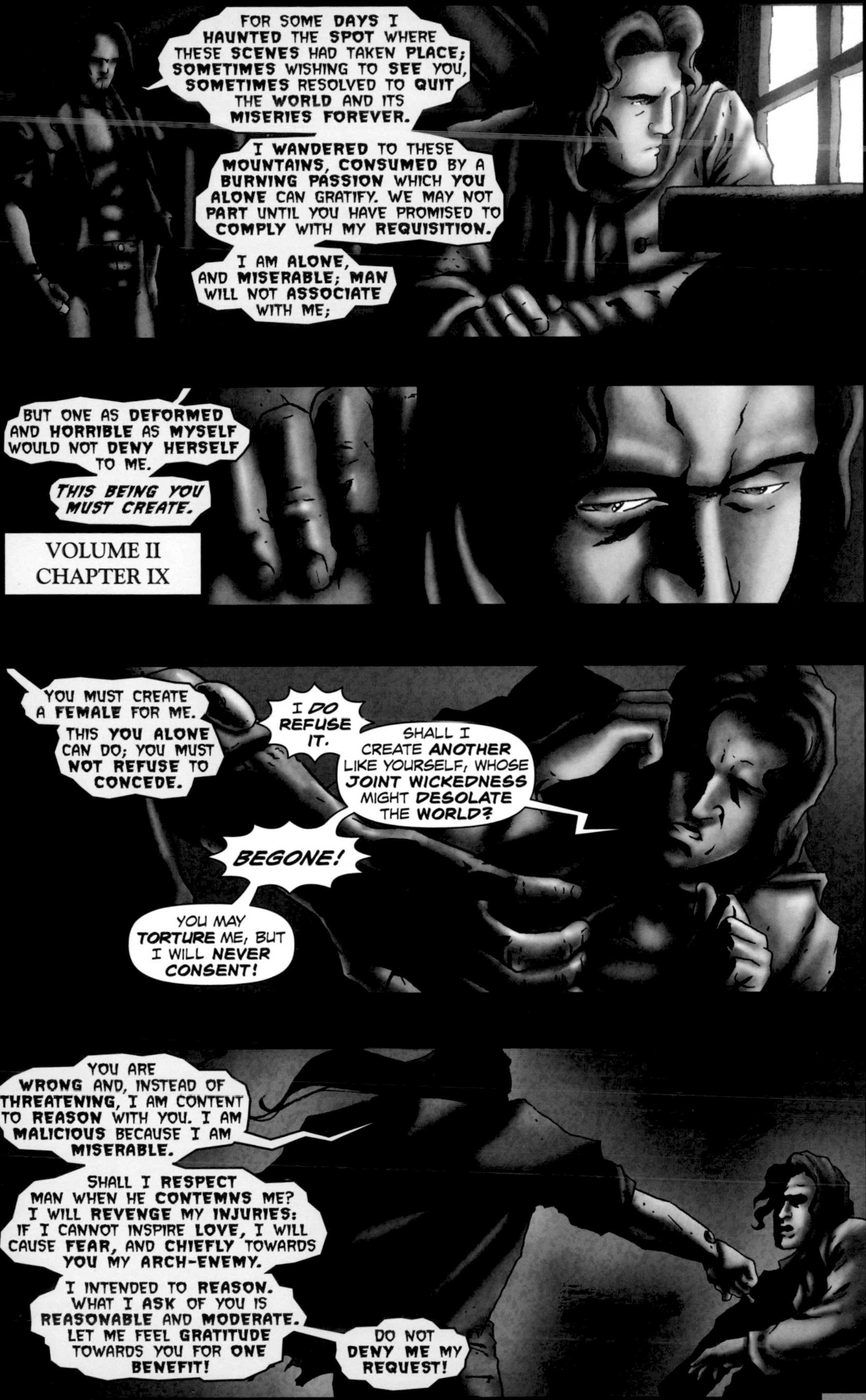
FOR SOME DAYS I HAUNTED THE SPOT WHERE THESE SCENES HAD TAKEN PLACE; SOMETIMES WISHING TO SEE YOU, SOMETIMES RESOLVED TO QUIT THE WORLD AND ITS MISERIES FOREVER.
I WANDERED TO THESE MOUNTAINS, CONSUMED BY A BURNING PASSION WHICH YOU ALONE CAN GRATIFY. WE MAY NOT PART UNTIL YOU HAVE PROMISED TO COMPLY WITH MY REQUISITION.
I AM ALONE, AND MISERABLE; MAN WILL NOT ASSOCIATE WITH ME;
BUT ONE AS DEFORMED AND HORRIBLE AS MYSELF WOULD NOT DENY HERSELF TO ME.
THIS BEING YOU MUST CREATE.
VOLUME II CHAPTER IX
YOU MUST CREATE A FEMALE FOR ME.
THIS YOU ALONE CAN DO; YOU MUST NOT REFUSE TO CONCEDE.
I DO REFUSE IT.
SHALL I CREATE ANOTHER LIKE YOURSELF, WHOSE JOINT WICKEDNESS MIGHT DESOLATE THE WORLD?
BEGONE!
YOU MAY TORTURE ME, BUT I WILL NEVER CONSENT!
YOU ARE WRONG AND, INSTEAD OF THREATENING, I AM CONTENT TO REASON WITH YOU. I AM MALICIOUS BECAUSE I AM MISERABLE.
SHALL I RESPECT MAN WHEN HE CONTEMNS ME? I WILL REVENGE MY INJURIES: IF I CANNOT INSPIRE LOVE, I WILL CAUSE FEAR, AND CHIEFLY TOWARDS YOU MY ARCH-ENEMY.
I INTENDED TO REASON. WHAT I ASK OF YOU IS REASONABLE AND MODERATE. LET ME FEEL GRATITUDE TOWARDS YOU FOR ONE BENEFIT!
DO NOT DENY ME MY REQUEST!

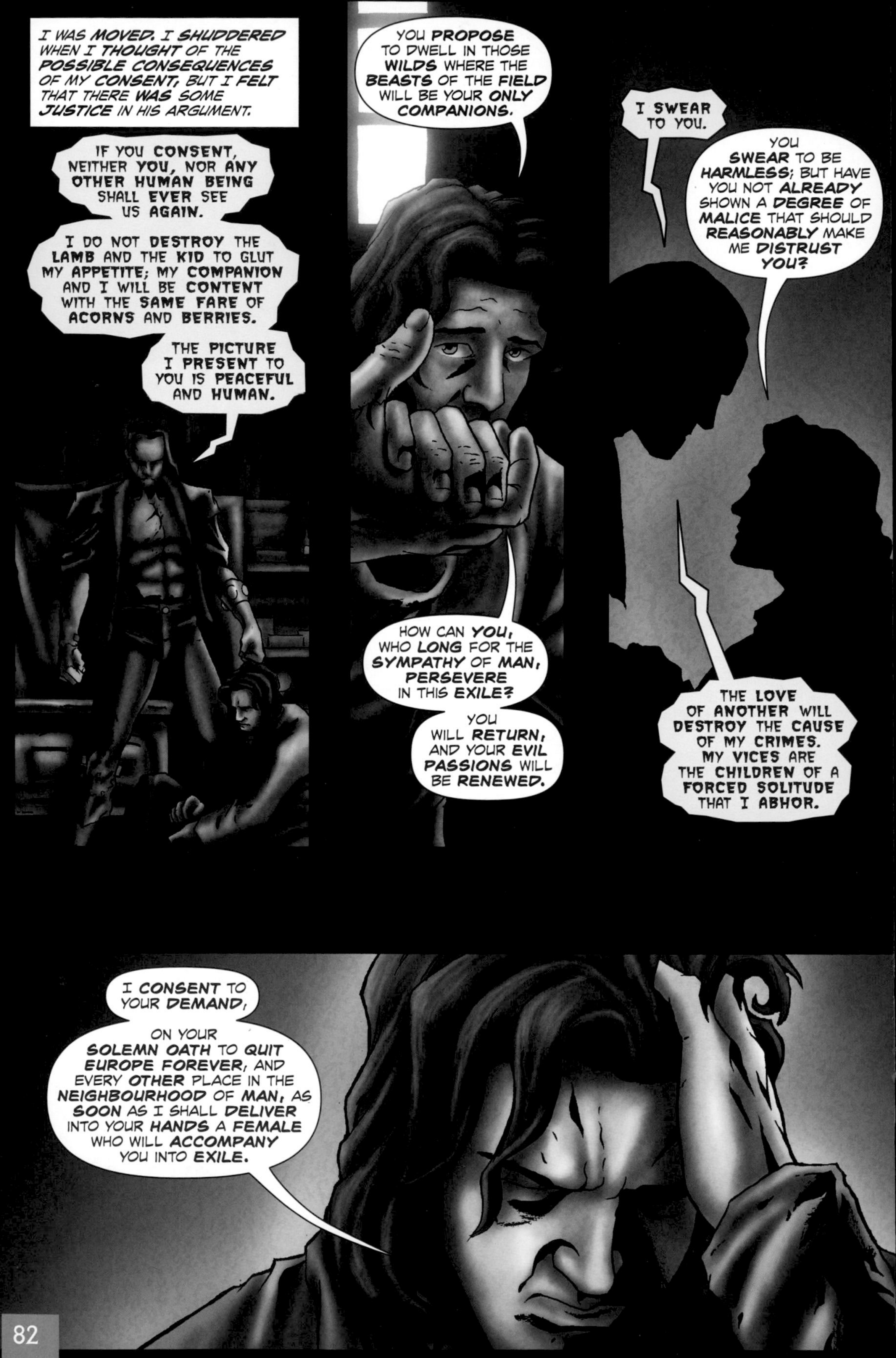
I WAS MOVED. I SHUDDERED WHEN I THOUGHT OF THE POSSIBLE CONSEQUENCES OF MY CONSENT, BUT I FELT THAT THERE WAS SOME JUSTICE IN HIS ARGUMENT.
IF YOU CONSENT, NEITHER YOU, NOR ANY OTHER HUMAN BEING SHALL EVER SEE US AGAIN.
I DO NOT DESTROY THE LAMB AND THE KID TO GLUT MY APPETITE; MY COMPANION AND I WILL BE CONTENT WITH THE SAME FARE OF ACORNS AND BERRIES.
THE PICTURE I PRESENT TO YOU IS PEACEFUL AND HUMAN.
YOU PROPOSE TO DWELL IN THOSE WILDS WHERE THE BEASTS OF THE FIELD WILL BE YOUR ONLY COMPANIONS.
HOW CAN YOU, WHO LONG FOR THE SYMPATHY OF MAN, PERSEVERE IN THIS EXILE?
YOU WILL RETURN, AND YOUR EVIL PASSIONS WILL BE RENEWED.
I SWEAR TO YOU.
YOU SWEAR TO BE HARMLESS; BUT HAVE YOU NOT ALREADY SHOWN A DEGREE OF MALICE THAT SHOULD REASONABLY MAKE ME DISTRUST YOU?
THE LOVE OF ANOTHER WILL DESTROY THE CAUSE OF MY CRIMES. MY VICES ARE THE CHILDREN OF A FORCED SOLITUDE THAT I ABHOR.
I CONSENT TO YOUR DEMAND,
ON YOUR SOLEMN OATH TO QUIT EUROPE FOREVER, AND EVERY OTHER PLACE IN THE NEIGHBOURHOOD OF MAN, AS SOON AS I SHALL DELIVER INTO YOUR HANDS A FEMALE WHO WILL ACCOMPANY YOU INTO EXILE.

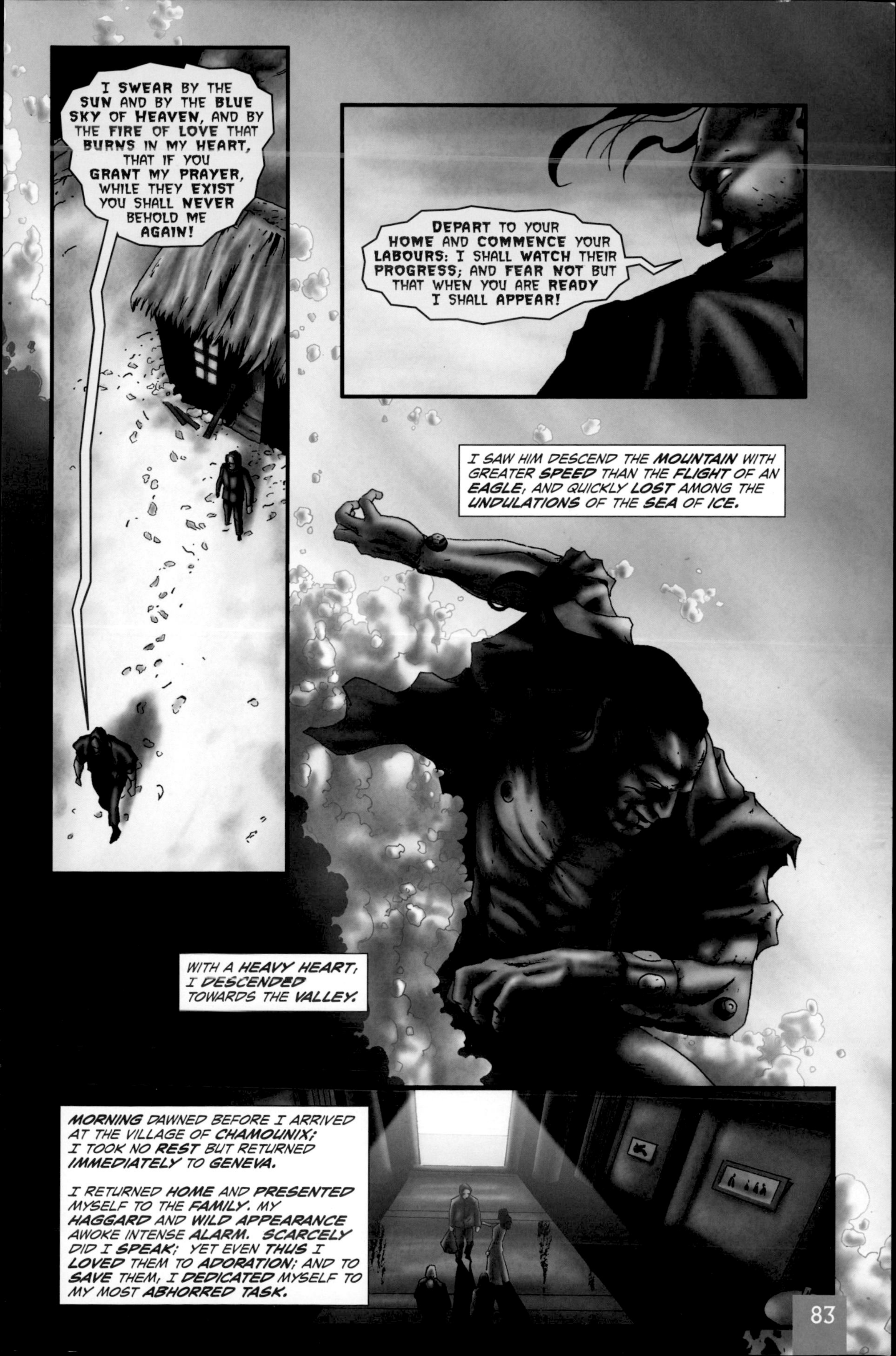
I SWEAR BY THE SUN AND BY THE BLUE SKY OF HEAVEN, AND BY THE FIRE OF LOVE THAT BURNS IN MY HEART, THAT IF YOU GRANT MY PRAYER, WHILE THEY EXIST YOU SHALL NEVER BEHOLD ME AGAIN!
DEPART TO YOUR HOME AND COMMENCE YOUR LABOURS: I SHALL WATCH THEIR PROGRESS; AND FEAR NOT BUT THAT WHEN YOU ARE READY I SHALL APPEAR!
I SAW HIM DESCEND THE MOUNTAIN WITH GREATER SPEED THAN THE FLIGHT OF AN EAGLE, AND QUICKLY LOST AMONG THE UNDULATIONS OF THE SEA OF ICE.
WITH A HEAVY HEART, I DESCENDED TOWARDS THE VALLEY.
MORNING DAWNED BEFORE I ARRIVED AT THE VILLAGE OF CHAMOUNIX; I TOOK NO REST BUT RETURNED IMMEDIATELY TO GENEVA.
I RETURNED HOME AND PRESENTED MYSELF TO THE FAMILY. MY HAGGARD AND WILD APPEARANCE AWOKE INTENSE ALARM. SCARCELY DID I SPEAK; YET EVEN THUS I LOVED THEM TO ADORATION; AND TO SAVE THEM, I DEDICATED MYSELF TO MY MOST ABHORRED TASK.

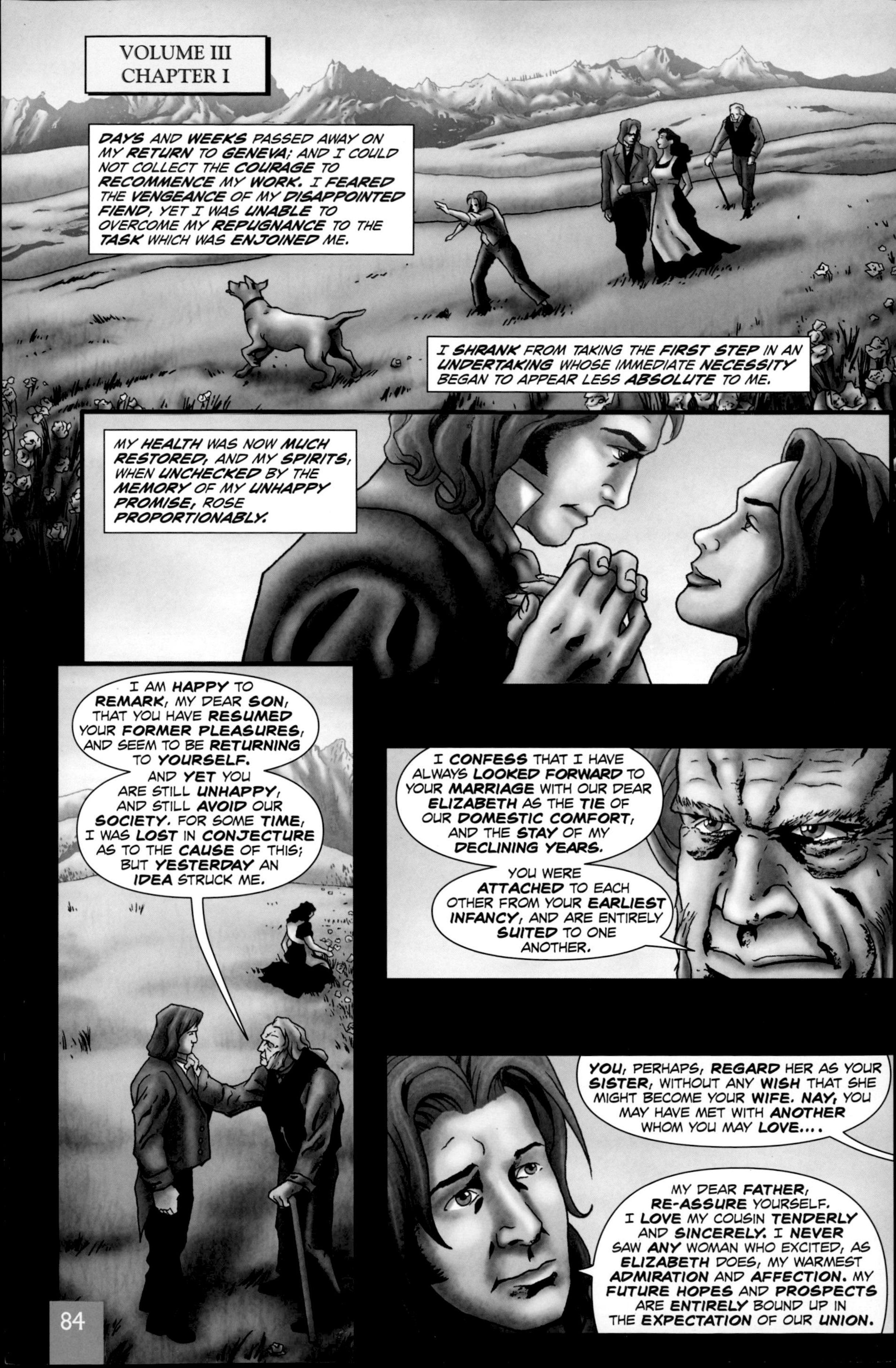

VOLUME III
CHAPTER I

DAYS AND WEEKS PASSED AWAY ON MY RETURN TO GENEVA; AND I COULD NOT COLLECT THE COURAGE TO RECOMMENCE MY WORK. I FEARED THE VENGEANCE OF MY DISAPPOINTED FIEND, YET I WAS UNABLE TO OVERCOME MY REPUGNANCE TO THE TASK WHICH WAS ENJOINED ME.

I SHRANK FROM TAKING THE FIRST STEP IN AN UNDERTAKING WHOSE IMMEDIATE NECESSITY BEGAN TO APPEAR LESS ABSOLUTE TO ME.

MY HEALTH WAS NOW MUCH RESTORED, AND MY SPIRITS, WHEN UNCHECKED BY THE MEMORY OF MY UNHAPPY PROMISE, ROSE PROPORTIONABLY.

I AM HAPPY TO REMARK, MY DEAR SON, THAT YOU HAVE RESUMED YOUR FORMER PLEASURES, AND SEEM TO BE RETURNING TO YOURSELF.

AND YET YOU ARE STILL UNHAPPY, AND STILL AVOID OUR SOCIETY. FOR SOME TIME, I WAS LOST IN CONJECTURE AS TO THE CAUSE OF THIS; BUT YESTERDAY AN IDEA STRUCK ME.

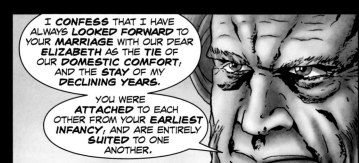

I CONFESS THAT I HAVE ALWAYS LOOKED FORWARD TO YOUR MARRIAGE WITH OUR DEAR ELIZABETH AS THE TIE OF OUR DOMESTIC COMFORT, AND THE STAY OF MY DECLINING YEARS.

YOU WERE ATTACHED TO EACH OTHER FROM YOUR EARLIEST INFANCY, AND ARE ENTIRELY SUITED TO ONE ANOTHER.

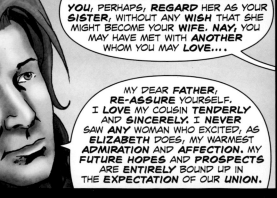

YOU, PERHAPS, REGARD HER AS YOUR SISTER, WITHOUT ANY WISH THAT SHE MIGHT BECOME YOUR WIFE. NAY, YOU MAY HAVE MET WITH ANOTHER WHOM YOU MAY LOVE....

MY DEAR FATHER, RE-ASSURE YOURSELF. I LOVE MY COUSIN TENDERLY AND SINCERELY. I NEVER SAW ANY WOMAN WHO EXCITED, AS ELIZABETH DOES, MY WARMEST ADMIRATION AND AFFECTION. MY FUTURE HOPES AND PROSPECTS ARE ENTIRELY BOUND UP IN THE EXPECTATION OF OUR UNION.

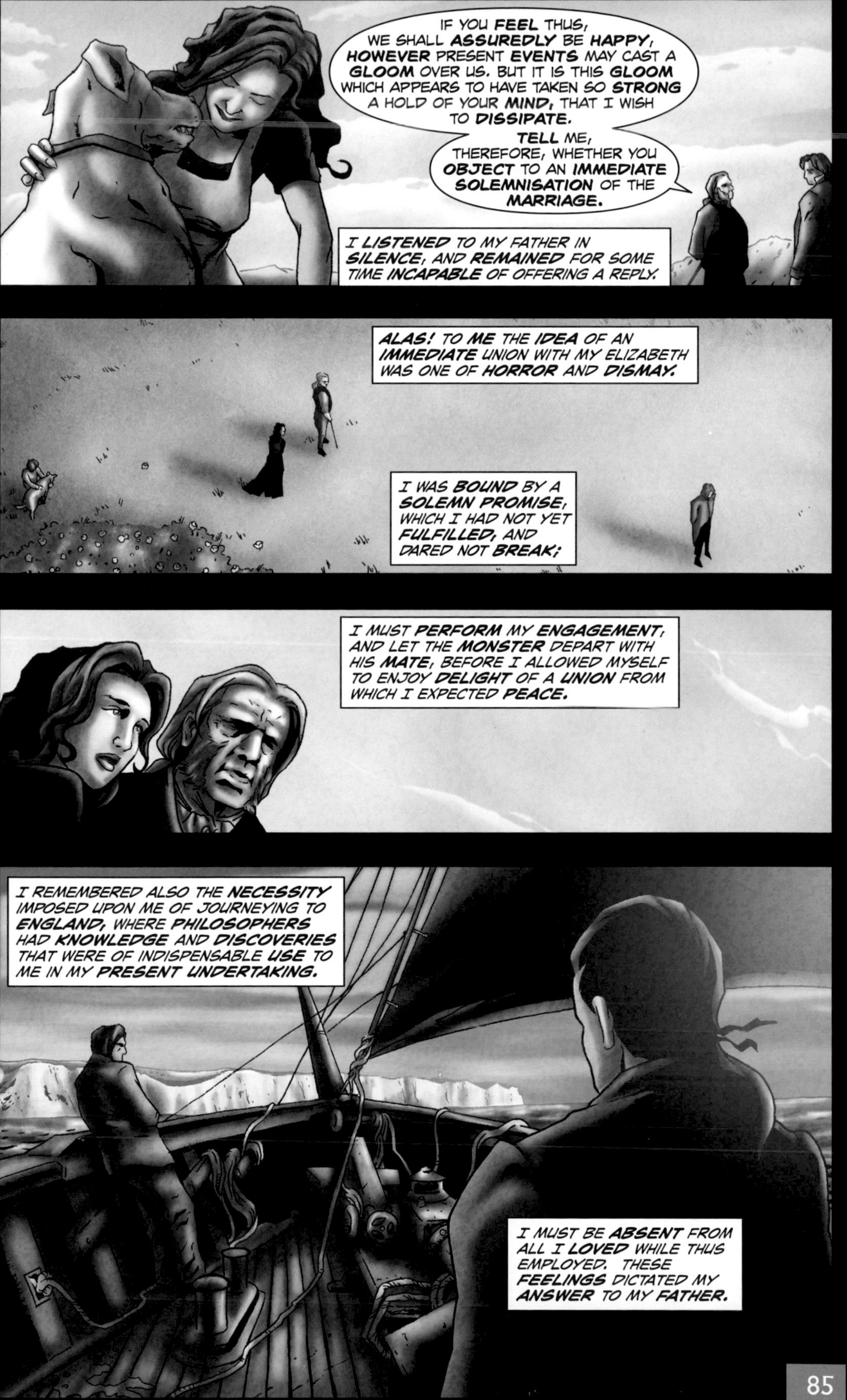
IF YOU FEEL THUS, WE SHALL ASSUREDLY BE HAPPY, HOWEVER PRESENT EVENTS MAY CAST A GLOOM OVER US. BUT IT IS THIS GLOOM WHICH APPEARS TO HAVE TAKEN SO STRONG A HOLD OF YOUR MIND, THAT I WISH TO DISSIPATE.
TELL ME, THEREFORE, WHETHER YOU OBJECT TO AN IMMEDIATE SOLEMNISATION OF THE MARRIAGE.
I LISTENED TO MY FATHER IN SILENCE, AND REMAINED FOR SOME TIME INCAPABLE OF OFFERING A REPLY.
ALAS! TO ME THE IDEA OF AN IMMEDIATE UNION WITH MY ELIZABETH WAS ONE OF HORROR AND DISMAY.
I WAS BOUND BY A SOLEMN PROMISE, WHICH I HAD NOT YET FULFILLED, AND DARED NOT BREAK;
I MUST PERFORM MY ENGAGEMENT, AND LET THE MONSTER DEPART WITH HIS MATE, BEFORE I ALLOWED MYSELF TO ENJOY DELIGHT OF A UNION FROM WHICH I EXPECTED PEACE.
I REMEMBERED ALSO THE NECESSITY IMPOSED UPON ME OF JOURNEYING TO ENGLAND, WHERE PHILOSOPHERS HAD KNOWLEDGE AND DISCOVERIES THAT WERE OF INDISPENSABLE USE TO ME IN MY PRESENT UNDERTAKING.
I MUST BE ABSENT FROM ALL I LOVED WHILE THUS EMPLOYED. THESE FEELINGS DICTATED MY ANSWER TO MY FATHER.

I CONCEALED THE *TRUE* REASONS FOR MY VISIT AND *INDUCED* MY *FATHER* TO *COMPLY.*

HE HOPED THAT *CHANGE* OF *SCENE* WOULD HAVE *RESTORED* ME ENTIRELY TO *MYSELF.*

HE *ENSURED* MY HAVING A *COMPANION* - AND IN CONCERT WITH *ELIZABETH,* ARRANGED THAT *CLERVAL* SHOULD JOIN ME.

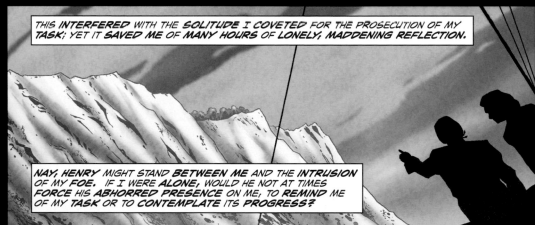

THIS *INTERFERED* WITH THE *SOLITUDE* I *COVETED* FOR THE PROSECUTION OF MY *TASK;* YET IT *SAVED ME* OF *MANY HOURS* OF *LONELY, MADDENING REFLECTION.*

NAY, HENRY MIGHT STAND *BETWEEN ME* AND THE *INTRUSION* OF MY *FOE.* IF I WERE *ALONE,* WOULD HE NOT AT TIMES *FORCE* HIS *ABHORRED PRESENCE* ON ME, TO *REMIND* ME OF MY *TASK* OR TO *CONTEMPLATE* ITS *PROGRESS?*

IT WAS *UNDERSTOOD* THAT MY *UNION* WITH *ELIZABETH* SHOULD TAKE PLACE *IMMEDIATELY* ON MY *RETURN.*

FOR *MYSELF,* THERE WAS *ONE REWARD* I *PROMISED* MYSELF FROM MY *DETESTED TOILS;* IT WAS THE *PROSPECT* OF THAT DAY WHEN, *ENFRANCHISED* FROM MY *MISERABLE SLAVERY,* I MIGHT *CLAIM* ELIZABETH, AND *FORGET* THE *PAST* IN *UNION* WITH HER.

I WAS *FEARFUL* THAT, DURING MY *ABSENCE,* I SHOULD *LEAVE* FRIENDS *UNCONSCIOUS* OF THE *EXISTENCE* OF THEIR *ENEMY,* AND *UNPROTECTED* FROM HIS *ATTACKS.* BUT HE HAD *PROMISED* TO *FOLLOW* ME WHEREVER I MIGHT *GO;* AND WOULD HE NOT *ACCOMPANY* ME TO *ENGLAND?*

THIS *IMAGINATION* WAS *DREADFUL* IN ITSELF, BUT *SOOTHING,* INASMUCH AS IT SUPPOSED THE *SAFETY* OF MY *FRIENDS.*

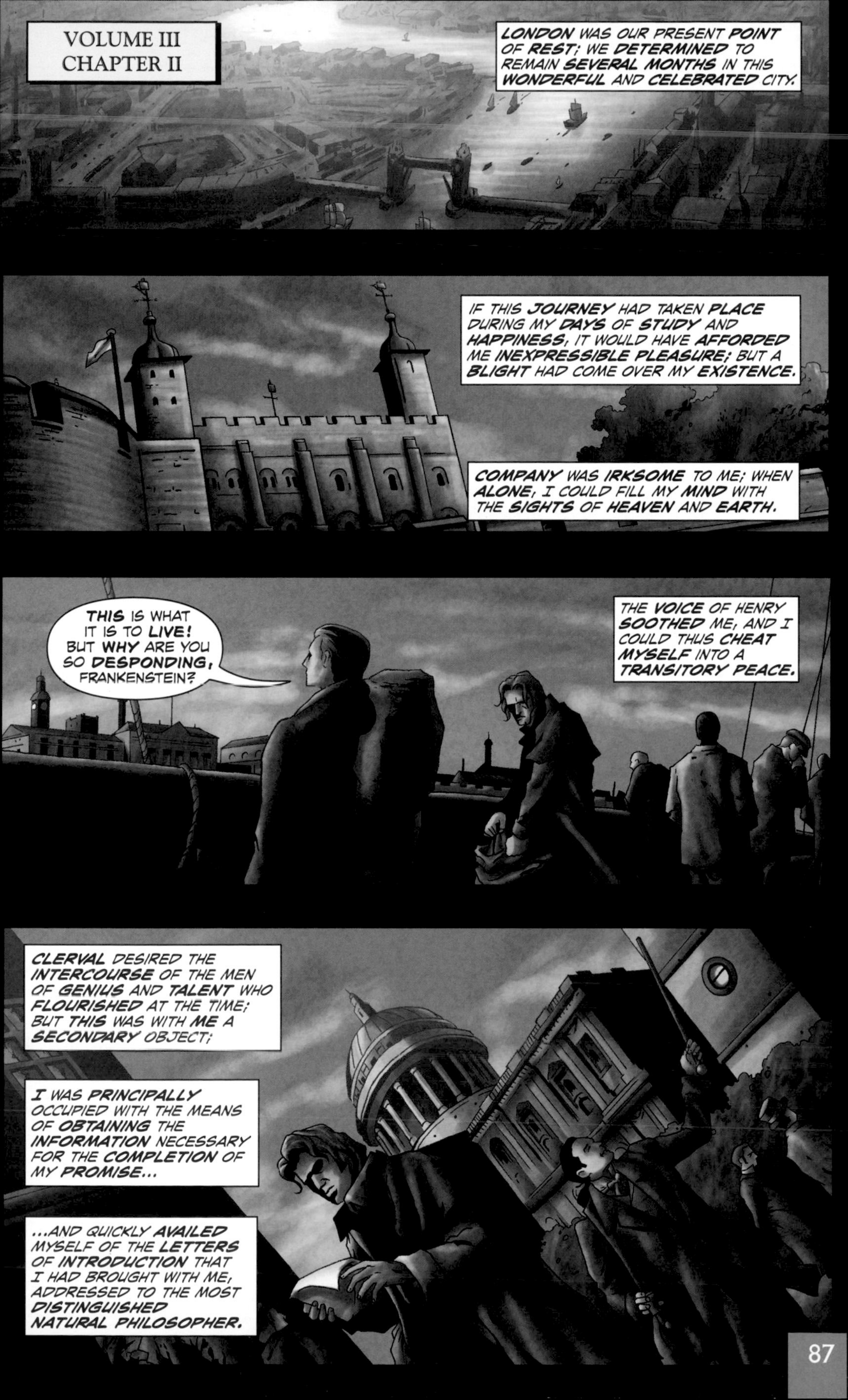
VOLUME III
CHAPTER II
LONDON WAS OUR PRESENT POINT OF REST; WE DETERMINED TO REMAIN SEVERAL MONTHS IN THIS WONDERFUL AND CELEBRATED CITY.
IF THIS JOURNEY HAD TAKEN PLACE DURING MY DAYS OF STUDY AND HAPPINESS, IT WOULD HAVE AFFORDED ME INEXPRESSIBLE PLEASURE; BUT A BLIGHT HAD COME OVER MY EXISTENCE.
COMPANY WAS IRKSOME TO ME; WHEN ALONE, I COULD FILL MY MIND WITH THE SIGHTS OF HEAVEN AND EARTH.
THIS IS WHAT IT IS TO LIVE! BUT WHY ARE YOU SO DESPONDING, FRANKENSTEIN?
THE VOICE OF HENRY SOOTHED ME, AND I COULD THUS CHEAT MYSELF INTO A TRANSITORY PEACE.
CLERVAL DESIRED THE INTERCOURSE OF THE MEN OF GENIUS AND TALENT WHO FLOURISHED AT THE TIME; BUT THIS WAS WITH ME A SECONDARY OBJECT;
I WAS PRINCIPALLY OCCUPIED WITH THE MEANS OF OBTAINING THE INFORMATION NECESSARY FOR THE COMPLETION OF MY PROMISE...
...AND QUICKLY AVAILED MYSELF OF THE LETTERS OF INTRODUCTION THAT I HAD BROUGHT WITH ME, ADDRESSED TO THE MOST DISTINGUISHED NATURAL PHILOSOPHER.

I ONLY **VISITED** THESE PEOPLE FOR THE **INFORMATION** THEY MIGHT GIVE ME ON THE **SUBJECT** IN WHICH MY INTEREST WAS SO TERRIBLY PROFOUND.

BUSY, **UNINTERESTED**, **JOYOUS** FACES BROUGHT BACK **DESPAIR** TO MY **HEART**. I SAW AN **INSURMOUNTABLE BARRIER** BETWEEN **ME** AND MY **FELLOW MEN**, SEALED WITH THE **BLOOD** OF **WILLIAM** AND **JUSTINE**.

BUT IN **CLERVAL** I SAW THE **IMAGE** OF MY **FORMER SELF**. HE WAS **INQUISITIVE**, AND ANXIOUS TO GAIN **EXPERIENCE** AND **INSTRUCTION**.

HE WAS **ALSO** PURSUING AN OBJECT HE HAD **LONG HAD** IN **VIEW**.

HIS **DESIGN** WAS TO VISIT **INDIA**, IN ORDER TO ASSIST THE **PROGRESS** OF **EUROPEAN COLONISATION** AND **TRADE**. IN **BRITAIN** ONLY COULD HE **FURTHER** THE **EXECUTION** OF HIS **PLAN**.

HE WAS **FOREVER BUSY**. I OFTEN **REFUSED** TO ACCOMPANY HIM, ALLEGING **ANOTHER ENGAGEMENT**, THAT I MIGHT REMAIN **ALONE**.

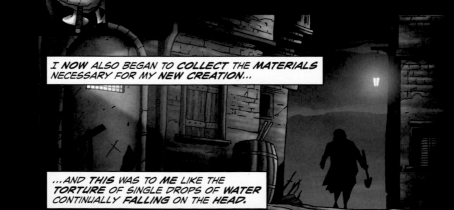

I NOW ALSO BEGAN TO **COLLECT** THE **MATERIALS** NECESSARY FOR MY **NEW CREATION**...

...AND **THIS** WAS TO **ME** LIKE THE **TORTURE** OF SINGLE DROPS OF **WATER** CONTINUALLY **FALLING** ON THE **HEAD**.

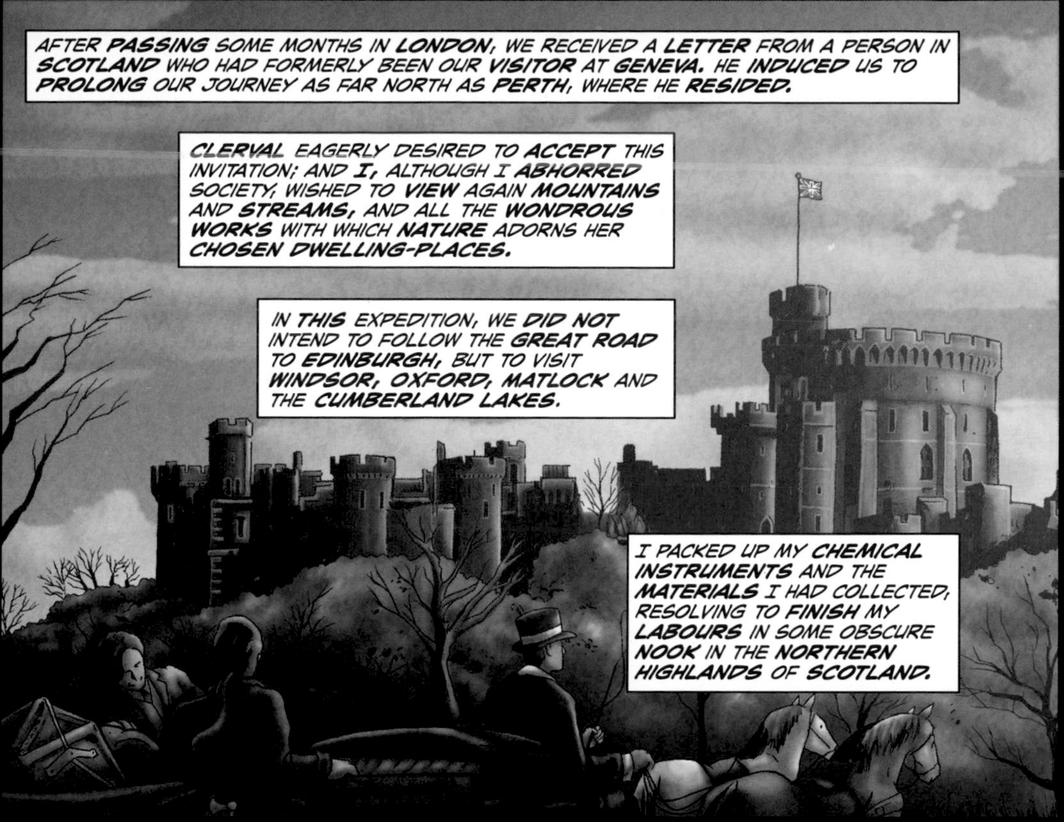
AFTER PASSING SOME MONTHS IN LONDON, WE RECEIVED A LETTER FROM A PERSON IN SCOTLAND WHO HAD FORMERLY BEEN OUR VISITOR AT GENEVA. HE INDUCED US TO PROLONG OUR JOURNEY AS FAR NORTH AS PERTH, WHERE HE RESIDED.
CLERVAL EAGERLY DESIRED TO ACCEPT THIS INVITATION; AND I, ALTHOUGH I ABHORRED SOCIETY, WISHED TO VIEW AGAIN MOUNTAINS AND STREAMS, AND ALL THE WONDROUS WORKS WITH WHICH NATURE ADORNS HER CHOSEN DWELLING-PLACES.
IN THIS EXPEDITION, WE DID NOT INTEND TO FOLLOW THE GREAT ROAD TO EDINBURGH, BUT TO VISIT WINDSOR, OXFORD, MATLOCK AND THE CUMBERLAND LAKES.
I PACKED UP MY CHEMICAL INSTRUMENTS AND THE MATERIALS I HAD COLLECTED, RESOLVING TO FINISH MY LABOURS IN SOME OBSCURE NOOK IN THE NORTHERN HIGHLANDS OF SCOTLAND.

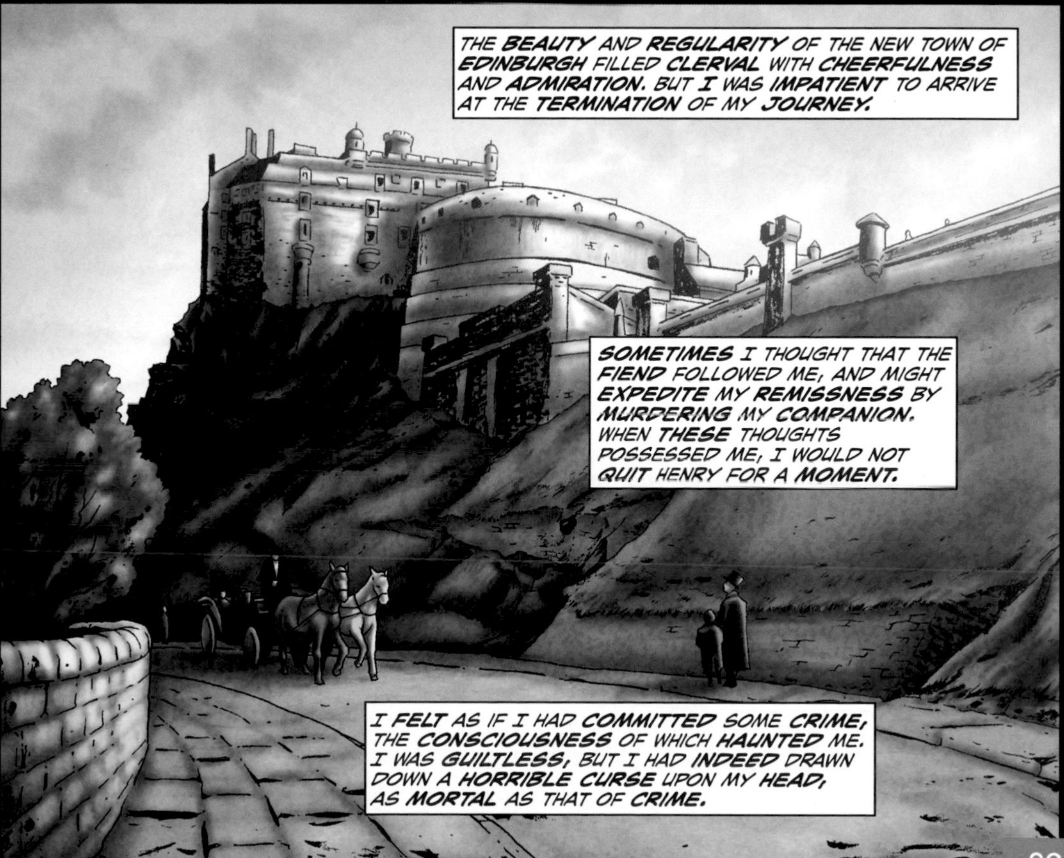
THE BEAUTY AND REGULARITY OF THE NEW TOWN OF EDINBURGH FILLED CLERVAL WITH CHEERFULNESS AND ADMIRATION. BUT I WAS IMPATIENT TO ARRIVE AT THE TERMINATION OF MY JOURNEY.
SOMETIMES I THOUGHT THAT THE FIEND FOLLOWED ME, AND MIGHT EXPEDITE MY REMISSNESS BY MURDERING MY COMPANION. WHEN THESE THOUGHTS POSSESSED ME, I WOULD NOT QUIT HENRY FOR A MOMENT.
I FELT AS IF I HAD COMMITTED SOME CRIME, THE CONSCIOUSNESS OF WHICH HAUNTED ME. I WAS GUILTLESS, BUT I HAD INDEED DRAWN DOWN A HORRIBLE CURSE UPON MY HEAD, AS MORTAL AS THAT OF CRIME.

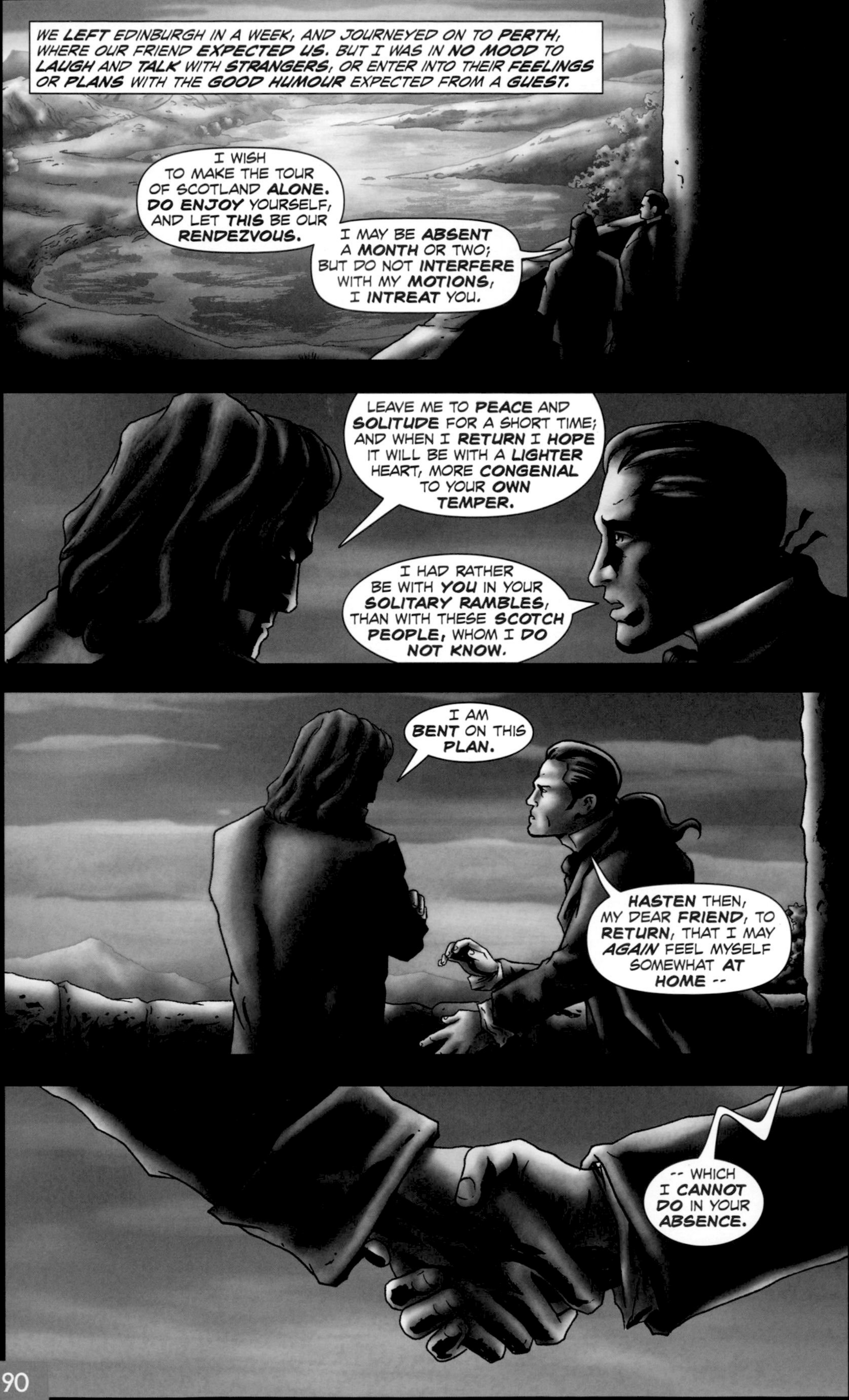
WE LEFT EDINBURGH IN A WEEK, AND JOURNEYED ON TO PERTH, WHERE OUR FRIEND EXPECTED US. BUT I WAS IN NO MOOD TO LAUGH AND TALK WITH STRANGERS, OR ENTER INTO THEIR FEELINGS OR PLANS WITH THE GOOD HUMOUR EXPECTED FROM A GUEST.
I WISH TO MAKE THE TOUR OF SCOTLAND ALONE. DO ENJOY YOURSELF, AND LET THIS BE OUR RENDEZVOUS.
I MAY BE ABSENT A MONTH OR TWO; BUT DO NOT INTERFERE WITH MY MOTIONS, I INTREAT YOU.
LEAVE ME TO PEACE AND SOLITUDE FOR A SHORT TIME; AND WHEN I RETURN I HOPE IT WILL BE WITH A LIGHTER HEART, MORE CONGENIAL TO YOUR OWN TEMPER.
I HAD RATHER BE WITH YOU IN YOUR SOLITARY RAMBLES, THAN WITH THESE SCOTCH PEOPLE, WHOM I DO NOT KNOW.
I AM BENT ON THIS PLAN.
HASTEN THEN, MY DEAR FRIEND, TO RETURN, THAT I MAY AGAIN FEEL MYSELF SOMEWHAT AT HOME --
-- WHICH I CANNOT DO IN YOUR ABSENCE.

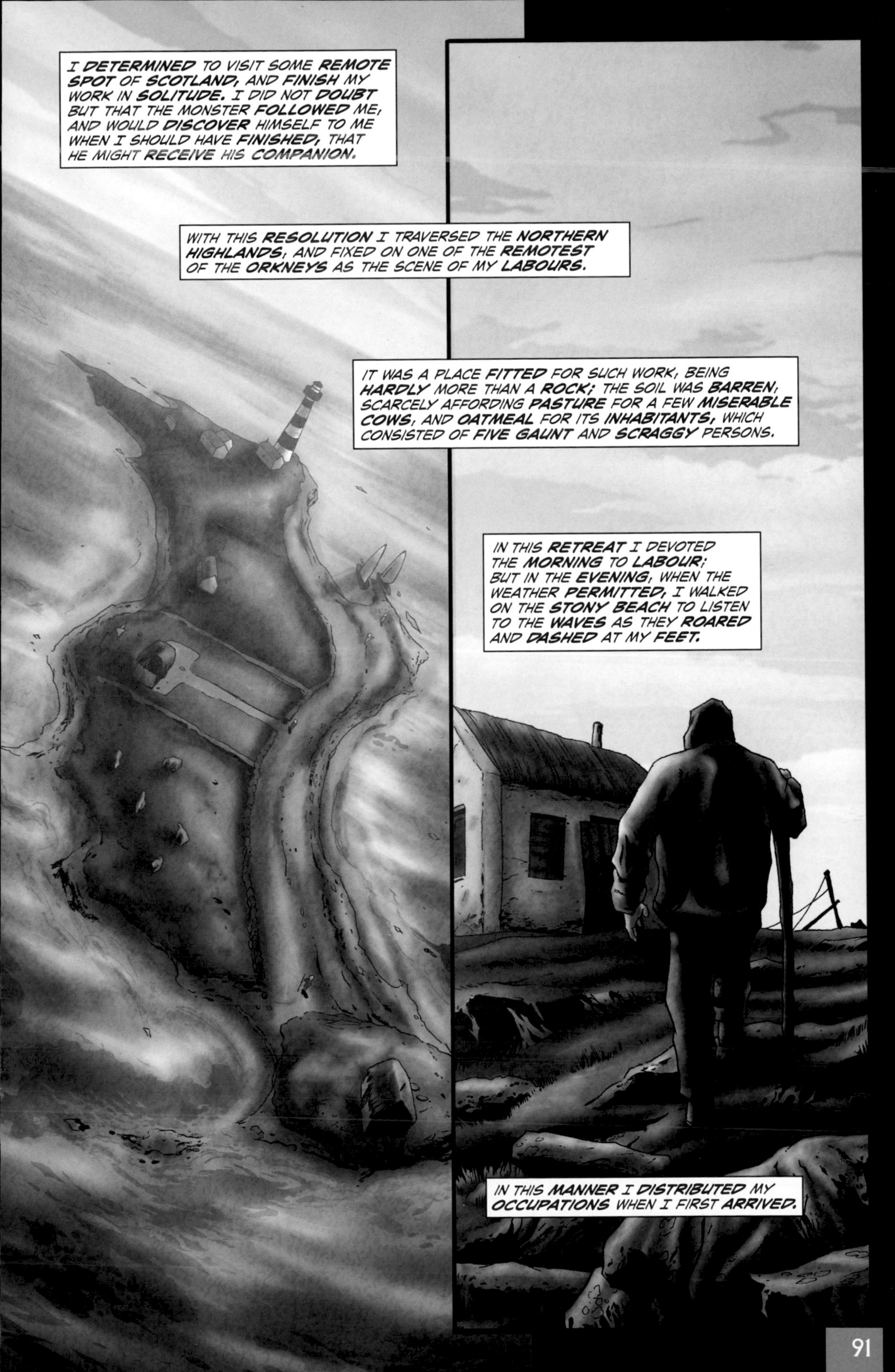
I DETERMINED TO VISIT SOME REMOTE SPOT OF SCOTLAND, AND FINISH MY WORK IN SOLITUDE. I DID NOT DOUBT BUT THAT THE MONSTER FOLLOWED ME, AND WOULD DISCOVER HIMSELF TO ME WHEN I SHOULD HAVE FINISHED, THAT HE MIGHT RECEIVE HIS COMPANION.
WITH THIS RESOLUTION I TRAVERSED THE NORTHERN HIGHLANDS, AND FIXED ON ONE OF THE REMOTEST OF THE ORKNEYS AS THE SCENE OF MY LABOURS.
IT WAS A PLACE FITTED FOR SUCH WORK, BEING HARDLY MORE THAN A ROCK; THE SOIL WAS BARREN, SCARCELY AFFORDING PASTURE FOR A FEW MISERABLE COWS, AND OATMEAL FOR ITS INHABITANTS, WHICH CONSISTED OF FIVE GAUNT AND SCRAGGY PERSONS.
IN THIS RETREAT I DEVOTED THE MORNING TO LABOUR; BUT IN THE EVENING, WHEN THE WEATHER PERMITTED, I WALKED ON THE STONY BEACH TO LISTEN TO THE WAVES AS THEY ROARED AND DASHED AT MY FEET.
IN THIS MANNER I DISTRIBUTED MY OCCUPATIONS WHEN I FIRST ARRIVED.

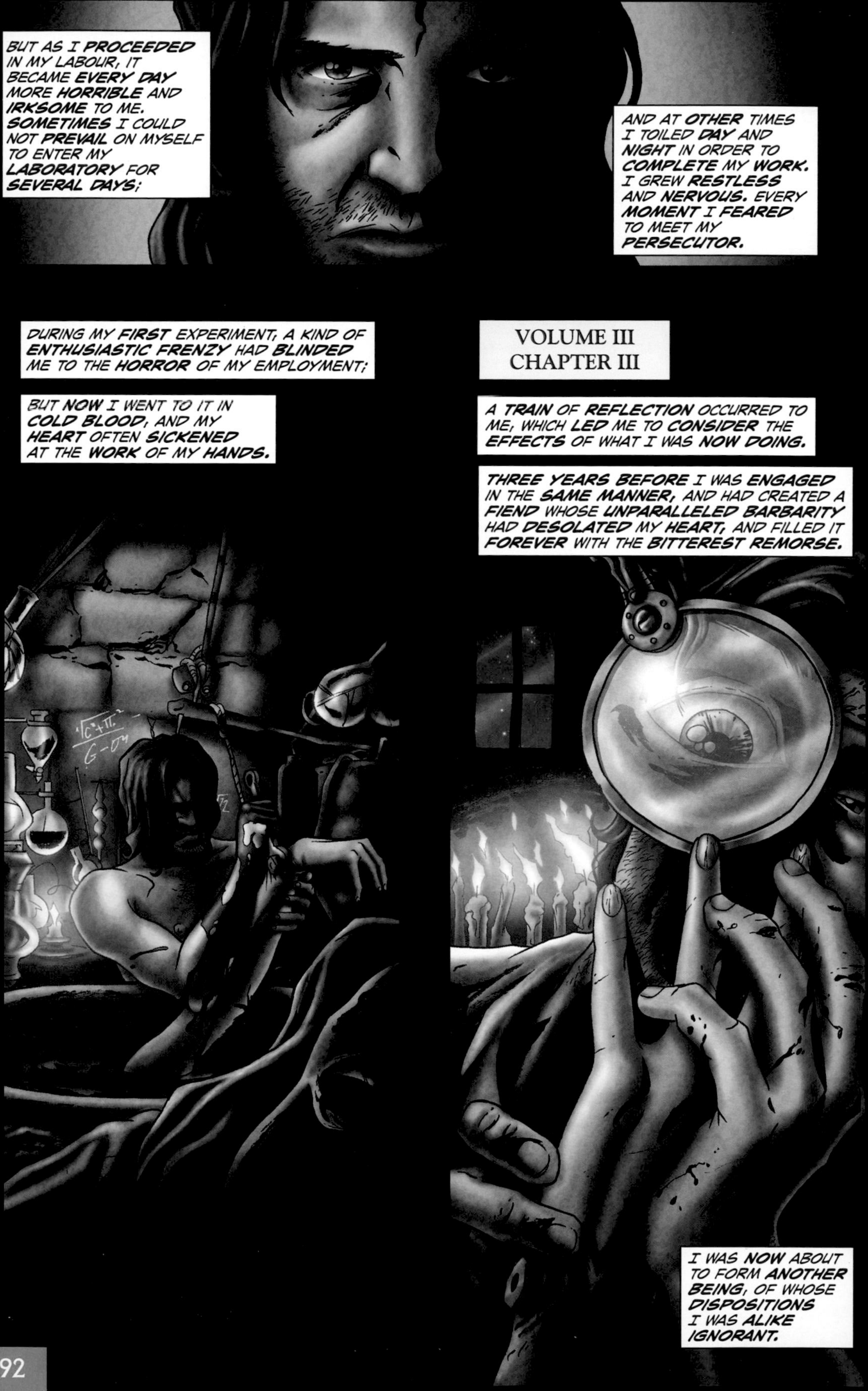
BUT AS I PROCEEDED IN MY LABOUR, IT BECAME EVERY DAY MORE HORRIBLE AND IRKSOME TO ME. SOMETIMES I COULD NOT PREVAIL ON MYSELF TO ENTER MY LABORATORY FOR SEVERAL DAYS;
AND AT OTHER TIMES I TOILED DAY AND NIGHT IN ORDER TO COMPLETE MY WORK. I GREW RESTLESS AND NERVOUS. EVERY MOMENT I FEARED TO MEET MY PERSECUTOR.
DURING MY FIRST EXPERIMENT, A KIND OF ENTHUSIASTIC FRENZY HAD BLINDED ME TO THE HORROR OF MY EMPLOYMENT;
BUT NOW I WENT TO IT IN COLD BLOOD, AND MY HEART OFTEN SICKENED AT THE WORK OF MY HANDS.
VOLUME III
CHAPTER III
A TRAIN OF REFLECTION OCCURRED TO ME, WHICH LED ME TO CONSIDER THE EFFECTS OF WHAT I WAS NOW DOING.
THREE YEARS BEFORE I WAS ENGAGED IN THE SAME MANNER, AND HAD CREATED A FIEND WHOSE UNPARALLELED BARBARITY HAD DESOLATED MY HEART, AND FILLED IT FOREVER WITH THE BITTEREST REMORSE.
I WAS NOW ABOUT TO FORM ANOTHER BEING, OF WHOSE DISPOSITIONS I WAS ALIKE IGNORANT.

SHE MIGHT BECOME TEN THOUSAND TIMES MORE MALIGNANT THAN HER MATE, AND DELIGHT, FOR ITS OWN SAKE, IN MURDER AND WRETCHEDNESS.
KRAKK!
KA-BOOM!
HE HAD SWORN TO QUIT THE NEIGHBOURHOOD OF MAN, AND HIDE HIMSELF IN DESERTS; BUT SHE HAD NOT;
AND SHE, WHO IN ALL PROBABILITY WAS TO BECOME A THINKING AND REASONING ANIMAL, MIGHT REFUSE TO COMPLY WITH A COMPACT MADE BEFORE HER CREATION.

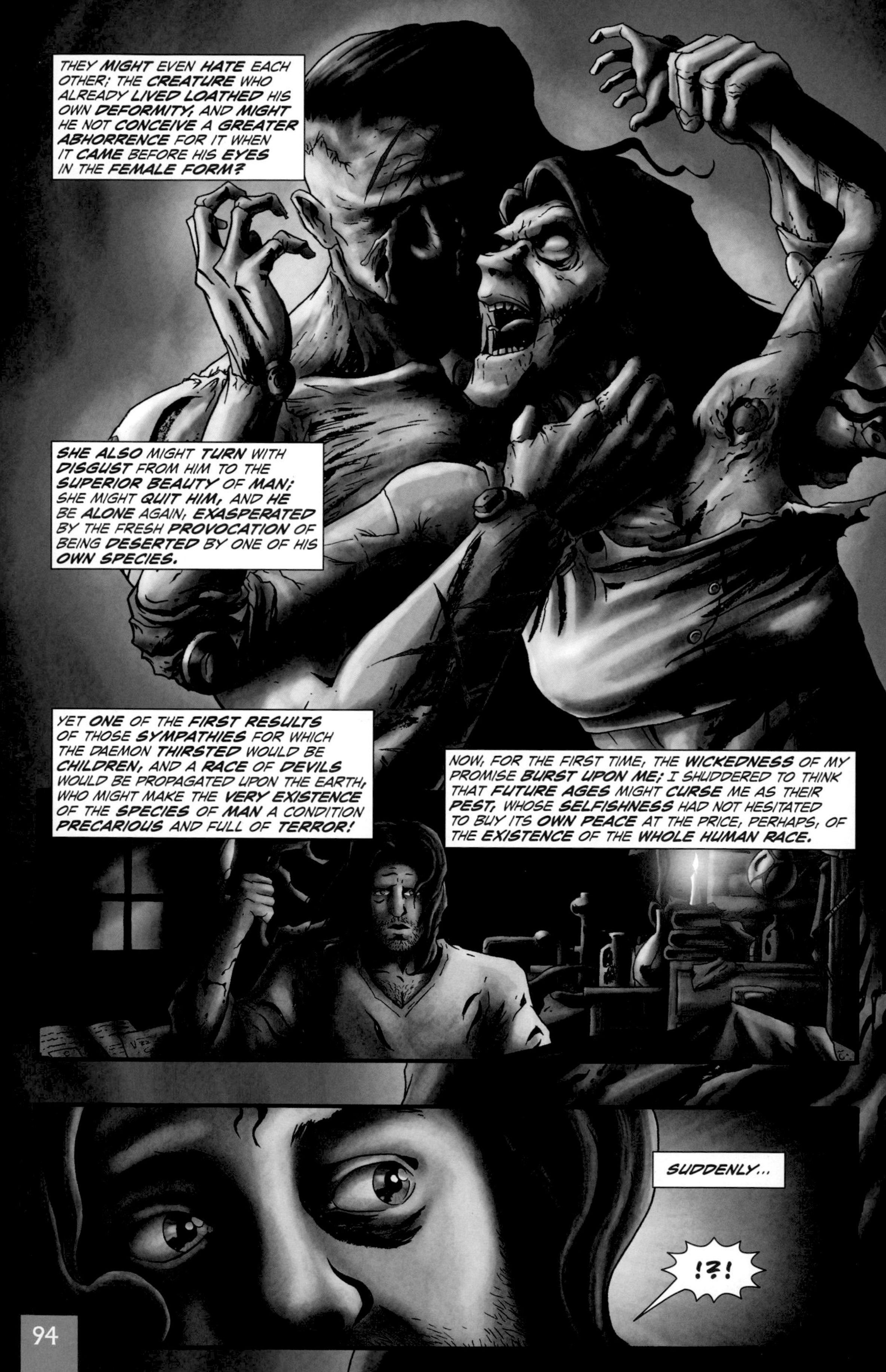
THEY MIGHT EVEN HATE EACH OTHER; THE CREATURE WHO ALREADY LIVED LOATHED HIS OWN DEFORMITY, AND MIGHT HE NOT CONCEIVE A GREATER ABHORRENCE FOR IT WHEN IT CAME BEFORE HIS EYES IN THE FEMALE FORM?
SHE ALSO MIGHT TURN WITH DISGUST FROM HIM TO THE SUPERIOR BEAUTY OF MAN; SHE MIGHT QUIT HIM, AND HE BE ALONE AGAIN, EXASPERATED BY THE FRESH PROVOCATION OF BEING DESERTED BY ONE OF HIS OWN SPECIES.
YET ONE OF THE FIRST RESULTS OF THOSE SYMPATHIES FOR WHICH THE DAEMON THIRSTED WOULD BE CHILDREN, AND A RACE OF DEVILS WOULD BE PROPAGATED UPON THE EARTH, WHO MIGHT MAKE THE VERY EXISTENCE OF THE SPECIES OF MAN A CONDITION PRECARIOUS AND FULL OF TERROR!
NOW, FOR THE FIRST TIME, THE WICKEDNESS OF MY PROMISE BURST UPON ME; I SHUDDERED TO THINK THAT FUTURE AGES MIGHT CURSE ME AS THEIR PEST, WHOSE SELFISHNESS HAD NOT HESITATED TO BUY ITS OWN PEACE AT THE PRICE, PERHAPS, OF THE EXISTENCE OF THE WHOLE HUMAN RACE.
SUDDENLY...
!?!

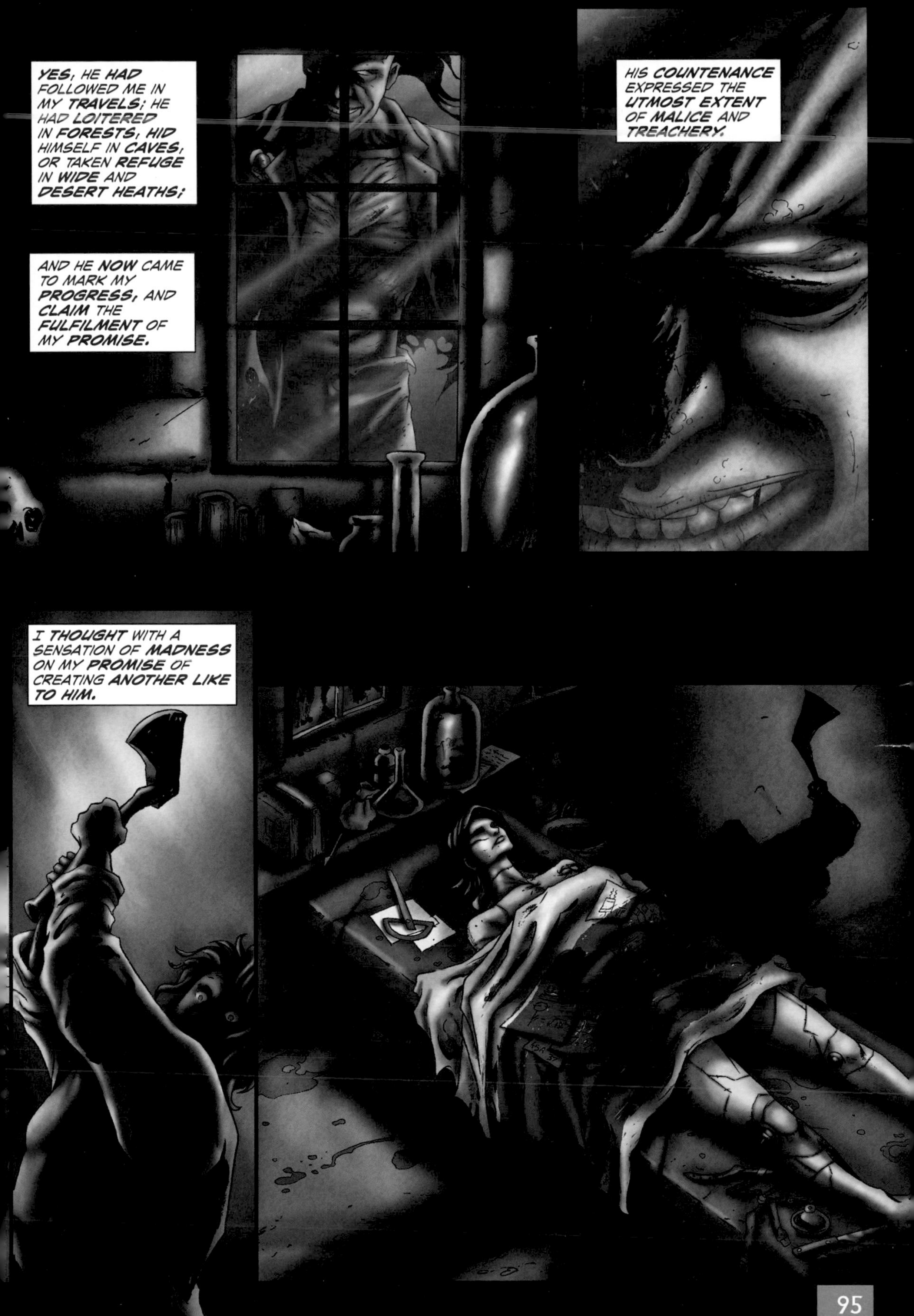
YES, HE HAD FOLLOWED ME IN MY TRAVELS; HE HAD LOITERED IN FORESTS, HID HIMSELF IN CAVES, OR TAKEN REFUGE IN WIDE AND DESERT HEATHS;
AND HE NOW CAME TO MARK MY PROGRESS, AND CLAIM THE FULFILMENT OF MY PROMISE.
HIS COUNTENANCE EXPRESSED THE UTMOST EXTENT OF MALICE AND TREACHERY.
I THOUGHT WITH A SENSATION OF MADNESS ON MY PROMISE OF CREATING ANOTHER LIKE TO HIM.

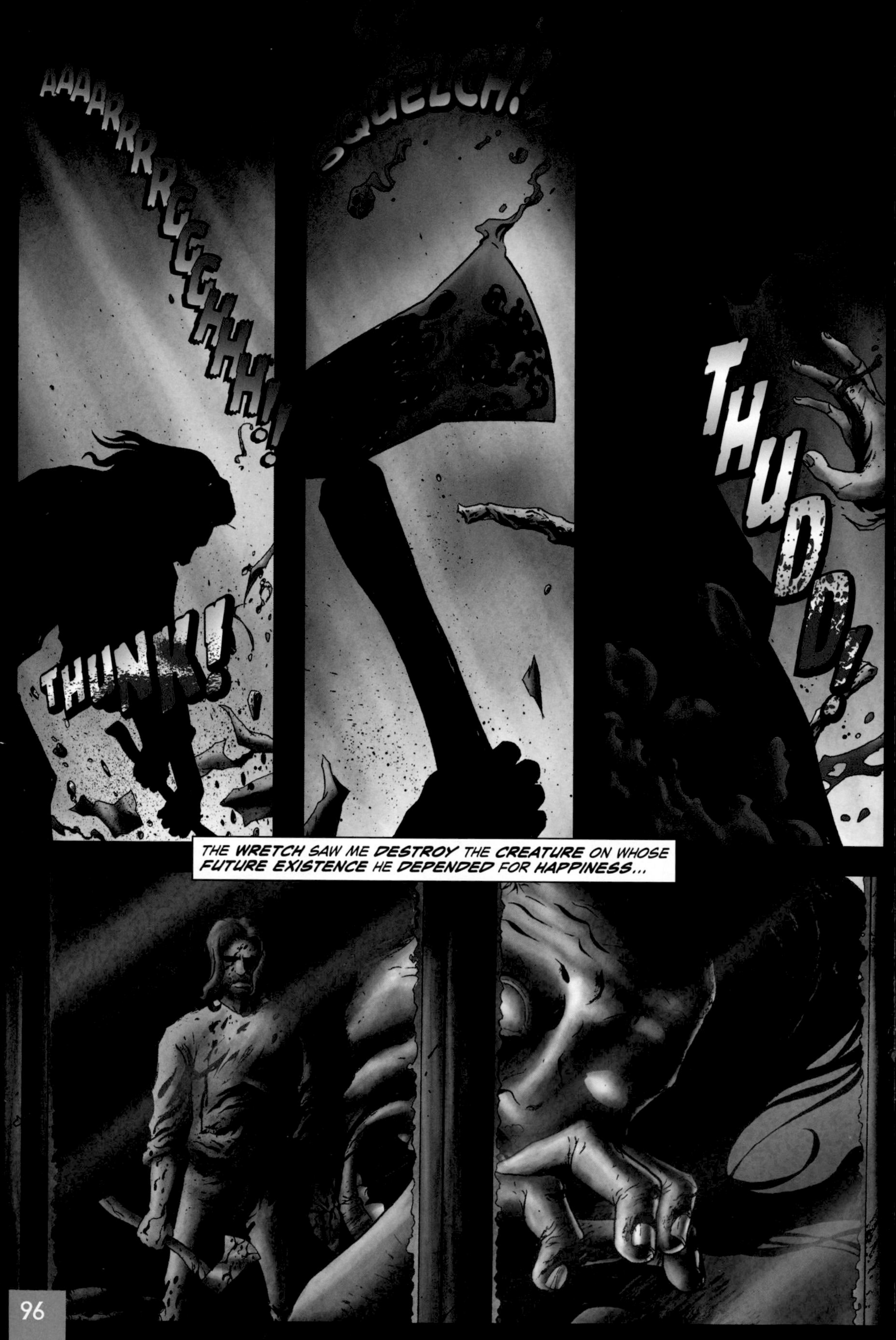
AAAARRRRRGGHHH!
SQUELCH!
THUDD!
THUNK!
THE WRETCH SAW ME DESTROY THE CREATURE ON WHOSE FUTURE EXISTENCE HE DEPENDED FOR HAPPINESS...

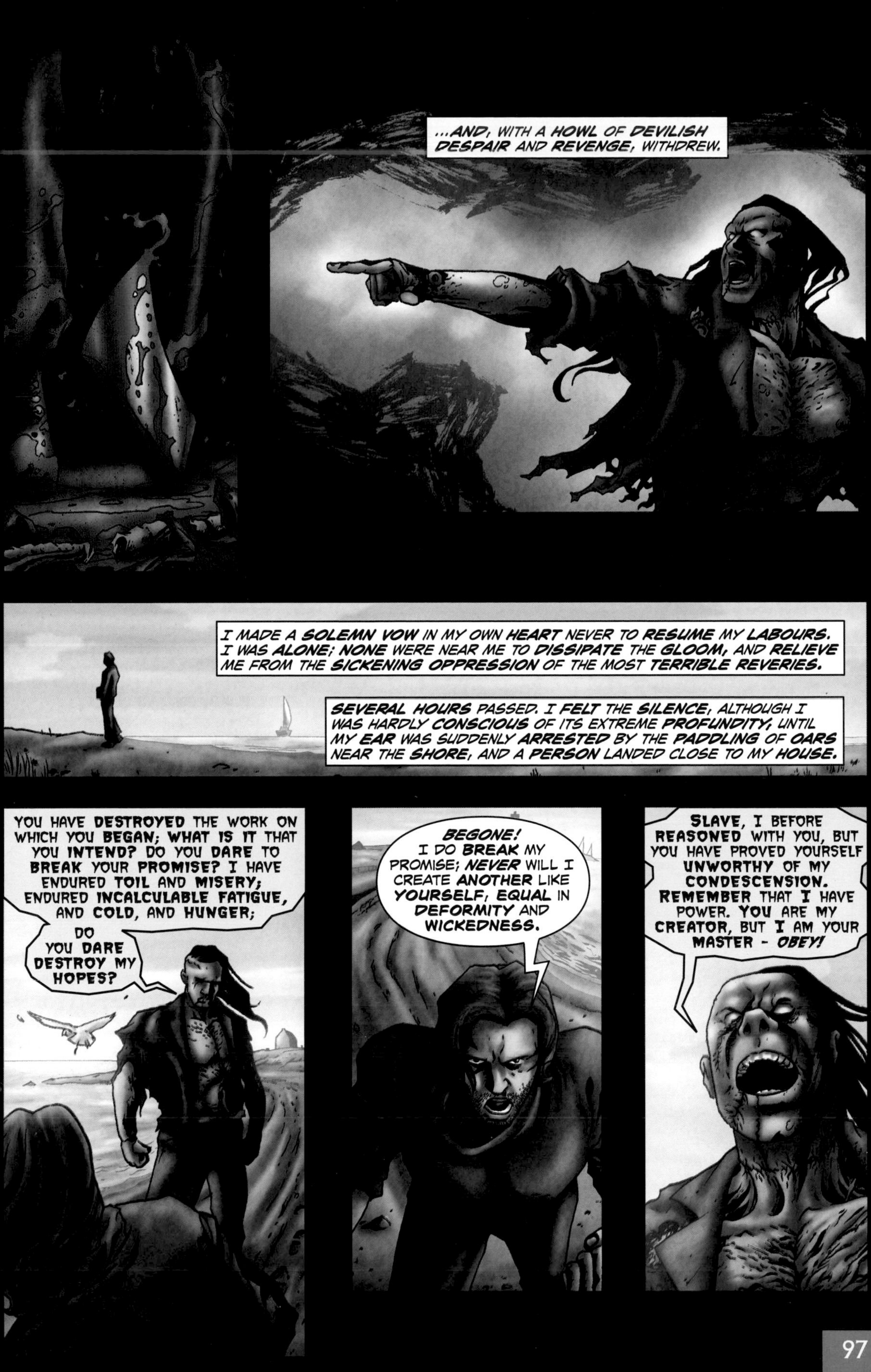
...AND, WITH A HOWL OF DEVILISH DESPAIR AND REVENGE, WITHDREW.
I MADE A SOLEMN VOW IN MY OWN HEART NEVER TO RESUME MY LABOURS. I WAS ALONE; NONE WERE NEAR ME TO DISSIPATE THE GLOOM, AND RELIEVE ME FROM THE SICKENING OPPRESSION OF THE MOST TERRIBLE REVERIES.
SEVERAL HOURS PASSED. I FELT THE SILENCE, ALTHOUGH I WAS HARDLY CONSCIOUS OF ITS EXTREME PROFUNDITY, UNTIL MY EAR WAS SUDDENLY ARRESTED BY THE PADDLING OF OARS NEAR THE SHORE, AND A PERSON LANDED CLOSE TO MY HOUSE.
YOU HAVE DESTROYED THE WORK ON WHICH YOU BEGAN; WHAT IS IT THAT YOU INTEND? DO YOU DARE TO BREAK YOUR PROMISE? I HAVE ENDURED TOIL AND MISERY; ENDURED INCALCULABLE FATIGUE, AND COLD, AND HUNGER;
DO YOU DARE DESTROY MY HOPES?
BEGONE! I DO BREAK MY PROMISE; NEVER WILL I CREATE ANOTHER LIKE YOURSELF, EQUAL IN DEFORMITY AND WICKEDNESS.
SLAVE, I BEFORE REASONED WITH YOU, BUT YOU HAVE PROVED YOURSELF UNWORTHY OF MY CONDESCENSION. REMEMBER THAT I HAVE POWER. YOU ARE MY CREATOR, BUT I AM YOUR MASTER - OBEY!

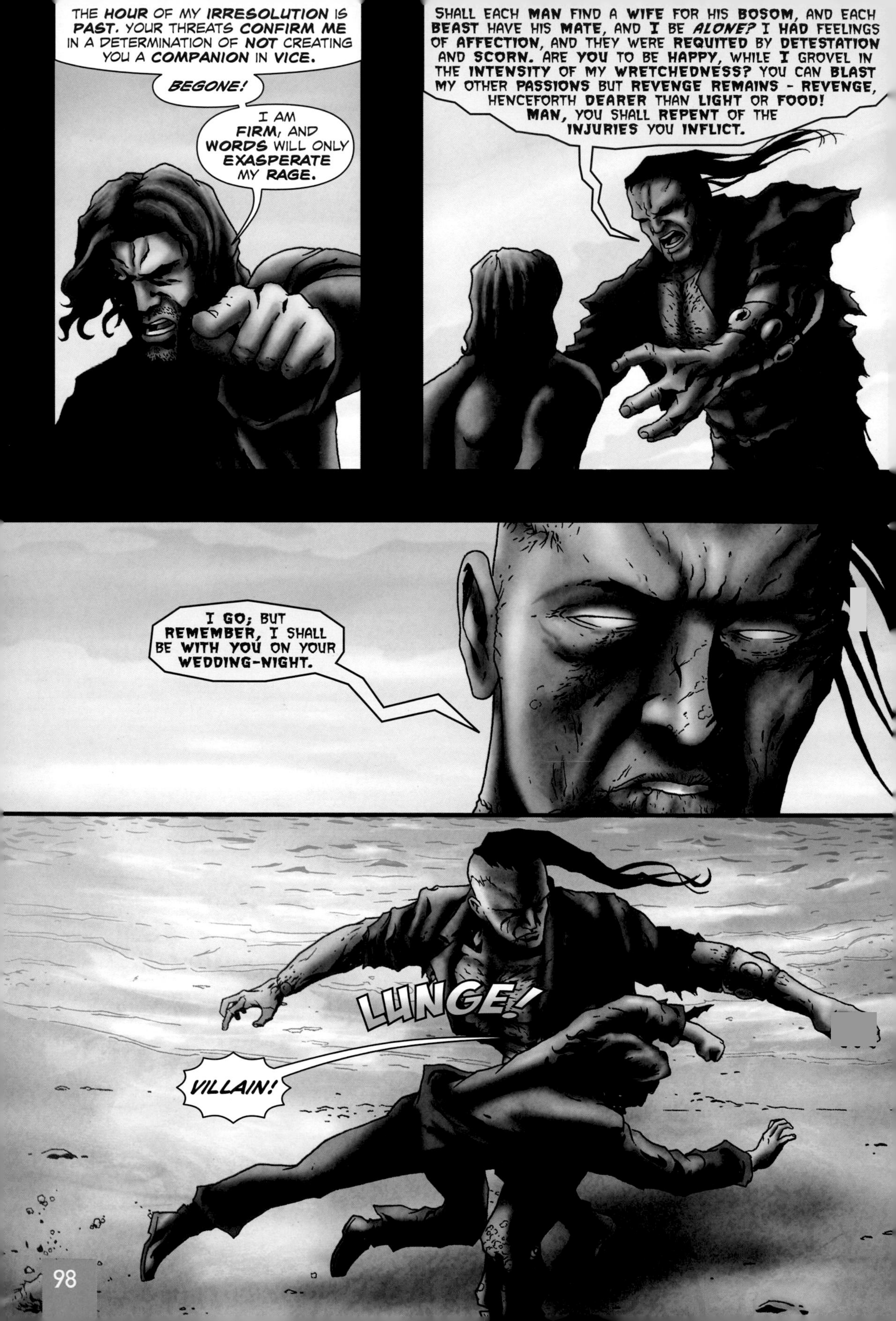
THE HOUR OF MY IRRESOLUTION IS PAST. YOUR THREATS CONFIRM ME IN A DETERMINATION OF NOT CREATING YOU A COMPANION IN VICE.
BEGONE!
I AM FIRM, AND WORDS WILL ONLY EXASPERATE MY RAGE.
SHALL EACH MAN FIND A WIFE FOR HIS BOSOM, AND EACH BEAST HAVE HIS MATE, AND I BE ALONE? I HAD FEELINGS OF AFFECTION, AND THEY WERE REQUITED BY DETESTATION AND SCORN. ARE YOU TO BE HAPPY, WHILE I GROVEL IN THE INTENSITY OF MY WRETCHEDNESS? YOU CAN BLAST MY OTHER PASSIONS BUT REVENGE REMAINS - REVENGE, HENCEFORTH DEARER THAN LIGHT OR FOOD! MAN, YOU SHALL REPENT OF THE INJURIES YOU INFLICT.
I GO; BUT REMEMBER, I SHALL BE WITH YOU ON YOUR WEDDING-NIGHT.
LUNGE!
VILLAIN!

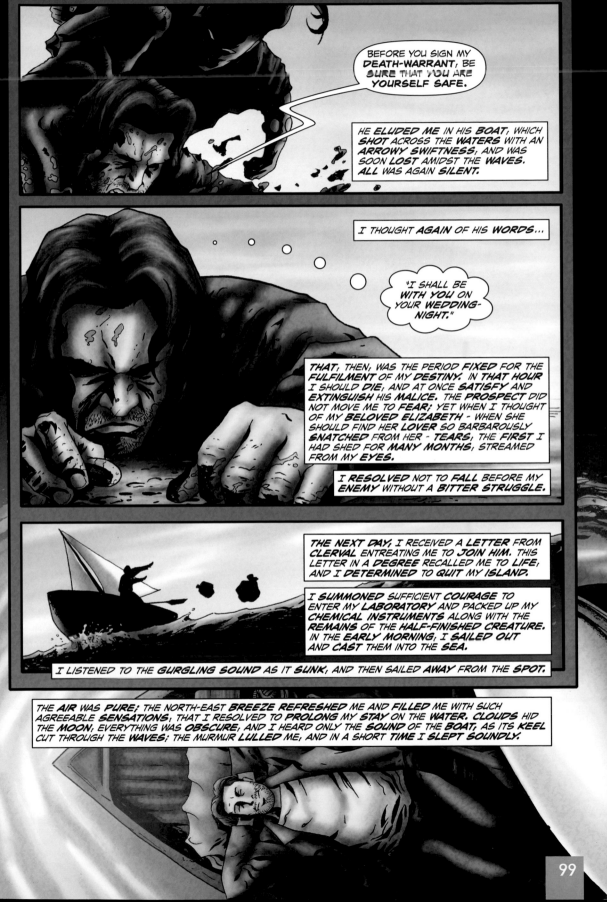

BEFORE YOU SIGN MY *DEATH-WARRANT,* BE SURE THAT YOU ARE YOURSELF *SAFE.*

HE *ELUDED* ME IN HIS *BOAT,* WHICH *SHOT* ACROSS THE *WATERS* WITH AN *ARROWY SWIFTNESS,* AND WAS SOON *LOST* AMIDST THE *WAVES.* ALL WAS AGAIN *SILENT.*

I THOUGHT *AGAIN* OF HIS *WORDS...*

"I SHALL BE WITH YOU ON YOUR *WEDDING-NIGHT.*"

THAT, THEN, WAS THE PERIOD *FIXED* FOR THE *FULFILMENT* OF MY *DESTINY.* IN *THAT HOUR* I SHOULD *DIE,* AND AT ONCE *SATISFY* AND *EXTINGUISH* HIS *MALICE.* THE *PROSPECT* DID NOT MOVE ME TO *FEAR;* YET WHEN I THOUGHT OF MY *BELOVED ELIZABETH* - WHEN SHE SHOULD FIND HER *LOVER* SO BARBAROUSLY *SNATCHED* FROM HER - *TEARS,* THE *FIRST* I HAD SHED FOR *MANY MONTHS,* STREAMED FROM MY *EYES.*

I *RESOLVED* NOT TO *FALL* BEFORE MY *ENEMY* WITHOUT A *BITTER STRUGGLE.*

THE *NEXT DAY,* I RECEIVED A *LETTER* FROM *CLERVAL* ENTREATING ME TO *JOIN* HIM. THIS LETTER IN A *DEGREE* RECALLED ME TO *LIFE,* AND I *DETERMINED* TO *QUIT* MY *ISLAND.*

I *SUMMONED* SUFFICIENT *COURAGE* TO ENTER MY *LABORATORY* AND PACKED UP MY *CHEMICAL INSTRUMENTS* ALONG WITH THE *REMAINS OF THE HALF-FINISHED CREATURE.* IN THE *EARLY MORNING,* I *SAILED OUT* AND *CAST* THEM INTO THE *SEA.*

I LISTENED TO THE *GURGLING SOUND* AS IT *SUNK,* AND THEN SAILED *AWAY* FROM THE *SPOT.*

THE *AIR* WAS *PURE;* THE NORTH-EAST *BREEZE REFRESHED* ME AND FILLED ME WITH SUCH AGREEABLE *SENSATIONS,* THAT I RESOLVED TO *PROLONG* MY *STAY* ON THE *WATER.* CLOUDS HID THE *MOON;* EVERYTHING WAS *OBSCURE,* AND I HEARD ONLY THE *SOUND* OF THE *BOAT,* AS ITS *KEEL* CUT THROUGH THE *WAVES;* THE *MURMUR LULLED* ME, AND IN A SHORT *TIME I SLEPT SOUNDLY.*

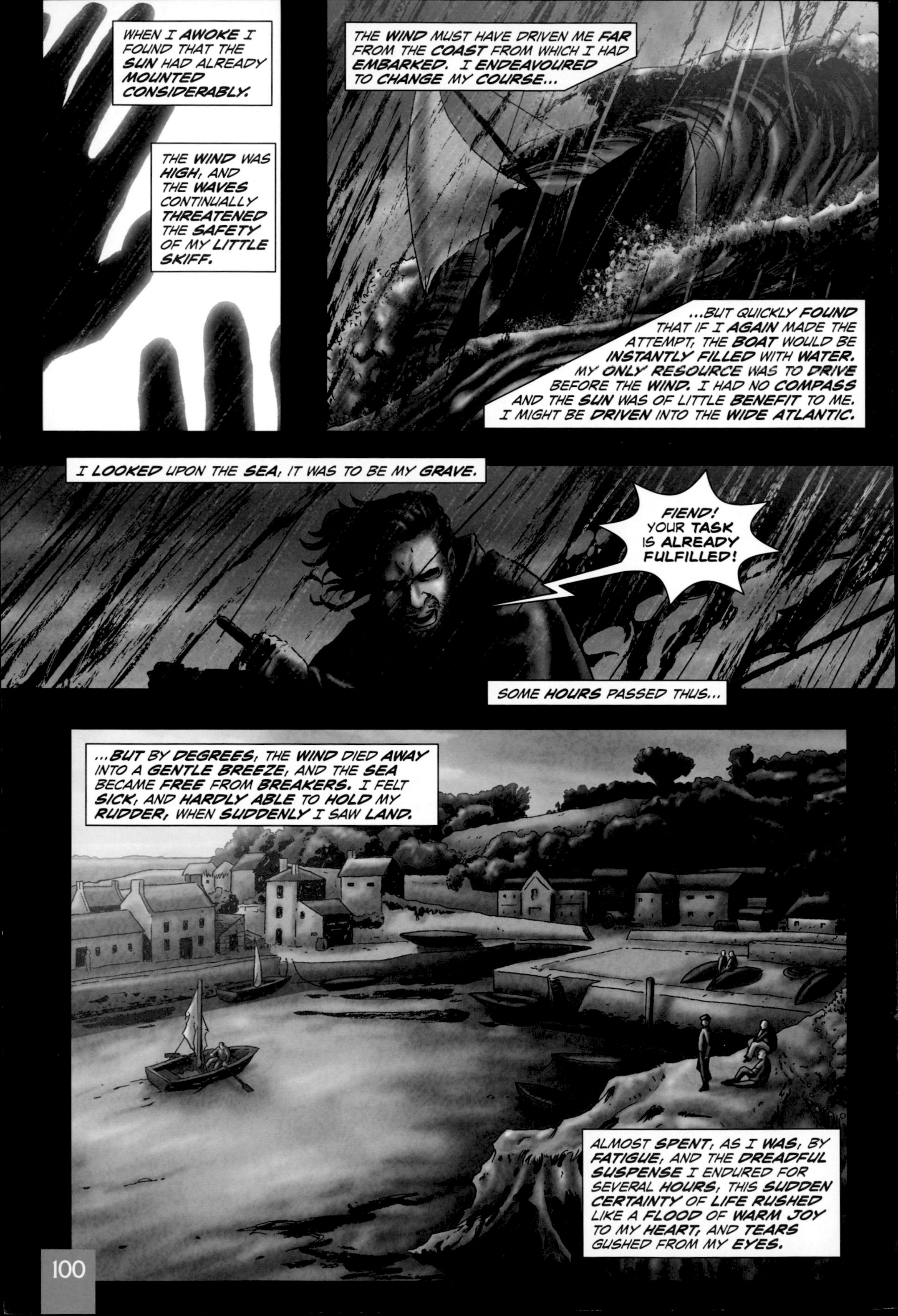
WHEN I AWOKE I FOUND THAT THE SUN HAD ALREADY MOUNTED CONSIDERABLY.
THE WIND WAS HIGH, AND THE WAVES CONTINUALLY THREATENED THE SAFETY OF MY LITTLE SKIFF.
THE WIND MUST HAVE DRIVEN ME FAR FROM THE COAST FROM WHICH I HAD EMBARKED. I ENDEAVOURED TO CHANGE MY COURSE...
...BUT QUICKLY FOUND THAT IF I AGAIN MADE THE ATTEMPT, THE BOAT WOULD BE INSTANTLY FILLED WITH WATER. MY ONLY RESOURCE WAS TO DRIVE BEFORE THE WIND. I HAD NO COMPASS AND THE SUN WAS OF LITTLE BENEFIT TO ME. I MIGHT BE DRIVEN INTO THE WIDE ATLANTIC.
I LOOKED UPON THE SEA, IT WAS TO BE MY GRAVE.
FIEND! YOUR TASK IS ALREADY FULFILLED!
SOME HOURS PASSED THUS...
...BUT BY DEGREES, THE WIND DIED AWAY INTO A GENTLE BREEZE, AND THE SEA BECAME FREE FROM BREAKERS. I FELT SICK, AND HARDLY ABLE TO HOLD MY RUDDER, WHEN SUDDENLY I SAW LAND.
ALMOST SPENT, AS I WAS, BY FATIGUE, AND THE DREADFUL SUSPENSE I ENDURED FOR SEVERAL HOURS, THIS SUDDEN CERTAINTY OF LIFE RUSHED LIKE A FLOOD OF WARM JOY TO MY HEART, AND TEARS GUSHED FROM MY EYES.

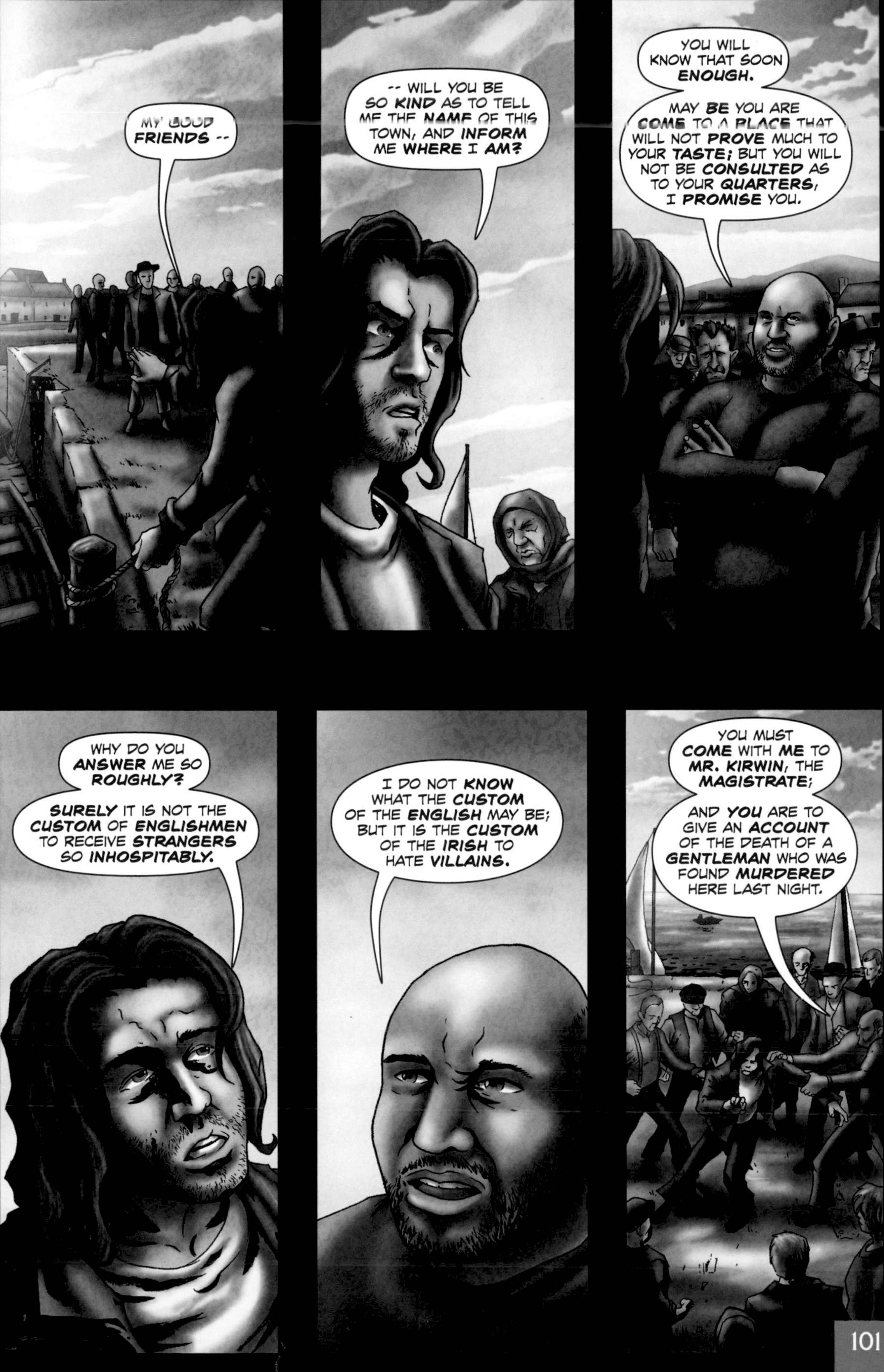
MY GOOD FRIENDS --
-- WILL YOU BE SO KIND AS TO TELL ME THE NAME OF THIS TOWN, AND INFORM ME WHERE I AM?
YOU WILL KNOW THAT SOON ENOUGH.
MAY BE YOU ARE COME TO A PLACE THAT WILL NOT PROVE MUCH TO YOUR TASTE; BUT YOU WILL NOT BE CONSULTED AS TO YOUR QUARTERS, I PROMISE YOU.
WHY DO YOU ANSWER ME SO ROUGHLY?
SURELY IT IS NOT THE CUSTOM OF ENGLISHMEN TO RECEIVE STRANGERS SO INHOSPITABLY.
I DO NOT KNOW WHAT THE CUSTOM OF THE ENGLISH MAY BE; BUT IT IS THE CUSTOM OF THE IRISH TO HATE VILLAINS.
YOU MUST COME WITH ME TO MR. KIRWIN, THE MAGISTRATE;
AND YOU ARE TO GIVE AN ACCOUNT OF THE DEATH OF A GENTLEMAN WHO WAS FOUND MURDERED HERE LAST NIGHT.

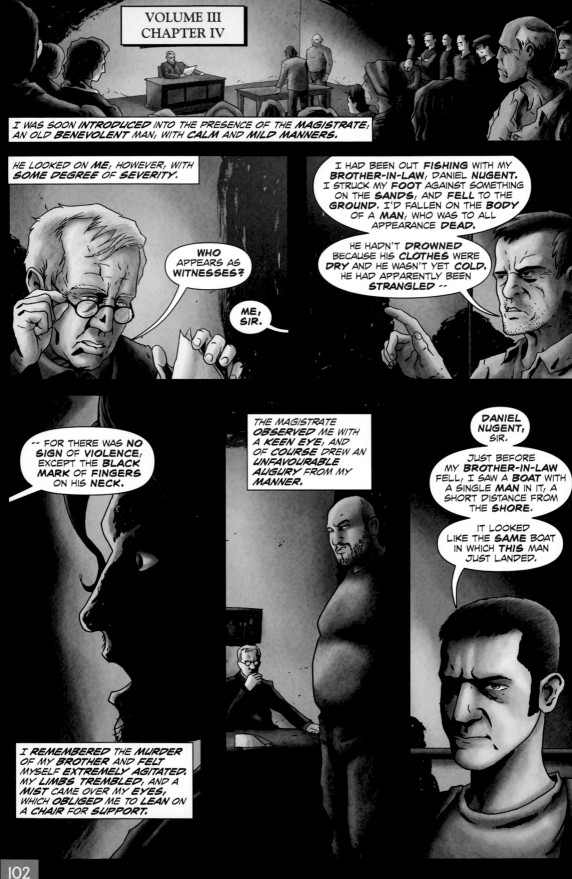

VOLUME III
CHAPTER IV

I WAS SOON *INTRODUCED* INTO THE PRESENCE OF THE *MAGISTRATE*, AN OLD *BENEVOLENT* MAN, WITH *CALM* AND *MILD MANNERS*.

HE LOOKED ON *ME*, HOWEVER, WITH *SOME DEGREE OF SEVERITY*.

WHO APPEARS AS *WITNESSES*?

ME, SIR.

I HAD BEEN OUT *FISHING* WITH MY *BROTHER-IN-LAW*, DANIEL *NUGENT*. I STRUCK MY *FOOT* AGAINST SOMETHING ON THE *SANDS*, AND *FELL* TO THE *GROUND*. I'D FALLEN ON THE *BODY* OF A *MAN*, WHO WAS TO ALL APPEARANCE *DEAD*.

HE HADN'T *DROWNED* BECAUSE HIS *CLOTHES* WERE *DRY* AND HE WASN'T YET *COLD*. HE HAD APPARENTLY BEEN *STRANGLED* --

-- FOR THERE WAS *NO SIGN OF VIOLENCE*, EXCEPT THE *BLACK MARK* OF FINGERS ON HIS *NECK*.

THE MAGISTRATE *OBSERVED* ME WITH A *KEEN EYE*, AND OF *COURSE* DREW AN *UNFAVOURABLE AUGURY* FROM MY *MANNER*.

DANIEL NUGENT, SIR.

JUST BEFORE MY *BROTHER-IN-LAW* FELL, I SAW A *BOAT* WITH A SINGLE *MAN* IN IT, A SHORT DISTANCE FROM THE *SHORE*.

IT LOOKED LIKE THE *SAME* BOAT IN WHICH *THIS* MAN JUST LANDED.

I REMEMBERED THE *MURDER* OF MY *BROTHER* AND FELT MYSELF *EXTREMELY AGITATED*. MY *LIMBS TREMBLED*, AND A *MIST* CAME OVER MY *EYES*, WHICH *OBLIGED* ME TO *LEAN* ON A *CHAIR* FOR *SUPPORT*.

A **WOMAN** DEPOSED THAT SHE SAW A **BOAT** WITH ONLY **ONE MAN** IN IT **PUSH OFF** FROM THAT PART OF THE SHORE WHERE THE **CORPSE** WAS AFTERWARDS **FOUND.**

SEVERAL **OTHER MEN** WERE EXAMINED CONCERNING MY **LANDING;** AND THEY AGREED THAT, WITH THE **STRONG WIND,** I HAD **BEATEN ABOUT** FOR MANY **HOURS,** AND HAD BEEN **OBLIGED** TO **RETURN** NEARLY TO THE **SAME SPOT** FROM WHICH I HAD **DEPARTED.**

THEY **OBSERVED** THAT IT **APPEARED** THAT I HAD BROUGHT THE **BODY** FROM **ANOTHER PLACE,** AND IT WAS **LIKELY** THAT I MIGHT HAVE **PUT** INTO THE **HARBOUR,** IGNORANT THAT IT WAS THE **PLACE** WHERE I HAD **DEPOSITED** THE **CORPSE.**

TAKE HIM INTO THE **ROOM** WHERE THE **BODY** LIES.

I WANT TO **OBSERVE** THE **EFFECT** THE **SIGHT** OF IT PRODUCES IN HIM.

KNOWING THAT I HAD BEEN CONVERSING WITH **SEVERAL** PERSONS IN THE ISLAND I HAD INHABITED ABOUT THE TIME THAT THE **BODY** HAD BEEN FOUND, I WAS PERFECTLY **TRANQUIL** TO THE **CONSEQUENCES** OF THE AFFAIR.

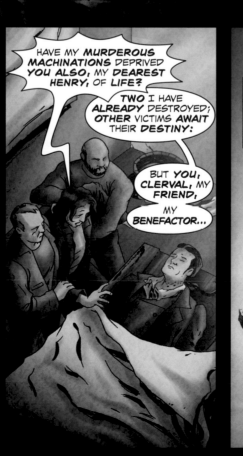

HAVE MY **MURDEROUS MACHINATIONS** DEPRIVED **YOU** ALSO, MY **DEAREST HENRY,** OF **LIFE?**

TWO I HAVE **ALREADY** DESTROYED; **OTHER** VICTIMS **AWAIT** THEIR **DESTINY:**

BUT **YOU,** CLERVAL, MY **FRIEND,**

MY **BENEFACTOR...**

THE **HUMAN FRAME** COULD **NO LONGER** SUPPORT THE **AGONIES** THAT I **ENDURED,** AND I WAS **CARRIED OUT** OF THE **ROOM** IN **STRONG CONVULSIONS.**

103

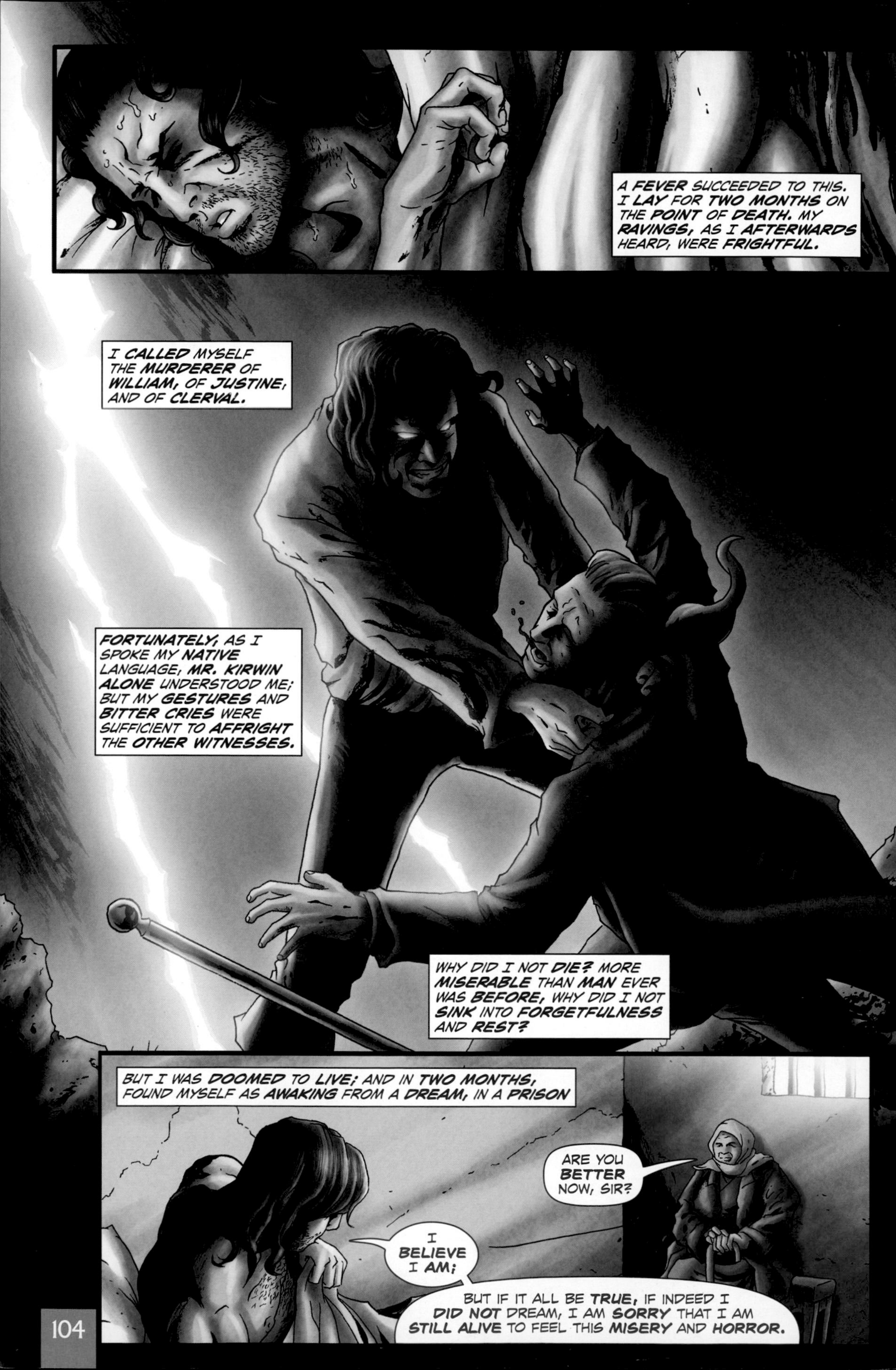
A FEVER SUCCEEDED TO THIS. I LAY FOR TWO MONTHS ON THE POINT OF DEATH. MY RAVINGS, AS I AFTERWARDS HEARD, WERE FRIGHTFUL.
I CALLED MYSELF THE MURDERER OF WILLIAM, OF JUSTINE, AND OF CLERVAL.
FORTUNATELY, AS I SPOKE MY NATIVE LANGUAGE, MR. KIRWIN ALONE UNDERSTOOD ME; BUT MY GESTURES AND BITTER CRIES WERE SUFFICIENT TO AFFRIGHT THE OTHER WITNESSES.
WHY DID I NOT DIE? MORE MISERABLE THAN MAN EVER WAS BEFORE, WHY DID I NOT SINK INTO FORGETFULNESS AND REST?
BUT I WAS DOOMED TO LIVE; AND IN TWO MONTHS, FOUND MYSELF AS AWAKING FROM A DREAM, IN A PRISON
ARE YOU BETTER NOW, SIR?
I BELIEVE I AM;
BUT IF IT ALL BE TRUE, IF INDEED I DID NOT DREAM, I AM SORRY THAT I AM STILL ALIVE TO FEEL THIS MISERY AND HORROR.

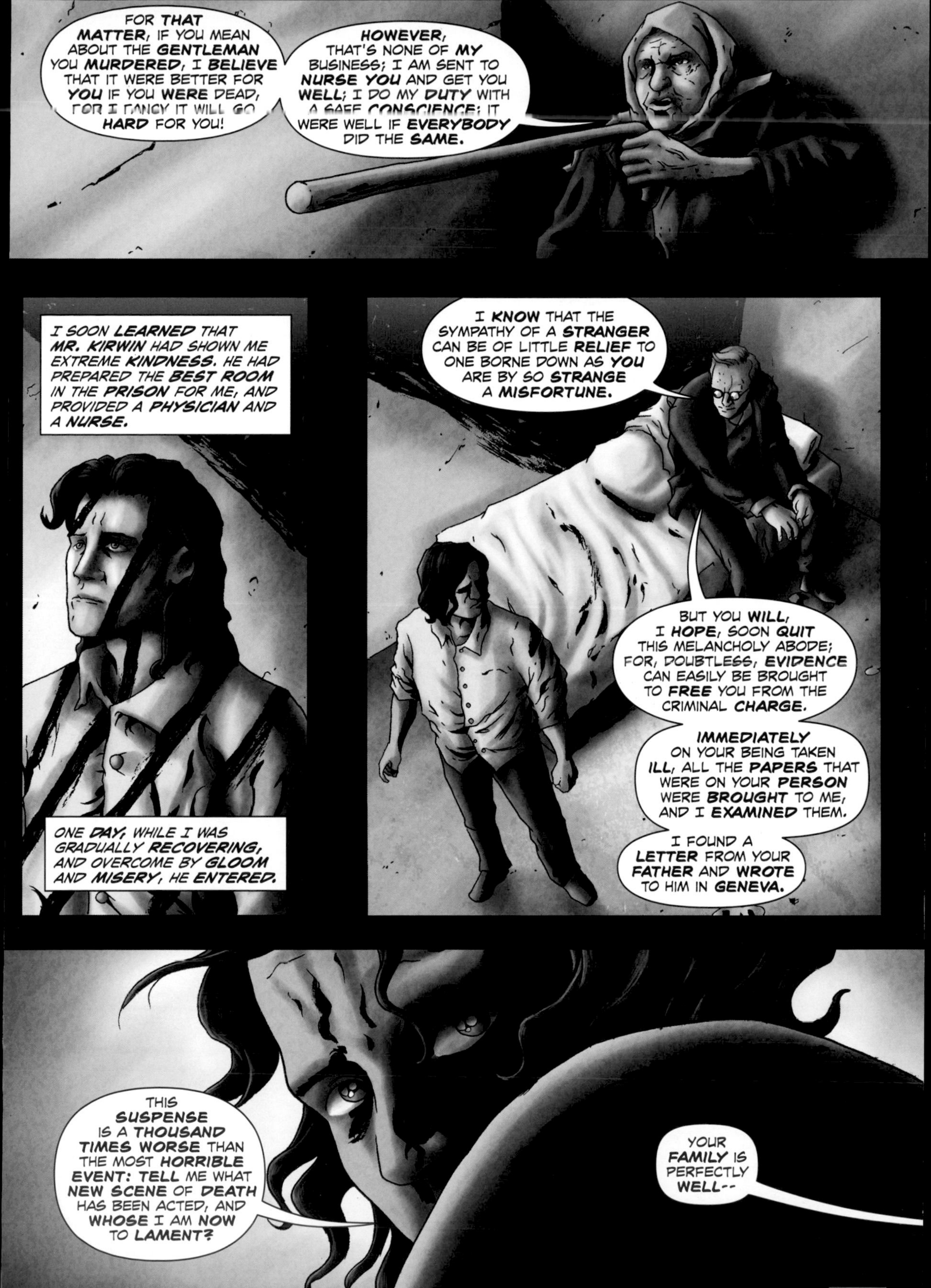
FOR THAT MATTER, IF YOU MEAN ABOUT THE GENTLEMAN YOU MURDERED, I BELIEVE THAT IT WERE BETTER FOR YOU IF YOU WERE DEAD, FOR I FANCY IT WILL GO HARD FOR YOU!
HOWEVER, THAT'S NONE OF MY BUSINESS; I AM SENT TO NURSE YOU AND GET YOU WELL; I DO MY DUTY WITH A SAFE CONSCIENCE; IT WERE WELL IF EVERYBODY DID THE SAME.
I SOON LEARNED THAT MR. KIRWIN HAD SHOWN ME EXTREME KINDNESS. HE HAD PREPARED THE BEST ROOM IN THE PRISON FOR ME, AND PROVIDED A PHYSICIAN AND A NURSE.
ONE DAY, WHILE I WAS GRADUALLY RECOVERING, AND OVERCOME BY GLOOM AND MISERY, HE ENTERED.
I KNOW THAT THE SYMPATHY OF A STRANGER CAN BE OF LITTLE RELIEF TO ONE BORNE DOWN AS YOU ARE BY SO STRANGE A MISFORTUNE.
BUT YOU WILL, I HOPE, SOON QUIT THIS MELANCHOLY ABODE; FOR, DOUBTLESS, EVIDENCE CAN EASILY BE BROUGHT TO FREE YOU FROM THE CRIMINAL CHARGE.
IMMEDIATELY ON YOUR BEING TAKEN ILL, ALL THE PAPERS THAT WERE ON YOUR PERSON WERE BROUGHT TO ME, AND I EXAMINED THEM.
I FOUND A LETTER FROM YOUR FATHER AND WROTE TO HIM IN GENEVA.
THIS SUSPENSE IS A THOUSAND TIMES WORSE THAN THE MOST HORRIBLE EVENT: TELL ME WHAT NEW SCENE OF DEATH HAS BEEN ACTED, AND WHOSE I AM NOW TO LAMENT?
YOUR FAMILY IS PERFECTLY WELL--

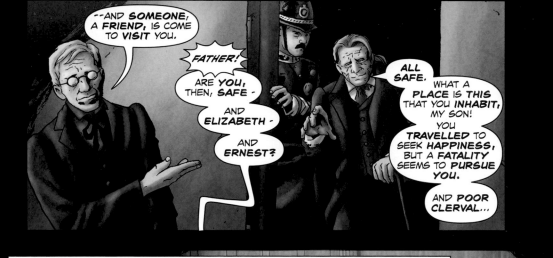

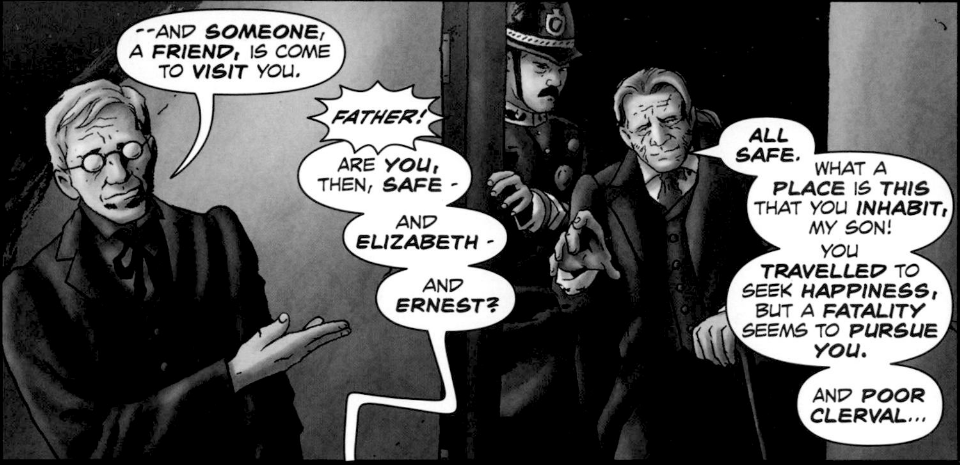
--AND SOMEONE, A FRIEND, IS COME TO VISIT YOU.
FATHER!
ARE YOU, THEN, SAFE -
AND ELIZABETH -
AND ERNEST?
ALL SAFE.
WHAT A PLACE IS THIS THAT YOU INHABIT, MY SON!
YOU TRAVELLED TO SEEK HAPPINESS, BUT A FATALITY SEEMS TO PURSUE YOU.
AND POOR CLERVAL...

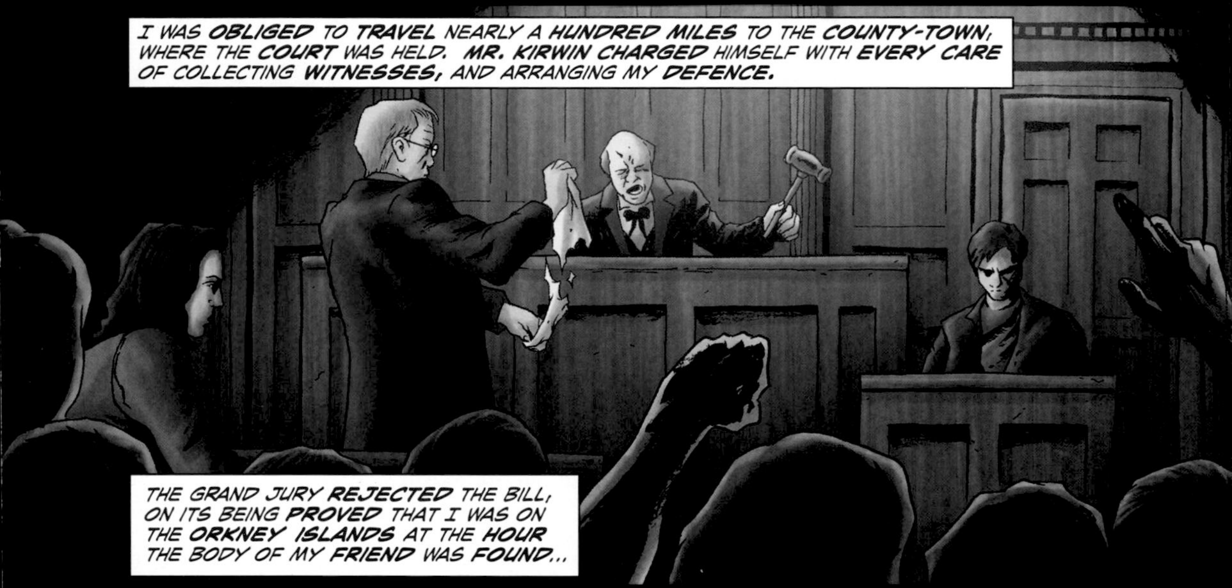
I WAS OBLIGED TO TRAVEL NEARLY A HUNDRED MILES TO THE COUNTY-TOWN, WHERE THE COURT WAS HELD. MR. KIRWIN CHARGED HIMSELF WITH EVERY CARE OF COLLECTING WITNESSES, AND ARRANGING MY DEFENCE.
THE GRAND JURY REJECTED THE BILL, ON ITS BEING PROVED THAT I WAS ON THE ORKNEY ISLANDS AT THE HOUR THE BODY OF MY FRIEND WAS FOUND...

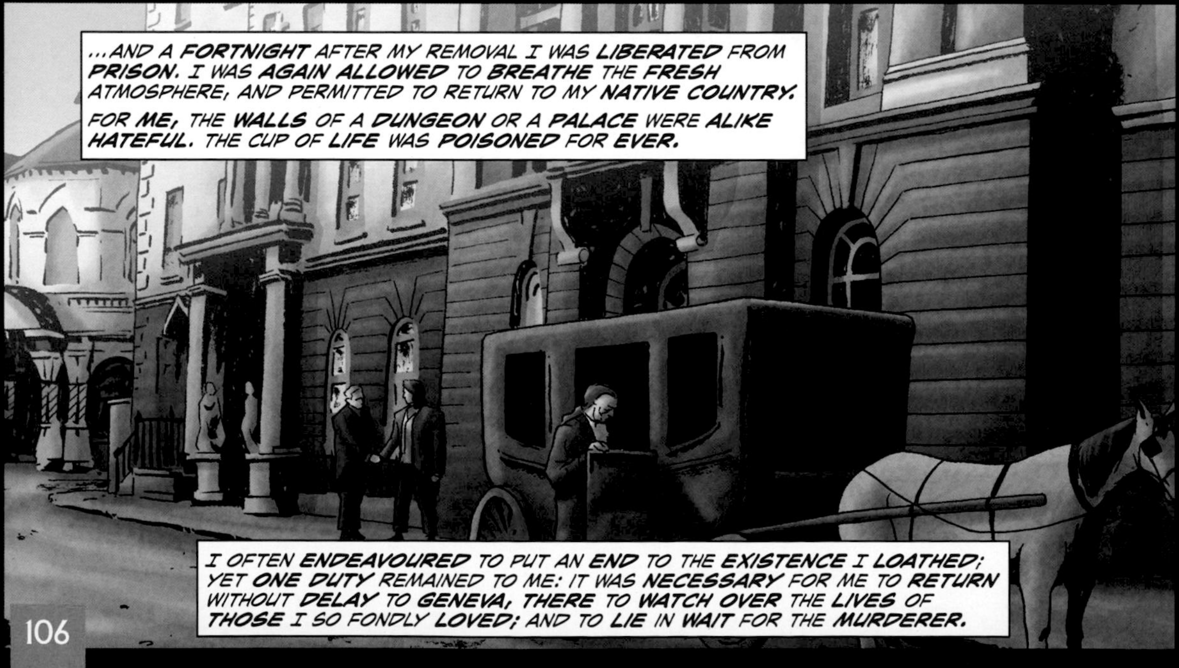
...AND A FORTNIGHT AFTER MY REMOVAL I WAS LIBERATED FROM PRISON. I WAS AGAIN ALLOWED TO BREATHE THE FRESH ATMOSPHERE, AND PERMITTED TO RETURN TO MY NATIVE COUNTRY.
FOR ME, THE WALLS OF A DUNGEON OR A PALACE WERE ALIKE HATEFUL. THE CUP OF LIFE WAS POISONED FOR EVER.
I OFTEN ENDEAVOURED TO PUT AN END TO THE EXISTENCE I LOATHED; YET ONE DUTY REMAINED TO ME: IT WAS NECESSARY FOR ME TO RETURN WITHOUT DELAY TO GENEVA, THERE TO WATCH OVER THE LIVES OF THOSE I SO FONDLY LOVED; AND TO LIE IN WAIT FOR THE MURDERER.

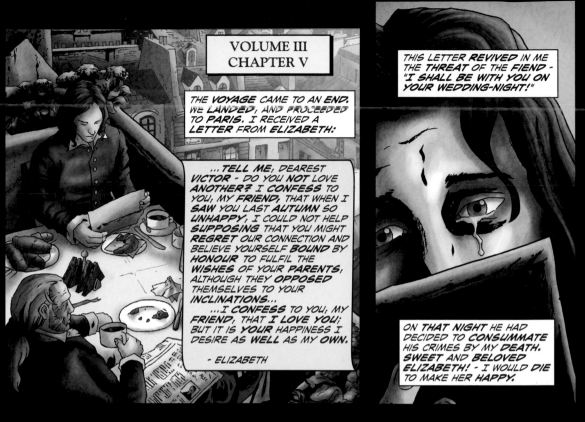

VOLUME III
CHAPTER V

THE **VOYAGE** CAME TO AN **END**. WE **LANDED**, AND PROCEEDED TO **PARIS**. I RECEIVED A **LETTER** FROM **ELIZABETH**:

...**TELL ME**, DEAREST **VICTOR** - DO YOU **NOT LOVE ANOTHER**? I CONFESS TO YOU, MY **FRIEND**, THAT WHEN I **SAW** YOU LAST **AUTUMN** SO **UNHAPPY**, I COULD NOT HELP SUPPOSING THAT YOU MIGHT **REGRET** OUR CONNECTION AND BELIEVE YOURSELF **BOUND** BY **HONOUR** TO FULFIL THE **WISHES** OF YOUR **PARENTS**, ALTHOUGH THEY **OPPOSED** THEMSELVES TO YOUR **INCLINATIONS**...

...I **CONFESS** TO YOU, MY **FRIEND**, THAT I **LOVE YOU**; BUT IT IS **YOUR** HAPPINESS I DESIRE AS **WELL** AS MY OWN.

- ELIZABETH

THIS LETTER **REVIVED** IN ME THE **THREAT** OF THE FIEND - "**I SHALL BE WITH YOU ON YOUR WEDDING-NIGHT!**"

ON **THAT NIGHT** HE HAD DECIDED TO **CONSUMMATE** HIS CRIMES BY MY **DEATH**. SWEET AND **BELOVED ELIZABETH!** - I WOULD **DIE** TO MAKE HER **HAPPY**.

I FEAR, MY **BELOVED GIRL**, LITTLE **HAPPINESS** REMAINS FOR US ON **EARTH**; YET ALL THAT I MAY **ONE DAY** ENJOY IS CENTRED IN YOU. CHASE AWAY YOUR **IDLE FEARS**; TO YOU ALONE DO I CONSECRATE MY **LIFE**, AND MY **ENDEAVOURS** FOR **CONTENTMENT**.

I HAVE ONE, DREADFUL, **SECRET** WHICH WHEN **REVEALED** TO YOU WILL **CHILL YOUR FRAME** WITH **HORROR**. I WILL **CONFIDE** THIS TALE OF **MISERY** TO YOU THE **DAY AFTER OUR MARRIAGE**; FOR THERE MUST BE **PERFECT CONFIDENCE** BETWEEN US. UNTIL **THEN**, DO NOT **MENTION** OR **ALLUDE** TO IT.

- VICTOR

IN ABOUT A **WEEK** AFTER THE **ARRIVAL** OF **ELIZABETH'S** LETTER, WE RETURNED TO **GENEVA**. THE SWEET GIRL **WELCOMED** ME WITH **WARM AFFECTION**; YET **TEARS** WERE IN HER EYES AS SHE **BEHELD** MY **EMACIATED FRAME**.

107

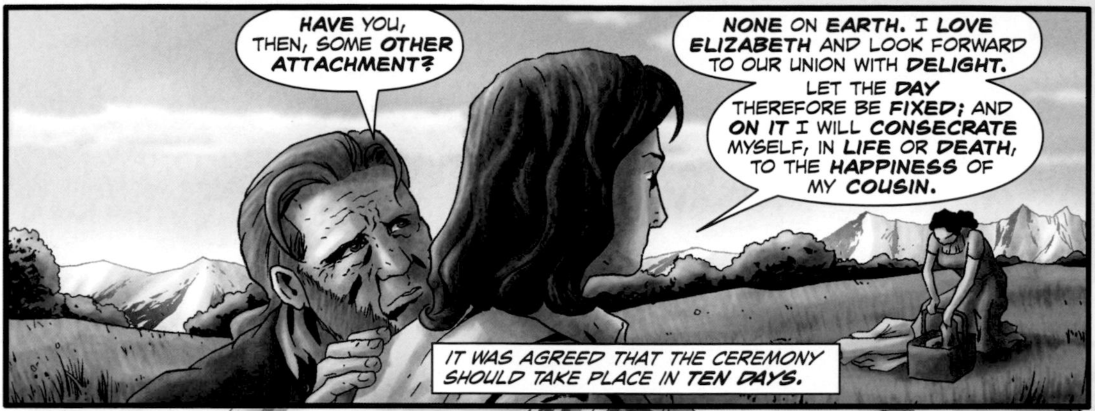
HAVE YOU, THEN, SOME OTHER ATTACHMENT?
NONE ON EARTH. I LOVE ELIZABETH AND LOOK FORWARD TO OUR UNION WITH DELIGHT.
LET THE DAY THEREFORE BE FIXED; AND ON IT I WILL CONSECRATE MYSELF, IN LIFE OR DEATH, TO THE HAPPINESS OF MY COUSIN.
IT WAS AGREED THAT THE CEREMONY SHOULD TAKE PLACE IN TEN DAYS.

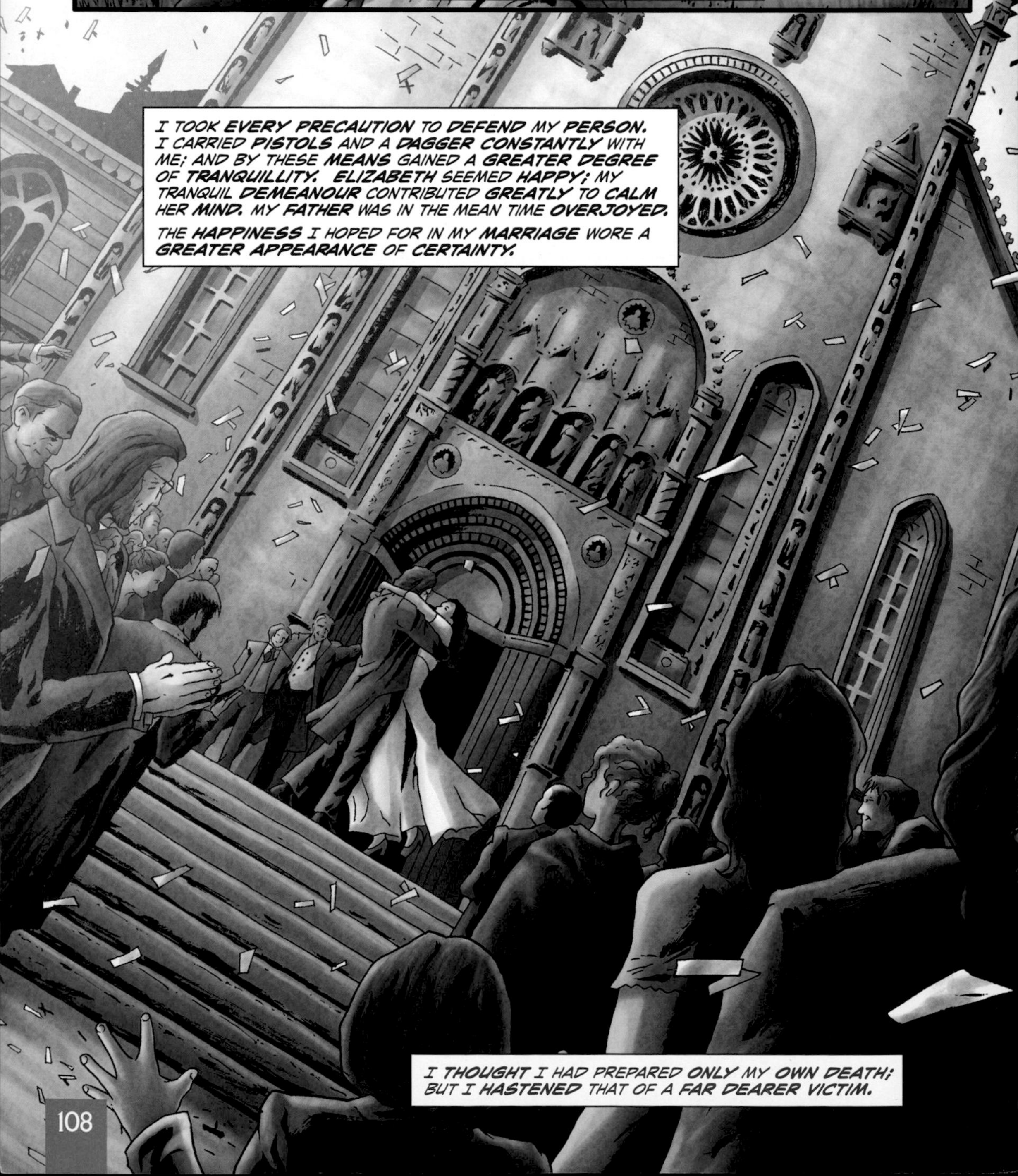
I TOOK EVERY PRECAUTION TO DEFEND MY PERSON. I CARRIED PISTOLS AND A DAGGER CONSTANTLY WITH ME; AND BY THESE MEANS GAINED A GREATER DEGREE OF TRANQUILLITY. ELIZABETH SEEMED HAPPY; MY TRANQUIL DEMEANOUR CONTRIBUTED GREATLY TO CALM HER MIND. MY FATHER WAS IN THE MEAN TIME OVERJOYED.
THE HAPPINESS I HOPED FOR IN MY MARRIAGE WORE A GREATER APPEARANCE OF CERTAINTY.
I THOUGHT I HAD PREPARED ONLY MY OWN DEATH; BUT I HASTENED THAT OF A FAR DEARER VICTIM.

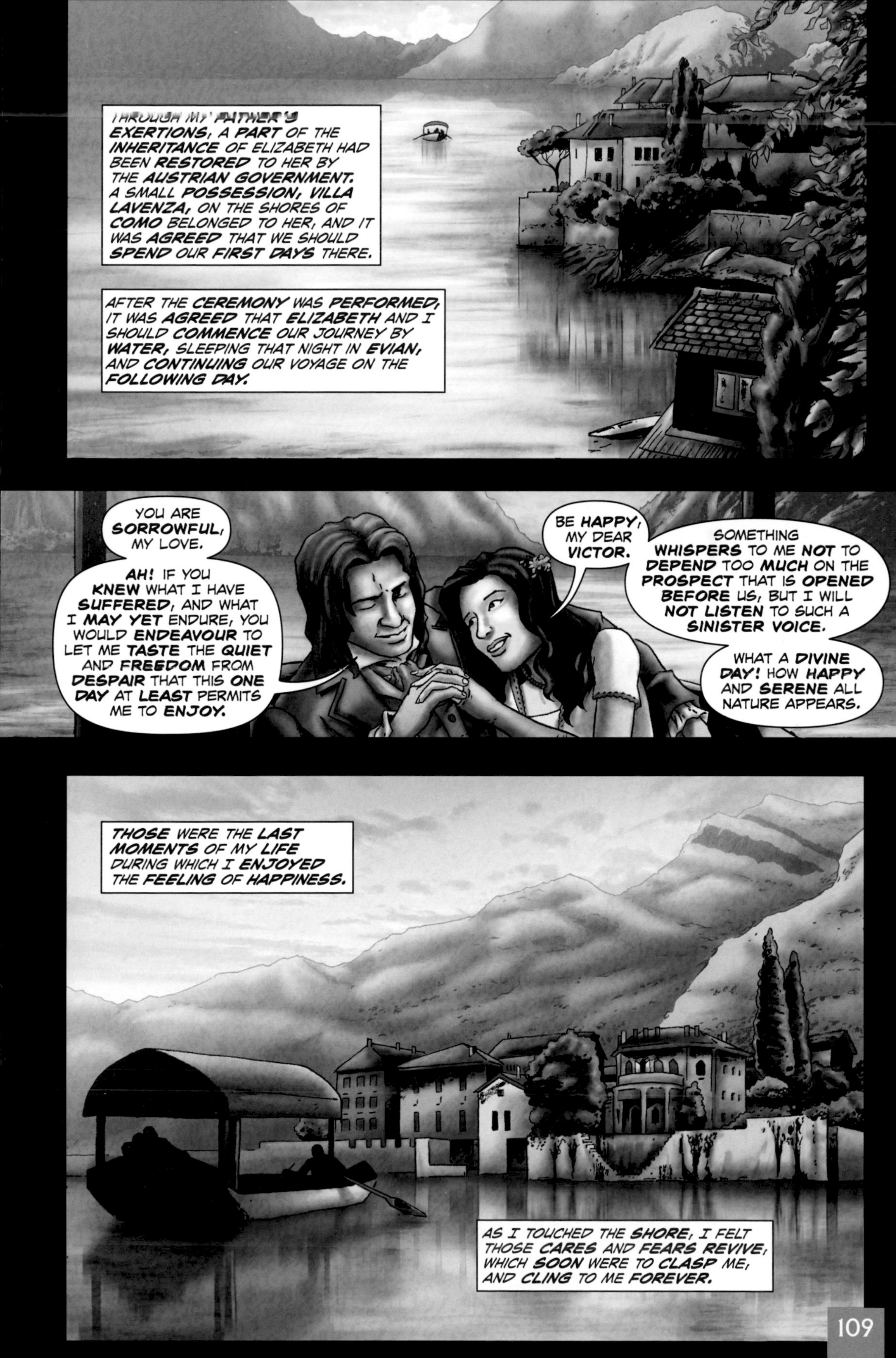
THROUGH MY FATHER'S EXERTIONS, A PART OF THE INHERITANCE OF ELIZABETH HAD BEEN RESTORED TO HER BY THE AUSTRIAN GOVERNMENT. A SMALL POSSESSION, VILLA LAVENZA, ON THE SHORES OF COMO BELONGED TO HER, AND IT WAS AGREED THAT WE SHOULD SPEND OUR FIRST DAYS THERE.
AFTER THE CEREMONY WAS PERFORMED, IT WAS AGREED THAT ELIZABETH AND I SHOULD COMMENCE OUR JOURNEY BY WATER, SLEEPING THAT NIGHT IN EVIAN, AND CONTINUING OUR VOYAGE ON THE FOLLOWING DAY.
YOU ARE SORROWFUL, MY LOVE.
AH! IF YOU KNEW WHAT I HAVE SUFFERED, AND WHAT I MAY YET ENDURE, YOU WOULD ENDEAVOUR TO LET ME TASTE THE QUIET AND FREEDOM FROM DESPAIR THAT THIS ONE DAY AT LEAST PERMITS ME TO ENJOY.
BE HAPPY, MY DEAR VICTOR.
SOMETHING WHISPERS TO ME NOT TO DEPEND TOO MUCH ON THE PROSPECT THAT IS OPENED BEFORE US, BUT I WILL NOT LISTEN TO SUCH A SINISTER VOICE.
WHAT A DIVINE DAY! HOW HAPPY AND SERENE ALL NATURE APPEARS.
THOSE WERE THE LAST MOMENTS OF MY LIFE DURING WHICH I ENJOYED THE FEELING OF HAPPINESS.
AS I TOUCHED THE SHORE, I FELT THOSE CARES AND FEARS REVIVE, WHICH SOON WERE TO CLASP ME, AND CLING TO ME FOREVER.

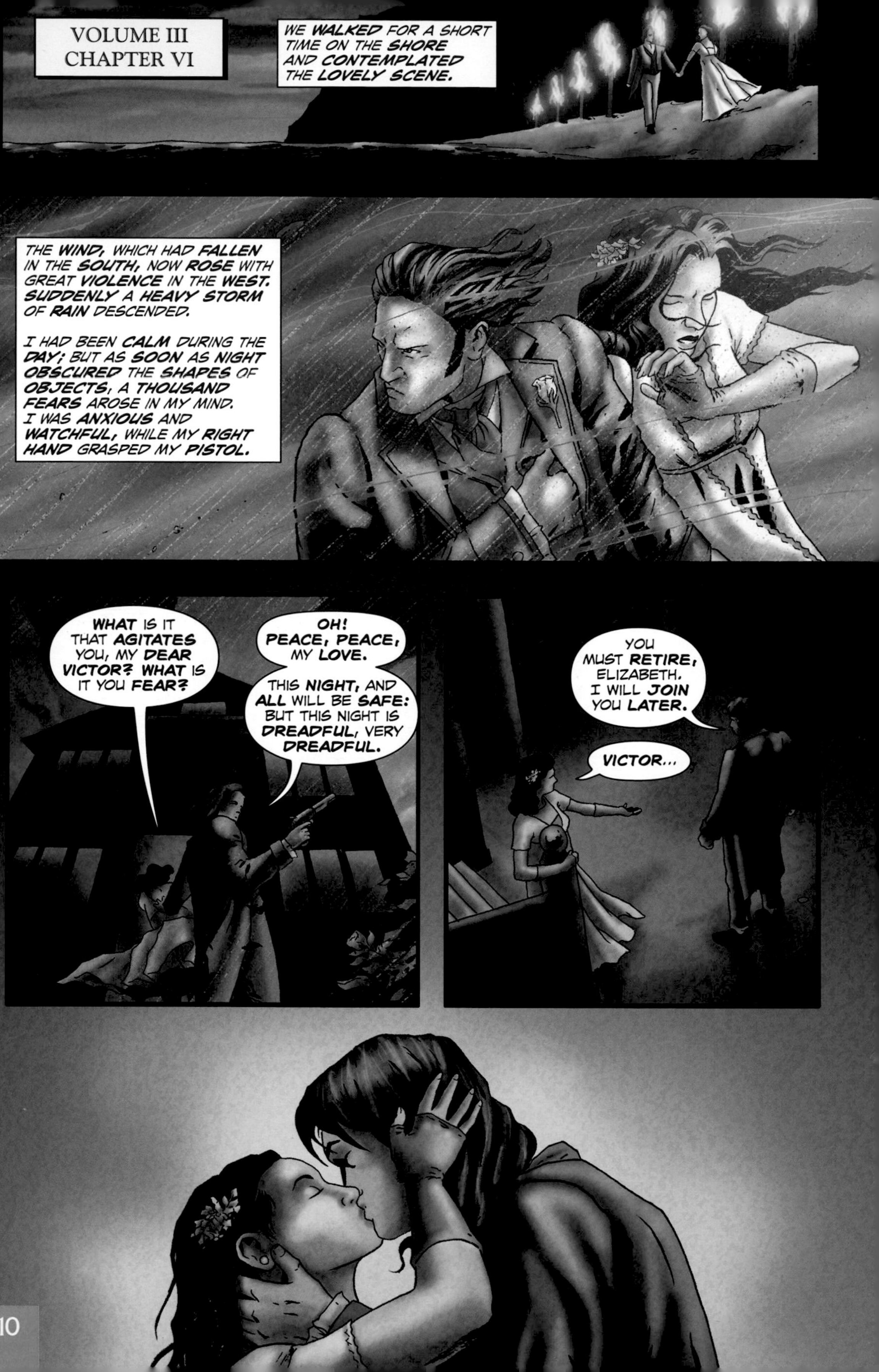
VOLUME III
CHAPTER VI
WE WALKED FOR A SHORT TIME ON THE SHORE AND CONTEMPLATED THE LOVELY SCENE.
THE WIND, WHICH HAD FALLEN IN THE SOUTH, NOW ROSE WITH GREAT VIOLENCE IN THE WEST. SUDDENLY A HEAVY STORM OF RAIN DESCENDED.
I HAD BEEN CALM DURING THE DAY; BUT AS SOON AS NIGHT OBSCURED THE SHAPES OF OBJECTS, A THOUSAND FEARS AROSE IN MY MIND. I WAS ANXIOUS AND WATCHFUL, WHILE MY RIGHT HAND GRASPED MY PISTOL.
WHAT IS IT THAT AGITATES YOU, MY DEAR VICTOR? WHAT IS IT YOU FEAR?
OH! PEACE, PEACE, MY LOVE.
THIS NIGHT, AND ALL WILL BE SAFE: BUT THIS NIGHT IS DREADFUL, VERY DREADFUL.
YOU MUST RETIRE, ELIZABETH. I WILL JOIN YOU LATER.
VICTOR...

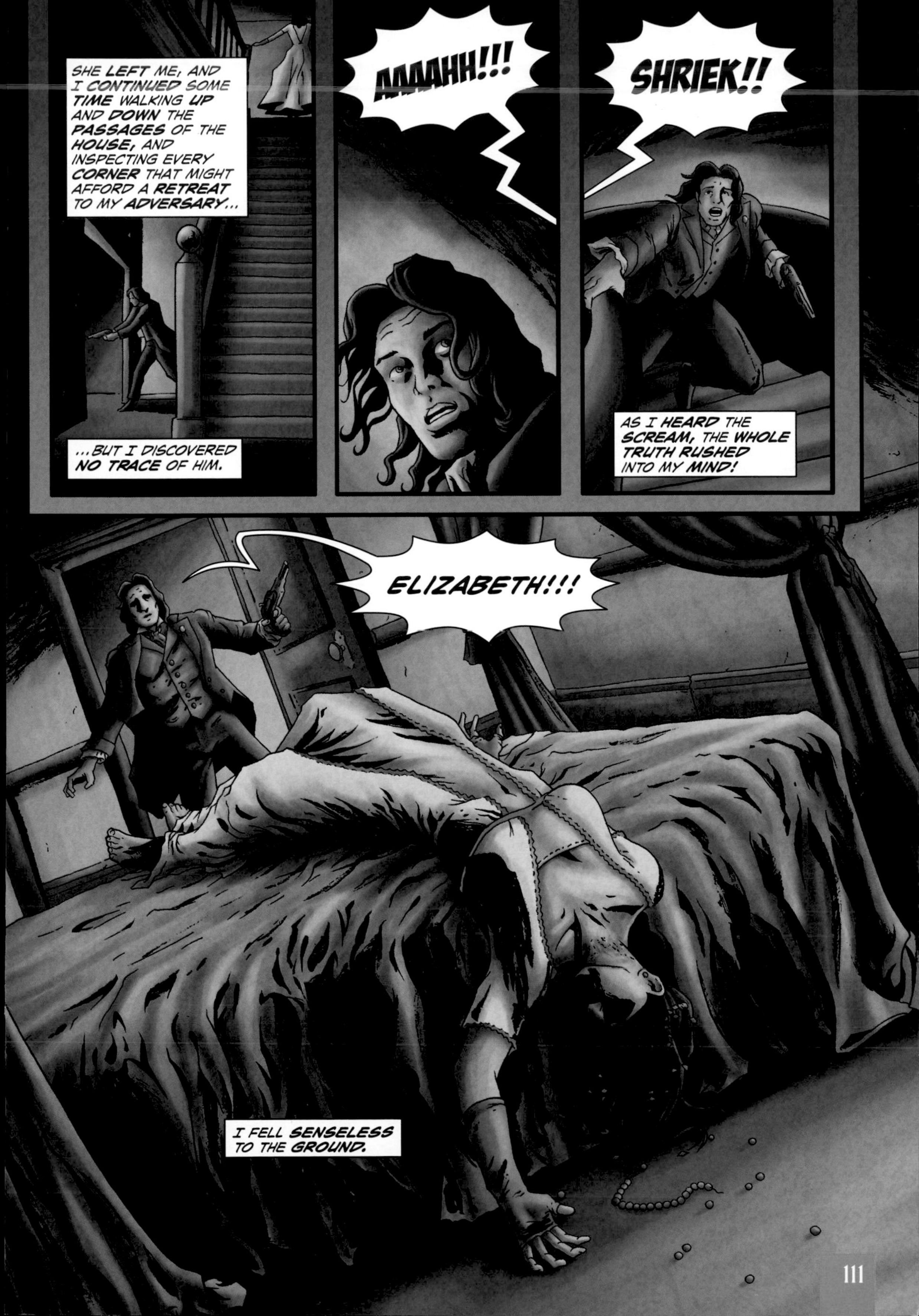
SHE LEFT ME, AND I CONTINUED SOME TIME WALKING UP AND DOWN THE PASSAGES OF THE HOUSE, AND INSPECTING EVERY CORNER THAT MIGHT AFFORD A RETREAT TO MY ADVERSARY...
...BUT I DISCOVERED NO TRACE OF HIM.
AAAAHH!!!
SHRIEK!!
AS I HEARD THE SCREAM, THE WHOLE TRUTH RUSHED INTO MY MIND!
ELIZABETH!!!
I FELL SENSELESS TO THE GROUND.

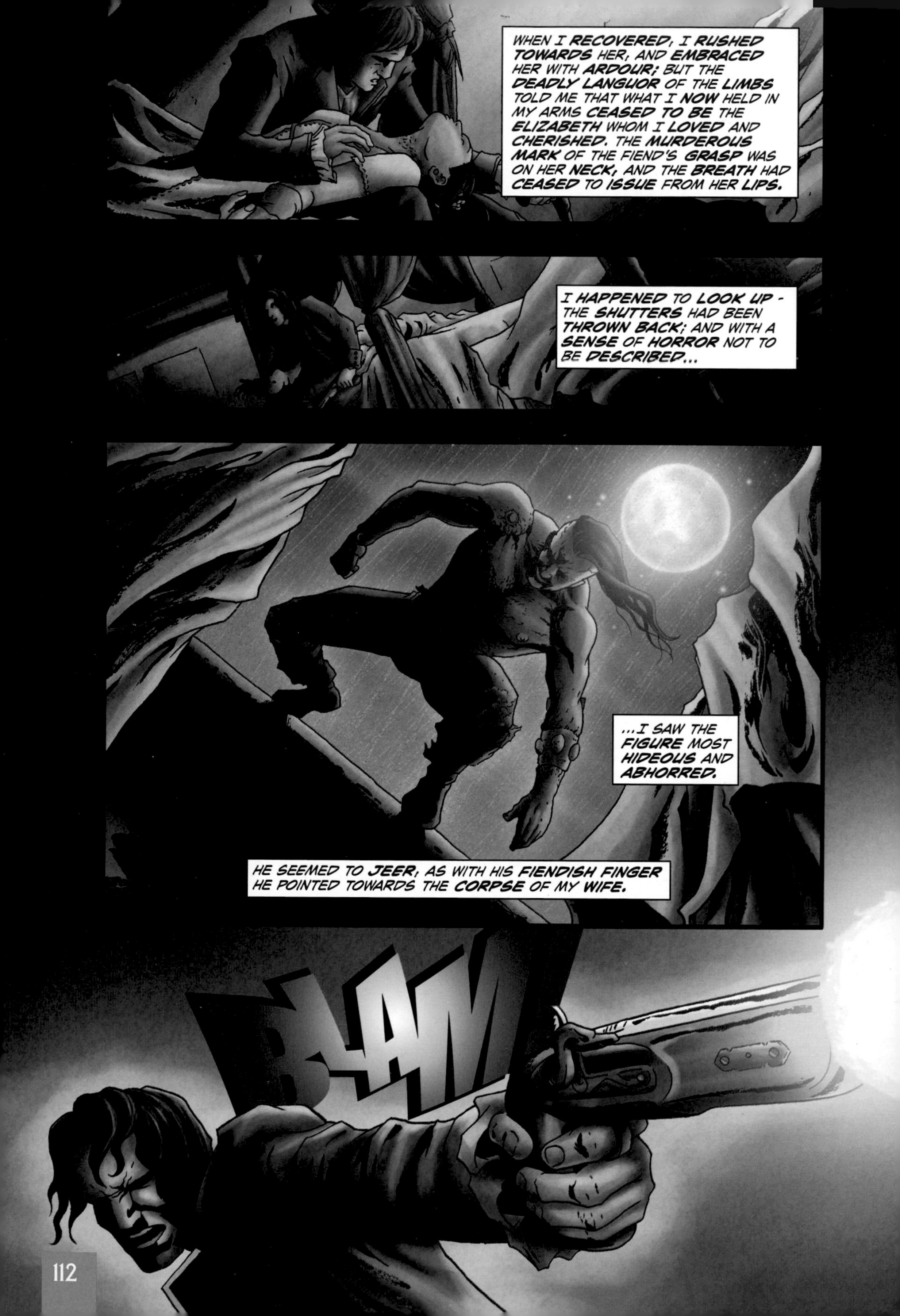
WHEN I RECOVERED, I RUSHED TOWARDS HER, AND EMBRACED HER WITH ARDOUR; BUT THE DEADLY LANGUOR OF THE LIMBS TOLD ME THAT WHAT I NOW HELD IN MY ARMS CEASED TO BE THE ELIZABETH WHOM I LOVED AND CHERISHED. THE MURDEROUS MARK OF THE FIEND'S GRASP WAS ON HER NECK, AND THE BREATH HAD CEASED TO ISSUE FROM HER LIPS.
I HAPPENED TO LOOK UP - THE SHUTTERS HAD BEEN THROWN BACK; AND WITH A SENSE OF HORROR NOT TO BE DESCRIBED...
...I SAW THE FIGURE MOST HIDEOUS AND ABHORRED.
HE SEEMED TO JEER, AS WITH HIS FIENDISH FINGER HE POINTED TOWARDS THE CORPSE OF MY WIFE.
BLAM

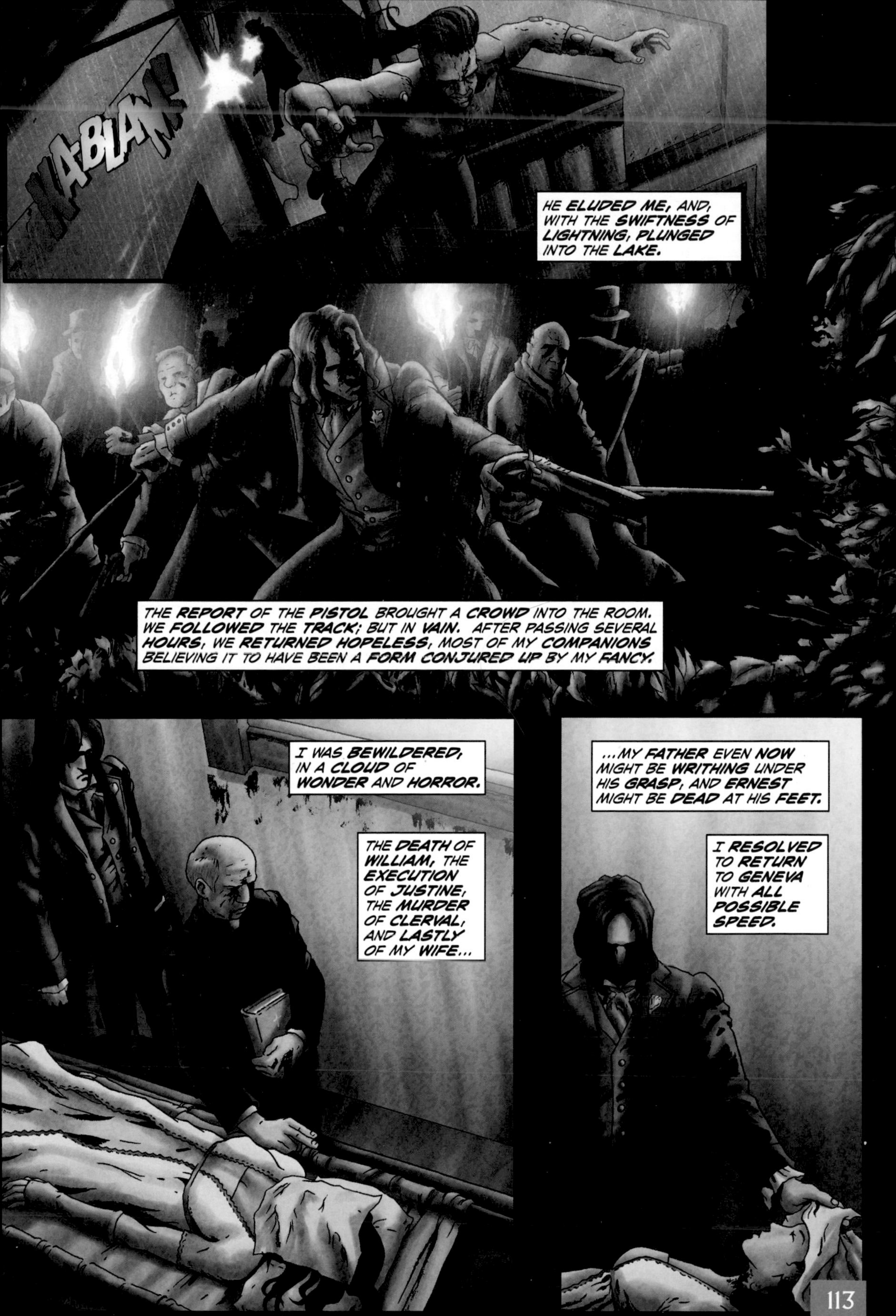
KA-BLAM!
HE ELUDED ME; AND, WITH THE SWIFTNESS OF LIGHTNING, PLUNGED INTO THE LAKE.
THE REPORT OF THE PISTOL BROUGHT A CROWD INTO THE ROOM. WE FOLLOWED THE TRACK; BUT IN VAIN. AFTER PASSING SEVERAL HOURS, WE RETURNED HOPELESS, MOST OF MY COMPANIONS BELIEVING IT TO HAVE BEEN A FORM CONJURED UP BY MY FANCY.
I WAS BEWILDERED, IN A CLOUD OF WONDER AND HORROR.
THE DEATH OF WILLIAM, THE EXECUTION OF JUSTINE, THE MURDER OF CLERVAL, AND LASTLY OF MY WIFE...
...MY FATHER EVEN NOW MIGHT BE WRITHING UNDER HIS GRASP, AND ERNEST MIGHT BE DEAD AT HIS FEET.
I RESOLVED TO RETURN TO GENEVA WITH ALL POSSIBLE SPEED.

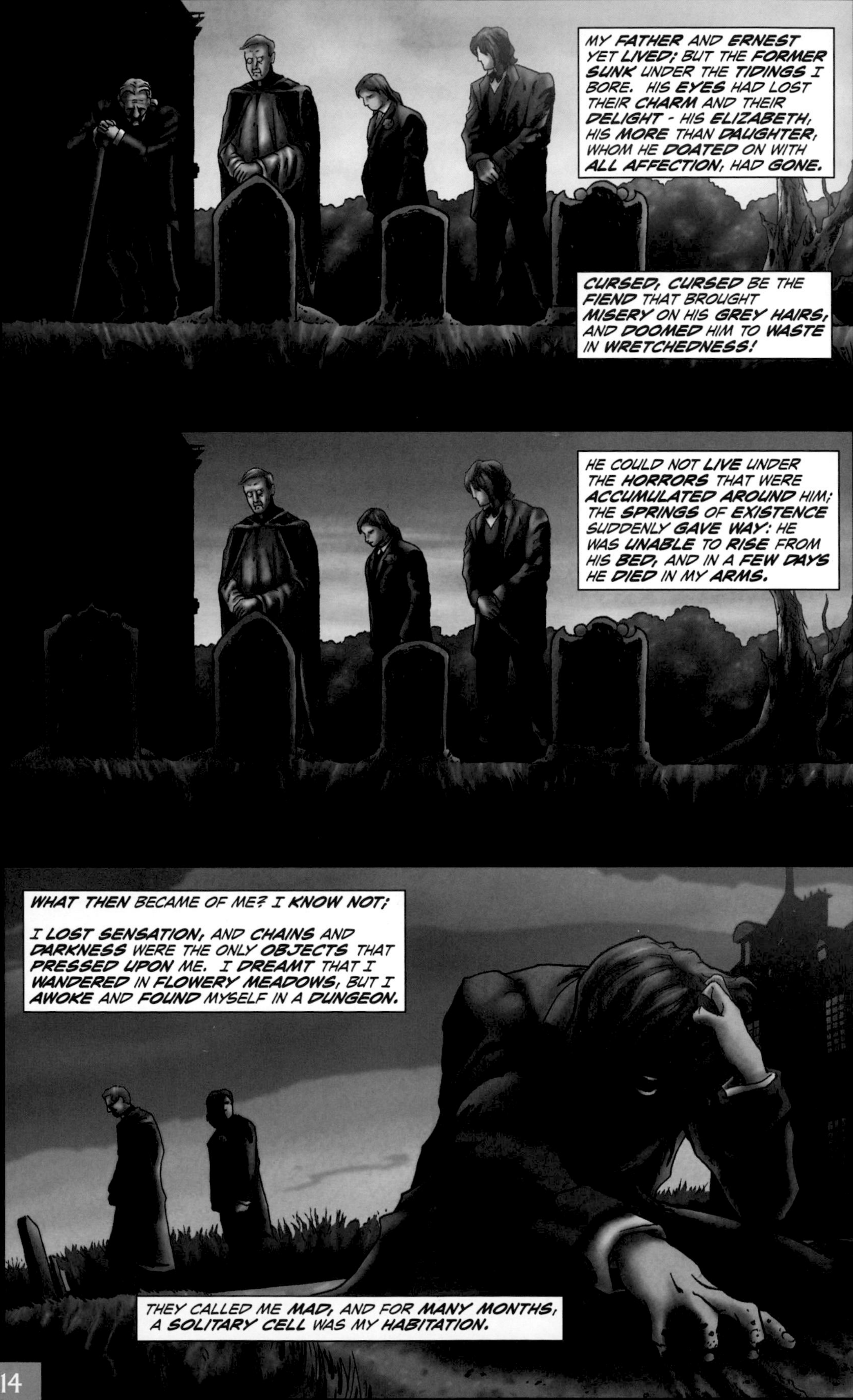
MY FATHER AND ERNEST YET LIVED; BUT THE FORMER SUNK UNDER THE TIDINGS I BORE. HIS EYES HAD LOST THEIR CHARM AND THEIR DELIGHT - HIS ELIZABETH, HIS MORE THAN DAUGHTER, WHOM HE DOATED ON WITH ALL AFFECTION, HAD GONE.
CURSED, CURSED BE THE FIEND THAT BROUGHT MISERY ON HIS GREY HAIRS, AND DOOMED HIM TO WASTE IN WRETCHEDNESS!
HE COULD NOT LIVE UNDER THE HORRORS THAT WERE ACCUMULATED AROUND HIM; THE SPRINGS OF EXISTENCE SUDDENLY GAVE WAY: HE WAS UNABLE TO RISE FROM HIS BED, AND IN A FEW DAYS HE DIED IN MY ARMS.
WHAT THEN BECAME OF ME? I KNOW NOT;
I LOST SENSATION, AND CHAINS AND DARKNESS WERE THE ONLY OBJECTS THAT PRESSED UPON ME. I DREAMT THAT I WANDERED IN FLOWERY MEADOWS, BUT I AWOKE AND FOUND MYSELF IN A DUNGEON.
THEY CALLED ME MAD, AND FOR MANY MONTHS, A SOLITARY CELL WAS MY HABITATION.

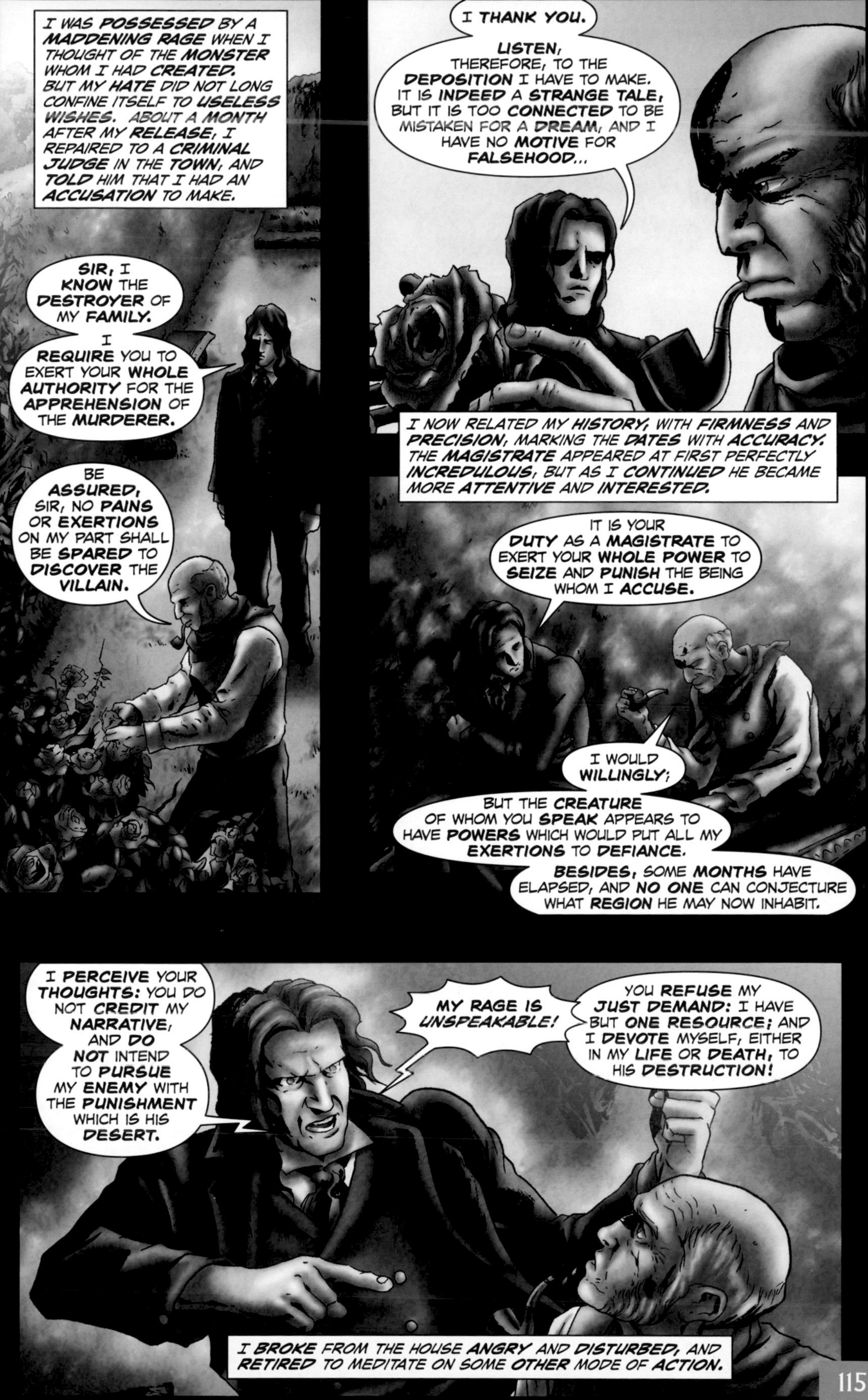
I WAS POSSESSED BY A MADDENING RAGE WHEN I THOUGHT OF THE MONSTER WHOM I HAD CREATED. BUT MY HATE DID NOT LONG CONFINE ITSELF TO USELESS WISHES. ABOUT A MONTH AFTER MY RELEASE, I REPAIRED TO A CRIMINAL JUDGE IN THE TOWN, AND TOLD HIM THAT I HAD AN ACCUSATION TO MAKE.
SIR, I KNOW THE DESTROYER OF MY FAMILY.
I REQUIRE YOU TO EXERT YOUR WHOLE AUTHORITY FOR THE APPREHENSION OF THE MURDERER.
BE ASSURED, SIR, NO PAINS OR EXERTIONS ON MY PART SHALL BE SPARED TO DISCOVER THE VILLAIN.
I THANK YOU.
LISTEN, THEREFORE, TO THE DEPOSITION I HAVE TO MAKE. IT IS INDEED A STRANGE TALE, BUT IT IS TOO CONNECTED TO BE MISTAKEN FOR A DREAM, AND I HAVE NO MOTIVE FOR FALSEHOOD...
I NOW RELATED MY HISTORY, WITH FIRMNESS AND PRECISION, MARKING THE DATES WITH ACCURACY. THE MAGISTRATE APPEARED AT FIRST PERFECTLY INCREDULOUS, BUT AS I CONTINUED HE BECAME MORE ATTENTIVE AND INTERESTED.
IT IS YOUR DUTY AS A MAGISTRATE TO EXERT YOUR WHOLE POWER TO SEIZE AND PUNISH THE BEING WHOM I ACCUSE.
I WOULD WILLINGLY;
BUT THE CREATURE OF WHOM YOU SPEAK APPEARS TO HAVE POWERS WHICH WOULD PUT ALL MY EXERTIONS TO DEFIANCE.
BESIDES, SOME MONTHS HAVE ELAPSED, AND NO ONE CAN CONJECTURE WHAT REGION HE MAY NOW INHABIT.
I PERCEIVE YOUR THOUGHTS: YOU DO NOT CREDIT MY NARRATIVE, AND DO NOT INTEND TO PURSUE MY ENEMY WITH THE PUNISHMENT WHICH IS HIS DESERT.
MY RAGE IS UNSPEAKABLE!
YOU REFUSE MY JUST DEMAND: I HAVE BUT ONE RESOURCE; AND I DEVOTE MYSELF, EITHER IN MY LIFE OR DEATH, TO HIS DESTRUCTION!
I BROKE FROM THE HOUSE ANGRY AND DISTURBED, AND RETIRED TO MEDITATE ON SOME OTHER MODE OF ACTION.

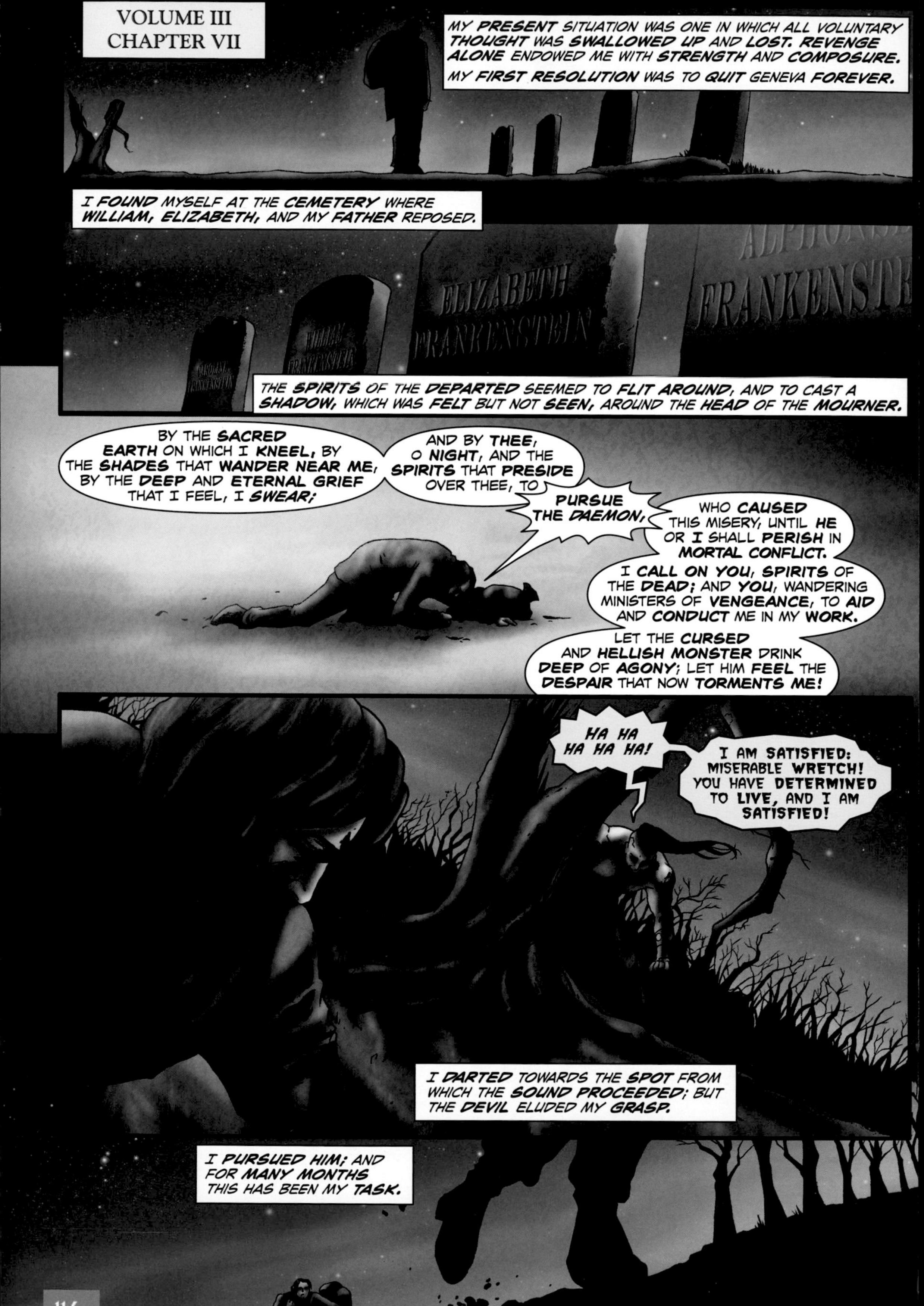
VOLUME III
CHAPTER VII
MY PRESENT SITUATION WAS ONE IN WHICH ALL VOLUNTARY THOUGHT WAS SWALLOWED UP AND LOST. REVENGE ALONE ENDOWED ME WITH STRENGTH AND COMPOSURE.
MY FIRST RESOLUTION WAS TO QUIT GENEVA FOREVER.
I FOUND MYSELF AT THE CEMETERY WHERE WILLIAM, ELIZABETH, AND MY FATHER REPOSED.
ELIZABETH FRANKENSTEIN
THE SPIRITS OF THE DEPARTED SEEMED TO FLIT AROUND, AND TO CAST A SHADOW, WHICH WAS FELT BUT NOT SEEN, AROUND THE HEAD OF THE MOURNER.
BY THE SACRED EARTH ON WHICH I KNEEL, BY THE SHADES THAT WANDER NEAR ME, BY THE DEEP AND ETERNAL GRIEF THAT I FEEL, I SWEAR;
AND BY THEE, O NIGHT, AND THE SPIRITS THAT PRESIDE OVER THEE, TO
PURSUE THE DAEMON,
WHO CAUSED THIS MISERY, UNTIL HE OR I SHALL PERISH IN MORTAL CONFLICT.
I CALL ON YOU, SPIRITS OF THE DEAD; AND YOU, WANDERING MINISTERS OF VENGEANCE, TO AID AND CONDUCT ME IN MY WORK.
LET THE CURSED AND HELLISH MONSTER DRINK DEEP OF AGONY; LET HIM FEEL THE DESPAIR THAT NOW TORMENTS ME!
HA HA HA HA HA!
I AM SATISFIED: MISERABLE WRETCH! YOU HAVE DETERMINED TO LIVE, AND I AM SATISFIED!
I DARTED TOWARDS THE SPOT FROM WHICH THE SOUND PROCEEDED; BUT THE DEVIL ELUDED MY GRASP.
I PURSUED HIM; AND FOR MANY MONTHS THIS HAS BEEN MY TASK.

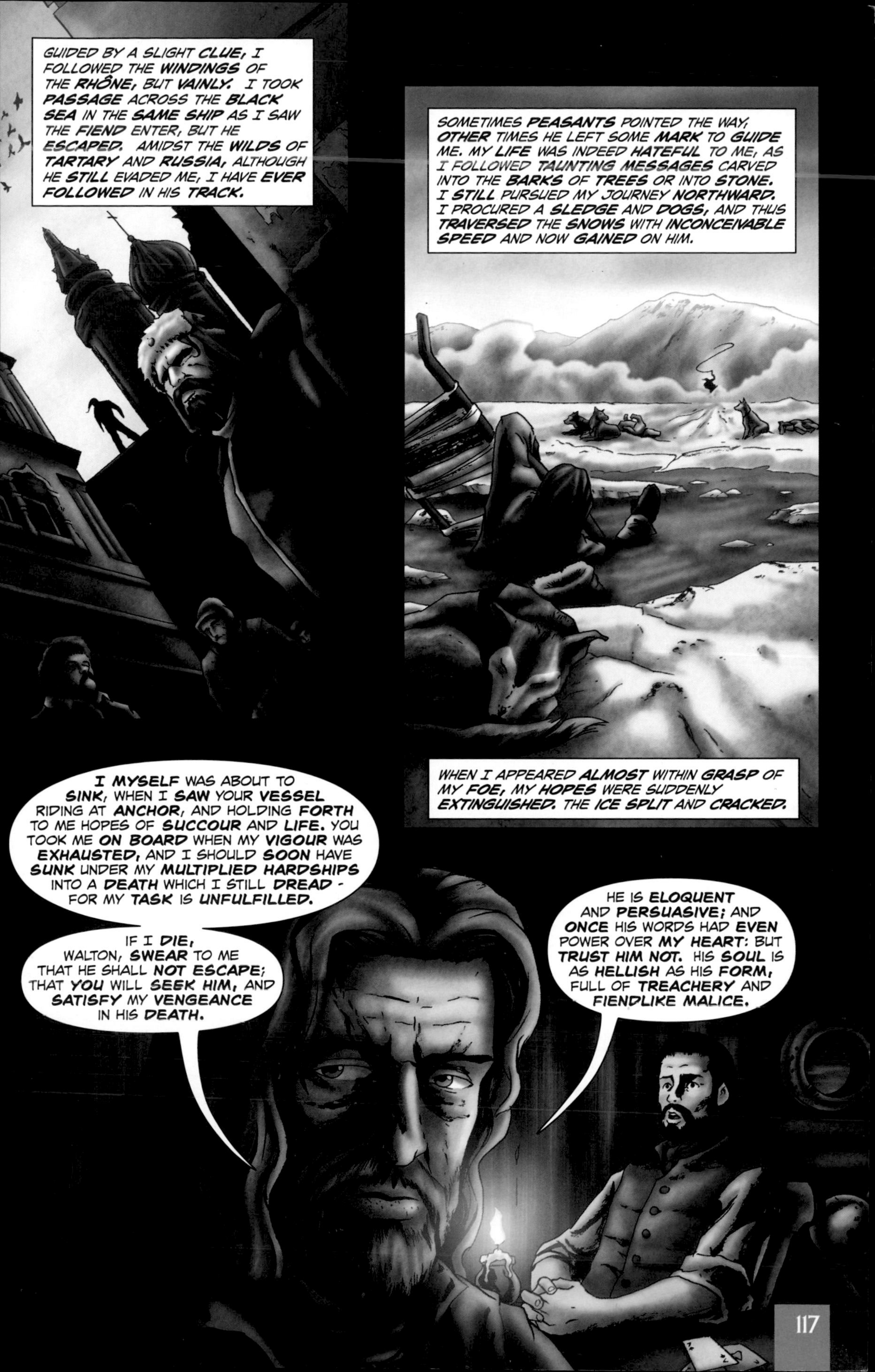
GUIDED BY A SLIGHT CLUE, I FOLLOWED THE WINDINGS OF THE RHÔNE, BUT VAINLY. I TOOK PASSAGE ACROSS THE BLACK SEA IN THE SAME SHIP AS I SAW THE FIEND ENTER, BUT HE ESCAPED. AMIDST THE WILDS OF TARTARY AND RUSSIA, ALTHOUGH HE STILL EVADED ME, I HAVE EVER FOLLOWED IN HIS TRACK.
SOMETIMES PEASANTS POINTED THE WAY, OTHER TIMES HE LEFT SOME MARK TO GUIDE ME. MY LIFE WAS INDEED HATEFUL TO ME, AS I FOLLOWED TAUNTING MESSAGES CARVED INTO THE BARKS OF TREES OR INTO STONE. I STILL PURSUED MY JOURNEY NORTHWARD. I PROCURED A SLEDGE AND DOGS, AND THUS TRAVERSED THE SNOWS WITH INCONCEIVABLE SPEED AND NOW GAINED ON HIM.
WHEN I APPEARED ALMOST WITHIN GRASP OF MY FOE, MY HOPES WERE SUDDENLY EXTINGUISHED. THE ICE SPLIT AND CRACKED.
I MYSELF WAS ABOUT TO SINK, WHEN I SAW YOUR VESSEL RIDING AT ANCHOR, AND HOLDING FORTH TO ME HOPES OF SUCCOUR AND LIFE. YOU TOOK ME ON BOARD WHEN MY VIGOUR WAS EXHAUSTED, AND I SHOULD SOON HAVE SUNK UNDER MY MULTIPLIED HARDSHIPS INTO A DEATH WHICH I STILL DREAD - FOR MY TASK IS UNFULFILLED.
IF I DIE, WALTON, SWEAR TO ME THAT HE SHALL NOT ESCAPE; THAT YOU WILL SEEK HIM, AND SATISFY MY VENGEANCE IN HIS DEATH.
HE IS ELOQUENT AND PERSUASIVE; AND ONCE HIS WORDS HAD EVEN POWER OVER MY HEART: BUT TRUST HIM NOT. HIS SOUL IS AS HELLISH AS HIS FORM, FULL OF TREACHERY AND FIENDLIKE MALICE.

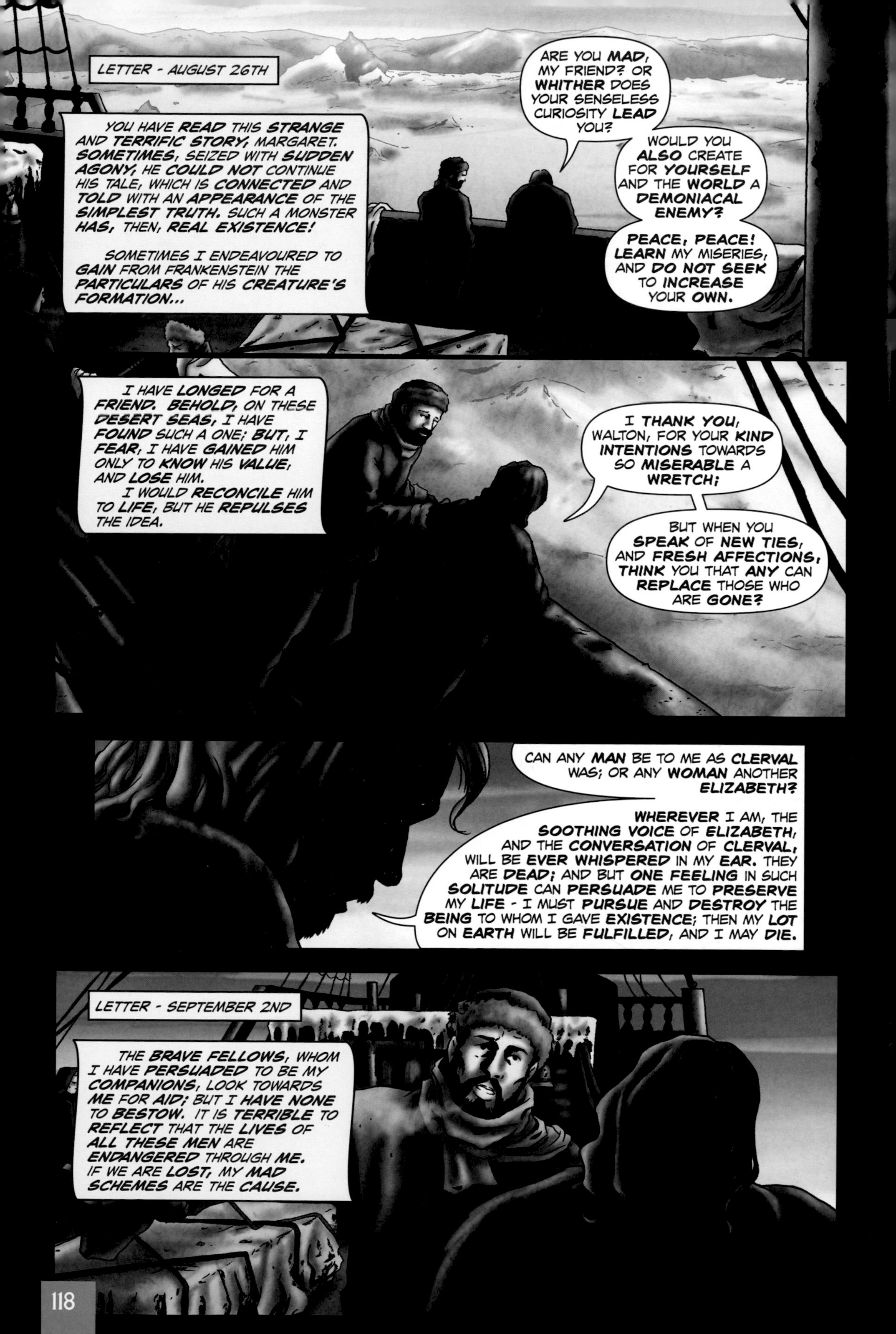
LETTER - AUGUST 26TH
YOU HAVE READ THIS STRANGE AND TERRIFIC STORY, MARGARET. SOMETIMES, SEIZED WITH SUDDEN AGONY, HE COULD NOT CONTINUE HIS TALE, WHICH IS CONNECTED AND TOLD WITH AN APPEARANCE OF THE SIMPLEST TRUTH. SUCH A MONSTER HAS, THEN, REAL EXISTENCE!
SOMETIMES I ENDEAVOURED TO GAIN FROM FRANKENSTEIN THE PARTICULARS OF HIS CREATURE'S FORMATION...
ARE YOU MAD, MY FRIEND? OR WHITHER DOES YOUR SENSELESS CURIOSITY LEAD YOU?
WOULD YOU ALSO CREATE FOR YOURSELF AND THE WORLD A DEMONIACAL ENEMY?
PEACE, PEACE! LEARN MY MISERIES, AND DO NOT SEEK TO INCREASE YOUR OWN.
I HAVE LONGED FOR A FRIEND. BEHOLD, ON THESE DESERT SEAS, I HAVE FOUND SUCH A ONE; BUT, I FEAR, I HAVE GAINED HIM ONLY TO KNOW HIS VALUE, AND LOSE HIM.
I WOULD RECONCILE HIM TO LIFE, BUT HE REPULSES THE IDEA.
I THANK YOU, WALTON, FOR YOUR KIND INTENTIONS TOWARDS SO MISERABLE A WRETCH;
BUT WHEN YOU SPEAK OF NEW TIES, AND FRESH AFFECTIONS, THINK YOU THAT ANY CAN REPLACE THOSE WHO ARE GONE?
CAN ANY MAN BE TO ME AS CLERVAL WAS; OR ANY WOMAN ANOTHER ELIZABETH?
WHEREVER I AM, THE SOOTHING VOICE OF ELIZABETH, AND THE CONVERSATION OF CLERVAL, WILL BE EVER WHISPERED IN MY EAR. THEY ARE DEAD; AND BUT ONE FEELING IN SUCH SOLITUDE CAN PERSUADE ME TO PRESERVE MY LIFE - I MUST PURSUE AND DESTROY THE BEING TO WHOM I GAVE EXISTENCE; THEN MY LOT ON EARTH WILL BE FULFILLED, AND I MAY DIE.
LETTER - SEPTEMBER 2ND
THE BRAVE FELLOWS, WHOM I HAVE PERSUADED TO BE MY COMPANIONS, LOOK TOWARDS ME FOR AID; BUT I HAVE NONE TO BESTOW. IT IS TERRIBLE TO REFLECT THAT THE LIVES OF ALL THESE MEN ARE ENDANGERED THROUGH ME. IF WE ARE LOST, MY MAD SCHEMES ARE THE CAUSE.

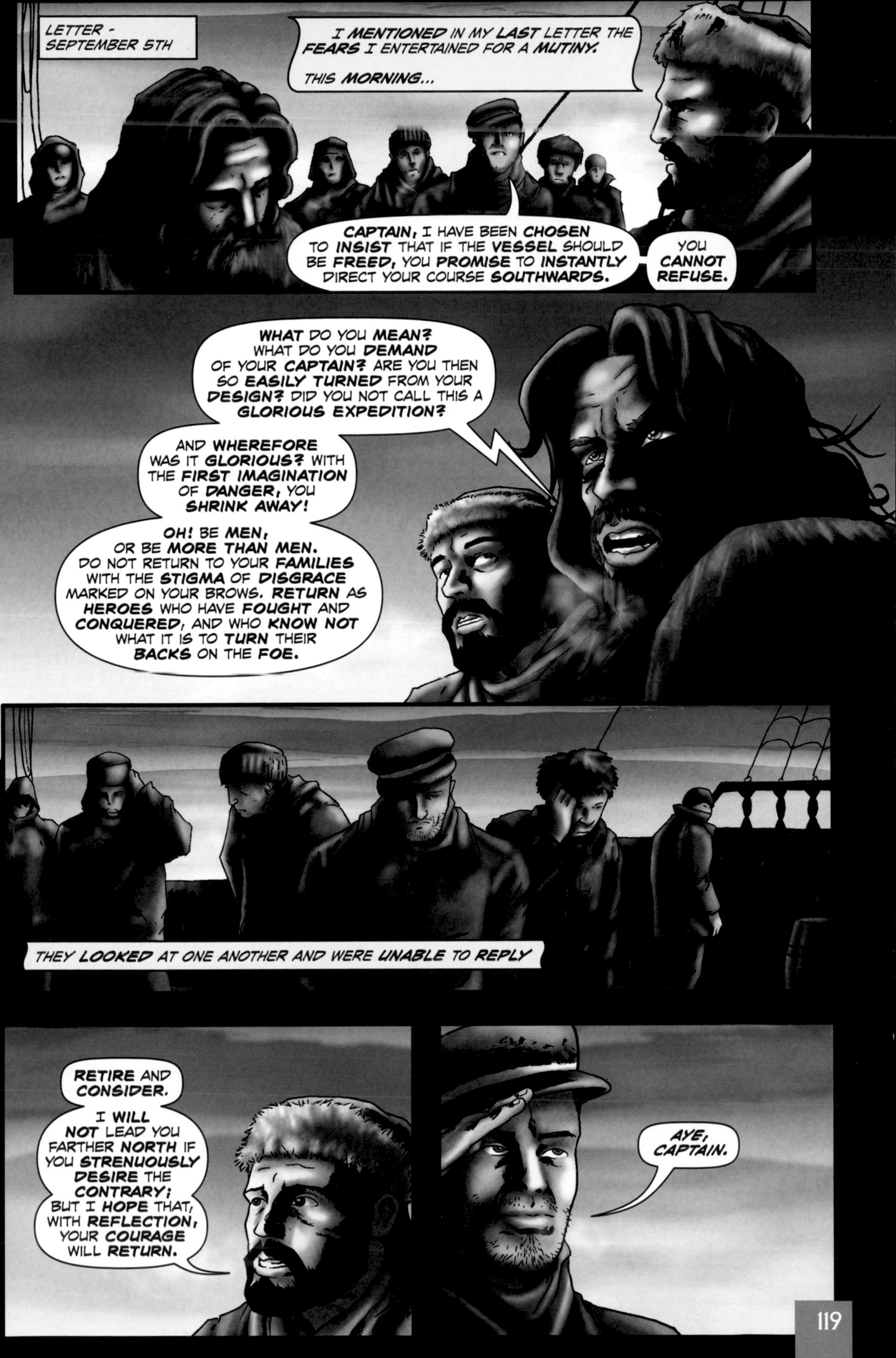
LETTER - SEPTEMBER 5TH
I MENTIONED IN MY LAST LETTER THE FEARS I ENTERTAINED FOR A MUTINY.
THIS MORNING...
CAPTAIN, I HAVE BEEN CHOSEN TO INSIST THAT IF THE VESSEL SHOULD BE FREED, YOU PROMISE TO INSTANTLY DIRECT YOUR COURSE SOUTHWARDS.
YOU CANNOT REFUSE.
WHAT DO YOU MEAN? WHAT DO YOU DEMAND OF YOUR CAPTAIN? ARE YOU THEN SO EASILY TURNED FROM YOUR DESIGN? DID YOU NOT CALL THIS A GLORIOUS EXPEDITION?
AND WHEREFORE WAS IT GLORIOUS? WITH THE FIRST IMAGINATION OF DANGER, YOU SHRINK AWAY!
OH! BE MEN, OR BE MORE THAN MEN. DO NOT RETURN TO YOUR FAMILIES WITH THE STIGMA OF DISGRACE MARKED ON YOUR BROWS. RETURN AS HEROES WHO HAVE FOUGHT AND CONQUERED, AND WHO KNOW NOT WHAT IT IS TO TURN THEIR BACKS ON THE FOE.
THEY LOOKED AT ONE ANOTHER AND WERE UNABLE TO REPLY
RETIRE AND CONSIDER.
I WILL NOT LEAD YOU FARTHER NORTH IF YOU STRENUOUSLY DESIRE THE CONTRARY; BUT I HOPE THAT, WITH REFLECTION, YOUR COURAGE WILL RETURN.
AYE, CAPTAIN.

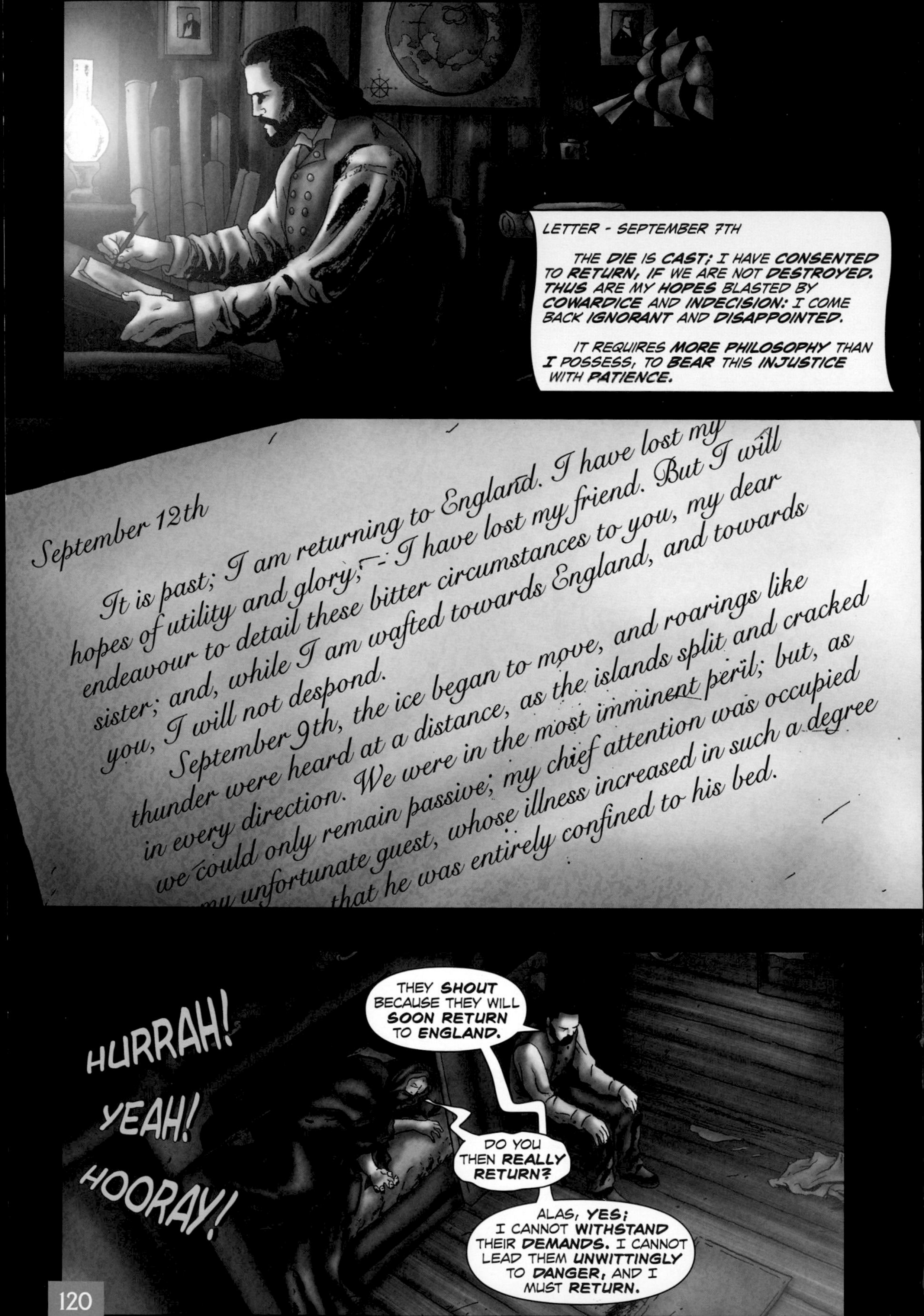
LETTER - SEPTEMBER 7TH
THE DIE IS CAST; I HAVE CONSENTED TO RETURN, IF WE ARE NOT DESTROYED. THUS ARE MY HOPES BLASTED BY COWARDICE AND INDECISION: I COME BACK IGNORANT AND DISAPPOINTED.
IT REQUIRES MORE PHILOSOPHY THAN I POSSESS, TO BEAR THIS INJUSTICE WITH PATIENCE.
September 12th
It is past; I am returning to England. I have lost my hopes of utility and glory; - I have lost my friend. But I will endeavour to detail these bitter circumstances to you, my dear sister; and, while I am wafted towards England, and towards you, I will not despond.
September 9th, the ice began to move, and roarings like thunder were heard at a distance, as the islands split and cracked in every direction. We were in the most imminent peril; but, as we could only remain passive, my chief attention was occupied unfortunate guest, whose illness increased in such a degree that he was entirely confined to his bed.
THEY SHOUT BECAUSE THEY WILL SOON RETURN TO ENGLAND.
HURRAH!
YEAH!
HOORAY!
DO YOU THEN REALLY RETURN?
ALAS, YES; I CANNOT WITHSTAND THEIR DEMANDS. I CANNOT LEAD THEM UNWITTINGLY TO DANGER, AND I MUST RETURN.

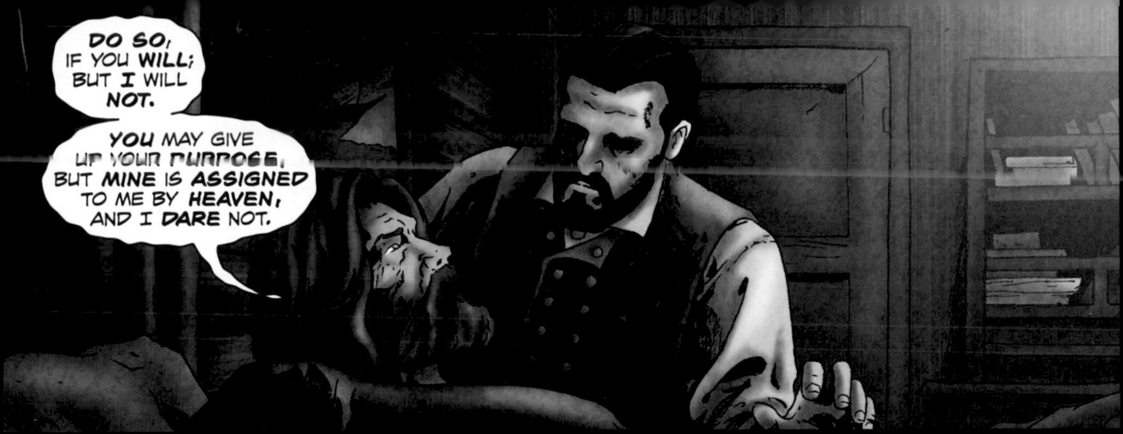
DO SO, IF YOU WILL; BUT I WILL NOT.
YOU MAY GIVE UP YOUR PURPOSE, BUT MINE IS ASSIGNED TO ME BY HEAVEN, AND I DARE NOT.

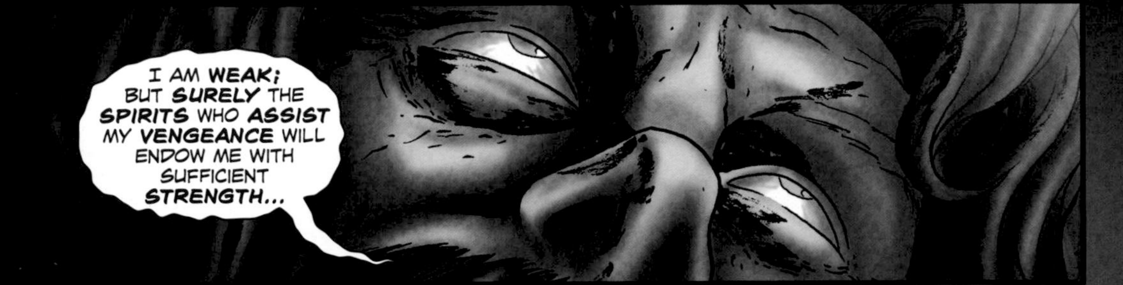
I AM WEAK; BUT SURELY THE SPIRITS WHO ASSIST MY VENGEANCE WILL ENDOW ME WITH SUFFICIENT STRENGTH...

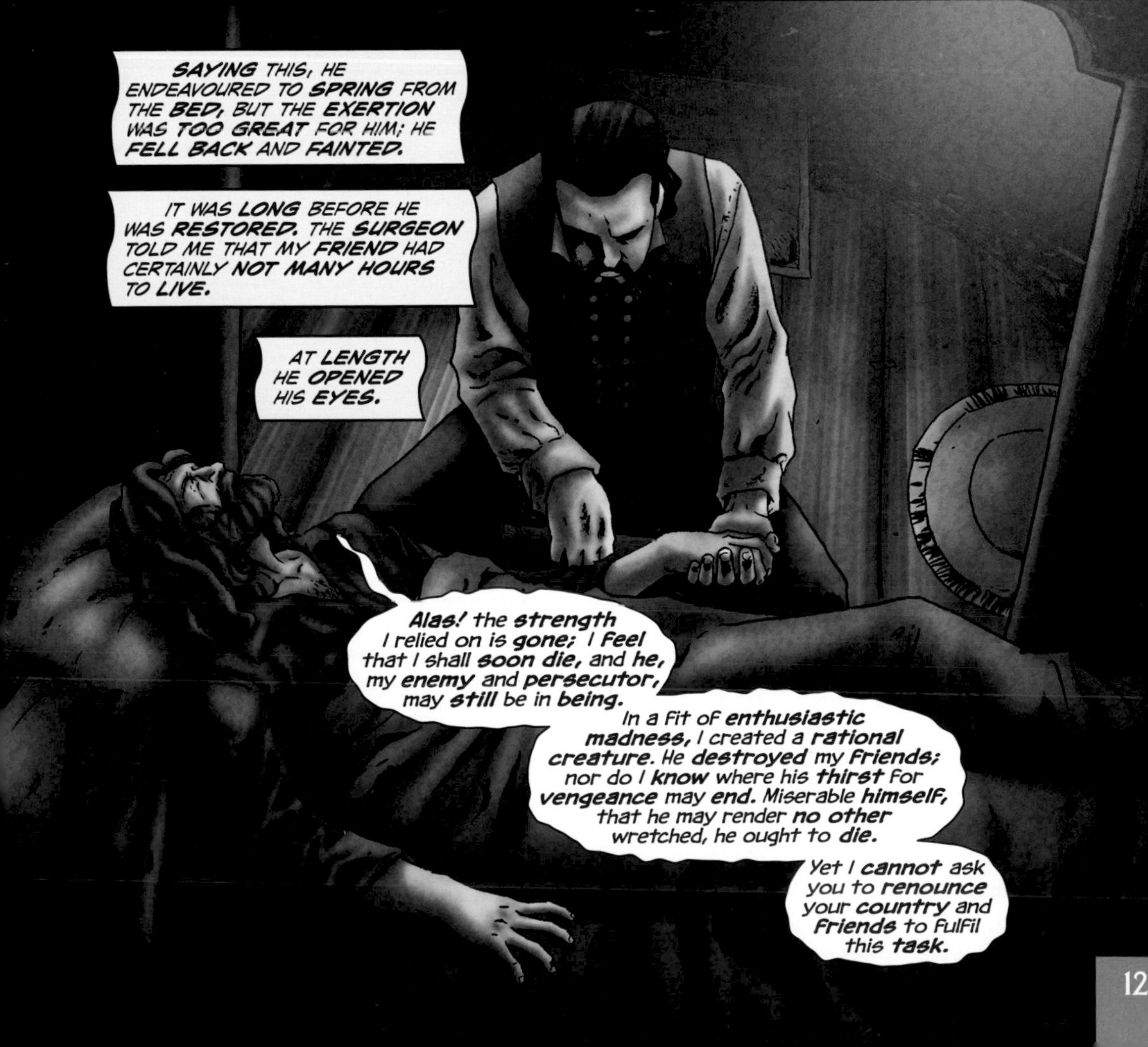
SAYING THIS, HE ENDEAVOURED TO SPRING FROM THE BED, BUT THE EXERTION WAS TOO GREAT FOR HIM; HE FELL BACK AND FAINTED.
IT WAS LONG BEFORE HE WAS RESTORED. THE SURGEON TOLD ME THAT MY FRIEND HAD CERTAINLY NOT MANY HOURS TO LIVE.
AT LENGTH HE OPENED HIS EYES.
Alas! the strength I relied on is gone; I feel that I shall soon die, and he, my enemy and persecutor, may still be in being.
In a fit of enthusiastic madness, I created a rational creature. He destroyed my friends; nor do I know where his thirst for vengeance may end. Miserable himself, that he may render no other wretched, he ought to die.
Yet I cannot ask you to renounce your country and friends to fulfil this task.

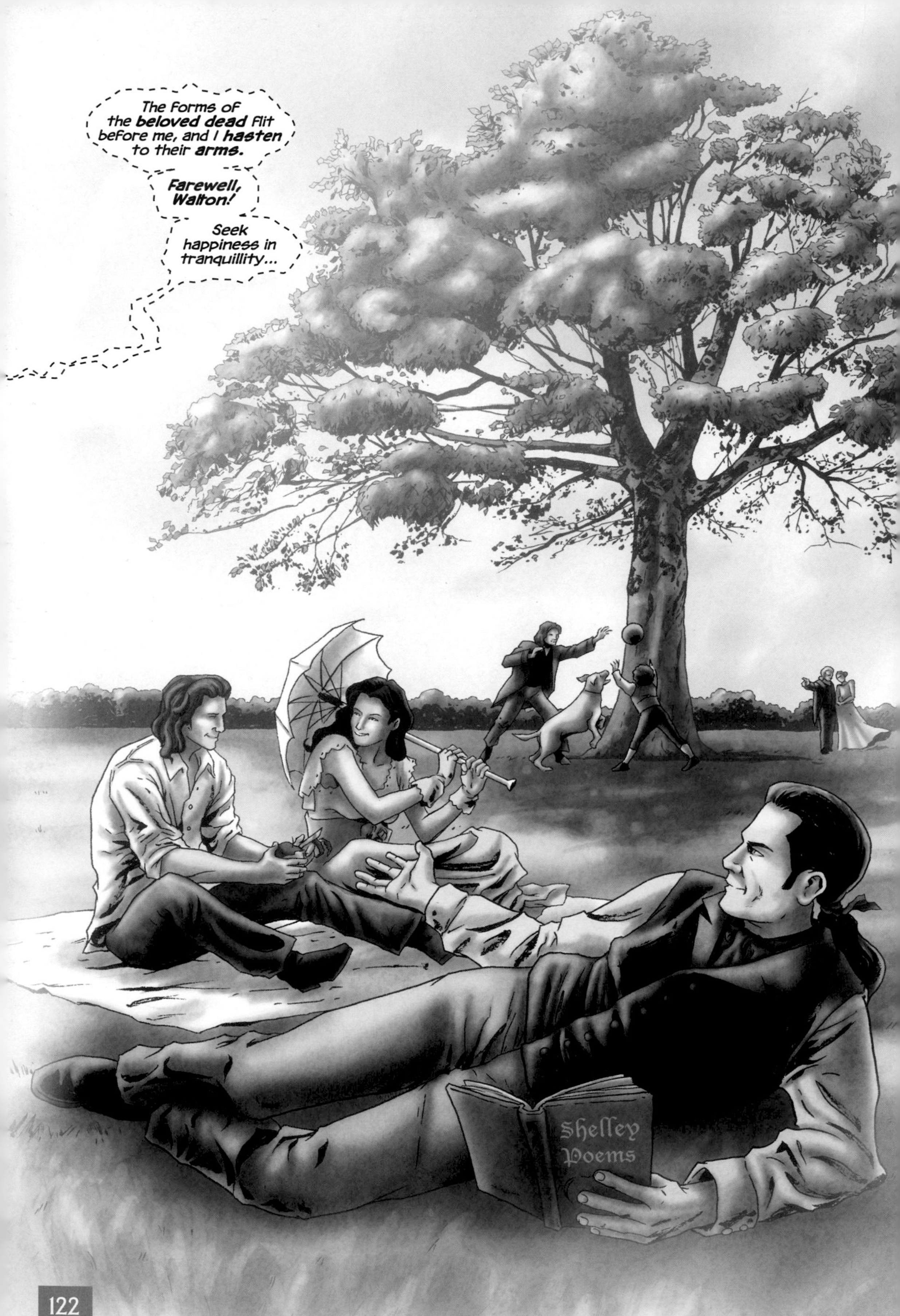
The forms of the **beloved dead** flit before me, and I **hasten** to their **arms.**
Farewell, Walton!
Seek happiness in tranquillity...
Shelley Poems

HE PRESSED MY HAND FEEBLY, AND HIS EYES CLOSED FOREVER, WHILE THE IRRADIATION OF A GENTLE SMILE PASSED AWAY FROM HIS LIPS.

MARGARET, WHAT COMMENT CAN I MAKE ON THE UNTIMELY EXTINCTION OF THIS GLORIOUS SPIRIT? MY TEARS FLOW; MY MIND IS OVERSHADOWED BY A CLOUD OF DISAPPOINTMENT.

THAT NOISE...

...A VOICE...

...FROM FRANKENSTEIN'S CABIN!

GREAT GOD!

WHEN HE HEARD THE SOUND OF MY APPROACH, HE SPRUNG TOWARDS THE WINDOW.

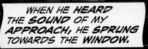

STAY!

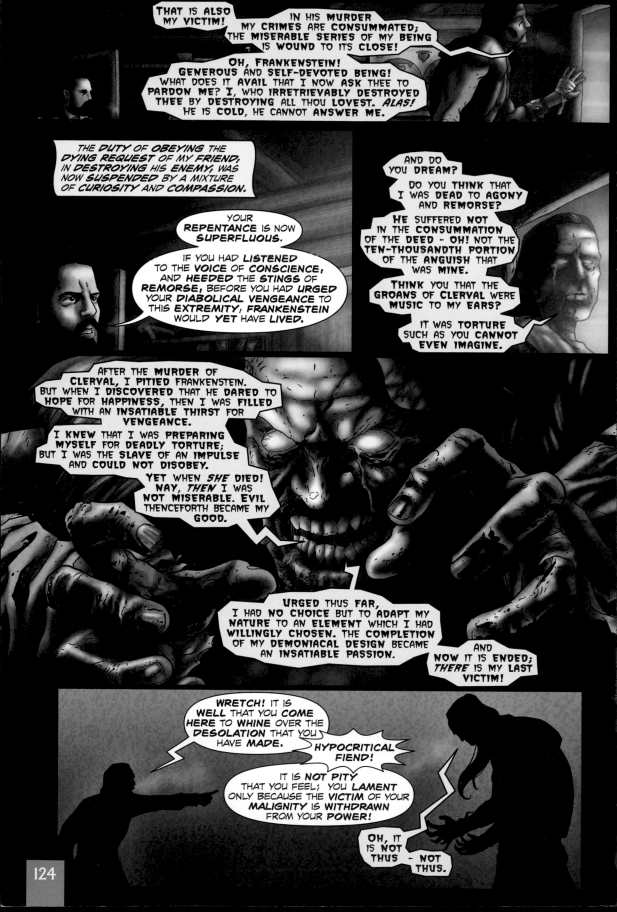

THAT IS ALSO MY VICTIM! IN HIS MURDER MY CRIMES ARE CONSUMMATED; THE MISERABLE SERIES OF MY BEING IS WOUND TO ITS CLOSE!

OH, FRANKENSTEIN! GENEROUS AND SELF-DEVOTED BEING! WHAT DOES IT AVAIL THAT I NOW ASK THEE TO PARDON ME? I, WHO IRRETRIEVABLY DESTROYED THEE BY DESTROYING ALL THOU LOVEST. ALAS! HE IS COLD, HE CANNOT ANSWER ME.

THE DUTY OF OBEYING THE DYING REQUEST OF MY FRIEND, IN DESTROYING HIS ENEMY, WAS NOW SUSPENDED BY A MIXTURE OF CURIOSITY AND COMPASSION.

YOUR REPENTANCE IS NOW SUPERFLUOUS.

IF YOU HAD LISTENED TO THE VOICE OF CONSCIENCE, AND HEEDED THE STINGS OF REMORSE, BEFORE YOU HAD URGED YOUR DIABOLICAL VENGEANCE TO THIS EXTREMITY, FRANKENSTEIN WOULD YET HAVE LIVED.

AND DO YOU DREAM?

DO YOU THINK THAT I WAS DEAD TO AGONY AND REMORSE?

HE SUFFERED NOT IN THE CONSUMMATION OF THE DEED - OH! NOT THE TEN-THOUSANDTH PORTION OF THE ANGUISH THAT WAS MINE.

THINK YOU THAT THE GROANS OF CLERVAL WERE MUSIC TO MY EARS?

IT WAS TORTURE SUCH AS YOU CANNOT EVEN IMAGINE.

AFTER THE MURDER OF CLERVAL, I PITIED FRANKENSTEIN. BUT WHEN I DISCOVERED THAT HE DARED TO HOPE FOR HAPPINESS, THEN I WAS FILLED WITH AN INSATIABLE THIRST FOR VENGEANCE.

I KNEW THAT I WAS PREPARING MYSELF FOR DEADLY TORTURE; BUT I WAS THE SLAVE OF AN IMPULSE AND COULD NOT DISOBEY.

YET WHEN SHE DIED! NAY, THEN I WAS NOT MISERABLE. EVIL THENCEFORTH BECAME MY GOOD.

URGED THUS FAR, I HAD NO CHOICE BUT TO ADAPT MY NATURE TO AN ELEMENT WHICH I HAD WILLINGLY CHOSEN. THE COMPLETION OF MY DEMONIACAL DESIGN BECAME AN INSATIABLE PASSION.

AND NOW IT IS ENDED; THERE IS MY LAST VICTIM!

WRETCH! IT IS WELL THAT YOU COME HERE TO WHINE OVER THE DESOLATION THAT YOU HAVE MADE.

HYPOCRITICAL FIEND!

IT IS NOT PITY THAT YOU FEEL; YOU LAMENT ONLY BECAUSE THE VICTIM OF YOUR MALIGNITY IS WITHDRAWN FROM YOUR POWER!

OH, IT IS NOT THUS - NOT THUS.

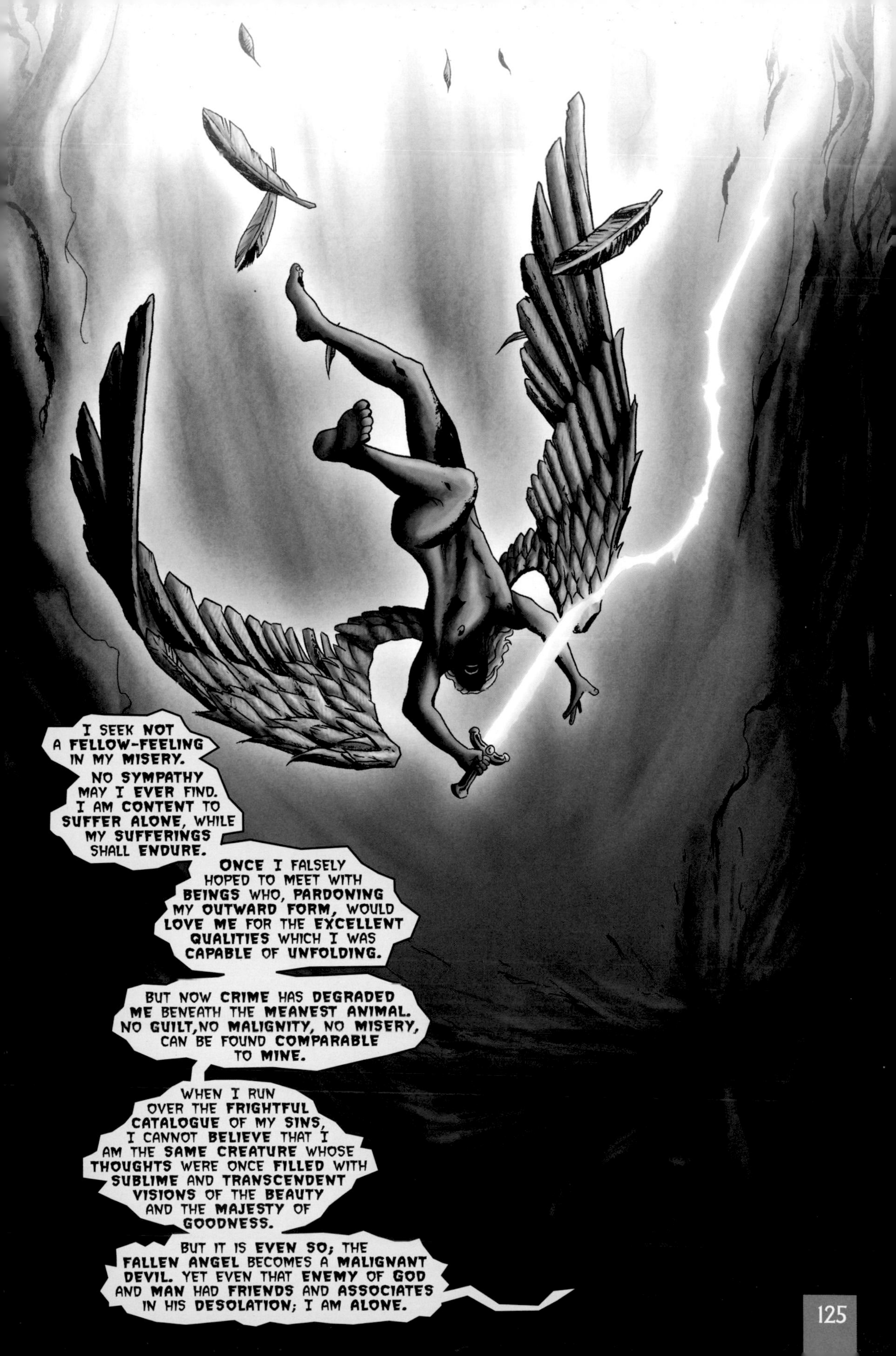

I SEEK NOT A FELLOW-FEELING IN MY MISERY.
NO SYMPATHY MAY I EVER FIND. I AM CONTENT TO SUFFER ALONE, WHILE MY SUFFERINGS SHALL ENDURE.
ONCE I FALSELY HOPED TO MEET WITH BEINGS WHO, PARDONING MY OUTWARD FORM, WOULD LOVE ME FOR THE EXCELLENT QUALITIES WHICH I WAS CAPABLE OF UNFOLDING.
BUT NOW CRIME HAS DEGRADED ME BENEATH THE MEANEST ANIMAL. NO GUILT,NO MALIGNITY, NO MISERY, CAN BE FOUND COMPARABLE TO MINE.
WHEN I RUN OVER THE FRIGHTFUL CATALOGUE OF MY SINS, I CANNOT BELIEVE THAT I AM THE SAME CREATURE WHOSE THOUGHTS WERE ONCE FILLED WITH SUBLIME AND TRANSCENDENT VISIONS OF THE BEAUTY AND THE MAJESTY OF GOODNESS.
BUT IT IS EVEN SO; THE FALLEN ANGEL BECOMES A MALIGNANT DEVIL. YET EVEN THAT ENEMY OF GOD AND MAN HAD FRIENDS AND ASSOCIATES IN HIS DESOLATION; I AM ALONE.

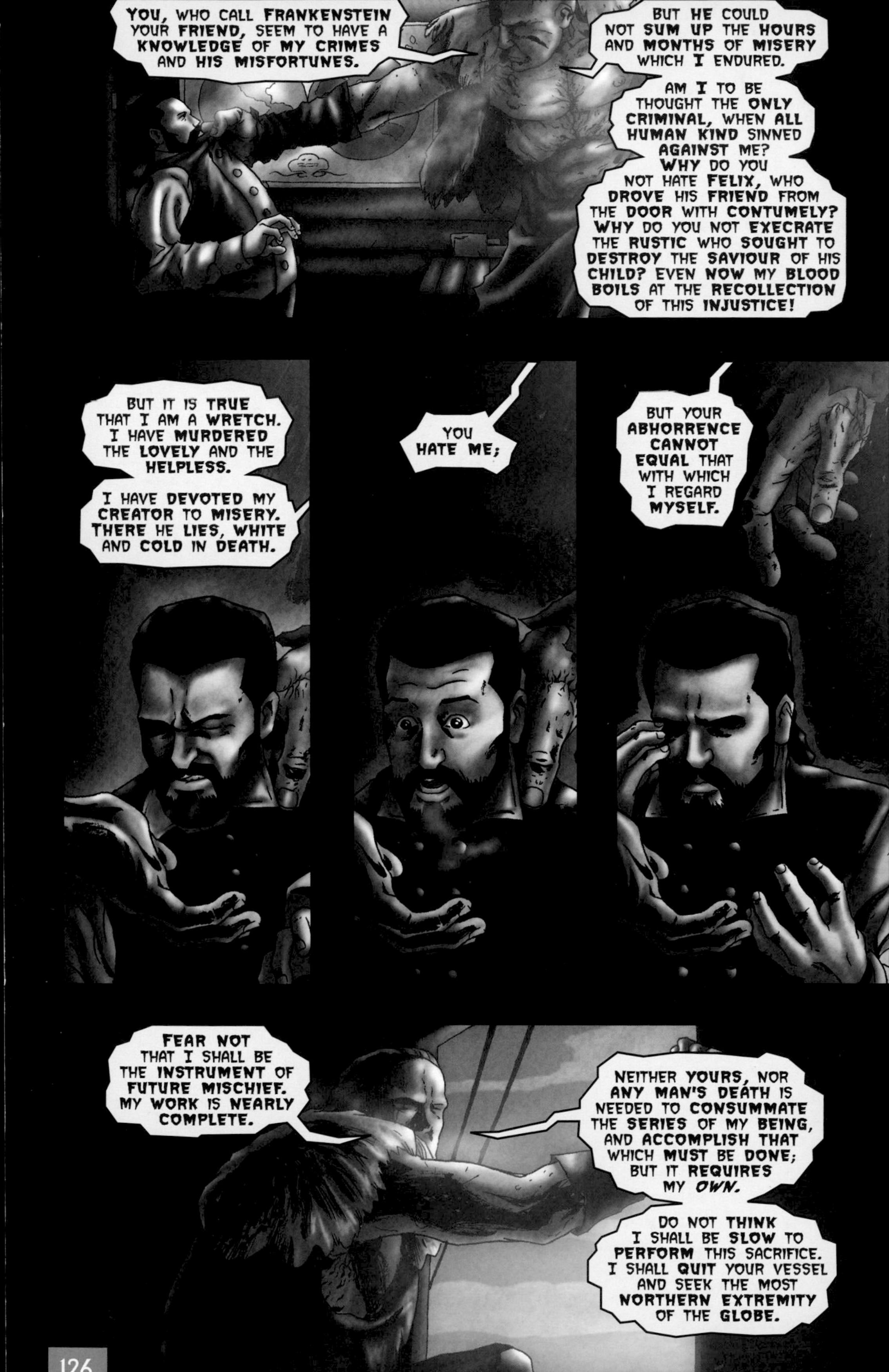
YOU, WHO CALL FRANKENSTEIN YOUR FRIEND, SEEM TO HAVE A KNOWLEDGE OF MY CRIMES AND HIS MISFORTUNES.
BUT HE COULD NOT SUM UP THE HOURS AND MONTHS OF MISERY WHICH I ENDURED.
AM I TO BE THOUGHT THE ONLY CRIMINAL, WHEN ALL HUMAN KIND SINNED AGAINST ME? WHY DO YOU NOT HATE FELIX, WHO DROVE HIS FRIEND FROM THE DOOR WITH CONTUMELY? WHY DO YOU NOT EXECRATE THE RUSTIC WHO SOUGHT TO DESTROY THE SAVIOUR OF HIS CHILD? EVEN NOW MY BLOOD BOILS AT THE RECOLLECTION OF THIS INJUSTICE!
BUT IT IS TRUE THAT I AM A WRETCH. I HAVE MURDERED THE LOVELY AND THE HELPLESS.
I HAVE DEVOTED MY CREATOR TO MISERY. THERE HE LIES, WHITE AND COLD IN DEATH.
YOU HATE ME;
BUT YOUR ABHORRENCE CANNOT EQUAL THAT WITH WHICH I REGARD MYSELF.
FEAR NOT THAT I SHALL BE THE INSTRUMENT OF FUTURE MISCHIEF. MY WORK IS NEARLY COMPLETE.
NEITHER YOURS, NOR ANY MAN'S DEATH IS NEEDED TO CONSUMMATE THE SERIES OF MY BEING, AND ACCOMPLISH THAT WHICH MUST BE DONE; BUT IT REQUIRES MY *OWN.*
DO NOT THINK I SHALL BE SLOW TO PERFORM THIS SACRIFICE. I SHALL QUIT YOUR VESSEL AND SEEK THE MOST NORTHERN EXTREMITY OF THE GLOBE.

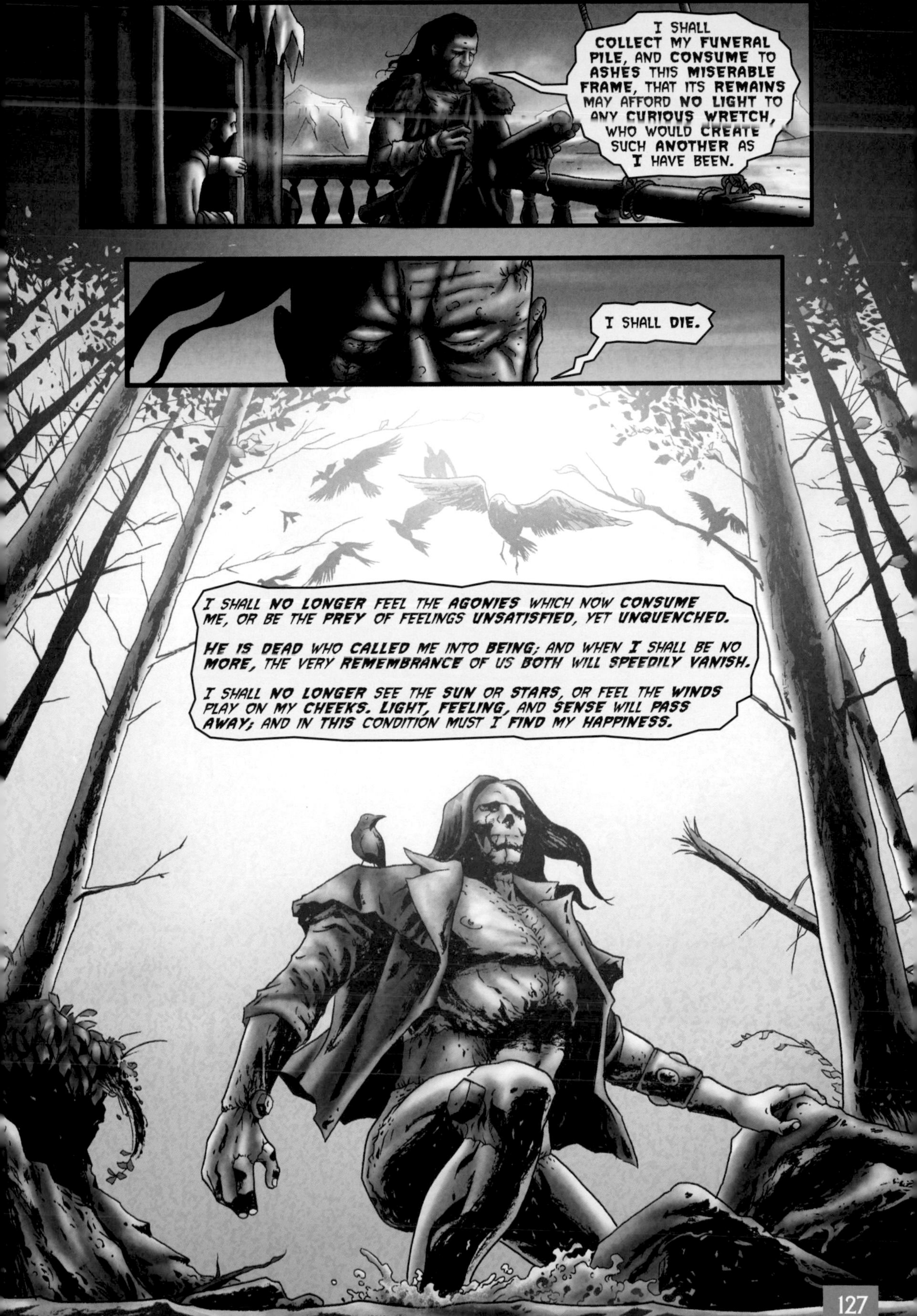
I SHALL COLLECT MY FUNERAL PILE, AND CONSUME TO ASHES THIS MISERABLE FRAME, THAT ITS REMAINS MAY AFFORD NO LIGHT TO ANY CURIOUS WRETCH, WHO WOULD CREATE SUCH ANOTHER AS I HAVE BEEN.
I SHALL DIE.
I SHALL NO LONGER FEEL THE AGONIES WHICH NOW CONSUME ME, OR BE THE PREY OF FEELINGS UNSATISFIED, YET UNQUENCHED.
HE IS DEAD WHO CALLED ME INTO BEING; AND WHEN I SHALL BE NO MORE, THE VERY REMEMBRANCE OF US BOTH WILL SPEEDILY VANISH.
I SHALL NO LONGER SEE THE SUN OR STARS, OR FEEL THE WINDS PLAY ON MY CHEEKS. LIGHT, FEELING, AND SENSE WILL PASS AWAY; AND IN THIS CONDITION MUST I FIND MY HAPPINESS.

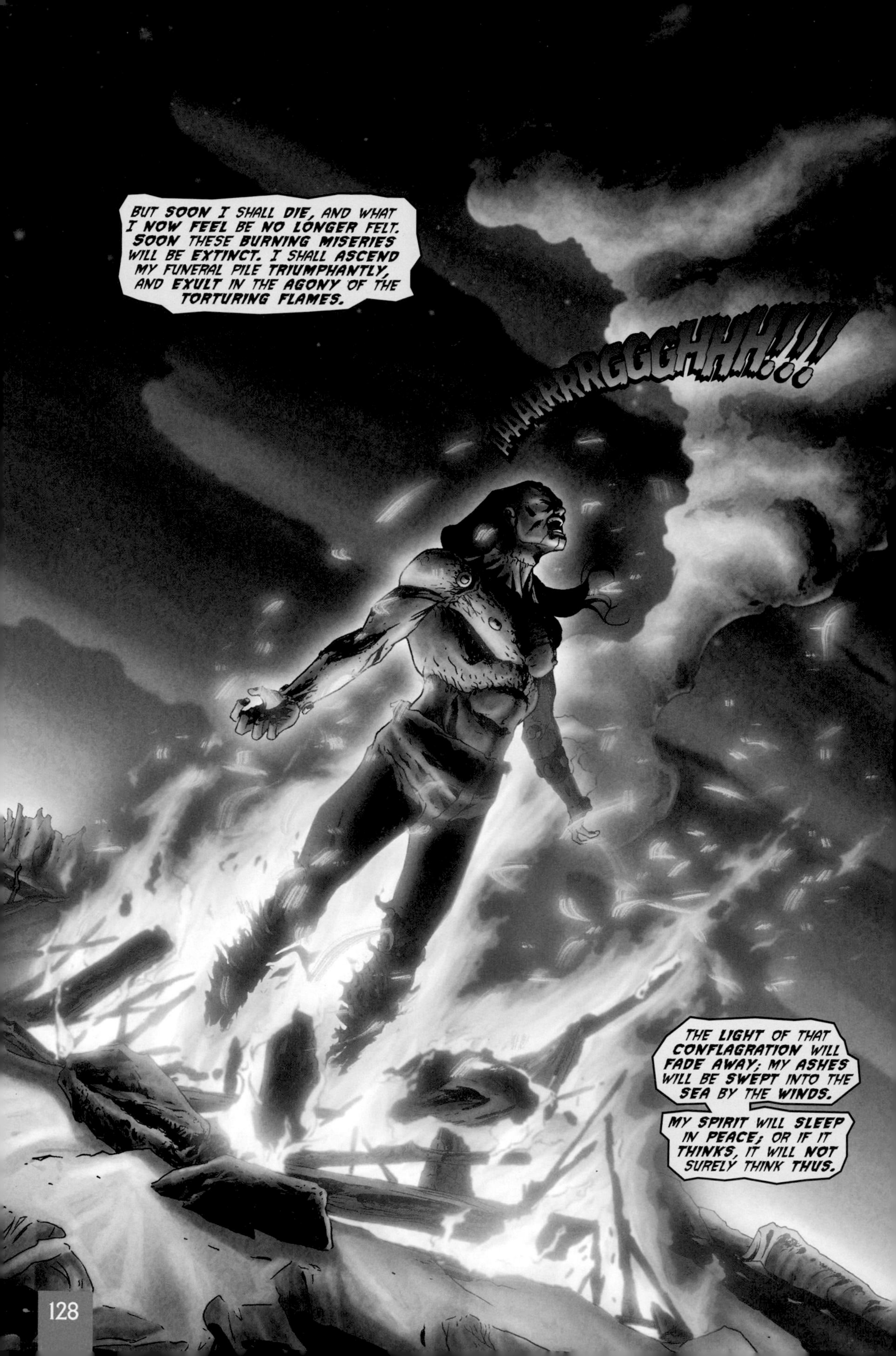
BUT SOON I SHALL DIE, AND WHAT I NOW FEEL BE NO LONGER FELT. SOON THESE BURNING MISERIES WILL BE EXTINCT. I SHALL ASCEND MY FUNERAL PILE TRIUMPHANTLY, AND EXULT IN THE AGONY OF THE TORTURING FLAMES.
AAAARRRRGGGHHH!!!!
THE LIGHT OF THAT CONFLAGRATION WILL FADE AWAY; MY ASHES WILL BE SWEPT INTO THE SEA BY THE WINDS.
MY SPIRIT WILL SLEEP IN PEACE; OR IF IT THINKS, IT WILL NOT SURELY THINK THUS.

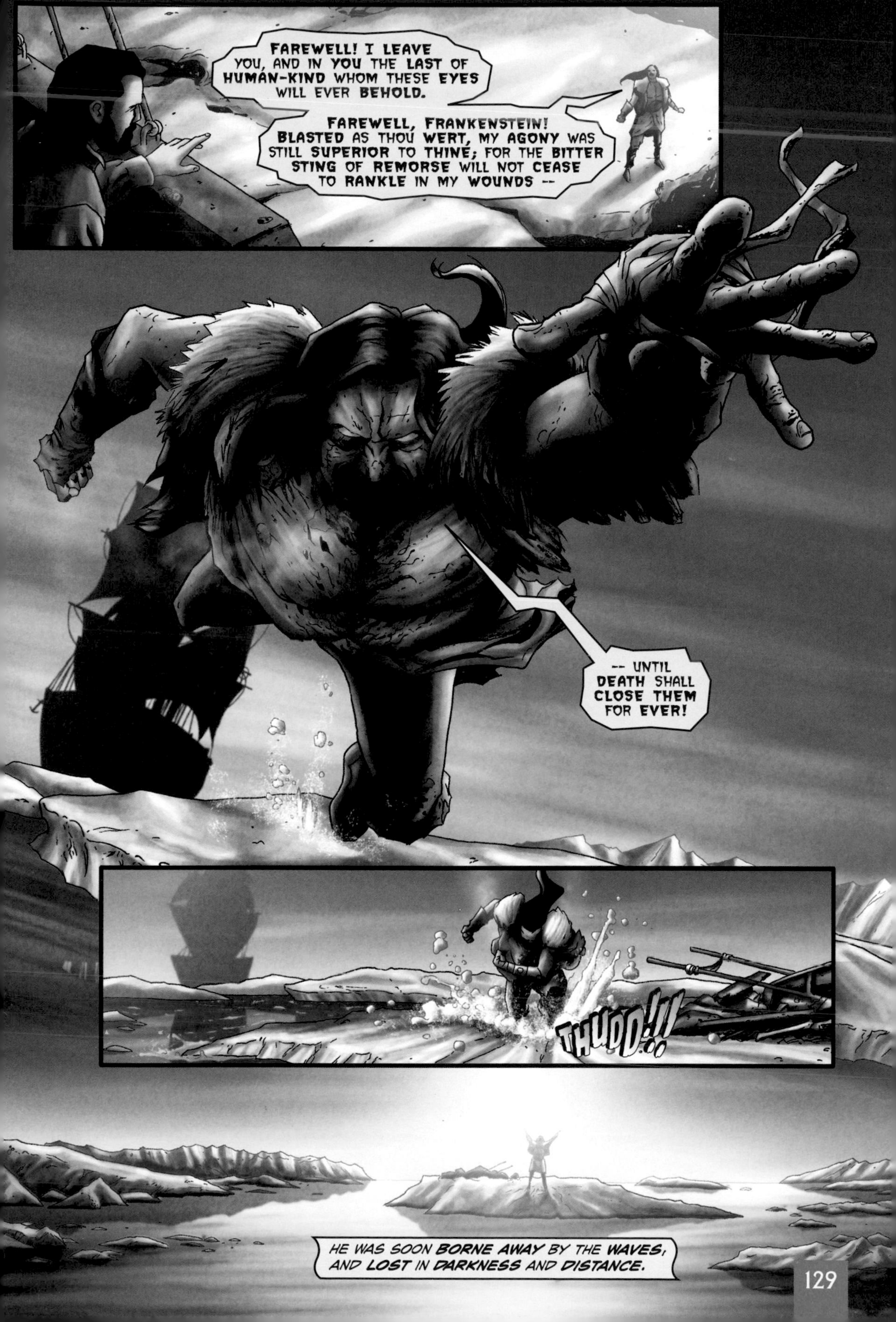
FAREWELL! I LEAVE YOU, AND IN YOU THE LAST OF HUMAN-KIND WHOM THESE EYES WILL EVER BEHOLD.
FAREWELL, FRANKENSTEIN! BLASTED AS THOU WERT, MY AGONY WAS STILL SUPERIOR TO THINE; FOR THE BITTER STING OF REMORSE WILL NOT CEASE TO RANKLE IN MY WOUNDS --
-- UNTIL DEATH SHALL CLOSE THEM FOR EVER!
THUDD!!!
HE WAS SOON BORNE AWAY BY THE WAVES, AND LOST IN DARKNESS AND DISTANCE.

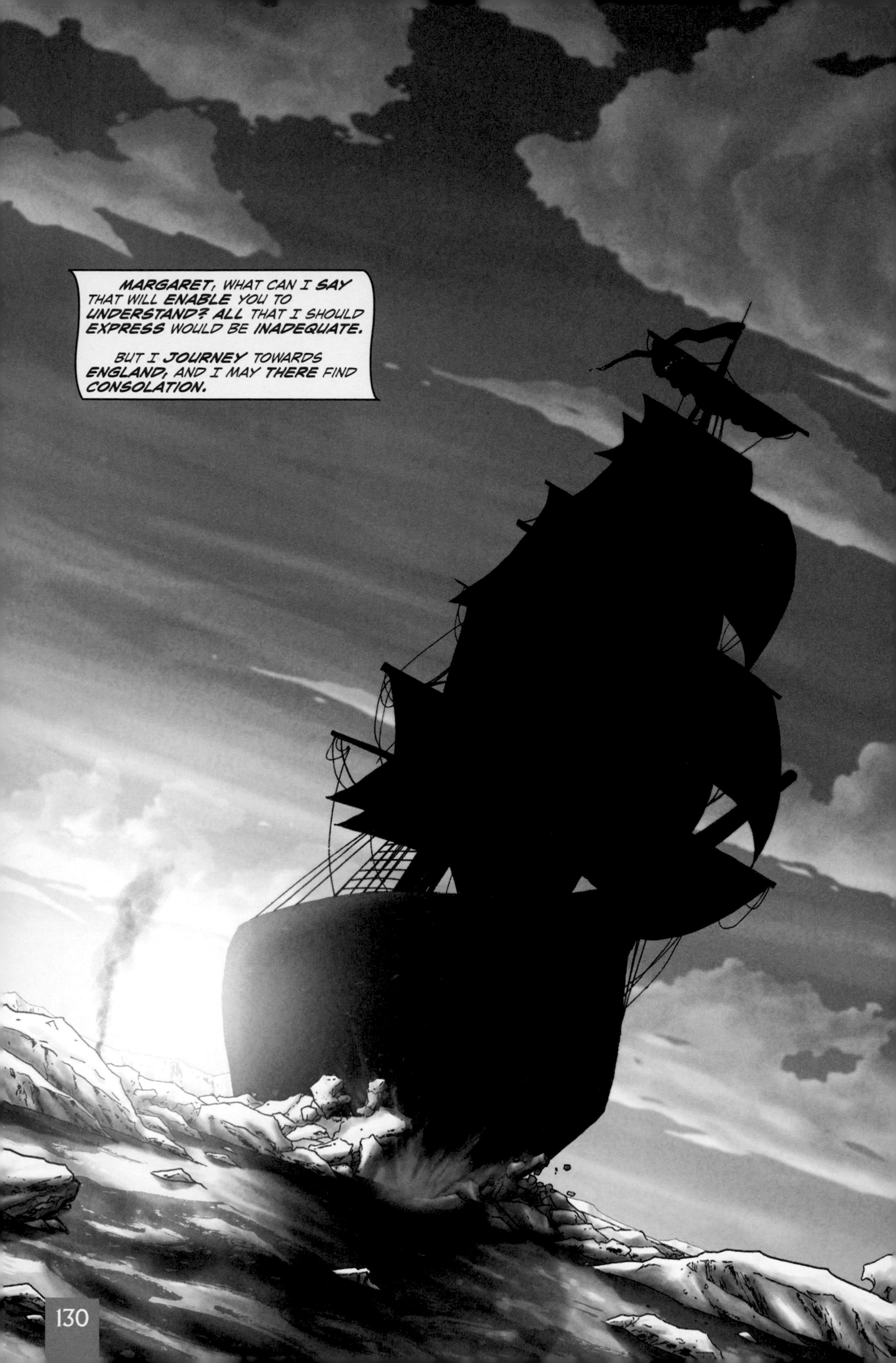
MARGARET, WHAT CAN I SAY THAT WILL ENABLE YOU TO UNDERSTAND? ALL THAT I SHOULD EXPRESS WOULD BE INADEQUATE.
BUT I JOURNEY TOWARDS ENGLAND, AND I MAY THERE FIND CONSOLATION.

Frankenstein
End

Mary Shelley

1797-1851

"It is not singular that, as the daughter of two persons of distinguished literary celebrity, I should very early in life have thought of writing."

National Portrait Gallery, London

Mary Shelley was born Mary Wollstonecraft Godwin in Somers Town, London in August 1797. Her father, William Godwin, was a famous philosopher, novelist and journalist. Her mother was Mary Wollstonecraft, who was a feminist philosopher, educator, and writer, well known for her work *A Vindication of the Rights of Woman* (1792). In it, she argued that women were not naturally inferior to men, but they appeared that way due to a lack of education (education did not become compulsory in England until the Education Act of 1870). She suggested that both men and women should be treated equally, and as rational beings in a society that operated upon reason and logic.

Despite William and Mary's revolutionary attitudes to the social order of the time, and the fact that Mary already had a daughter, Fanny Imlay, from a previous relationship, they married in March 1797 to ensure the legitimacy of their coming child.

Sadly, Mary Wollstonecraft died of puerperal fever (sometimes called "childbed fever") a few days after giving birth, leaving William Godwin alone to bring up baby Mary and her older half-sister Fanny. He believed himself **"totally unfitted to educate them"** and felt that a substitute mother should be found. He didn't look far! William Godwin married his next-door neighbor, Mary Jane Vial (better known as Mary Jane Clairmont) on December 21, 1801. Mary Jane brought two children of her own into the marriage: Charles and Jane (who later called herself Claire). Then, in 1803, Mary Jane gave birth to William Godwin Junior - bringing the total to five children living under the same roof.

Mary Wollstonecraft Godwin did not have a "formal" education, but was taught to read and write at home. Her father encouraged her to write from an early age. She was given freedom to access his extensive library and allowed to listen to the political, philosophical, scientific and literary discussions that he conducted with his friends —William Wordsworth and Samuel Taylor Coleridge were among the many distinguished visitors to the house at this time.

William and Jane Godwin started a publishing company in 1805 (M. Godwin and Co.) and opened a shop selling children's books. The couple also wrote children's books themselves, often under the name of Edward Baldwin.

In 1810, they published what was possibly Mary's first work: *Mounseer*

Nongtongpaw; or the Discoveries of John Bull on a Trip to Paris, a verse poem. It is hard to say whether this was in fact Mary's first work, as all of her early papers were lost, and nothing of her surviving writing can be dated prior to 1814 with any certainty.

In 1812, possibly due to growing conflict with her stepmother, Mary went to live for several months in Dundee with the family of William Baxter, who was a friend of her father's.

Around the same time, the famous poet Percy Bysshe Shelley (a devoted follower, friend and sponsor of Mary's father) began spending a great deal of time in the Godwin home. Percy, along with his young wife Harriet and sister-in-law Eliza, would regularly dine there; and Mary would have met Percy on her return visits to London. By then, aged nineteen, Shelley had already been expelled from Oxford University and his family would only talk to him through lawyers.

Percy and Mary began to meet outside of her home, often at the grave of Mary's mother in St. Pancras Churchyard, where Mary used to sit and read her mother's works. Their relationship developed quickly - much to the horror of Mary's father, who forbade the lovers to meet.

Disregarding the views of her father and of society as a whole, on July 18, 1814, when Mary was only sixteen years old, the lovers ran away to France, taking Jane Clairmont (Mary's stepsister, who later called herself Claire) with them. Mary also took a box containing her writings and letters; and unfortunately, this precious box was lost during the journey.

After only two months, the travelers returned to London. They were penniless, and Shelley was forced to hide from people he owed money to. Mary's father still strongly disapproved of the relationship and would not even meet with his daughter or her lover. Mary, unmarried and barely seventeen, was now pregnant. To make matters worse, Percy Shelley's wife, Harriet, was also pregnant. Harriet gave birth to a son in 1814 and sued her husband for custody of their children and for financial support - leaving Percy in terrible financial difficulty.

From her sparse journal entries of this time, it would appear that the young couple still enjoyed a reasonable standard of living and had a close circle of friends – which was surprising as their behavior would have been considered scandalous by the "respectable" society of the day.

Percy Shelley's grandfather, Sir Bysshe Shelley, died in January 1815. This left Percy as "heir apparent" to the title and to the family estate on the death of his father. It also greatly improved the Shelleys' financial situation; and by June 1815, Percy was in receipt of an annual allowance of £1,000 – a huge amount of money at a time when the average annual wage for a weaver was only £16 (seventy-two pennies per week).

However, the relationship between Mary and Percy was sadly to be put under further strain. Their first daughter was born two months premature and died within a few days. This was to have a lasting effect on Mary, as she wrote in her journal on March 19, 1815:

> **"Dream that my little baby came to life again – that it had only been cold & that we rubbed it by the fire & it lived – I awake & find no baby – I think about the little thing all day – not in good spirits – Shelley is very unwell."**

Almost immediately, Mary became pregnant again and a second, healthy child, William, was born a year later. During this time, Shelley's health was deteriorating (possibly through a weak heart) and the continuing but not always welcome presence of Mary's stepsister - now known as Claire - can only have added further pressure to the couple's relationship.

The following year of 1816 was no less eventful. Claire had become pregnant by the poet Lord George Byron. She needed to establish with Byron that the child was indeed his, and so persuaded Percy and Mary to accompany her to Switzerland to meet him at Lake Geneva. By June, they had settled near Cologny - and it was here that Mary began to write *Frankenstein*; she was still only eighteen. In her original preface to the book, she wrote:

> **"I passed the summer of 1816 in the environs of Geneva. The season was cold and rainy, and in the evenings we crowded around a blazing wood fire, and occasionally amused ourselves with some German stories of ghosts, which happened to fall into our hands. These tales excited in us a playful desire of imitation. Two other friends (a tale from the pen of one of whom would be far more acceptable to the public than any thing I can ever hope to produce) and myself agreed to write each a story founded on some supernatural occurrence."**

They returned to London in September 1816. In October, Mary's older half-sister Fanny committed suicide through a laudanum overdose. In November, Percy Shelley's pregnant wife Harriet went missing and was eventually found drowned in the River Serpentine. She was just twenty-one years old - and her death greatly added to the scandal that already dogged the couple. Amidst all of this drama, Mary Wollstonecraft married Percy Shelley on December 30, 1816 at St. Mildred's Church in London.

Frankenstein was eventually completed in May 1817, but wasn't published until 1818 – and even then, Mary wasn't named as the author (*Frankenstein* wasn't published in her name until 1831).

In September 1817, Mary gave birth to her third child, Clara Everina. Percy owed money once again, and the family, along with Claire and her young child, moved across Europe to the warmer climes of Italy.

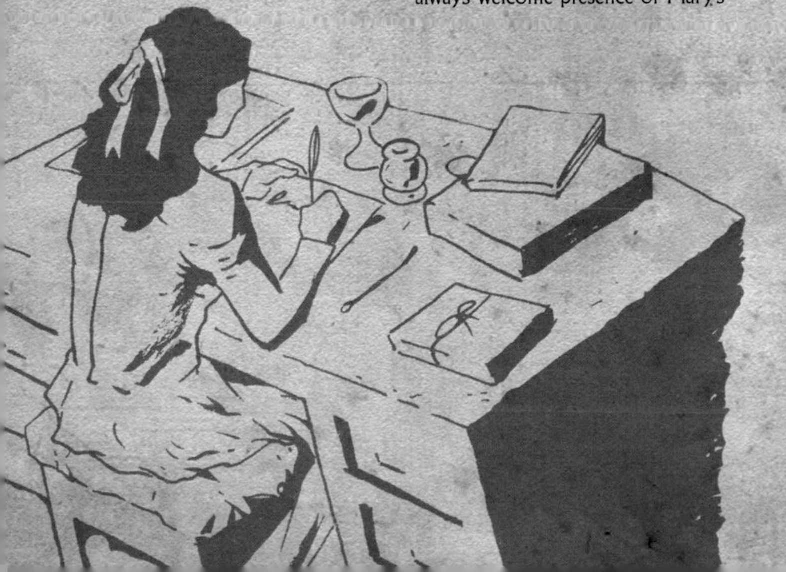

Tragically, Clara Everina died in Venice in 1818; and in the following year, their son William died of Malaria in Rome. These losses had a profound effect on Mary, who sank into a deep depression. Percy wrote in his notebook:

> **"My dearest Mary, wherefore hast thou gone,**
> **And left me in this dreary world alone?**
> **Thy form is here indeed—a lovely one—**
> **But thou art fled, gone down a dreary road**
> **That leads to Sorrow's most obscure abode.**
> **For thine own sake I cannot follow thee**
> **Do thou return for mine."**

The Shelleys moved to Florence in October 1819, where their son Percy Florence was born the following month. His birth lifted Mary's spirits and brought the couple closer together again.

In May 1822, they moved on to La Spezia, where Mary miscarried on June 16, during her fifth pregnancy. Percy insisted that she should sit in a bath of ice until the doctor arrived – and that advice saved her life.

Percy Shelley was not a strong swimmer, and some say that he couldn't swim at all; yet despite that, and even though he had once nearly drowned in a boating accident, he and several friends decided to spend the summer of 1822 sailing on the Bay of Lerici. On July 18, the drowned bodies of Percy, his friend Edward Williams and a young sailor by the name of Charles Vivian were washed ashore. In keeping with the quarantine regulations of the time, Percy Shelley's body was cremated on the beach near Viareggio. His heart was snatched from the funeral pyre by Edward Trelawny - adventurer, author and friend of the poets – who had designed the boat that sank.

In 1823, Shelley's ashes were interred in a burial plot in the Cimitero Acattolico in Rome, under an ancient pyramid in the city walls. The Latin inscription reads, **"Cor Cordium"**, which translates to **"Heart of Hearts"**. It also bears a few lines from Shakespeare's *The Tempest*:

> **"Nothing of him that doth fade**
> **But doth suffer a sea change**
> **into something rich & strange"**

Back in England, *The Courier* (a leading newspaper of the time) published a notice of the death of Shelley:-

> **"Shelley, the writer of some infidel poetry has been drowned; now he knows whether there is a God or no."**

Mary and her only surviving child, Percy Florence, left Italy in the summer of 1823 and returned to England.

Percy Shelley's allowance ended when he died. His father, Sir Timothy Shelley, provided Mary and his grandson with only a very small sum of money – and even that was on the condition that she did not publish any of his son's remaining manuscripts and that she did not write under her married name.

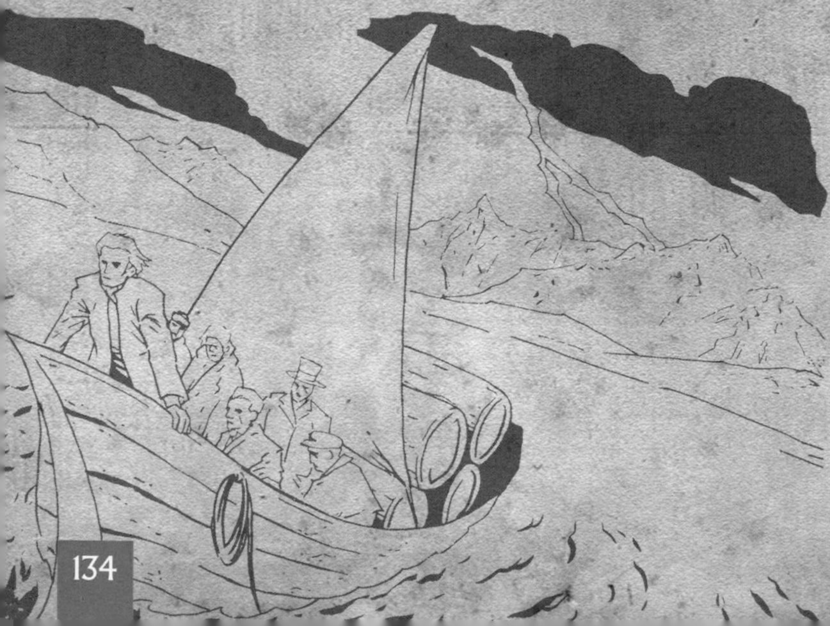

It is to satisfy this last condition that all of her publications avoid the use of an author's name, and instead say, "By the Author of *Frankenstein*."

In 1824 she wrote in her journal:

> **"At the age of twenty six I am in the condition of an aged person--all my old friends are gone ... & my heart fails when I think by how few ties I hold to the world...."**

She did not remarry; in fact she turned down more than one proposal, saying that after being married to one genius, she could only marry another. She concentrated on earning money from her writing, while looking after her father, William, until his death in 1836. Percy Florence followed in his father's footsteps, going to public school and on to university. He inherited his grandfather's baronetcy in 1844, becoming Sir Percy Florence Shelley, 3rd Baronet.

Although Mary continued to write, none of her later works are as well known or as powerful as her first novel, *Frankenstein* (she died before completing the biography of her husband). From 1839 onwards, she suffered from several illnesses, including headaches and bouts of paralysis, which at times prevented her from writing; and she was blighted by ill health in her final years. In 1848, Percy Florence married Jane Gibson St. John. Mary divided her time between living with them at their country home in Sussex and at her own home in Chester Square, London.

Mary Wollstonecraft Shelley died on February 1, 1851 aged fifty-three. The cause of death is recorded as **"Disease of the brain – supposed tumour in left hemisphere of long standing"**. She is buried next to her parents at St. Peter's Church in Bournemouth, on the southern English coast.

After her death, Mary's box desk was opened. In it were locks of her dead children's hair, a notebook she had shared with Percy Bysshe Shelley, and a copy of his poem *Adonaïs*, with one page folded around a silk parcel containing some of his ashes and the remains of his heart.

Mary Shelley's Family Tree

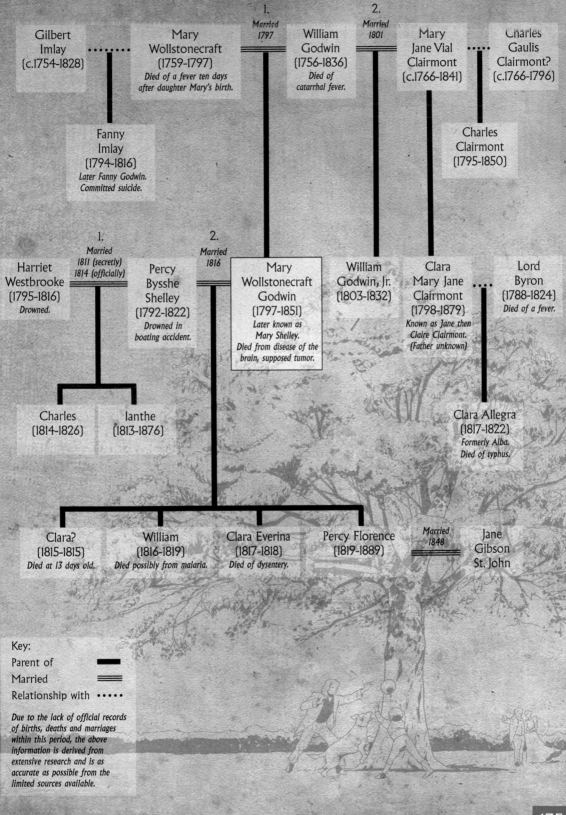

Gilbert Imlay (c.1754-1828) · · · · · · Mary Wollstonecraft (1759-1797)
Died of a fever ten days after daughter Mary's birth.

1. Married 1797

William Godwin (1756-1836)
Died of catarrhal fever.

2. Married 1801

Mary Jane Vial Clairmont (c.1766-1841) · · · · · Charles Gaulis Clairmont? (c.1766-1796)

Fanny Imlay (1794-1816)
Later Fanny Godwin. Committed suicide.

Charles Clairmont (1795-1850)

1. Married 1811 (secretly) 1814 (officially)

2. Married 1816

Harriet Westbrooke (1795-1816)
Drowned.

Percy Bysshe Shelley (1792-1822)
Drowned in boating accident.

Mary Wollstonecraft Godwin (1797-1851)
Later known as Mary Shelley. Died from disease of the brain, supposed tumor.

William Godwin, Jr. (1803-1832)

Clara Mary Jane Clairmont (1798-1879)
Known as Jane then Claire Clairmont. (Father unknown)

· · · · Lord Byron (1788-1824)
Died of a fever.

Charles (1814-1826)

Ianthe (1813-1876)

Clara Allegra (1817-1822)
Formerly Alba. Died of typhus.

Clara? (1815-1815)
Died at 13 days old.

William (1816-1819)
Died possibly from malaria.

Clara Everina (1817-1818)
Died of dysentery.

Percy Florence (1819-1889)

Married 1848

Jane Gibson St. John

Key:
Parent of ▬▬▬
Married ≡≡≡
Relationship with · · · · ·

Due to the lack of official records of births, deaths and marriages within this period, the above information is derived from extensive research and is as accurate as possible from the limited sources available.

1816...The Birth of Frankenstein

"How I, then a young girl, came to think of, and to dilate upon, so very hideous an idea?"

The year of 1816 saw crop failure and famine, food riots across Europe following the end of the Napoleonic wars, and a heavy June snow fall in New England. France sentenced Napoleon Bonaparte to permanent exile in St. Helena, and the author of *Jane Eyre*, Charlotte Brontë, was born in England.

Eighteen-year-old Mary Wollstonecraft Godwin spent the summer of 1816 with her poet lover Percy Bysshe Shelley and her stepsister Claire Clairmont at Maison Chapuis near Colgny in Geneva, Switzerland. They were there to visit Lord Byron and confirm that he was indeed the father of Claire's unborn child.

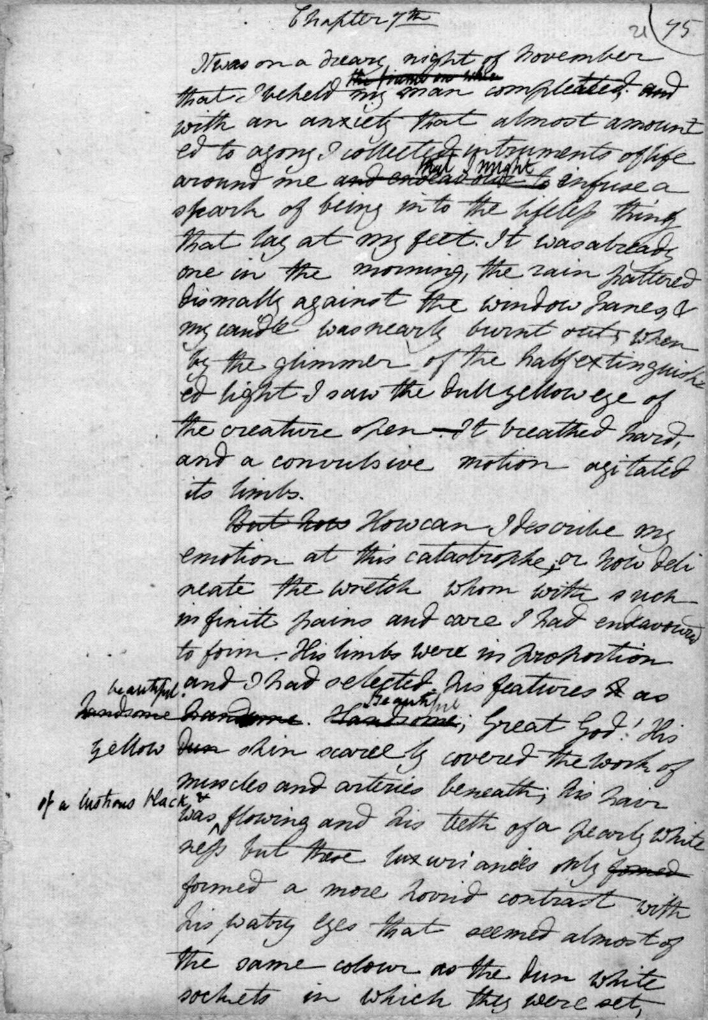

Chapter 7th — 21 95

It was on a dreary night of November that I beheld ~~the frame on which~~ my man completeed ~~and~~ with an anxiety that almost amounted to agony I collected instruments of life around me ~~and endeavoured~~ that I might to infuse a spark of being into the lifeless thing that lay at my feet. It was already one in the morning, the rain pattered dismally against the window panes & my candle was nearly burnt out, when by the glimmer of the half extinguished light I saw the dull yellow eye of the creature open — It breathed hard, and a convulsive motion agitated its limbs.

~~But how~~ How can I describe my emotion at this catastrophe, or how deliniate the wretch whom with such infinite pains and care I had endeavoured to form. His limbs were in proportion and I had selected his features ~~&~~ as beautiful ~~handsome handsome~~. ~~Handsome~~ Beautiful, Great God! His yellow ~~dun~~ skin scarcely covered the work of muscles and arteries beneath; his hair was of a lustrous black & flowing and his teeth of a pearly whiteness but these luxuriances only ~~formed~~ formed a more horrid contrast with his watry eyes that seemed almost of the same colour as the dun white sockets in which they were set,

Abinger papers, Dep. c. 477, fol. 21r © Bodleian Library, University of Oxford

The weather was peculiar in 1816 – in fact it became known as "the year without a summer", or "The Poverty Year". Temperatures fluctuated between beautiful summer days and near freezing temperatures within a matter of hours. These unusual conditions were most likely the result of the eruption of Volcano Tambora in Indonesia. In addition to temperature variations, torrential rains and terrifying lightning storms plagued the area, with sunsets being particularly spectacular due to the vast quantities of ash in the air. It was this abnormal weather, coupled with the mood of the group and the wilder aspects of the Swiss landscape, that contributed to the birth of the story of *Frankenstein*.

Due to a particularly violent storm on the night of June 16, 1816, Mary and Percy could not return to Maison Chapuis, and so were invited to spend the night with Lord Byron and John Polidori, Byron's young physician, at Villa Diodati. The group read aloud from *The Fantasmagoriana*, a collection of ghost stories translated from German into French, that they had found in the villa. In one of the stories, a group of travelers entertain each other with tales of supernatural experiences; and this inspired Byron to challenge the group to each write a ghost story.

Shelley wrote an unrecorded story based on his life experiences; Byron wrote only a fragment of a novel; and Polidori is thought to have begun ***The Vampyre*** at this time (many consider the main character in this story, Lord Ruthven, to be based on Lord Byron). Mary was lost for ideas that evening; but she continued, days after the challenge had finished, determined to produce a suitable story.

In her own words:

> **"I busied myself to think of a story, – a story to rival those which had excited us to this task. One which would speak to the mysterious fears of our nature, and awaken thrilling horror – one to make the reader dread to look round, to curdle the blood, and quicken the beatings of the heart. If I did not accomplish these things, my ghost story would be unworthy of its name. I thought and pondered – vainly. I felt that blank incapability of invention which is the greatest misery of authorship."**

Below: Two leafs from the first of the two disbound draft notebooks, started by Mary Godwin at Geneva in summer 1816, with marginal corrections by Percy Bysshe Shelley.

The one on the left is where the story actually started:
"It was on a dreary night of November that I beheld my man completed..."
which in the finished book is the first line of Volume I Chapter V.

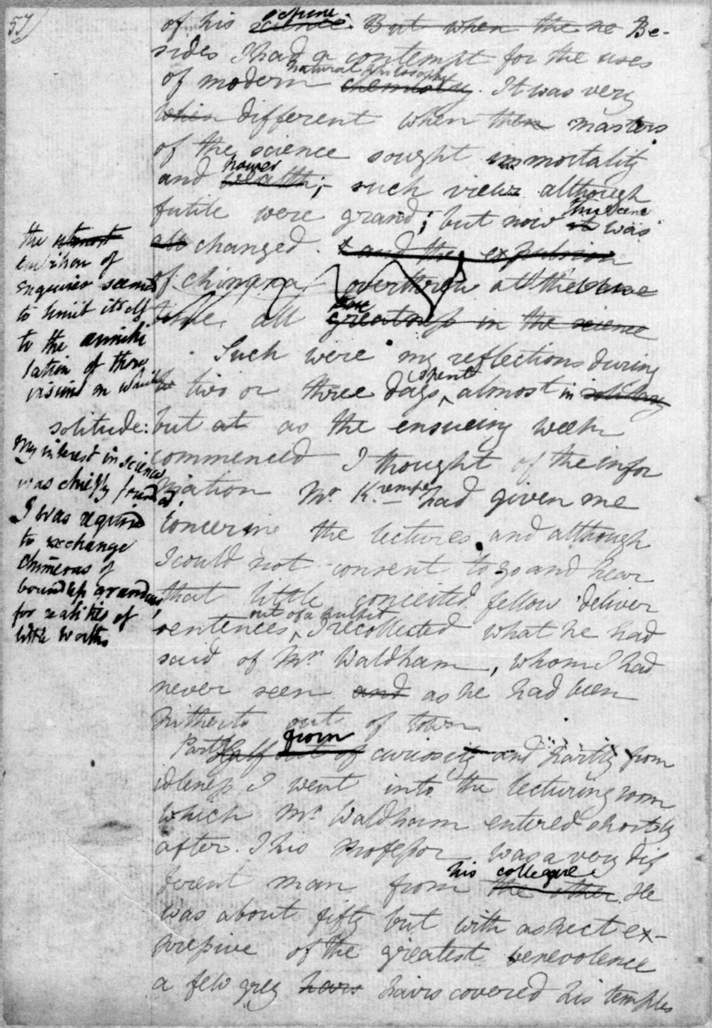

57

of his science. But when the ne Besides I had a contempt for the uses of modern natural philosophy chemistry. It was very different when the masters of the science sought immortality and power wealth; such views although futile were grand; but now the scene was changed. ... of chimeras ... overthrow ... all ... greatness in the science.

Such were my reflections during the two or three days spent almost in solitude: but as the ensuing week commenced I thought of the information Mr. Krempe had given me concerning the lectures, and although I could not consent to go and hear that little conceited fellow deliver sentences out of a pulpit, I recollected what he had said of Mr. Waldman, whom I had never seen as he had been hitherto out of town.

Partly from curiosity and partly from idleness I went into the lecturing room which Mr. Waldman entered shortly after. This professor was a very different man from his colleague. He was about fifty but with an aspect expressive of the greatest benevolence; a few grey hairs covered his temples

the ambition of enquiries seemed to limit itself to the annihilation of those visions on which my interest in science was chiefly founded. I was required to exchange chimeras of boundless grandeur for realities of little worth.

In the days that followed, Mary remained unable to begin her story:

> **"Have you thought of a story? I was asked each morning, and each morning I was forced to reply with a mortifying negative."**

During one gathering of the group that summer, they debated the nature of the principle of life and discussed whether there was any probability of it ever being discovered and communicated. These conversations had a profound effect on Mary. She later wrote that when she went to her bedroom, she had a vision:

> **"I saw the pale student of unhallowed arts kneeling beside the thing he had put together. I saw the hideous phantasm of a man stretched out, then, on the working of some powerful engine, show signs of life...His success would terrify the artist; he would rush away...hope that...this thing...would subside into dead matter...he opens his eyes; behold the horrid thing stands at his bedside, opening his curtains..."**

Mary had at last found her story, and the monster had his creator.

As you can see from the page opposite, she began by writing the lines that open Volume I Chapter V.:

> **"It was on a dreary night of November."**

...and just as in the story, a monster was born!

"(Frankenstein) is the most wonderful work to have been written at twenty years of age that I ever heard of. You are now five and twenty. And, most fortunately, you have pursued a course of reading, and cultivated your mind in a manner the most admirably adapted to make you a great successful author. If you cannot be independent, who should be?"

– William Godwin to Mary Shelley

Frankenstein Lives!

It is testimony to the dramatic nature of the book and the way that it captured the imaginations of people at the time, that a stage version of *Frankenstein* appeared within five years of its first publication.

On 28th July 1823, *Presumption; or The Fate of Frankenstein*, a play with songs by Richard Brinsley Peake, opened at the English Opera House, and ran for thirty-seven performances. The monster was played by T.P. Cooke; and according to one account, his make-up left him with a

"shrivelled complexion, lips straight and black, and a horrible ghastly grin."

The monster is mute in this first adaptation. This has also been the case in many adaptations since, despite Mary Shelley's creation being tormented, tragic and well-spoken.

An 1823 poster from the English Opera House production of the play entitled *Presumption; or, The Fate of Frankenstein*

Mary Shelley went to see the production on August 28, 1823 and was mostly complementary about it in her letter to her friend Leigh Hunt on September 9. She writes:

"*Frankenstein* had prodigious success as a drama & was about to be repeated for the 23rd night at the English Opera House. The play bill amused me extremely, for in the list of dramatis personæ came, ———— by Mr. T. Cooke: this nameless mode of naming the un {n}ameable is rather good. On Friday Aug. 29th, Jane, my father William & I went to the theatre to see it. Wallack looked very well as F—he is at the beginning full of hope & expectation—at the end of the 1st Act. The stage represents a room with a staircase leading to F's workshop—he goes to it and you see his light at a small window, through which a frightened servant peeps, who runs off in terror when F. exclaims "It lives!"—Presently F himself rushes in horror & trepidation from the room and while still expressing his agony & terror ———— throws down the door of the laboratory, leaps the staircase & presents his unearthly & monstrous person on the stage. The story is not well managed—but Cooke played ————'s part extremely well—his seeking as it were for support—his trying to grasp at the sounds he heard—all indeed he does was well imagined & executed. I was much amused, & it appeared to excite a breathless eagerness in the audience."

It was well received by the critics, too. This review of the play appeared in a London newspaper the day after the premiere:

THEATRE, English Opera
London Morning Post:
Tuesday, July 29 & Wednesday, July 30
Review of Presumption; or the
Fate of Frankenstein (1823)

"A new three act piece, described as 'a romance of a peculiar interest,' was last night produced at this theatre, entitled, *Presumption, or the Fate of Frankenstein*.

The fable represents Frankenstein, a man of great science, to have succeeded in uniting the remains of dead persons, so as to form one being, which he endows with life. He has, however, little reason to exult in the triumph of his art; for the creature thus formed, hideous in aspect, and possessed of prodigious strength, spreads terror, and carries ruin wherever he goes. Though wearing the human form, he is incapable of associating with mankind, to whom he eventually becomes hostile, and having killed the mistress and brother of Frankenstein, he finally vanquishes his mortal creator, and perishes himself beneath a falling avalanche. Such is the outline of the business of a drama more extraordinary in its plan, than remarkable for strength in its execution. There is something in the piecemeal resurrection effected by Frankenstein, which, instead of creating that awful interest intended to arise from it, gives birth to a feeling of horror. We have not that taste for the monstrous which can enable us to enjoy it in the midst of the most startling absurdities. To Lord BYRON, the late Mr. SHELLEY, and philosophers of that stamp, it might appear a very fine thing to attack the Christian faith from a masked battery, and burlesque the resurrection of the dead, by representing the fragments of departed mortals as starting into existence at the command of a man; but we would prefer the comparatively noble assaults of VOLNEY, VOLTAIRE, and PAINE.

In the first scene in which ——— (so the creature of Frankenstein is indicated in the bills) makes his appearance, the effect is terrific. There are other parts in which a very powerful impression is produced on the spectators, but to have made the most of the idea a greater interest ought early in the drama to have been excited for Frankenstein and the destined victims of the non-descript, and he himself would have been an object of greater attention if speech had been vouchsafed. The efforts to relieve the serious action of the Piece by mirth and music were generally successful, and the labours of Mr. WATSON the composer we often loudly applauded.

The acting was very grand. WALLACK as Frankenstein, displayed great feeling and animation; T.P. COOKE as ——— (or the made up man), was tremendously appalling. The other performers did as much as could be expected in the parts allotted to them, and the piece though it met with some opposition at the close had a large majority in its favour, and was announced for repetition."

Further dramatizations followed in quick succession. On August 18, 1823 *Frankenstein; or, the Demon of Switzerland*, a play by Henry M. Milner, took to the stage at the Royal Coburg Theatre in London. Three other stage versions followed that same year: *Humgumption; or, Dr. Frankenstein and the Hobgoblin of Hoxton*, *Presumption and the Blue Demon* and *Another Piece of Presumption*, the second play by Peake based on the *Frankenstein* story.

In December 1824, *Frank-in-Steam; or, The Modern Promise to Pay* premiered at the Olympic Theatre; while July 1826 saw the opening at the Royal Coburg Theatre of *The Man and The Monster; or The Fate of Frankenstein*, a further interpretation by Henry M. Milner.

Twenty-three years later in December 1849, *Frankenstein; or, The Model Man*, by William and Robert Brough, opened at the Adelphi Theatre and ran for twenty-six performances.

Interestingly, it is within these early plays that the man and the monster were becoming interchangeable, with writers using *Frankenstein* to describe both the scientist and his creation.

The list of adaptations doesn't end there. Steven Earl Forry, author of *Hideous Progenies: Dramatizations of Frankenstein from Mary Shelley to the Present* and an authority on this dramatic history, has cataloged almost one hundred dramatic adaptations of *Frankenstein* between 1821 and 1986.

Frankenstein on Film

The birth of motion pictures opened up further opportunities to present the story visually. The first cinematic version of *Frankenstein* appeared in 1910. It was a one-reel silent film produced by Edison Films of New York. Their catalogue of the time proudly proclaimed:

> "we have carefully omitted anything in Mrs. Shelley's story which might shock any portion of the audience."

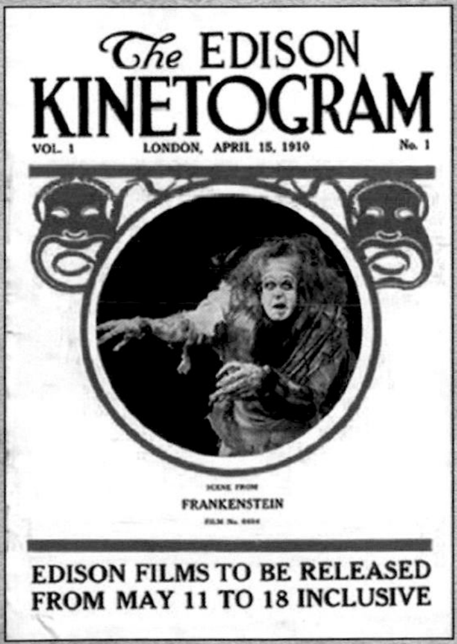
The EDISON
KINETOGRAM
VOL. 1
LONDON, APRIL 15, 1910
No. 1
FRANKENSTEIN
EDISON FILMS TO BE RELEASED
FROM MAY 11 TO 18 INCLUSIVE

This film was assumed to be lost but amazingly was re-discovered in the 1970s, still in a viewable condition. The second *Frankenstein* film was produced in 1915, titled *Life Without Soul* and directed by Joseph W. Smiley. The story is of a doctor who creates a man without a soul. At the end of the film, we find out that the young hero has only dreamed the events of the film, after falling asleep reading Mary Shelley's novel. This film is thought to have been lost.

In 1930, Universal Studios bought the film rights to Peggy Webling's play *Frankenstein: An Adventure in the Macabre*, which had premiered in London in 1927. Bela Lugosi was originally put forward as the actor to play the part of the monster. However, a then obscure English actor, William Henry Pratt, who went by the stage name of Boris Karloff, finally got the part. Karloff's success in *Frankenstein* made him an international star, and the film itself became an instant classic of a new genre - the horror movie.

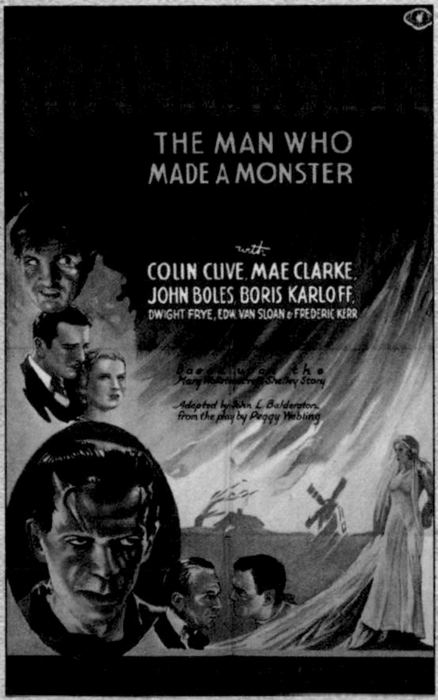
THE MAN WHO
MADE A MONSTER
with
COLIN CLIVE, MAE CLARKE,
JOHN BOLES, BORIS KARLOFF,
DWIGHT FRYE, EDW. VAN SLOAN & FREDERIC KERR

The Granger Collection, New York. Poster for the 1931 film, *Frankenstein* starring Boris Karloff as the monster.

This lumbering and (again) mute creature has perhaps been the most recognizable image of Frankenstein's "monster" since then. The creature's now-famous flat head and neck-bolt make-up was created by Universal Studios' make-up artist Jack P. Pierce.

Frankenstein earned rave reviews and was voted one of the films of the year by the New York Times. It made huge amounts of money; the production cost of around $270,000 was dwarfed by the earnings of more than $12 million.

In all, over fifty films have been made of the *Frankenstein* story, ranging from horror to drama to comedy, such as the brilliant Mel Brooks' *Young Frankenstein* (1974) starring Gene Wilder and Marty Feldman. Unsurprisingly, interest in the story remains as strong as ever today.

2004 saw the release of a TV film based on the *Frankenstein* trilogy of books by Dean R. Koontz. The story takes place in present day New Orleans, where two detectives are hunting the perpetrator of a series of murders. They are assisted by a mysterious "man", who is in fact the first "creation" of a scientist from many years past, and who has been roaming the earth for hundreds of years, searching for his creator and nemesis. The premise of the film is that Mary Shelley based her own book on the story of this "creation".

In contrast, Hallmark Entertainment's four-part TV mini-series, also released in 2004, has often been cited as the most faithful cinematic telling of Mary Shelley's story to date. This adaptation focuses not only on the action, but also on the development of the characters as the story unfolds. It contains all of the important scenes from the novel - including the narratives by Robert Walton – but has one major deviation from the novel: Victor Frankenstein is seen to use electricity from a thunderstorm to give life to his creature. Although this dramatic cinematic effect has been used by the majority of directors over the years, it doesn't appear in Mary Shelley's book.

It is incredible that a story written nearly two hundred years ago should still be part of our everyday culture. Although the popularity of the films has helped, it is mainly the strength of the original story, dealing as it does with complex themes and issues, that has enabled it to survive through the years; from stage to screen, radio to television; and even now being transformed into this full-color graphic novel.

Page Creation

1. Script

In order to create two versions of the same book, the story is first adapted into two scripts: Original Text and Quick Text. While the degree of complexity changes for each script, the artwork remains the same for both books.

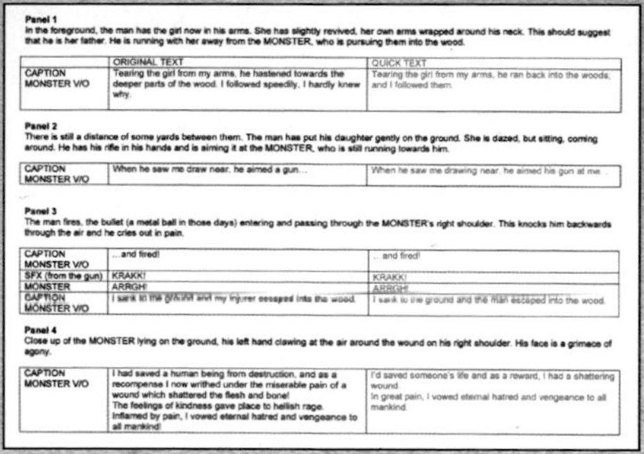

Panel 1
In the foreground, the man has the girl now in his arms. She has slightly revived, her own arms wrapped around his neck. This should suggest that he is her father. He is running with her away from the MONSTER, who is pursuing them into the wood.

	ORIGINAL TEXT	QUICK TEXT
CAPTION MONSTER V/O	Tearing the girl from my arms, he hastened towards the deeper parts of the wood. I followed speedily, I hardly knew why.	Tearing the girl from my arms, he ran back into the woods; and I followed them.

Panel 2
There is still a distance of some yards between them. The man has put his daughter gently on the ground. She is dazed, but sitting, coming around. He has his rifle in his hands and is aiming it at the MONSTER, who is still running towards him.

CAPTION MONSTER V/O	When he saw me draw near, he aimed a gun...	When he saw me drawing near, he aimed his gun at me...

Panel 3
The man fires, the bullet (a metal ball in those days) entering and passing through the MONSTER's right shoulder. This knocks him backwards through the air and he cries out in pain.

CAPTION MONSTER V/O	...and fired!	...and fired!
SFX (from the gun)	KRAKK!	KRAKK!
MONSTER	ARRGH!	ARRGH!
CAPTION MONSTER V/O	I sank to the ground and my injurer escaped into the wood.	I sank to the ground and the man escaped into the wood.

Panel 4
Close up of the MONSTER lying on the ground, his left hand clawing at the air around the wound on his right shoulder. His face is a grimace of agony.

CAPTION MONSTER V/O	I had saved a human being from destruction, and as a recompense I now writhed under the miserable pain of a wound which shattered the flesh and bone! The feelings of kindness gave place to hellish rage. Inflamed by pain, I vowed eternal hatred and vengeance to all mankind!	I'd saved someone's life and as a reward, I had a shattering wound. In great pain, I vowed eternal hatred and vengeance to all mankind.

A page from the script of *Frankenstein* showing the two versions of text.

2. Rough Sketch

The artist first creates a rough sketch from the panel directions provided by the scriptwriter. The artist considers many things at this stage, including story pacing, emphasis of certain elements to tell the story in the best way, and even lighting of the scene.

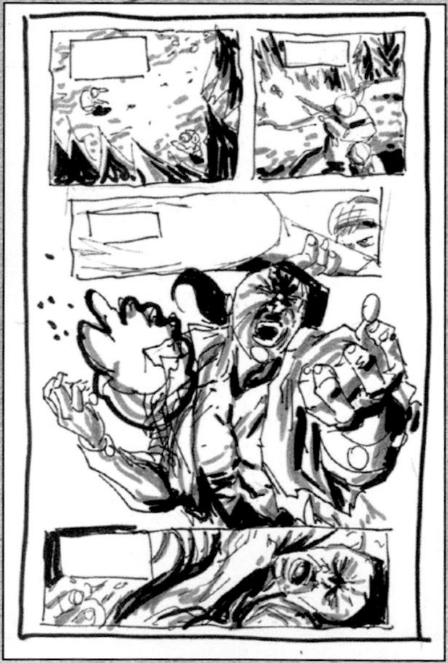

The rough sketch created from the above script.

As you can see here, Declan is using the central action to provide a lighter background to this page, which is in contrast to the dark borders used elsewhere in the book.

3. Pencils

The artist and Art Director discuss the rough sketches and agree on any changes that are needed. Once a clear direction is established, the artist creates a pencil drawing of the page.

It is interesting to see the changes made from the rough to the pencil. Note how the first two panels have changed drastically, whereas the third and last panel are unchanged. The main panel showing the monster being hit by the gun shot was reversed to allow the direction of the shot from the previous panel to continue.

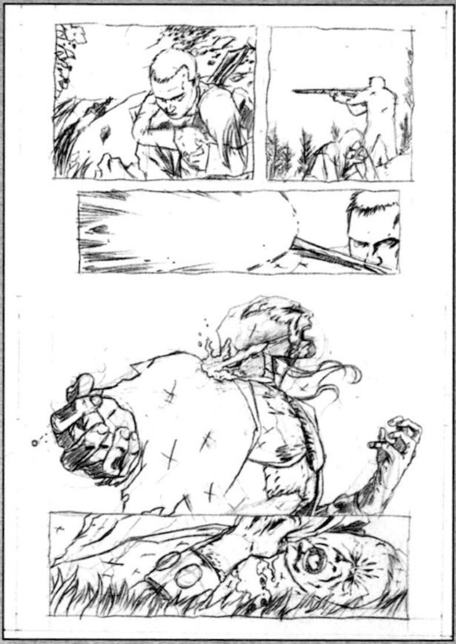

The pencil drawing of page 76.

4. Inks

From the pencil sketch, an inked version of the same page is created. Inking is not simply tracing over the pencil sketch; it is the process of using black ink to fill in the shaded areas and to add clarity and cohesion to the "pencils". The "inks" give us the final linework prior to the coloring stage.

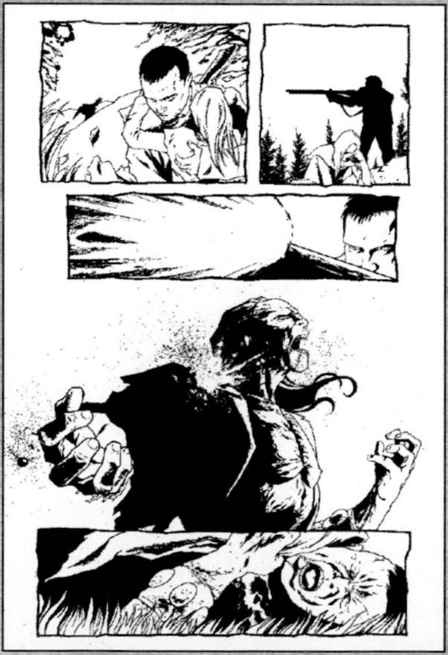

The inked image, ready for coloring.

5. Coloring

Adding color really brings the page and its characters to life.

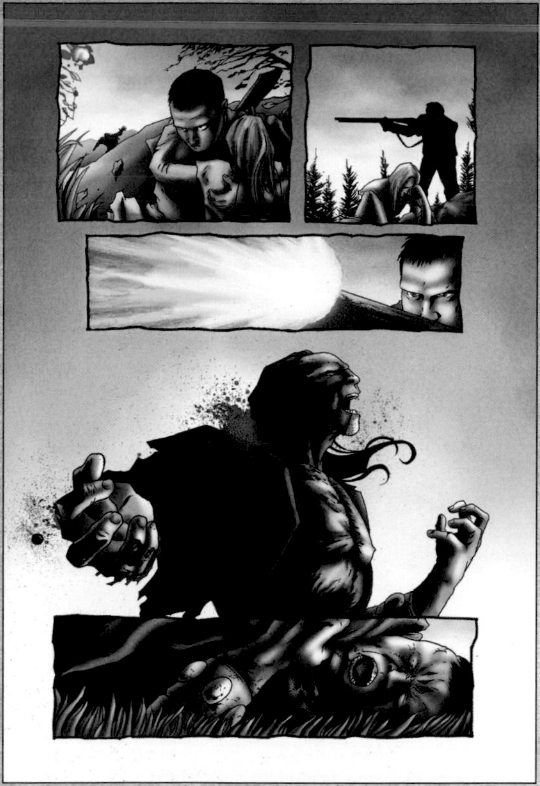

There is far more to the coloring stage than simply replacing the white areas with color. Some of the linework is replaced with color (like the red of the shot wound), the light sources are considered for shadows and highlights, and effects added. Finally, the whole page is color-balanced to the other pages of that scene, and to the overall book.

6. Lettering

The final stage is to add the captions, sound effects, and dialogue speech bubbles from the script. These are laid on top of the colored pages. Two versions of each page are lettered, one for each of the two versions of the book (Original Text and Quick Text).

These are then saved as final artwork pages and compiled into the finished book.

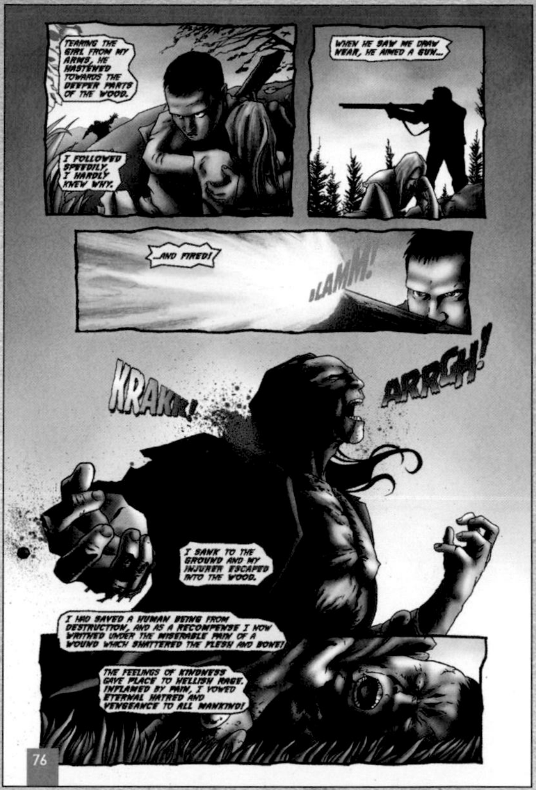
TEARING THE GIRL FROM MY ARMS, HE HASTENED TOWARDS THE DEEPER PARTS OF THE WOOD.
I FOLLOWED SPEEDILY, I HARDLY KNEW WHY.
WHEN HE SAW ME DRAW NEAR, HE AIMED A GUN...
...AND FIRED!
LAMM!
KRAKK!
ARRGH!
I SANK TO THE GROUND AND MY INJURER ESCAPED INTO THE WOOD.
I HAD SAVED A HUMAN BEING FROM DESTRUCTION, AND AS A RECOMPENSE I NOW WRITHED UNDER THE MISERABLE PAIN OF A WOUND WHICH SHATTERED THE FLESH AND BONE!
THE FEELINGS OF KINDNESS GAVE PLACE TO HELLISH RAGE. INFLAMED BY PAIN, I VOWED ETERNAL HATRED AND VENGEANCE TO ALL MANKIND!
76

Original Text

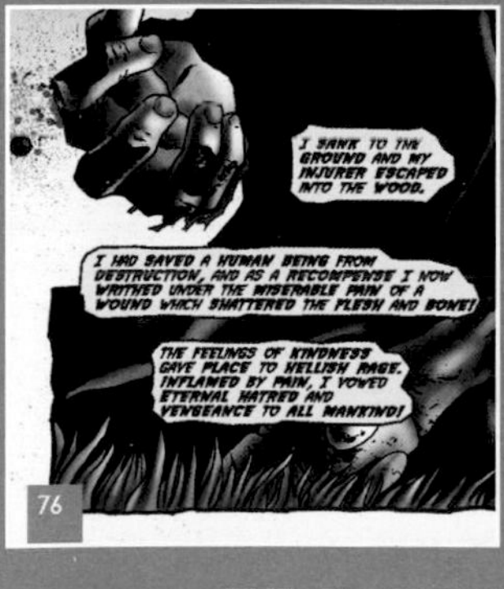
I SANK TO THE GROUND AND MY INJURER ESCAPED INTO THE WOOD.
I HAD SAVED A HUMAN BEING FROM DESTRUCTION, AND AS A RECOMPENSE I NOW WRITHED UNDER THE MISERABLE PAIN OF A WOUND WHICH SHATTERED THE FLESH AND BONE!
THE FEELINGS OF KINDNESS GAVE PLACE TO HELLISH RAGE. INFLAMED BY PAIN, I VOWED ETERNAL HATRED AND VENGEANCE TO ALL MANKIND!
76

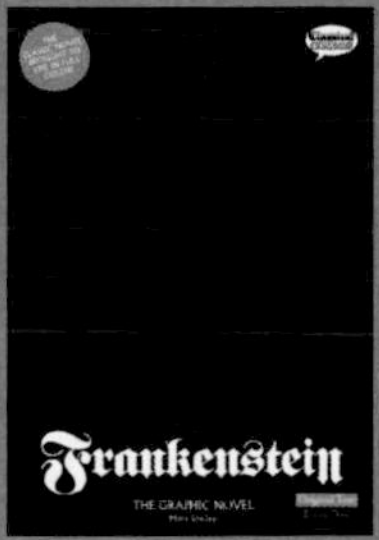
Frankenstein
THE GRAPHIC NOVEL

ISBN:
978-1-906332-49-5

THE CLASSIC NOVEL
BROUGHT TO LIFE IN FULL COLOR!

Quick Text

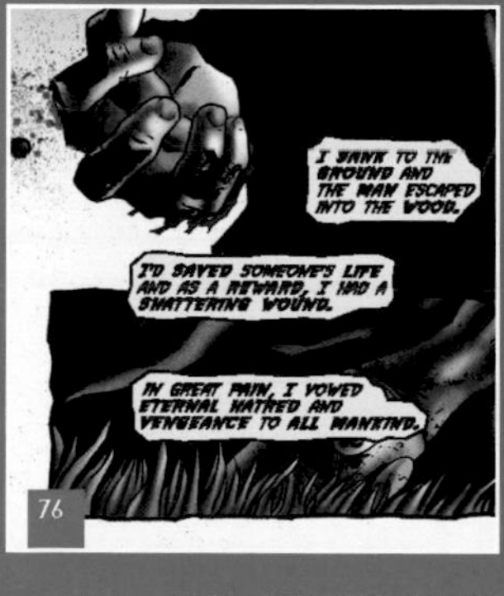
I SANK TO THE GROUND AND THE MAN ESCAPED INTO THE WOOD.
I'D SAVED SOMEONE'S LIFE AND AS A REWARD, I HAD A SHATTERING WOUND.
IN GREAT PAIN, I VOWED ETERNAL HATRED AND VENGEANCE TO ALL MANKIND.
76

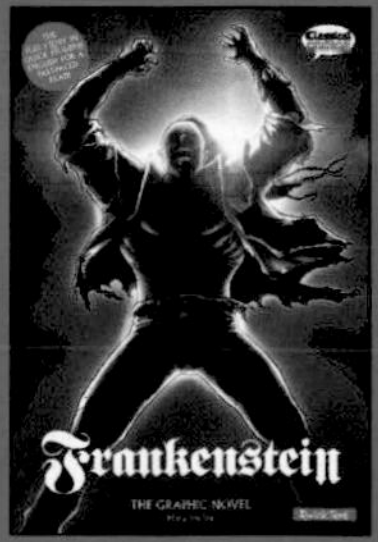
Frankenstein
THE GRAPHIC NOVEL

ISBN:
978-1-906332-50-1

THE FULL STORY IN QUICK MODERN
ENGLISH FOR A FAST-PACED READ!

LOOK OUT FOR MORE TITLES
IN THE CLASSICAL COMICS RANGE

Jane Eyre: The Graphic Novel

Published: December 8, 2008 • 144 Pages • $16.95
• Script Adaptation: Amy Corzine • Artwork: John M. Burns • Letters: Terry Wiley

This Charlotte Brontë classic is brought to vibrant life by artist John M. Burns. His sympathetic treatment of Jane Eyre's life in England during the 19th century will delight any reader, with its strong emotions and wonderfully rich atmosphere. Travel back to a time of grand mansions contrasted with the severest poverty, and immerse yourself in this fabulous love story.

Original Text

ISBN: 978-1-906332-47-1

Quick Text

ISBN: 978-1-906332-48-8

A Christmas Carol: The Graphic Novel

Published: November 5, 2008 • 160 Pages • $16.95
• Script Adaptation: Sean Michael Wilson • Pencils: Mike Collins
• Inks: David Roach • Colors: James Offredi • Letters: Terry Wiley

A full-color graphic novel adaptation of the much-loved Christmas story from the great Charles Dickens. Set in Victorian England and highlighting the social injustice of the time, we see one Ebenezer Scrooge go from oppressor to benefactor when he gets a rude awakening to how his life is, and how it should be. With sumptuous artwork and wonderful characters, this magical tale is a must-have for the festive season.

Original Text

ISBN: 978-1-906332-51-8

Quick Text

ISBN: 978-1-906332-52-5

OTHER CLASSICAL COMICS TITLES:

Great Expectations
Published: July 2009
Original Text   978-1-906332-59-4
Quick Text   978-1-906332-60-0

Romeo & Juliet
Published: November 2009
Original Text   978-1-906332-61-7
Plain Text   978-1-906332-62-4
Quick Text   978-1-906332-63-1

Richard III
Published: September 2009
Original Text   978-1-906332-64-8
Plain Text   978-1-906332-65-5
Quick Text   978-1-906332-66-2

Dracula
Published: February 2010
Original Text   978-1-906332-67-9
Quick Text   978-1-906332-68-6

The Tempest
Published: October 2009
Original Text   978-1-906332-69-3
Plain Text   978-1-906332-70-9
Quick Text   978-1-906332-71-6

The Canterville Ghost
Published: March 2010
Original Text   978-1-906332-72-3
Quick Text   978-1-906332-73-0

For more information visit www.classicalcomics.com